# TALONS & TALISMANS I

Book One
Libri Mysteriorum

Edited by Rob Howell
& Chris Kennedy

New Mythology Press
Coinjock, NC

Copyright © 2021 by Rob Howell and Chris Kennedy.

All rights reserved. No part of this publication may be reproduced, distributed or transmitted in any form or by any means, including photocopying, recording, or other electronic or mechanical methods, without the prior written permission of the publisher, except in the case of brief quotations embodied in critical reviews and certain other noncommercial uses permitted by copyright law.

Chris Kennedy/New Mythology Press
1097 Waterlily Rd., Coinjock, NC, 27923
http://chriskennedypublishing.com/

Publisher's Note: This is a work of fiction. Names, characters, places, and incidents are a product of the author's imagination. Locales and public names are sometimes used for atmospheric purposes. Any resemblance to actual people, living or dead, or to businesses, companies, events, institutions, or locales is completely coincidental.

Cover Art and Design by Jake Caleb (https://www.jcalebdesign.com/)

The stories and articles contained herein have never been previously published. They are copyrighted as follows:

TAMING FIRE by Kacey Ezell © 2021 by Kacey Ezell
MELTING ICE by David Shadoin © 2021 by David Shadoin
WHY NOT by Kevin Steverson © 2021 by Kevin Steverson
THE EMPTY HOUSE by J.T. Evans © 2021 by J.T. Evans
SMALL FAVORS by Jon R. Osborne © 2021 by Jon R. Osborne
A LESSER GOD by Mark Wandrey © 2021 by Mark Wandrey
THROUGH A SPYGLASS DARKLY by G. Scott Huggins © 2021 by G. Scott Huggins
FORTUNE'S EXPENSIVE SMILE by Julie Frost © 2021 by Julie Frost
COLD HANDS, WARM HEART by Benjamin Tyler Smith © 2021 by Benjamin Tyler Smith
WIDOW'S FEAST by Casey Moores © 2021 by Casey Moores
A GIFT FOR MOTHER by Melissa Olthoff © 2021 by Melissa Olthoff
THE TIME OF THE DRAGON by Rick Partlow © 2021 by Rick Partlow
A SONG OF MERCY by Josh Hayes © 2021 by Josh Hayes
MYTHICAL CREATURES by Kevin J. Anderson © 2021 by Kevin J. Anderson
THE NAME OF THE MONSTER by D.J. Butler © 2021 by D.J. Butler

Talons & Talismans/Chris Kennedy and Rob Howell -- 1st ed.
ISBN: 978-1648552229

# Preface by Rob Howell

Welcome to *Talons & Talismans*! This is the first in a series of anthologies we at New Mythology Press call the *Libri Mysteriorum*, or the Books of Mysteries.

The *Libri Mysteriorum* will focus on different fantasy themes, providing our authors with a chance to create something they might not have had the opportunity to write about before. In this case, their writing prompt was beasts and monsters.

We ended up with fifteen stories in this anthology including selkies, medusae, dragons, werewolves, ogres, zombies, and more. These come from bestselling authors like Kevin J. Anderson, Rick Partlow, Dave Butler, Mark Wandrey, and other great writers at the top of their game.

However, one of my primary motivations for editing anthologies isn't simply to work with some of the best names in the business, it's also to work with up-and-coming talent. This is why nearly all of New Mythology's anthologies will include four spots for open submission. It's our goal to provide good opportunities for the next generation of authors, and they really came through.

Melissa Olthoff and Casey Moores have proven, beyond any doubt, that they can write. This is their second time winning a spot in one of our open submissions. Once is lucky, twice is good, and so they are. They've earned my attention on other projects they want to do, and you'll note we listed their stories as being part of their own universe. You *will* see more from them.

The other two winners were Julie Frost, who is a great werewolf-whisperer and J.T. Evans. His story is perhaps my favorite in the anthology. It's got that feel-good vibe and courageous stance against fear that I love. No one who knows my tastes will be surprised that I chose his submission.

We got so many great submissions, I had to do *two* separate *Talons & Talismans* anthologies. That's right, we've got fifteen more great stories coming in a month. That one includes Dave Butler with a follow-up to his story in here, plus Aaron Rosenberg, Sam Witt, Mel Todd, and Quincy J. Allen among others.

And it allowed me to include stories from four more of the open submissions. Of the stories we received, an amazing seventeen were worthy stories. Picking four for each anthology was a huge challenge and it's really an honor to see the next generation in action.

But, speaking of action, it's time to let you get to the stories, starting with Kacey Ezell teaming up with another newer writer, David Shadoin. They're U.S. Army helicopter pilots and they take us on a whirling introduction of *their* new setting.

Exciting stuff is coming for the readers of New Mythology Press, and we're glad to have you along for the ride.

— Rob Howell
Publisher, New Mythology Press

\* \* \* \* \*

# Table of Contents

**TALONS & TALISMANS I** ................................................. 1

Preface by Rob Howell ..................................................... 3

Table of Contents ............................................................ 5

Taming Fire by Kacey Ezell ............................................. 7
    An Alliance of Spirits Story

Melting Ice by David Shadoin ...................................... 35
    An Alliance of Spirits Story

Why Not by Kevin Steverson ....................................... 63
    A Balance of Kerr Story

The Empty House by J.T. Evans .................................. 93

Small Favors by Jon R. Osborne ................................ 119
    An Accords Universe Story

A Lesser God by Mark Wandrey ................................ 151
    A Traveling Gods Story

Through a Spyglass Darkly by G. Scott Huggins ...... 185

Fortune's Expensive Smile by Julie Frost ................. 213

Cold Hands, Warm Heart by Benjamin Tyler Smith .... 239
    A Necrolopolis Story

Widow's Feast by Casey Moores ................................ 279
    A Deathmage War Story

A Gift For Mother by Melissa Olthoff ....................... 309
    A Scourge of the Angels Story

The Time of the Dragon by Rick Partlow ................. 341

A Song of Mercy by Josh Hayes ................................ 373

Mythical Creatures by Kevin J. Anderson ................ 397

The Name of the Monster by D.J. Butler..........................415
    A Tales of Indrajit & Fix Story

About the Editors ................................................................445

Excerpt from A Reluctant Druid.........................................447
    Book One of The Milesian Accords

Excerpt from *Responsibility of the Crown*..............................453
    Book One of The Endless Ocean

# Taming Fire
# by Kacey Ezell
## An Alliance of Spirits Story

"**M**y Lady, I must protest! You *cannot* marry the Butcher!"

Chyldin's strident squawking echoed down the stone corridor that led from Lovinah's council chambers to the tower that housed her rooms. Not for the first time, the Lady of Fryktmarch reflected that they really needed some kind of carpeting or tapestries, to dampen the piercing echo of her councilors' voices, if for no other reason.

"Chyldin," Lovinah said, keeping her tone even as she walked. "The matter is closed."

"But my lady, he is our greatest enemy!"

At that, Lovinah halted and spun, her straight black hair flaring out around her as she came nose to beak with his raptor's eyes and hooked visage. She swallowed a low growl that threatened to rumble up out of her throat and narrowed her blue-black eyes to glare at one of the Vapaana who'd raised her from childhood.

"*War* is our greatest enemy, Chyldin," she said, speaking slowly. "The war with the Elves has decimated our population, destroyed our crops and our herds, and forced our people to pull back to these forested mountains in order to hold off their expansion. We have been at war my entire life, as you well know!"

Chyldin took a step back and held up two pale-fingered hands.

"I do know, my lady," he said, "and no one wants an end to the war more than I—"

"Then let me end it." Lovinah let the growl ripple through her words as she stared down one of her most trusted councilors.

"Forgive me, my lady, but this is not the way! Kaldir the Bastard is a butcher! He's slaughtered armies of Men and Vapaana since he was barely out of leading strings! You must see that this offer of alliance is nothing but an insult! *They are laughing at us!*"

"Let them laugh," Lovinah said, lifting her chin and shaking her hair back between her horns. They were the same color as her deep blue eyes, and she knew the contrast between them and her golden-furred face had a powerful effect on her people. Chyldin was no exception. He lowered his eyes in instinctive submission, then glanced back up.

"My lady—"

"No. I am not a child, old friend. You and the others have raised me well. I am Lady of Fryktmarch, and I alone lead our people. I *will* protect them from the ravages of further, endless war. Our people deserve time to recover, to rebuild their lives, to bear their children, and raise them free of the fear of never-ending violence. Samir's offer of alliance may be a backhanded one, but what care I for Elven sensibilities? I would marry the Destroyer Herself if that bought time for our people."

"But if you would just wait—"

"War waits for no one, Chyldin. We cannot afford to do so, either."

"But—"

"You are dismissed, Chyldin," Lovinah said, her voice devoid of the growl, but cold and crisp as the mountain glacier that ran up to the southern perimeter wall of Fryktmarch. Chyldin opened his beak, then closed it and bowed his feathered raptor's head. He said nothing else, but his shoulders slumped.

Lovinah pushed away the uncomfortable thought that Chyldin, like all the councilors who had raised her since her father's death, had aged rapidly. As a rule, Vapaana were long-lived people by the standards of Men. Not as long as the near-immortal Elves, but long enough. Still, the burdens and sorrows of loss after loss, struggle after struggle—it was no wonder Chyldin looked old and careworn.

*This damn war*, Lovinah thought as she turned her sword-straight back on him and resumed her unhurried progress toward her chambers. *It has to end. I will end it. Even if I must marry a butcher.*

She pushed these thoughts to the side and focused on climbing the worn spiral stairs to her tower chambers. Fryktmarch was ancient and had been the home of the most powerful of the Vapaana sorcerers for as long as anyone could remember. As a people, the Vapaana were an independent and fractious lot, but by and large, they followed the path Fryktmarch set.

Out of habit, Lovinah reached within herself to the pulsing well of her own sorcerous power. She felt it rise at her touch, like an eager cub coming out to play. She took the power and wove it through her being like a caress, reveling in the pleasure that slid along her nerves at the sensations it brought. She reached out to trail her hand along the stone wall of the tower and felt the spirits of Fryktmarch's stone stir in welcoming response.

"Lady Lovinah?"

Lovinah blinked, and the image of sleepy giants smiling faded from her eyes, replaced by the half-indulgent, half-worried smile of her handmaiden.

"My lady, is something wrong? Why are you just standing here at the top of the stairs?"

"No, Xiscine," Lovinah said with a smile. "I was just woolgathering. Council is closed. Finally."

"And are they happy?" Xiscine asked, stepping aside and holding the door to Lovinah's chambers open.

"No," Lovinah said. "Not at all."

"But they will not block the alliance?"

"I believe they would if they could, but they cannot. The ruler of Fryktmarch has always chosen their own mate, and much to their chagrin, I am of age to do so." Lovinah let out a sigh of relief as she finally crossed the threshold into the sanctuary of her own rooms. By long tradition, no one came here but herself and Xiscine, and Lovinah relished the privacy of the space. A leader didn't often have the option to let their guard down, but here, if nowhere else, Lovinah felt safe.

The chamber itself was not particularly large, but it felt airy. Stone arches vaulted toward the ceiling, and large windows made up three-fourths of the walls.

Lovinah had communed with the glass spirits as a teenager, when she'd renewed her ancestors' plea to create windows as hard as steel, transparent from the inside, and opaque from the outside. Her power and charisma had charmed the glass spirits, and the windows had shone crystal clear and unbreakable ever since.

She approached them now, after kicking off her slippers and reveling in the feel of the naked stone and soft, plush woven rugs under her feet. The mountains unfolded before her, capped with snow, and appearing darkly brooding from the winter-gray foliage of the great, powerful forest that blanketed the slopes.

"We could hold here forever," Lovinah said out loud. "These mountains are impassable, save for a few spots firmly in our control. Neither Elves nor Men could ever oust us here, and if it came to that, I believe I could even awaken the Spirit of the Forest to defend us. But would that be enough?"

"You could make it enough." Xiscine's calm certainty bolstered Lovinah, as it always had. They'd been girls together, as Xiscine's parents had given their daughter into the care of a council wise enough to realize their child-queen would need a friend and confidante. The Vapaana didn't have nobility as Men and Elves did, but Fryktmarch was treacherous in its own ways, and Xiscine's steady loyalty helped Lovinah navigate it. "You are powerful enough to do anything."

"You say that because you love me," Lovinah said, turning with a teasing smile to regard her handmaiden.

"I do love you," Xiscine said, "but it is also true." Light rippled across the faceted lenses of her bulbous, compound eyes as she stepped up to join Lovinah at the window. "You are the most powerful sorceress the Vapaana have seen in generations. You can take how many forms? Three?"

"Four," Lovinah said, ducking her head.

"Four? Lovinah!"

"I woke up this morning a viper," Lovinah said, her words soft, but excitement hammered in her chest.

"Bear, cat, bat, and now viper?" Xiscine turned and grasped her by the shoulders, her fingers tight with shock. "Lovinah, having *two* forms is rare enough! *No one* has ever held four forms before! Not in any of the recorded histories!"

"I know. I keep waiting for my power to plateau but…it doesn't. The well inside me just gets deeper every day."

Xiscine pulled her lady into a hug so hard and tight that Lovinah could feel the hard, round nubs of her handmaiden's spinnerets under her gown. "You really *can* do anything," Xiscine whispered in Lovinah's ear.

"I don't know about anything, Xiscine, but I hope I can do what's needed."

\* \* \*

The journey to the Elven capital city of Alfhild took but a few days. As a concession to her councilors' fears, Lovinah allowed them to select her honor guard, and therefore she ended up traveling with nearly a full cohort of mages. She rather thought she'd have been safer to have gone quietly and quickly in stealth, flying as a bat, and taking only Xiscine in her spider form.

But, as her council had pointed out before she could even propose the plan, that was impractical. This was a political marriage, the start of an alliance that would be tenuous at best. Lovinah knew well enough that in matters such as these, appearances were paramount. Doubly so when dealing with the Elves, whose High Lord was known for his interest in fashion, excess, and displaying his vast wealth for others to admire—and find intimidating.

Lovinah had no intention of letting Samir of the Elves intimidate her over her clothing or anything else, but the pride of her people demanded she represent them well. So, she traveled in her ornate carriage, leading a baggage wain filled with trunks of gowns, accessories, and jewels…and a small cohort of battle-hardened mages to watch her back.

"Not that they're likely to be of much use when we pass the gates of Alfhild," Lovinah said quietly to Xiscine on the last day of their trip. "They'll be quartered with the Elven army, and we shall be alone in the beast's den."

"How fortunate, then, that your magic is more powerful than any three of our mages put together," Xiscine said, her tone dry. Her body swayed as the carriage rocked over the rutted forest path, but she didn't look up from her lap, where her hands and spinnerets moved in quick, competent flashes as she wove a new length of silk.

Lovinah laughed and rolled her eyes. "You have too much confidence in me, but I do not think the threats we face will be overt enough to be defended by magic. Not primarily, in any case."

Xiscine did look up then, and smiled. "You refer to the Elves' legendary Game of Court?"

"Everyone plays it, at every court," Lovinah said with a sigh. She leaned her head back against the wall of the carriage and closed her eyes. "Even at Fryktmarch. The difference is that there, I am the lady, and if I prefer plain speech and honest truth, I mostly get it. In Alfhild, High Lord Samir rules, and he…"

"He prefers lies," Xiscine said. Her tone held no judgement or censure. She simply stated a fact.

Lovinah felt herself smile. "Perhaps, though we probably shouldn't say so. I'm sure he prefers that *he* knows the truth, in any case."

"Secrets, then?"

"Oh, yes. From our dealings thus far, I can say with certainty that Elves love their secrets, and Samir is the most secretive of all."

"I am extraordinarily good at learning secrets," Xiscine said with a tiny smile.

"Xiscine," Lovinah said, raising her head and letting her smile drop away, "you must promise me you will take the greatest care. I *cannot* allow you to put yourself in danger simply to learn a few bits of juicy gossip on my account."

"My lady," Xiscine said, the light from the carriage window reflecting in her compound eyes, "I am in no danger. I am simply a maid, not a battle mage, not the Lady of Fryktmarch. No one knows or will expect me to have enough magic to change shape, and if they did, who can tell one web crawler from another? I've been trained since childhood to serve and protect you, and so I will, but you must trust me to do my job and not limit me out of misplaced fear for my safety."

Lovinah stared at her for a long moment, then swallowed the protest that rose within. Xiscine was right, after all. She gave a slow nod, then smiled. "I can always tell when you're serious with me, because you call me 'My lady', instead of 'Lovinah.'"

"I know," Xiscine said with her own smile, then bent her head to her work once more.

Lovinah leaned her head back again and closed her eyes, wishing, rather than expecting, to drift off into a doze for the rest of the trip. She didn't have much success, but before too long, they halted at the gates of Alfhild.

After a reassuringly brief pause to identify themselves, they moved forward again, and Lovinah had to fight to keep herself from gawping out the carriage window. She'd never seen an Elven city up close before, and it truly was a beautiful place to behold.

Samir's palace was no exception to the general splendor. Lovinah loved her home, but Fryktmarch looked exactly like what it was—a mountain fortress, grim and poised for violence. Samir's triple-spired castle glittered and shone by comparison.

The Elven guards who led them from the gate of the city directed them onto a long, curving carriage path that ran up to an area clearly designed for dismounting. As she stepped out, Lovinah looked up and realized that it had also clearly been designed to display and showcase the High Lord's visitors. Hundreds of balconies overlooked the courtyard, some mounted in the great southern trees that surrounded them, some carved into those blindingly white towers that pierced the canopy and arrowed up into the achingly blue sky. She could see Elves of all ages and descriptions looking down upon her, some straining to get a glimpse. She smiled and lifted a hand to wave at a young face that peered between the elegant branches of one of the tree balconies. The child's eyes widened, and he or she ducked behind one of the adult Elves standing nearby.

"This way, please, my lady."

Lovinah pushed down her disappointment at the child's fear and focused her eyes on the captain of her guard, who beckoned her forward toward the doors of the palace. His lion's mane stood out in a stiff ruff around his face, broadcasting his unease. *I'm too exposed here*, Lovinah realized. *He doesn't like it. I shouldn't either, I suppose. This is not the time to forget such things.*

She gave her captain a smile that she hoped reassured him and lifted the skirts of her travelling gown so she could walk forward quickly to the door. It swept open at her approach, and with a deep breath, Lovinah held her head high and went to meet the beast in his den.

\* \* \*

The game began almost immediately.

Lovinah had known it would, but knowing didn't keep her from having to fight not to be knocked off balance by the swift efficiency of the Elven court. She'd only just arrived in her rooms when a page brought a message from the Elven High Lord. She looked at the scrap of parchment and summoned every bit of her will not to crumple it and throw it across the room.

"Thank you, young one," she said instead, smiling down at the page. "You may inform your High Lord that I will do as he requests."

It hadn't, strictly speaking, been a request, but the young Elven page was well enough versed in court etiquette not to correct a high-ranking visitor, and simply nodded. Lovinah smiled down at him or her—it was so hard to tell with Elven youngsters—and stepped back while Xiscine closed the door to the quarters they'd been assigned.

"What is it?" Lovinah's handmaiden asked as soon as they were alone.

"Samir. I'm to be ready to sign the marriage accords in an hour."

"An hour? We haven't even unpacked yet!"

Lovinah smiled tightly.

"That's not an accident, I'm sure. Samir means to keep me off balance and wrongfooted at the meeting, no doubt. Can you get me ready in time? If not, I can cast a glamour—"

"No," Xiscine said, firmly cutting her off as her compound eyes glinted in the afternoon sunlight. "No need to exert your energy. Your dark blue gown with the silver embroidery is close at hand and easy to put on. You go into the bathroom and wash up while I get it out. We'll do something simple and elegant with your hair, but I know just the thing…"

Xiscine trailed off as she turned to rummage through the various trunks and boxes that had just been carried in from their baggage wagon. Lovinah smiled after her, and went obediently to wash herself as she'd been bid.

Not quite an hour later, as she followed the page down the labyrinthine hallways of Samir's palace, Lovinah caught a glimpse of herself in a reflective glass case. Xiscine, as ever, had outdone herself. She'd brushed Lovinah's hair until it glimmered in the light and let it fall in loose waves down her back. A simple silver chain held it away from her face, complete with a thumb-sized sapphire that rested on her forehead, providing both adornment...and a little extra power. The sapphire was a focus stone, one whose spirit had been tuned to Lovinah's particular grasp, and it could be used to funnel power to her from ambient energy that usually lay dormant everywhere.

It also brought out the blue in her eyes and the beautiful midnight silk of the gown. Xiscine had used a pulse of her own little magic to convince the dress to unwrinkle, and it flowed around Lovinah as she walked, catching the light like moonlight on the ocean.

So rather than arriving disheveled and out of sorts, Lovinah met the High Lord of the Elves with her head held high. Her confident demeanor never slipped, not even when Samir arrived, followed closely by his brother.

Who immediately drew his sword.

"My apologies," Samir said, stepping forward and putting a hand on Kaldir's shoulder. "The High Commander is feeling a bit *edgy* after his long ride back. I assure you, he *will* remember his manners and the protections afforded by guest-right."

Lovinah didn't answer, simply shifted her gaze to meet the eyes of her longtime enemy and soon-to-be husband. Then she blinked slowly and smiled. The coiled energy she'd gathered waited, just below the level of her skin.

Kaldir held her gaze and sheathed his blade.

"My apologies as well," he said. His voice was dark, and deeper than his brother's. It reminded Lovinah of the shadows beneath the forest canopy on a moonlit night. She felt her smile deepen. "I know not what came over me."

"I do," she said.

"My Lady of Fryktmarch! Don't you look…pretty!"

The surprise that underlaid Samir's sudden practiced bonhomie made Lovinah's smile grow even more, and she turned to him and inclined her head, as one would to an equal.

"High Lord Samir, I thank you for the welcome and the compliment alike. Your home is lovely."

"Yes, it is, rather. Not quite like your hut in the mountains, I am certain. Can I offer you some refreshment after your long journey? You must be exhausted!"

*Now he thinks of that!* Lovinah thought, holding back a snort of humor.

"I am well enough, my lord," she said. "Perhaps we should instead discuss the terms of our agreement?"

"My, how blunt! It's fascinating how your kind disregard the niceties of state affairs."

"I never saw the need for insincere small talk when there's business at hand." Lovinah smiled up at the High Lord of the Elves as she said it, making sure he saw the sharp points of her canine teeth.

"Hmm. You will find time spent in my court most painful, then, I should think," he said, a thread of malice in his tone. He walked toward a low table. "Painful, perhaps, but instructive. Ah! Here we are."

Lovinah joined him at the table and looked down upon the formal document that would cement the alliance between the Vapaana and the Elves. She'd read it multiple times already, of course, both in its present form and in several previously proposed draft versions. The wrangling over the details of this particular document had consumed her life for the past several months.

And now, here they were. In the end, it was fairly straightforward. They would ally with the Elves against the ever-rapacious nations of Mankind. They would send battlemages to augment the storied Elven forces, and in return, the Elves would protect the Vapaana homeland. And it would all be cemented by her marriage to the Elven general, Kaldir, the High Lord's brother. Kaldir the Bastard. Kaldir the Butcher.

Her eyes ran over the script, confirming that nothing had been altered from the language they'd agreed upon. Then, satisfied, she plucked a quill out of the inkpot on the table and signed her name without fanfare: Lovinah, Lady of Fryktmarch.

"My lord?" she said, turning and offering the quill. She saw the High Lord's eyes narrow at her lack of formality, but she did not show her smile. *He offends easily. That is a weakness I can use, someday.*

He took the quill and bent over the document, signing his name with a great many more flourishes than she'd used.

"And now," he said, "it is done. To the wedding and the feast!"

\* \* \*

*Will this thrice-damned day never end?*

Lovinah held herself still in her seat at her wedding feast and carefully schooled her features not to show any of the ache between her eyes or the tension she felt twisting through her musculature. The Elven marriage ceremony earlier had been interminable, and damn near incomprehensible due to their stupid habit of using overly ornate and formal language. But she'd stood through it all, her spine straight and her chin held high as she sought to project the image of herself as calm, deep water, undisturbed by the petty splashing of those around her.

It was a lie, of course. Anyone who'd ever met Lovinah knew she was fire first and always, but the Elves didn't care, and here in their stronghold, she played a dangerous game of pretense for the highest stakes imaginable.

So: Calm. Still. Deep.

Powerful.

For the thousandth time that night, she cut her eyes to watch her new husband through her lashes. If she was fire hiding behind water, he appeared to be metal encased in ice. She had to admit, his initial reaction to draw down on her in the reception room had rather pleased her. At least that was an honest response in this den of lying vipers.

Vipers she could handle. The lies made her head hurt.

She'd found a servant and managed to procure a glass of honest water. She lifted it to her lips and took another look around the sumptuously decorated ballroom. It was beautiful in the way that all of the Elven finery was beautiful: intricate, ornate…and artificial. Her heart longed for a clearing she knew near Fryktmarch, where the arching branches of ancient oaks formed soaring vaults above the forest floor.

That's where she would have celebrated her marriage if it had been up to her.

Which brought her back to her husband again. They'd spoken briefly earlier, and she smiled in remembered pleasure that he'd seemed surprised to find she had both a mind of her own and the will to speak plainly. She had to admit, he wasn't exactly what she'd expected, either. He'd stifled his sighs and mouthed platitudes well, but he watched the members of the court as if they were enemy combatants lying in ambush, and more than once she saw his fingers twitch toward the hilt of his famous sword.

In fact, the only time he'd seemed to take any pleasure in the evening at all had been when speaking with his nieces. Lovinah had departed from the table in search of something non-alcoholic by that point, but she'd watched from across the room as he interacted with the two young Elven girls. The cold, arrogant lines of his face had softened into a genuine smile, and for the first time, Lovinah realized her husband was a truly beautiful specimen of masculinity.

Then his brother had intervened, and the mask of the Butcher slammed back into place. Lovinah watched and wondered at the reason. One thing became clear: Kaldir hated the Elven court as much as she did. *How interesting.*

"Lady Lovinah!"

Lovinah turned at the call and came face to face with an Elven noble whose name she didn't care enough to remember. He strode toward her, coming close enough to loom with his greater height. She refused to move and simply looked up at the arrogant smile that seemed to be a racial trait of the Elves.

"How exciting this must be for you," he said. He pitched his voice oddly, so that it had a slower, singsong quality to it. Almost as if he were speaking to a child.

"How so, my lord?" she asked.

"Well, as I understand it, this is your first trip to Alfhild. What an adventure for a…girl such as yourself. To see the majesty of the city and the glory of the Elven Empire!"

Lovinah couldn't help it, she quirked her lips in a tiny smile.

"If you say so, lord…"

"Deleon."

"Lord Deleon."

His brow wrinkled for a tiny moment as he reminded her of his name, and then smoothed as he returned to his condescending smile. "Of course, I imagine it's quite an intimidating prospect, as well. Especially for one so…unspoiled as yourself." His eyes tracked down her body and back up again, and Lovinah felt a jolt of amusement.

*Is he thinking to seduce me?*

"I do not easily intimidate," she said, and let her smile grow enough to show the sharp points of her predator's teeth. He blinked, and his pale skin went even whiter as two of his bodyguards stepped up to flank him on either side.

Suddenly, Lovinah was done. Sick and tired of it all. She was here for one reason and one reason only—to cement the treaty between the Elves and her people. She'd endured Samir's thinly-veiled threats and insults, she'd married the Bastard, and now it was finished. She saw no further need to put up with being treated like an exhibit at a curiosity show for the entertainment of these dissolute, false-faced, scheming worms of the Elven court.

She gathered her power through the focus stone, pulling in the energies latent in the air, in the wood around her, in the stone beneath her feet—

A hand on her arm. Kaldir—she knew by the way the air currents moved around his powerful form. She looked up at him anyway. *I don't need your help.*

*Or do I?*

The thought came from nowhere, intruding into her consciousness as her new husband spoke some nonsense about visits to a marsh and lovely views. It was merely more false patter like everything else in the room, and she started to pull her arm out of his grasp when he did the damnedest thing.

He *winked* at her.

*What in seven hells?* Lovinah forced her face to remain neutral, refused to let her jaw drop as Kaldir went on to protest Lord Deleon's monopoly on her attention and insist that she owed him a dance.

Longing for home hit her like two fists to her gut, and she fought to keep her breathing even. At a real wedding between her people, there would have been much dancing, and the happy couple would have been in the midst of it all. But here, things were different. It wasn't the done thing to dance with one's spouse, for the Elves used dancing as a tool to advertise shifting alliances and political connections.

*Trust the Elves to strip the joy from everything,* Lovinah thought as Deleon and his two guards backed down. Kaldir released her arm, and for the first time since they'd met, looked suddenly uncertain.

Lovinah reached down, captured his hand with her own, and moved toward the dance floor, careful not to advertise that she was leading him rather than the other way around. This was a display, like everything else. Better to project the image of unity and equality, if they were really going to do this. She wound her fingers through his, careful not to catch his delicate skin with her claws.

"That was a decent bluff," she said as she turned to face him, "though you appear not to have thought it through."

"I hadn't expected everyone to back off so quickly, if I'm honest," he admitted, and Lovinah felt a flash of incredulous gratitude. *An honest Elf? Is such a thing possible?*

He put his hand on her side, slightly higher than it should properly go. She leaned into him and used her free hand to correct his placement, covering the movement with a toss of her dark hair. For just a moment, gratitude and trepidation flashed across his face before his habitual arrogance returned.

*He's miserable, and he doesn't know the dance. He wants out of here as much as I do!*

She smiled up at him, letting him see her teeth as an idea took hold. She could get them out of there and give the Elven court something to whisper about for decades.

"Then follow my back lead," she said, "and let's give them a show."

They twirled out onto the floor, and Lovinah took a moment to enjoy the feeling of her husband's powerful body responding to her cues. He moved like the warrior he was, and the quickness with which he picked up on her lead spoke to his intelligence. When the steps called for her to turn in his arms and lean back against his chest, he bent to speak in her ear.

"You got your wish, Lady. They're all watching you."

"Not me," she said as she twirled back out to the length of their extended arms. "Us."

"Do you enjoy their attention?"

"No more than you do. Are you ready?"

"For what?"

"To get out of here. As I said, follow my lead." She met his eyes and smiled again, then *pulled* on the energy that lived in the core of her being. She spun it like fiber in her mind, working in the memory of cold to chill her blood, and the cunning of the wild to shape her mind and body. Fire rushed to her brain, and she spindled it as well, pushing it down, feeding it into the teeth that elongated into her twin fangs as she flowed into her pit viper form.

Screams erupted from the crowd. Lovinah laughed, but it came out as a hiss, which only caused more screaming. To his credit, Kaldir never let go of her, simply shifting his grip so he held the long, muscled tube of her body in his surprisingly gentle left hand. His right gripped the hilt of his sword, blade glittering in the candlelight of the ballroom as he drew it in a motion that seemed as unconscious as breathing.

She flexed and wound up his wrist and forearm, twining herself around the length of his arm until she could rise up next to his ear and look out over his shoulder.

"Well done," she murmured and caught his tiny tensing as the air spirits translated words that only he would be able to hear. "Now we can leave. Sheathe your sword and blame it on my uncontrollable magic."

"You're anything but uncontrolled," he murmured. She felt the words along her skin as it echoed through his chest.

"A useful thing for you to know, perhaps. As useful as being underestimated by one's enemies."

He snorted softly, as if he'd like to chuckle but couldn't, and inclined his head toward her. She rewarded his acknowledgement of her point by sliding up around the back of his neck and hissing over his other shoulder, letting the crowd see a flash of fang. Fear rose from them, its stench thick and cloying on her tongue. Through the focus stone still on her forehead, she pulled on that fear and wove it into something a little different, a little more subtle. She took the energy of their terror and twisted it into something more like…awe.

Glamours weren't complicated, but they could be tiring, especially when one attempted to affect so many minds as this. However, Lovinah was not the leader of her people for nothing. She called silently to the spirits of air and flickering light in the room, and they came, bolstering her power as their energy flowed in through the sapphire, mingling with the emotions of the crowd.

"As you can see…" Kaldir said, projecting his voice to the back of the ballroom. Even to her un-glamoured eyes, he shone with the layers of her power surrounding him. "…my wife's magic is unpredictable. With your permission, High Lord, we will retire."

Lovinah swiveled and found Samir lounging in his ornate chair on a dais. "Far be it for me to keep a newlywed from his bride, brother!" He raised a goblet and laughed at his own quip. Lovinah felt Kaldir swallow, and heat began to radiate from his cheeks, though she kept his complexion and expression appearing as icy as ever. "Go! Go to your marriage bed!" Samir continued.

Kaldir bowed with the same grace and economy of motion he'd used when dancing with her, then walked unhurriedly toward the exit of the vast room. The crowd parted for them, and Lovinah couldn't resist hissing once more as the Elven nobility stared at her with varying degrees of horror and envy.

*Who said an Elven wedding couldn't be fun?*

\* \* \*

Lovinah hated carriages. She preferred to ride a horse if she must travel in humanoid form. Or better yet, dispense with form altogether, and run on her own four paws, or stretch her wings, soaring high above road and forest alike. But one must observe the niceties. Plus, Kaldir could do none of those things, and it would be rude of her to leave him to travel alone in their first 24 hours of married life.

Especially when she'd so thoroughly glamoured him the night before. She hadn't really intended to do that, but he'd caught the edge of her power as it spilled over the crowd. She'd realized it on the way out of the ballroom, so she'd gotten him back to his own warriors, then sought her own chambers for the remainder of the evening.

Newlyweds they may be, but she'd be damned if she was going to consummate her marriage with the groom under the magical duress of a glamour.

The carriage jolted, pulling Lovinah from her thoughts. Xiscine fidgeted on the bench next to her.

"You could shift," Lovinah murmured quietly. Kaldir appeared to still be under some of the lingering effects of the glamour, and she didn't want to jolt him into full awareness. "I'm sure you'd be more comfortable."

"I'll not leave you to appear unattended."

Lovinah snorted softly. "We are wed, Xiscine. No one would impugn my virtue for riding in a carriage apparently alone with him."

"I'm not worried about that." Xiscine turned to Lovinah and gave her a tight, wintry smile. "*He* needs to see you are not unattended."

"He won't hurt me, dear one. This may not be a love match, but it is a political one. He would gain nothing by harming me."

Xiscine looked as if she was going to say something else, but Kaldir chose that moment to stir. Lovinah felt a wave of fatigue as he started to speak, so she answered his thanks briefly, but kept most of her attention out the window while he and Xiscine spoke.

*Oh, clever girl,* Lovinah thought as she listened to her friend spar with her husband. Kaldir's questions about their shifting abilities might have been innocuous...but then again, they might be something else. As she kept her eyes on the moonlight streaming through the trees on either side of the road, Lovinah realized she was indeed very glad that Xiscine had insisted on remaining humanoid with her.

"So, your abilities have energy limits? Does it change based on what you're trying to perform with magic?"

"You won't be able to control us that easy, Butcher." Xiscine's tart answer made Lovinah stifle a smile and turn away from the window.

"Gentle, Xiscine. He is allowed to be curious. She has a point, though. You think about it in terms of limited amount of energy, much like that used in running or fighting. It's a more complicated relationship," Lovinah said. Prudence and caution made her end her explanation, though, in truth, she enjoyed teaching and talking about magic. Maybe one day—if she could ever trust him—she might be able to explain further. With a mind as sharp as his, she imagined that discussion would be both deep and stimulating. She turned back to the window.

"Then your ability to shapeshift takes a lesser toll than the illusion you cast on the guests?" Kaldir pressed.

"Shapeshifting is no mere ability; it's who we are. It defines us. We would not be called Beasts by your people if we could simply teach our ability to our young," she answered without looking at him.

"Ladies, I'm not here to control anyone," Kaldir said. "Prior to yesterday's negotiations, I didn't even know I was being traded like our wheat in the market. But I understand the need to protect one's best weapons against a former enemy commander. So let me ask you this instead; what do you hope to get from this alliance-based marriage?"

Kaldir's question rolled through Lovinah's mind. What did she want from her marriage? She wanted what anyone wanted: love, connection, partnership, children. None of those, however, would be possible for her in this match. *So, what do I hope to gain?*

"Peace, High Commander," Lovinah finally said, her words falling into the carriage like snowflakes onto stone. "I wish this union to save my people further pain and anguish. I wish that for your people, as well, so when there was an offer on the table to put in a temporary peace and give all a chance to sit at the same table and understand each other, I chose it. War waits for no one, so one must act to stop war."

Lovinah closed her eyes and leaned her head against the window. Kaldir didn't push the matter further, and Lovinah thanked the Creator for small mercies as the carriage rattled on down the road in comparative silence.

A few moments later, Xiscine shifted next to her, pulling Lovinah from her not-quite-rest. She opened her eyes and sat up, looking out once more to see if she could determine why they were slowing...and then stopping.

Adrenaline jolted through her system, burning away the remainder of her pensive ennui as one of her battle mages strode by the carriage, his form already hazy as he began to shift into his predatory wolf form.

"Why have we stopped?" Xiscine asked, her voice high and sharp.

"Lady Lovinah, I think it a prudent time now to tel—" Kaldir was speaking low and fast, but Lovinah already had the carriage door open. Another of her mages ran by, her body flowing into the form of a great hunting eagle. Lovinah felt the combined effort of her honor guard's pull on the energies of wind, rocks, trees as they arrayed themselves in a defensive formation.

Whatever Kaldir had to say could wait. Lovinah took her place behind her mages and delved into the core of her own internal well. With a thought, she flowed into the form of one of the great mountain cats that lived near Fryktmarch. At least a score of men and women stepped forward from the shadows under the trees, their weapons glinting in the moonlight.

Lovinah let out a snarl of mingled joy and rage. She could already taste the blood of these ambushers on her fangs.

*  *  *

With a whisper, Lovinah stroked the ego of the earth spirits beneath her paws, and they responded, buckling up with enough energy that the archer in front of her lost her footing and stumbled. The arrow streaked toward Oonire as she beat her wings against the air, climbing to relay images of the battlefield from her raptor's eyes. It went wide, causing relief to ripple down Lovinah's spine.

The archer cursed and picked herself up, spreading her feet wide as she pulled another arrow from her quiver, but by then Lovinah was on her.

She let out a snarl as she sprang from the shadows, letting her weight hit the woman square in the back. Her claws dug into the woman's shoulders, and her powerful jaws closed on the back of her neck. She felt the satisfying *crunch* as she crushed vertebrae and spinal cord alike, and the hot, iron tang of Man-blood filled her mouth with savage glee and battle lust for more.

The woman under her gave one last shudder and went limp, and Lovinah raised her bloodstained face to look around and sprint back to her warriors. Despite the lingering triumph of her kill, an icy coldness settled in her gut. Her mages were performing well, but the view Oonire passed to her mind via the spirits of light and air was grim.

There were just too many. With Men, there were always too many. That was their greatest strength. No matter how many fell beneath her mages' claws and fangs, there were always more Men.

Slowly, the enemy corralled Lovinah and her people, forcing them into the center of a circle of flashing blades and stinging arrows. She sang out to the tree spirits, to the air spirits...but despite all that she could do, the Men still kept coming.

Lovinah raked her claws down the lower torso of a sword-wielding man. His entrails spilled out over her paws, but he jabbed weakly at her with the point of his weapon, and a line of fire pierced her shoulder as his strike scored. She hissed in pain, but she could handle it...for the moment.

Kaldir's shout rang out through the small clearing, and in one sickening instant, Lovinah *knew* her worst nightmare had just come true. It had all been a plot—a trap designed to kill her and reignite the war between her people and the lying Elves.

She whipped her head around to see her treacherous Butcher of a husband. He lifted the infamous Frostfang, and the blade glittered in the moonlight.

\* \* \* \* \*

## Kacey Ezell Biography

Kacey Ezell is an active duty USAF instructor pilot with 3000+ hours in the UH-1N Huey and Mi-171 helicopters. When beating the air into submission, she writes sci-fi/fantasy/horror/noir/alternate history fiction. She is a two-time Dragon Award Finalist for Best Alternate History and won the 2018 Year's Best Military and Adventure Science Fiction Readers' Choice Award. She has written multiple bestselling novels published with Chris Kennedy Publishing, Baen Books, and Blackstone Publishing. She is married with two daughters. You can find out more and join her mailing list at www.kaceyezell.net.

\* \* \* \* \*

# Melting Ice
# by David Shadoin
## An Alliance of Spirits Story

Kaldir parried a spear that had gotten through the front lines, sliced off one of the hands holding it, and buried his blade, Frostfang, in the now defenseless chest. A swordsman fought his way through to him, but swiftly fell to his bluish-silver blade.

Kaldir, the High Commander of the renowned Legion, looked up to gauge the situation.

He tracked several enemies as they attempted to fight through the center, surprising the back rows of 1$^{st}$ Spear. Arrows from 1$^{st}$ and 2$^{nd}$ Rangers landed in the breach. The high commander moved forward, two hands on Frostfang. An overhead swing gashed an axe man's shoulder, and he forced it through the joint. He continued the movement into a low sweep, severing legs from bodies. He hacked through several sets of armor and flesh, leaving a wake of body parts behind him as he moved to plug the gap.

"On me!" he directed his Guard and the nearest Spears still standing. "Five by five, drive them back into the abyss." A dozen Elves fell in behind their high commander. They stepped forward and left any who opposed this new wall of steel bleeding out on the ground. His Guard protected his flanks with their glaives, while Frostfang danced in his hands, winning back the field where it had seemed lost.

"Spears take point! Shields up, blades out!" Kaldir called out. He and his four guards allowed the remaining Spears to step forward to line up behind some of 2nd Shield's members who had fought back to them.

With the breach plugged and the latest push by Man foiled, Kaldir took a moment to survey the field. An acrid, metallic stench filled his nostrils, and he saw that his troops had pushed them back into the woods at the edge of the field.

His reprieve didn't last long. He dispatched yet another swordsman who had gotten through with a feint and stab.

*War waits for no one.*

With the trap set and the prey in position, Kaldir used his blade to direct flashes of sunlight at 1st and 2nd Ranged companies. Two flaming arrows shot downrange on both flanks of the current field, signaling the final pincer, and 1st Mounted drove into the left flank of the retreating Men. Outmatched and confused, the forces of Men ran toward what seemed to be their unmolested right flank…right into the waiting wall of 1st Spear. Their foes were breaking but needed one more nudge to ensure they retreated without regrouping.

Kaldir nodded at one of his guardsmen, who blew the Horn of Val-Tivar and signaled 2nd Mounted to begin their charge. A second shining wall of fresh horses and blades bore down from the hillside. The Elven front lines parted for their arrival, and the cavalry crashed into the heart of the remaining enemies. They broke, steel, madness, and fear driving them as far away as their legs would take them.

Less than an hour later, Kaldir trudged back up the hill toward his tent, his armor sporting new dents and scratches. Mud caked his boots and blood ran down the left side of his armor. He couldn't remember getting cut, so he was fairly confident it wasn't his own. Victory belonged to his men, but it had cost them half of 2nd Shield, part of 1st Spear, and one of his subordinate commanders.

He lifted the flap and ducked into his tent, then slowly removed his armor. Without help, it wasn't easy, but he took great care to put each piece back in its proper place on the stand for the camp hands to clean. He rolled his shoulders and belted Frostfang back at his waist. He exited his tent to find a messenger waiting for him.

"Letter from the High Lord, sir." The messenger held out the letter.

A camp hand had left a basin outside his tent. He cupped his hands in the cool, clear water, splashed his face, and toweled the last bits of mud and blood away before accepting the message. He stepped back into his tent, poured himself a glass of wine, and sat to read the letter.

*Return when you have won; the empire is at stake.*

An involuntary shiver ran down his spine. The High Lord hadn't asked for the Legion, only for Kaldir to return, meaning an enemy from within.

Kaldir drained his glass and packed his saddle bags, intending to leave under the cover of darkness, alone. He loathed the idea of leaving his army here on the night of victory, and the captain of his personal guard would not be pleased, either, but clearly, time was of the essence.

He packed light; no armor, only his sword, bow, some rations, and a waterskin. He wrote a note directing which commander would be in charge of what tasks that remained. Before midnight, he rode eastward with a nagging feeling that he might be riding into a terrible fate.

* * *

The first night passed in a blur. Only saddle-borne meditation and smooth riding over the plains allowed him to continue all night. At sunset on the second day, Kaldir passed through an ethereal glade that put him in a calmer mood. He relaxed, taking in the sights. With his defenses down and drifting in and out of another meditative rest, he was mildly surprised to notice the light of a fire dancing in the trees.

*Who would be in in the Forest of the Elders?* he thought.

Then he heard the last thing he'd ever expected to hear in this forest: a beastly voice growling out a conversation.

Kaldir jolted back to full alertness. He dismounted quietly and tapped the back of the front right hoof of the horse, a signal common to all Elven mounts as a command to wait. He slowly drew his bow from the saddle, then slid three arrows free of his quiver. With a deep, silent breath, he moved away from his horse and glided between the trunks, taking great care to not step on any sticks or other debris that might give him away.

About two furlongs closer, Kaldir found a group of Vapaana—though his soldiers preferred the pejorative Changeling, or worse, when they faced them in the field—gathered around a small campfire. They appeared relaxed and at ease as they took an evening meal.

He counted at least eight of them, and he thought he might have heard a few more rummaging around the tents. For a scouting party, they seemed quite comfortable in enemy territory. One in particular caught his attention, if only because all the others seemed to defer to her. She sat on the far side of the fire, covered from head to toe in bristling golden fur, with a long mane of stark black hair. A pair of blue-tinged black horns spiraled out of her temples, providing a subtle illusion when seen against her mane. As she followed the conversation, Kaldir noted that her eyes seemed to match the blackness of the night sky, soaking in the light of the fire and letting none of it escape.

He had a moment of intuition and ducked behind the trunk before one of the party happened to look his way. He'd seen enough.

He needed to carry a warning back to the Beacon and ensure the guards were on high alert. He crawled slowly over to the other side of the trunk, leaned out just enough to ensure no Changeling eyes were still curious about what hid just outside of the firelight, and slunk away as quietly as he'd come.

Once back to his mount, Kaldir mounted and trotted along the path he had chosen, and when he was certain the party wouldn't hear him, urged the stallion into a full gallop.

It had been several months since Kaldir had seen the Elven capital of Alfhild, and despite his best efforts to spot it during his ride, it still sprang out of the forest and surprised him. The builders of Alfhild hid its soaring stone spires in the heart of a redwood and giant oak forest.

Kaldir rode up to a gate. "It's High Commander Kaldir with an urgent message! Open the gate!"

The guards at the post above jumped at the sound of Kaldir's voice, and as he slowed his approach, the gates began to swing outward. As soon as he thought there was enough room, Kaldir rode through the center, brushing by both doors.

Soon an inordinate number of stalls, Elves, and animals forced Kaldir to slow down. Kaldir had never been good at remembering when certain celebrations were scheduled, but he was sure there wasn't one he'd forgotten. He fumed at the delay, trying to calm the fires of impatience that grew within him. He searched for a distraction and was met by a familiar sight that loomed behind the throng.

In the center of Alfhild stood a triplet of cylindrical towers made from sparkling white quartz stone. They reflected the sun and served as a beacon for all Elves—hence its name. The castle descended from the spires to a wide three-story keep of the same ivory stone. Giant oak doors framed the base of the Beacon. Windows of stained glass were intermixed with arrow loops along the second and third story. Archers patrolled the ramparts atop the keep, between the towers. Inside the gate, a stone courtyard could be seen, an addition his half-brother had deemed necessary to their civilization. His family's standard draped over the gate and hung from the ramparts: dark blue banners with a silver-gray sword beneath a golden crescent moon and two golden stars. The richly embroidered cloth snapped in the wind.

Kaldir finally drew up to the gate, where the last of the crowd parted for him. Word of his arrival had beaten him here, as a stable hand and two of the castle's footmen awaited him.

The stable girl grabbed his horse's reins as he tossed them down and gracefully dismounted in one fluid motion. She wasted no time, and the horse didn't even break stride, following her to his much-needed grooming and rest. The lead footman, a younger Elf by the name of Filir, stepped forward.

"The High Lord has asked us to escort you to the Library's inner sanctum to discuss urgent matters."

"I sent word that I had an urgent message for the High Lord, yet I see no High Lord, nor even a captain of the guard!" Kaldir snarled at the two servants. Both of the servants flinched. Kaldir reminded himself that they couldn't make Samir or the captain appear. The chill of winter returned to his voice, replacing the fire of his temper. "Thank you for your assistance, Filir, but you may both go back to whatever it is the High Lord normally requires of you. I will see myself to the appointed meeting place."

He felt several pairs of Elven eyes following his back as he strode up to the keep's main entrance. Summoning the full power of his influence, Kaldir projected his next words as if he were on the battlefield and felt the satisfying reverberations as they bounced off the heavy doors in front of him.

"You are not here to gawk," he snapped, never turning his head. "Do not let me catch you idle. Get to it." Several murmured, "High Commander," in response, accompanied by bows following his proclamation. He opened the door and stepped inside the Beacon.

Kaldir made his way as directly as the castle pathways allowed. The Inner Sanctum itself was a small den hidden in the center of the Library, with only two entrances and exits, surrounded by floor to ceiling bookshelves of the Elves' most prized literary works, including several books on tactics and strategy Kaldir had studied. Five ornate, padded, dark oak chairs stood next to three small side tables of similar design. Only Elves with permission from the High Lord or the Chief Librarian were allowed in this room, and it was one of Samir's favorite meeting locations.

Two lamps lit the room, creating a smoky haze that burned Kaldir's eyes and tickled his throat while he awaited his half-brother. Enough time had passed that Kaldir began to wonder if he should go to his quarters and clean up when the door opposite his seat opened.

His half-brother Samir, the High Lord of the Elves, strode in like he'd always intended this time as the meeting time, and he didn't have a care in the world about urgent messages.

It had been at least a year since Kaldir had seen him, but not much had changed in that time. Where Kaldir's symmetrical face, glowing blond shoulder-length locks, and lean-muscled body qualified him as one of the fairest of the Fair Folk, Samir was his antithesis. His platinum mane was unkempt on the best of days, as he wore it straight down his back, and his stormy blue eyes darted around constantly, seeking the next threat. Some claimed he—and not Kaldir—was the real bastard of the half-brothers. That had done nothing to quell Samir's conspiratorial nature and caused him to jump at his own shadow.

But it had also made him cunning, and Kaldir was never sure exactly which facet of his brother's character he was about to encounter.

"Brother! So good of you to make it back so quickly! I could've sworn I just sent that note yesterday. I trust you have good news from the West?" Samir used familial recognition, with no obvious scorn or sarcasm. *So, an issue of family matters, then,* thought Kaldir.

"High Lord, you'll get the full report when the Legion has returned and proper accounting can be done. However, to ease your mind, I've returned only after ensuring victory on the field and the forces of Man have surrendered the area completely. But there is another matter—"

"Those are good tidings indeed, Brother!" Samir cut him off, his smile beaming...but his eyes didn't quite match the forced cheeriness. "No need to be so formal, Kaldir; as you can see, I've seen to it that your homecoming is as relaxed as you prefer. No officials, no stuffy court-aged nobles, no fanfare. Please, do sit down and act like you've noticed the efforts I've made."

Kaldir let out his breath and closed his mouth, swallowing his exasperation. He rolled his shoulders and attempted to put a smile on his face.

"My beloved brother, Samir. I apologize for my rude and boorish behavior and for not recognizing the work you've done to make me feel more welcome in your home. I'll try to enjoy this time with my only brother, but I have one thing weighing heavily on my mind that we should discuss at your earliest convenience..." Kaldir trailed off, unsure how to proceed.

"That's a much better tone, brother. Apology accepted, as always. We may not share the same mother, but we're still family, and my daughters would take it amiss if their favorite uncle was not enjoying his victorious return. Speaking of, they would very much like to see you tonight after the banquet. Ensure you make time for them before riding off again, won't you?" Samir's predatory grin stayed plastered to his pasty-white face, reminding Kaldir of a possum he'd once found taking residence in a tree near his home.

Having been ignored for a second time, Kaldir struggled to maintain his façade. Samir *was* family though; the High Lord and his daughters were Kaldir's only blood relations.

"Of course, Samir. I would never dream of visiting the Beacon without seeing the two most precious gems that help light it." Kaldir always referred to his nieces as the source of the Beacon's glow, much to their delight.

"Now that we've had a chance to exchange pleasantries like normal brothers, we can discuss some business. I was told you had an urgent message that seemed to have manifested on your journey home; is that correct?" Samir waited expectantly.

"I did, but you've summoned me here to help you protect your empire, brother. How can I be of service?" Maybe Samir already knew the Changelings were mounting an offensive and needed him to break it before it gained strength? Maybe something worse was driving them into Elven-held lands, and the fate of all living creatures might hang in the balance? At this point, Kaldir wouldn't be surprised if Samir's cavalier attitude was just a cover for the paralyzing fear of the news he was about to deliver.

Samir turned back to Kaldir, and his smile had widened, if that was even possible, the mirth finally touching those menacing blue eyes in a way that would make normal prey run in fright.

"Yes, brother, I did. Thank you for recognizing that. You know I'd never ask anything of you of this magnitude unless I thought it was for the good of the empire." Samir slowly paced around the room, directing his words to both Kaldir and the books that surrounded them. "The Beasts have been growing restless again, and have entreated me to relinquish part of the empire in the North without bloodshed. It seems your time up there still weighs on their small minds, Butcher."

Kaldir didn't miss his brother's use of the most derogatory name of the species or the venom he put into it with a hiss. "I will deal with their insurrection swiftly, Brother, of that you can be assured. On that note—"

"I wasn't DONE, Kaldir." Samir's voice whip-cracked his half-brother into brooding silence as he pushed a stray strand of his platinum bangs back into place from his forehead.

Kaldir ground his teeth to keep his mouth shut and not storm out of the room.

Samir stared down his half-brother, an attempt to will him into obedience and silence, before continuing, "As I was saying, they've sent several messages to entreat me for a truce between our nations and have communicated a set of terms that I find agreeable. We're preparing to receive them, and I need you to be at your peak of decorum and etiquette for the finalization of official negotiations."

Samir stopped pacing just off Kaldir's left shoulder, and Kaldir felt his brother's gaze attempting to penetrate the back of his own skull. "Now you may speak."

Just as Kaldir drew breath to respond, one of the doors opened.

"They have arrived, High Lord!" Keylin, an Elf of middling height with dirty blonde hair draped down her back, stood at the door. She was an old staple of the castle, having served the previous High Lord as well as his heir. "High Commander." She nodded at Kaldir. "Congratulations."

"Who has arrived?" Kaldir asked.

"Follow me and see." Samir continued in a low tone, just audible enough for Kaldir, "Just try to enjoy the festivities, High Commander."

Kaldir didn't break stride, but wondered what Samir meant. Samir and Keylin discussed other castle business as they made their way to the receiving room. Kaldir walked behind them in silence, trying to determine what his brother had planned.

Inside the reception chamber, gazing at him from across the table, was a pair of familiar black irises surrounded by golden fur, with a black mane and two curling horns. He barely noticed the others standing behind her.

Without a conscious thought, Frostfang leapt into his hand, held in a ready stance. He felt Samir's hand on his shoulder.

"My apologies," his brother said. "The High Commander is feeling a bit *edgy* after his long ride back. I assure you, he *will* remember his manners and the protections afforded by guest-right." A soft squeeze on his shoulder was the only warning the High Lord would give him, and Kaldir slowly sheathed the silver-blue blade.

"My apologies as well. I know not what came over me." *That explains the ease of the "scouting party" I found.*

Samir turned with a broad smile. "I hope she accepts your apology. Otherwise, your marriage will be more interesting than even I expect."

\* \* \*

Kaldir's fingers rubbed his temples as he stared into his own visage, noting the crinkles on the sides of his eyelids, the downward slope of his eyebrows, and the thinning mouth that gave away the anger that smoldered just beneath the surface. He had been summoned home by his brother to be sent off like chattel, negotiated as a pawn in Samir's half-baked scheme at an attempt for peace. Sold to a Vapaana for High Lord and empire.

Here his anger faltered. For the empire. A peace so desperately sought between the powerful but sparse Vapaana and the long-lived

Elves rested on his ability to maintain his composure and perform his duty. He didn't have to be happy with his fate, but he'd accept it head-on and whole-heartedly.

*But what is Samir playing at? Why give up his High Commander when any high-ranking noble would have done the trick? The Lady of the Vapaana doesn't seem so particular about who her consort would be. What was her name again?*

Lovinah. Lovely name. But she didn't seem to care who she married, so long as that someone was high enough in the families that the Elves would think twice about endangering the peace. *So why did Samir choose me?*

Kaldir continued to swirl the possibilities of the gains and losses, the strategies, and the cryptic messages in play while he dressed in his most exquisite outfit: a baroque silver cape on his left shoulder, over an ivory tunic that fastened on his right-hand side with red oak toggles. He buckled Frostfang over satin swordsman's breeches that flared out at his knees and tightened around his calves above his dark leather boots.

A servant knocked on the door, ready to usher him to the banquet. Before he knew it, he was seated next to his new bride, a striking contrast in a midnight blue formal gown over her golden fur, her jet-black hair pulled back out of her face. Elven custom dictated that their union be cemented by the two families breaking bread together at this feast.

Several tables stood before them, each filled with fresh vegetables, roast pig, and fresh baked bread interspersed with jugs of wine from the southern edges of the empire. Banners hung above each table, with lace streamers darting to and fro between them. The silver chandeliers had been polished to a sparkling sheen and tiny mirrors amplified the lit candles within, creating a multitude of lights that danced on every surface of the hall. The court nobles had put on their best attire of silvers, golds, and greens, a stark contrast to the earthy tones their Vapaana guests wore. Samir had ensured the first part of this treaty-enforced partnership was an extravagant celebration of his empire's most recent victory.

Kaldir shook his head to clear the stars from his vision. He vaguely heard Lady Lovinah state something to him. He grunted as a response, assuming that was probably good enough to keep her occupied while he studied the room. *What purpose do these nobles have for being here tonight?* Few of the Elves who would support him were in attendance, which included none of the Legion, save those serving as castle guards for the event.

Lovinah leaned over. "I know I'm not your first choice of mates, and to be honest, you haunt my nightmares, Butcher, but eventually we will have to acknowledge each other and provide each the necessary attention if we are to make this union work."

Kaldir wasn't sure what drew his focus, but between his infamous moniker and some unseen force, he was now staring into the Changeling lady's stark blue eyes as she addressed him. *Blue? They were black as night earlier.* For now, he shoved down his resentment and tried to be a better dining partner. "My lady, how unbecoming of me. May I offer you something to eat and fill your wine glass?" He reached for the nearby roast.

"It's a start," she replied, her now black eyes flashing hungrily at the small portion of pork and vegetables he'd placed on her plate. "The first thing you should learn about your new bride is I'm not as dainty as your kind." She reached for more of the roast pig. When he went to pour her wine, though, her clawed hand covered her glass. "While I appreciate the gesture, I would prefer to keep my mind clear and my senses intact whilst feasting in a den of wolves."

Kaldir studied his new partner a little closer this time. *Very shrewd of her.* Her eyes darted from one table to the next, presumably learning and planning, much as he would do. He wondered whether she was planning her escape routes, her best points of attack, or trying to learn the power struggles of the court. Several times, she seemed to glance sidelong beyond Kaldir's far hand, where Samir, High Lady Elska, and their two daughters sat in their proper place at the head table.

As the food and wine flowed, many of the nobles in attendance paid their respects to their union. On the surface, one wouldn't notice any misgivings. The noble Elves greeted his new bride with her proper title of 'Lady Lovinah,' even managing to keep ugly sneers from besmirching their otherwise beautiful faces, but the small talk was just that, talk. No well wishes, no requests that the lady visit the Southern Marsh of the Nesals or the Jadirs' Northern Tower, no obvious ploys or schemes to gain their favor. Kaldir was greeted only as 'High Commander,' and they very rarely even spoke to him. The nobles who backed Samir made it clear they didn't trust or like Kaldir. Those nobles who weren't friends of the High Lord also gave Kaldir a chilled felicitation, still holding it against him that a bastard controlled the military forces for a corrupt and gluttonous High Lord.

"I believe I need some air. The doublespeak and feigned deference for this union is growing tiresome." Lovinah stood up beside him as the latest culprits rejoined their compatriots and threw furtive glances back at the head table.

Kaldir turned to exchange pleasantries with the graceful, hazel-eyed High Lady Elska and her two daughters. "High Lady, it is a pleasure to see you at these sordid affairs, as always. Might I complement your house on the delicacies prepared for our new union?"

"High Commander, I see you haven't forsaken your good manners in your barbarity abroad. We would be ashamed to have started this union with any feast of lesser merit," Elska replied, a bit tartly.

"That's a lovely dress you have for the evening, as well. My bride and I are honored you've given nothing short of your best work."

She nodded without looking at him further and allowed him to address his two nieces, Rynska and Tamir. Rynska was the spitting image of her mother, while Tamir's golden eyes clashed with her reddish-golden hair.

"My fairest of ladies, you both grow more beautiful than the white lotus of the Crystal Lake each time I see you." This elicited rosy spots on their cheeks and small fits of giggles. They caught him up on all they'd learned since his last visit and fired a volley of questions in his direction, each growing bolder, until Samir sat back down in his seat between them and Kaldir.

"My ladies, the High Commander shouldn't be telling children of the horrors of his war. Hopefully you've had a chance to congratulate him on his nuptials, as he has many guests he must entertain and entreat."

Kaldir winced at the hint and turned back to find the Lady of Fryktmarch was still away.

With his bride apparently indisposed, Kaldir picked up his glass of wine and started a methodical route around the hall. He kept to the shadows at the edge of the room, just outside the light provided by the sconces on each pillar. Here the mood was quieter, conspiratorial almost, as they drank slowly and spoke in soft tones, their platinum and white tresses practically touching.

He heard part of one conversation. "As if the Bastard needed any further attention..."

A pair of Elves from the Freyling clan spoke in low tones. "The High Lady told her father that the High Lord has been trying to find a way to keep Kaldir away. No better scheme than sending him into the heart of Beast territory, and we'll no longer need to fear the Legion." Before he could be noticed, he moved on. *The Freylings think this is an attempt by Samir to get rid of me?*

He came to another cluster. "No, no, no! You have it all wrong. No one close to the High Lord truly *wants* peace. We have the tactical advantage from this marriage. Think about it! What would happen if the lady dies? Who gains the lands?" some Elf mumbled in response. "You think our High Lord would leave the empire vulnerable to the Beasties by letting them take the High Commander, and thus, our Legion hostage? You can trust that my brother Nintilith has his Men ready, and he intends to prove he can be an esteemed battle commander…"

The drunkard spotted Kaldir and quickly changed his tune. "I see the groom has joined us, and we should all toast his health and good fortune!" Several pairs of eyes turned in his direction, narrowed in suspicion and distrust, but raising their glasses half-heartedly.

Kaldir raised his in a full salute and drained it. He inclined his head and injected a little stagger into his step as he walked away; maybe they would think he was three sheets to the wind and assume he hadn't heard.

Unfortunately, his covert stroll had been discovered. Every Elf had noticed his absence from the head table, and he felt more eyes following him. He hid behind his now empty glass, raising it to his lips as if he expected to drain the nonexistent drink while he searched for an escape.

The Vapaana retinue at a nearby table watched him intently, but two of the guard were looking elsewhere. Following their gazes, he finally found his new golden bride.

Lady Lovinah seemed to be entangled with one of the High Lord's biggest benefactors, the head of the Nesal clan, Deleon. His eyes glowed with malice, and his sharp grin would give children nightmares.

The lady stared him down, though, holding her own by keeping her stance relaxed and inviting no immediate quarrel. Some of the Elves nearby even laughed at a response she gave that caused a brief bit of discomfort to cross Deleon's face. She said something else that caused Deleon's two private guards to stand behind him, though they made no move toward the lady. The fire light nearest them increased in intensity.

*Curious,* noted Kaldir.

As he was watching, Kaldir became aware that his bit of theater hadn't shaken any of his own enemies nearby. If the nobles wanted a spectacle, it was time to give them one.

Kaldir placed his chalice on a nearby table and strode across the hall to where Lovinah was coiling to strike. He put one hand on her arm, feeling the bristling of her fur and the quivering of tension, drawing a resentful gaze. His other hand he placed on Deleon's shoulder, closer to his neck than would normally be considered proper.

"My lord, I know you're trying to convince her to visit your keep in the marshlands," Kaldir said. "A wonderful summer vista view, if I do say so." He winked at Lovinah, an awkward gesture for him, but hopefully it would keep blades from being drawn—and play into his illusion of drunkenness. "However, I must protest that you've taken her attention for far too long…she owes me a dance." He squeezed Deleon's shoulder, attempting to pinch the nerve attached to his neck just enough to remind the old noble how dangerous he was.

Deleon winced. "Of course, High Commander. I feel we've had a fruitful conversation, but this night does belong more to the celebration than business and politics. Please excuse us." He backed away as Kaldir released his grip. Kaldir was certain Deleon would attempt to make him pay for that slight. However, his more pressing concern was surviving the night—and this dance he abruptly realized he didn't know.

It seemed Lovinah realized his lack, too, as she transferred his grip to her hand and led him onto the floor.

"It was a decent bluff, though you appear not to have thought it through," she told him.

"I hadn't expected everyone to back off that quickly, if I'm honest," he replied attempting to remember the form he'd been taught growing up. She gently corrected his hand placements, making it all look graceful.

"Then follow my back lead, and let's give them a show." She grinned, a feral look that reached her eyes, now a shade of midnight blue. A haze seemed to engulf his senses as he followed his new partner around the floor, and he knew they'd become the center of attention. His feet moved as if in a duel; it seemed that making blades sing and dancing with a partner matched up better than he'd thought.

\* \* \*

The haze cleared from Kaldir's eyes. He shook his head as the carriage hit a bump and woke him from his reverie. He remembered bits and pieces of the night before, almost like he'd drunk too much wine, but much seemed a blur, except those midnight blue eyes staring back at him from his memories. Had he threatened his half-brother with a *viper*?

*A glamour or illusion then, something to occupy our minds with elation and enhance the optics*, he mused, and heard a sigh from the far corner of the carriage. Lovinah sat there, staring out the window. It was hard to gauge her expression; the fur and hair hid the more subtle moods a face might hold and made her look angrier.

*For a glamour to have worked on me for that long while not being the primary target, she must hold great power.* Kaldir had seen the Vapaana's powers at work before, both from powerful mages on the battlefield and lighter touches by what he'd assumed were those of lesser power. But she'd enchanted them all in a simple dance…

*She was dangerous.*

"Thank you," Kaldir stated aloud, looking out his own window and attempting to determine where they were on their journey. He felt Lovinah's gaze turn on him slowly.

"You're welcome." Her gravelly reply was barely more than a growl. He glanced back over at her questioningly.

"She used quite a bit of energy to make you look brilliant," Lovinah's arachnidan handmaiden, Xiscine, chimed in. Her compound eyes glittered in the moonlight from the window, sending a chill across his skin. Kaldir hadn't noticed her sitting on the bench beside him, across from her lady. She seemed to phase in and out of the background.

It would only stand to reason that the Vapaana retinue was nearby somewhere. Kaldir had studied the race's many traits during previous campaigns, but he knew nothing for certain. He thought they were able to take the physical prowess of whichever beasts they could transform into, meaning their carriage's slow trot was an easy loping pace for many of them. He didn't know if they were naturally that fast in their humanoid form.

"So, your abilities have energy limits?" he asked. "Does it change based on what you are trying to perform with magic?"

"You won't be able to control us that easy, Butcher." Xiscine's jaw was a bit stiff, clicking in response.

"Gentle, Xiscine. He is allowed to be curious. She has a point though. You think about it in terms of a limited amount of energy, much like that used in running or fighting. It's a more complicated relationship." Lovinah's gaze drifted back out of the window.

"Then your ability to shapeshift takes a lesser toll than the illusion you cast on the guests?" Kaldir pressed.

"Shapeshifting is no mere ability; it's who we are. It defines us. We would not be called Beasts by your people if we could simply teach our ability to our young."

A deft dodge from the lady, but it provided some insight, nonetheless.

"Ladies, I'm not here to control anyone. Prior to yesterday's negotiations, I didn't even know I was being traded like our wheat in the market. But I understand the need to protect one's best weapons against a former enemy commander. So let me ask you this instead; what do you hope to gain from this alliance?" Kaldir had a good idea of what they wanted, but not every piece on the table had been revealed yet.

He sat in silence after his question. Xiscine didn't look at anyone or anything, staring into the seat next to her mistress, clearly letting her lady choose to answer, or not. When the silence grew uncomfortable and Kaldir had gone back to watching trees pass, he heard Lovinah answer, though muffled and quiet.

"Peace, High Commander." Kaldir turned back to her, though she still seemed lost in her own train of thought. "I wish this union to save my people further pain and anguish. I wish that for your people, as well, so when there was an offer on the table to put in a temporary peace and give all a chance to sit at the same table and understand each other, I chose it. War waits for no one, so one must act to stop war." She said nothing further and closed her eyes, effectively ending the conversation.

Kaldir set that sentiment against what Samir had told him about the alliance and its purpose for their empire. *His empire*, he corrected himself. He'd been adding up the pieces of the puzzle the High Lord was leaving him, not quite willing to name his objective, but enough to give Kaldir warning.

*When the time comes, can I do what was being asked of me?*

Kaldir had been fighting in wars for several hundred years now. Samir's plan would only entrench the two sides in a longer war, waged until one of the two races ceased to exist. The alternative was to tell the two Changelings about his suspicions, putting an already rocky union off to a worse start. It might still ignite the impending conflict, but his conscience would be clear. He would much prefer an open battle over the possible surprise slaughter. The more he thought about it, the more he realized there was something about Lovinah, something she'd said, that made the equation make more sense if he balanced it with her in it rather than without.

As if on cue, the carriage slowed to a halt. If Kaldir's intuition was correct, he expected to step out to see several Men—or he could stay in the carriage and wait. Out his window he saw one of Lovinah's battle guards stalk by, eyes glowing slightly, and his form seemed hazy.

"Why have we stopped?" Xiscine leaned against the opposite door, trying to get a better view. Another of the guard passed by her window, their form also hazy.

"Lady Lovinah, I think it a prudent time now to tel—"

But Lovinah opened the door and stepped out, black eyes now sapphires ablaze, and her form going hazy as well. Xiscine followed her lady after glancing back at Kaldir.

*A test or challenge, maybe?* He decided it didn't matter and stepped down from his side of the carriage.

Six Vapaana warriors stood arrayed against at least two companies of Men, and Kaldir could see archers in the trees on either side of the road.

Lovinah had transformed into a giant mountain cat. He couldn't see Xiscine anywhere.

The Men on the road wielded swords, maces, axes, and spears.

The two sides faced off for a moment, then the lion in the center roared his challenge. An arrow flew out of the tree line and pierced his shoulder. A great paw reached up, and with dexterous precision, swept the thorn out, and the Vapaana charged into battle.

The great beasts were a fearsome sight, but their attackers were either too bold, or too ignorant to know better, as they held their ground and used the advantage of numbers. Kaldir saw a tigress dodge an axe and leave gashes in the Man swinging it. A bear took a spear to the side while fending off two swords with its great claws.

In the center of the fray, Lovinah flowed through the attacks, sweeping aside strikes while assisting her guard where she could. The High Commander recognized that his wife fought as if this battle would decide the fate of the universe.

*In her mind, it might,* he realized. He also observed something he hadn't noticed in his previous campaigns to their homelands. The Men seemed to be struggling against unseen foes. They would swipe at branches randomly if they were near the trees, and even the road seemed to buck underneath them. *More Changeling magic at work, but it won't be enough.* There were too many, and the archers sent arrow after arrow into the Beasts. The mercenaries slowly encircled the party. While members on both sides had attained new injuries, only a few of the assaulters and one of the Vapaana appeared unable to continue.

Kaldir searched the tree line. Just behind the archer on the right—a female from the realm of Man—stood the Nesal cousin, Nintilith. The wicked grin on the Elf's face made him look like a goblin.

Kaldir refocused on the main battle, where the mercenaries had almost surrounded his wife's entourage. They would go down swinging, but if something didn't change, they *would* go down.

Lovinah led her small force toward what she thought was a weak link. The Men were ready for her, and they forced her back. She let out a mighty growl while staying out of spear's reach. Her sapphire eyes saw him staring. In that brief moment, their gazes locked.

Her fire wasn't going to die easily. It would blaze like a forest fire in her fight for what she believed in. In her soul, Kaldir could see she believed in their union and would fight for it, too. In her soul, Kaldir saw his equal, someone he could respect, someone he should care for, and who would care for him in return if he let her. She was as pure a being as anyone he'd ever met. She truly wanted peace for all, and she had the power to make it happen.

Stark against the sudden heat of raw adrenaline, Kaldir felt the cool solidity of Frostfang in his hand. The hand-and-a-half sword shone in the moonlight, giving him an eerie glow. He strode into battle and thrust into the chest of one of the swordsmen.

Then an arrowhead sliced across Kaldir's sword arm, leaving a red gash in his tunic. He saw Nintilith, bow in hand, staring him down.

Kaldir's battlefield instincts kicked in, and he yelled, "Two at a time, attack toward me. Keep stepping forward. Focus earth movement right between us. Whoever's at the back, keep the attackers covered."

He circled the group slightly, taking Nintilith and his archer out of play, but leaving his other side exposed. That also placed the downed Changeling, a curious looking ram that could have existed in the Northern Mountains, between him and the trapped defenders. His sword flashed low, taking another mercenary unaware.

Between Kaldir's command and the man now writhing in pain at his feet, a few of the nearby fighters noticed they were no longer safe. Their attention drawn, one spearman took a blow to the head from the lion. He was out before he hit the ground. The bear swept his claw through the line, knocking weapons flying.

A sword swing from his right forced Kaldir to duck when he heard a rustle on the wind pass dangerously close to his left ear. He looked up to see if he could place a tree between himself and another archer, and saw Changeling magic had already entangled him in branches that had suddenly moved and grown. His attention returned just in time to duck an axe. The wielder paid for his miss when his arm returned without the hand or the axe.

The ground shook, throwing everyone near Kaldir off balance. The one-handed former axeman stumbled forward as half his shoulder simply vanished into the maw of one of the Vapaana. Blue eyes, now only a couple hands away, burned bright in Kaldir's vision. Lovinah. They'd broken the encirclement. Kaldir finished disarming his current opponent, literally.

He commanded, "Tigress and Bear, take the flanks. No one outside of you. Lion, Panther, Lady Lovinah, and"—he looked at a beast he didn't recognize—"whatever you are, drive the wedge up the center. I'll finish the Elf and any remaining archers."

He hoped their answering growls indicated understanding as Kaldir stepped back toward the grove where he'd last seen Nintilith. A piercing pain emanated from his left abdomen. Examining himself, he saw an arrow nestled in his side. He swiped down with Frostfang and cut the shaft off, leaving the tip in. That was going to be a problem later, but he had to survive the fight for later to matter.

Nintilith's female partner nocked another arrow.

"Lovinah!" Kaldir called for support, hoping she'd understand. The female archer was taking aim, focusing solely on Kaldir. She didn't see the trees sway behind her. As she released the arrow, an expression of surprise broke the concentration on her features. There was no thrum of the bow string, no arrow flashing across the span. The branches had frozen her and the arrow in place, a disturbingly peaceful statuette. A thick branch lay across her throat, clamping down tightly, and her face turned blue.

Kaldir stepped closer to the grove, sword in guard, searching for the missing Elf. A shuffling step was the only warning he got. He spun to his right as Nintilith sliced down where he'd been a moment before. Kaldir swept his blade at his foe, but Nintilith stepped back out of reach, Frostfang passing through the air harmlessly. Their dance had begun.

"How could you align yourself with the Beasts?" Nintilith spat at him.

"How could you believe you could ever be a commander?" Kaldir retorted.

"The High Lord has promised me your title and lands, should I return with your bastard head. I wonder if he'll still give me at least your title if I only return with an ear..." A feint followed by a cross swing forced Kaldir to deflect.

*So, Samir wants me dead.*

Kaldir let his instincts take over. Frostfang became an extension of his arm. They traded several searching blows, each feeling out their opponent for weakness. Nintilith was neither particularly skilled with the blade, nor strong enough to overpower Kaldir...normally. But Kaldir's wound throbbed with pain, slowing his steps and reactions. It was enough to balance the scale.

"You seemed to have improved, Nintilith. Must be nice that you can now beat our younglings in a fair contest. You should probably forget commanding the Legion, however. That requires respect and skill you don't have."

"You're cocky for someone about to die, High Commander." Nintilith struck.

Kaldir ducked under Nintilith's wild swing and countered with his own overhead slash. Nintilith deflected Frostfang to the ground. He raised his blade for a killing blow aimed at Kaldir's skull.

Kaldir dropped to one knee and lifted Frostfang to parry.

The resounding clang sang across the grove.

Nintilith held him there, pinning Kaldir under his own block.

Kaldir gripped the hilt with his right hand and the guard in his left, putting his back into holding off Nintilith's blade. Pain from his stomach wound seared Kaldir.

"I have something I must confess, Kaldir." Nintilith's breath was labored, but a smile again crossed his ugly features.

"You don't need to confess your inability to understand when you've lost. I'll make you pay for that just fine." Kaldir's arms were heavy under Frostfang. He needed to hold just a bit longer.

"I plan to post your betrothed's head on—"

Two golden-furred paws grabbed Nintilith's head, claws gouging his eyes. "You talk too much, little sword." Lovinah's indigo eyes flashed with visceral pleasure, and she snapped his neck.

Nintilith's sword fell to the ground, and the High Commander took a relieved breath.

He stood and dusted off his knees, sheathing Frostfang. "That went rather well," he said, scanning the field for any movement or hidden enemies. He inhaled slowly, trying not to look as if he'd just been fighting for his life. "Perfect timing...does this count as our first argument, or first tryst?"

"We should return to Fryktmarch with haste. I feel trouble on the wind. It's haunting our footsteps."

"It seems the High Lord took the initiative, but we've won the opening skirmish. Without me there to talk him down, he will not take this loss well." Kaldir walked back to the carriage and unhitched the horses. "I never asked if you know how to ride."

"You still have much to learn...Kaldir." And with that, she bounded off into the woods, her guard out to either side, like a pack. Kaldir's breath labored under the pain in his side as he climbed onto his mount.

Then Lovinah's voice floated back to him, as if carried by the breeze. "War waits for no one, so we must be prepared for when war comes."

*We? An intriguing revelation, indeed.*

With that unsettling thought, Kaldir spurred his mount after his wife.

\* \* \* \* \*

## David Shadoin Biography

David "Shady" Shadoin is a troublemaking, corn-fed Nebraska boy the United States Air Force managed to turn into a somewhat decent pilot of whirly birds. An avid reader from a young age, literally the picture definition of 'bookworm' in Webster's, he has always found inspiration in listening to rock music while reading Fantasy and Sci Fi novels and drinking single malt scotch. This love of written adventure set up Shady to moonlight as an author trying to find a good outlet for creative ideas that start with nothing more than a misplaced pop culture reference and some D&D dungeons. While travelling to the farthest reaches of the US as a young pilot, he met a wonderful, patient woman, Stef, whom he conned into marrying him. She is responsible for encouraging this new habit, and he loves her for it very much.

* * * * *

# Why Not
# by Kevin Steverson
## A Balance of Kerr Story

### Chapter 1

Garl dodged the log thrown at him. It wasn't hard to do. Sargil, like the others in his clan, was predictable.

He didn't care what his brother thought, or anyone else in his clan. Garl had no intention of staying in the huge clan-house every night with the rest.

He showed up every morning in time to eat, and then go to the caves to work. Only the little ones stayed back with the elders. All the rest went to the holding caves and cared for the eggs. They turned them daily and kept the fire burning to keep it warm enough.

The work was boring, but it kept his clan in good standing with the Elves. At least they didn't have to feed the young ones, or worse, the older ones. Others did that.

"Where do you go every night?" demanded Sargil. "What do you do?"

"I sleep in the nesting caves," answered Garl, "not here on the floor with the rest."

"You are clan Long Tooth!" shouted Sargil. Another log flew at him to smash against the even bigger logs of the wall. "You stay here with the rest of us!"

"Why?" Garl asked. The question wasn't directed at his brother.

"All the clans stay together," Elder Lorth answered. "It has always been this way. There is strength in numbers."

"But why?" Garl asked again. "We have nothing to fear. The other clans know us. They won't attack us. The Elves wouldn't tolerate such an act. We aren't in the time of our ancestors."

"You cannot question an Elder!" Sargil yelled. He reached for another log. The closest one was burning, one end in the firepit. He brandished it, the light making crazy shadows in the clan house.

"Put it down," Elder Lorth said. "He can ask why. He's always asked why. It is his nature. Much like your temper is yours."

"Bah," Sargil muttered. He threw the log back into the fire pit and stormed out.

"Garl, you are nearing the time to find a mate from one of the other clans and bring her here. The time for 'why' is nearly over. I won't say this in front of your brother, but he's right. The old ways are the best ways. No, we don't fear attack in the night like the days of old, but if it happens, we'll fight as a clan, like we live as one. It's time for you to decide."

"Decide?"

"All must decide. Will you stay, find a mate, and remain here in your clan, or will you go and find your own way?"

"I have a choice? Why have I not been told this before? I do not remember any other leaving."

"The last to choose to go was Lunthak, before you were born. It happens. More so in other clans, ones who don't prosper like clan Long Tooth. In the hills to the south, there are clans. Others choose to go west to the far mountains."

"I...I feel this isn't my place," Garl said, looking off. It was the first time he'd ever told anyone.

Elder Lorth nodded his big head as if he'd expected it. "I suspected this would be your answer."

Garl looked at his father's father. "How did you know? Is it because you are Shaman? Did Lothar show you I would?"

Elder Lorth held two fingers out together and made a waving motion, simulating lightning coming down. With his other hand he reached up to the string of small animal skulls around his neck. "No, the God of Lightning—may he strike with a vengeance forever—did not."

"Then how?"

"You're like your father. He stayed with the clan but regretted it. It weighed heavy on him."

"I was never told this," Garl said. "Why?"

The old one grinned, his few remaining teeth showing. "And the questioning you get from your mother."

He stared into the flames of the fire pit and spoke without looking at Garl. "Lothar didn't have to show me you'd choose to leave. You question the way things are, the way they have always been, and you long to be elsewhere. It's within you. I always knew it. You aren't like your brother. He remembers your parents. The memory of their deaths fuels his anger. Anger defines him."

"I was but crawling when they were killed."

"Yes, you were too young to remember the night half the clan died. That's why the emperor sent us here to watch over the eggs until they hatch. The Slashing clan now has the job we once had here in Zar. Not a year goes by they don't lose members, but never in the numbers we did that night."

"What do I do?" Garl asked.

"Ever the questions," Elder Lorth remarked.

"How else will I learn?"

"It's simple. You leave."

"That's it?"

"Yes. There's nothing to be said. It would only anger your brother and the others more. Were I younger, it would anger me. I've been shown there is other than anger and rage in all we do."

"I don't want to be angry all the time."

"Then go." Elder Lorth made the sign of lightning. "May Lothar guide you to where you belong."

\* \* \*

Later that afternoon, Garl looked around. It was the first time he'd been alone, and he couldn't wait any longer. Others would be back for more of the eggs. He wiped the sweat from his forehead. The fires had been allowed to burn down, but it was still hot in the nesting cave.

He looked up toward the ceiling. Two feet above his head was the opening for smoke to escape. With the fires low, there was little smoke, and it was easy to see. He grabbed the closest egg, raised it high, and pushed it up into the opening. He put the heavy egg in the thick netting hanging there. It almost didn't fit. The egg he'd chosen was the largest of the new ones.

When it was secure, he turned and went back to the rest. He picked up two of the smaller ones and carried them to the front of the cave, around the bend. Outside in the sunlight, he squinted and waited.

Two others passed him, going back for more. He placed his two in the next cart in line. He put them as gently as his big hands could manage on the straw. One of them was already cracked and moved back and forth. He waved a hand to get the attention of the nearest Overseer.

"Egg hatch early," Garl said. The Elven language was difficult for his tongue.

The black-haired Elf walked over and looked up at Garl as if he'd lost his mind, daring to speak to him. He looked at the egg and to the driver. "Take this cart to the closest empty cage and put the hatching egg in it. Go now!"

The light-brown haired Elf sitting in the seat nodded but didn't speak. She flicked the reins, and the cart moved away quickly. The eggs would go to separate cages, out of sight of each other. There, the dragons would hatch and grow, secluded by themselves. Garl knew that was to slowly drive the poor creatures insane. They'd remain alone, fed and cared for by lesser Elves who were forbidden to talk to them.

When they were still young, their wings would be clipped, and training would begin, enforced by long poles enchanted with lightning spells. When they were fully grown, they would be kept in chains and used by the Elven armies at the onset of battle.

Garl was only in his teens, but he knew this year was different. More eggs had been taken from caves near the coast, beyond the mountain ranges in Zar. Many Elves had died to acquire the eggs, especially the few blue ones.

Later, he made his way up the mountain to the opening in the roof of the nesting cave. In the light of the moon, he looked for the dark, soot-covered rocks. Working his way to them, he reached down for the hidden rope. He untied it from the limb lying across the opening and began pulling. Slowly, carefully, he pulled the netting out, the egg still secured inside.

He wrapped the rope a few times around the netting and tied it. He slung it over his shoulder and moved away from the edge of the city. Once he grabbed his bag hidden in the forest, he started running, his long legs taking huge strides. He ran for hours.

*　*　*

The next morning, miles away, Garl stopped. He was exhausted. He sat with his back against a huge oak tree, ate the last of a rough loaf of bread and pieces of dried deer meat, and then closed his eyes. He slept restlessly, checking on the egg several times. Near noon, he was awakened by the sound of cracking. He took it out of the netting and watched.

Slowly, more cracks formed as the egg wobbled back and forth. Finally, a dark blue nose pushed through, breaking pieces off. An hour later it was free from the egg. Garl reached down and picked up the baby. It leaned back and stared up into his face.

"Hello, little one," Garl said.

The little blue-eyed baby blinked sleepily several times, leaned his head forward, and nestled it against Garl's chest. In that moment, Garl knew he'd made the right decision. Leaving his clan wasn't a hard one to make. Stealing an egg was, but he'd done it anyway.

They weren't disturbed. Even if an animal or anything else were to discover them, they would remain so. There are very few creatures on the entire planet of Kerr willing to disturb an Ogre, much less one cradling a Dragon in his arms.

* * * * *

## Chapter 2

Garl crouched behind the huge boulder.

The last Troll stopped, raised its face to the sky, and inhaled deeply. It looked around, squinting in the bright light. It couldn't see what it smelled. It said something Garl couldn't understand. The two others stopped and started to come back.

Garl came around the boulder, his bone club held high. He brought it down with all his might.

The Troll raised an arm to protect itself, but it didn't stop the force of the blow, and it went flying. The next came at him with hands extended, its dirty claws brandished like bone blades. It jumped back as Garl brought the club back around.

Both Trolls shuffled toward him. They weren't as big as he was, even if they stood straight, but they were larger than any others he'd fought. When the third came up behind them, one arm dangling, he realized they might be more than he could handle.

From the corner of his eye, he saw a flash of blue. The young Dragon hit the injured Troll with all four feet extended, his claws buried as they both went rolling.

Garl used the distraction to his advantage. He threw his club with both hands, and it went spinning to hit the one closest to him square in the face. It dropped, dazed.

The last turned its head when the sound of crackling and the smell of burnt flesh washed over them. Garl grabbed it by the arm, spun, and smashed its head against the boulder over and over. He dropped the lifeless body and used his club on the dazed one. All three were dead.

"Rynok!" Garl shouted.

The Dragon looked over, and with a flap of his wings and the strength of his legs, jumped over all three bodies. "I got him," he said.

"I saw," Garl admitted. "I told you to stay out of sight. You could have been hurt."

"I wasn't," Rynok assured him. He looked pleased with himself. "I breathed on him, too!"

"I smelled," Garl said. He shook his head. "It's time we moved on from here. That makes five Trolls we've seen in the last week. Something is stirring them up, causing them to leave the mountains."

"Why?"

"You ask a lot of questions."

"How else will I learn?"

* * *

Garl stood at the edge of the forest on a cliff looking out over the rolling sea. He'd never seen this much water in his life. In the past, they'd stayed on the edge of lakes, some bigger than others, but nothing like this. He inhaled deeply. He now knew the cause of the scent growing stronger the last few days.

Rynok had tried to describe to him what he'd seen from high above, but the young Dragon had been at a loss for words when he did so. Calling it "big water" didn't do it justice. Garl looked up and spied him soaring in the constant breeze. He rolled and swooped in delight. Leaving him to his play, Garl looked for a way down to the sands below.

The easiest way down was to follow the creek as it cut its way through the hills. It was the same one they'd followed for weeks, from the stream bubbling out of the ground, until it widened to a distance he couldn't jump over. It ended in a waterfall as tall as he was, falling to a pool formed in the rocks and sand, moving on to the sea in three small channels.

Garl sat in the sand, his arms around his knees, as the water lapped over his bare feet every fourth or fifth wave. The sun felt good on his shoulders. He shifted, digging his feet deeper. Rynok dozed behind him in the softer sand, his belly full of the last of the two large fish he'd snagged. He'd said they were easy to see, with their fins sticking out.

Garl had plans for the rows of sharp teeth left on the piles of bones. He picked one up and started working them out of the jaws while he thought about hardening a new wooden club, one with the teeth embedded that could be used as a saw. At the very least, he could make spear tips.

The last few years, he and Rynok had lived off the land, hunting and fishing. Always fishing, especially. Some places they stayed for months before moving on. It was time to settle permanently.

"Why not here?" he asked himself aloud.

* * *

Silas counted the shadows in the dark. He added three more to the count to include the little ones secured to their fathers' backs. *Twenty of us*, he thought. *Can so many move far enough to keep from being found?* He put his hand on his wife's shoulder to reassure her. His teenage children needed none. They were resolved, his daughter helping to keep the younger children together.

Nessille moved toward them, her darkened form huge in the dimly lit night. "We go," she said. She spoke the Human language haltingly.

Silas knew it was not an indication of her intelligence. That was a mistake many other races made, including their Elven masters. He could only speak a little of the Ogre language, but what he did know conveyed whole sentences and thoughts in only a few words. It was all about the emphasis and tone of each sound. It was far more difficult than the Elven language he spoke so well.

The two words she said also conveyed urgency and excitement, followed by finality. On a moonless night, the group moved deeper into Zar, away from the cities and toward the hills and mountains of the west. For the first two hours they moved at the fastest pace the youngest could handle. Afterward, Nessille carried the three smallest for hours more.

They left their village, the empty clan house on the hill, and the livestock free to roam with gates flung wide far behind. *Why not?* Silas asked himself for the hundredth time. In a few days, the Elves would come back, still angered, and gather the Humans like they did the Ogres. They were to be fed to the Dragons, too, blamed for the loss of the new blues. *Let them hunt us.*

\* \* \* \* \*

# Chapter 3

Dragon Master Xenth looked up from the scroll he was studying. Unlike most in his profession, he had the gift of magic. Not enough to join the ranks of mages in Zar, but enough to use scrolls, items, and cast a few spells. Captain Naroz, the head trainer, was breathing heavily as he approached him. "What is it?"

"Sir, they're gone!"

"Who are gone?"

The trainer stood straight, took a deep breath, brushed his long black hair back, and gave his report. "I sent a squad to gather the Humans from the village with tainted meat. The ones who caused us to lose all the new Blues, like you ordered."

Xenth waved his hand in a small circle, indicating for the trainer to get on with the report.

"They're gone. They're just gone. The cattle roam free in the village and the woods around. The firepit in every hut is cold. From what the squad leader says, they've been gone for over a week."

Xenth pursed his lips in frustration. Not only would he have to inform the Commander of the Army all the new Blue Dragons had perished again, but he would also have to let one of the emperor's advisors know an entire village of Human slaves had disappeared. He could lie and say they'd been fed to other Dragons, but if the lie was discovered, he'd be the next snack, because he'd ordered the death of the clan of Ogres overseeing the livestock and the Humans in the area.

"Send a platoon to find them. Tell the lieutenant to bring them back if you can, or kill them if you must. I want resolution before I make my report."

"Shall we send a squad of scouts with them?"

"No, don't bother, the soldiers should be able to track them well enough. Oh, and tell them they aren't to return without taking care of this."

* * *

Garl watched Rynok circle lower and lower, enjoying the constant breeze from the ocean and the warm air radiating from the sands as they made flight easier than it could have been, given his size. The Dragon didn't have a fish in his claws. Garl didn't expect it, though. Rynok had been inland most of the morning, hunting meat for the Ogre. With several mighty flaps of his wings kicking up sand, Rynok landed gracefully.

"No luck this morning?" Garl asked. He continued to scrape the hide of the last large deer Rynok had caught. He turned the wooden frame over and reached for another of the tooth knives.

Rynok turned his long neck, bringing his head closer to Garl. He inspected the hide. "No, I saw several. Others hunted them, so I let them be. You always tell me to avoid others. I think these are some of the others."

Garl dropped his knife and spun toward his friend. "What? You saw others? Were they Elves?"

"I don't know. I've never seen an Elf," Rynok answered. "From what you've described, I don't believe so. The hair wasn't right."

"Hair?"

"Yes, you say they have black hair. The small ones I saw didn't. Their hair was the color of the coconuts you like. Brown. Some were lighter."

"Not black?" Garl pondered out loud. "They could be lesser Elves. They aren't soldiers or scouts. Only the upper caste is afforded those opportunities."

He paused a moment, realizing what the Dragon had said. "Wait. What do you mean by 'small ones?'"

"I counted more than twenty small ones; some were very small and held by others. I also saw one like you. But now that I recall the details, the hair was wrong on that one, too."

"You saw an Ogre? What was wrong with the hair?"

"It was longer than yours, and tied in the back."

"A female," Garl stated. He looked down at his leather britches and shirt. They weren't stained as some of his others were. He brushed his chest and stomach with a large hand. These he'd made recently. Barefooted, he looked around for his boots. They were inside his cabin on the edge of the cliff, near the stairs he'd cut into it.

"Did they see you?"

"I don't think so. I was colored as the sky. Much lighter than my natural color."

All Dragons had the ability to change colors to match what was around them. Garl knew there were lizards with the same ability. "Good. You might have frightened them if they saw you."

"Why?"

"Well, because you're a Dragon."

"Why does that matter? I don't frighten you. You're not a Dragon."

"I know. It's just that...well, the Red Dragons in Zar aren't sane. They're used in battle to kill scores of enemy soldiers. Everyone associates all Dragons with them. Well, the other clans and the Human slaves did, anyway."

"I am blue."

Garl reached out and patted his friend on the side of his jaw. "Yes, you are. The only one I've ever seen live beyond a week or two."

"Why?"

"More questions," Garl said, lifting a hand to ward off the statement from his big blue friend. "I know, I know. It's how you learn." In many ways, despite his enormous size, Rynok was still young.

"They ate, got sick, and starved. And speaking of that, we'll need several deer in case they're hungry when they get here."

"And fish," Rynok said. "Lots of fish." He crouched, ready to spring high before flapping his wings. Before he made the leap, he asked, "How do you know they will come here?"

"I asked Lothar in prayer," Garl answered. "The God of Lightning answers prayer."

"You asked for them to come here? You didn't know they were close until I saw them and told you. This seems very suspicious to me."

"I didn't pray for those you saw," Garl explained. "I prayed for a mate. You saw a female. Seems like Lothar answered."

"Are you sure he does?" Rynok asked. He tilted his head and studied Garl with one eye. "Why would a God answer you?"

"The shamans never said. They just taught us all to pray." Garl shrugged his shoulders. "And to stay out of the storms, lest we anger him, and he shows us why he reigns over lightning."

"I have lightning. Did he give it to me?"

"I don't think that's how it works. Now go get some meat. We have guests coming."

\* \* \* \* \*

## Chapter 4

Rynok landed again long before he should have been back. "What's wrong now?" Garl asked. The Dragon's body language was more than enough to make him realize something was wrong.

"They're coming faster," Rynok said. "There's another group chasing them. The new ones ride big, antlerless deer, and they smell different than the first group. Also, there's something else. Something sharp, tangy. I can taste something on the tip of my tongue. I do not think I like it." He added one more thing. "Oh, and they all have black hair."

"Steel," Garl said. "You smell steel. The second group are High Elves. Soldiers. They must be trying to capture…or kill the first group."

"That's not right, is it?" Rynok asked. He dug deep furrows in the sand with his front feet. "You said we only kill for food or in defense. They will not eat the others, will they?"

"No. Elves don't eat Elves. They don't kill lesser Elves, either." He reached up and scratched the side of his face. "Humans they kill. They don't care about the slaves. Wait, did you say the sharp smell was what was different? Or was there more?"

"More. I know the smell of something alive. It was the steel, whatever that is. They smelled different."

"They're chasing Humans. Why is an Ogre with the slaves?"

Rynok shook his massive head. "I don't know. I only know you. I would like to meet your mate and the others. I don't want to meet those with steel."

"I didn't say she was my mate," Garl said quickly. "I said I prayed for one. There is a difference. She could be an elder, for all we know. Or already mated to another."

"Does that matter?"

"Of course it matters! It...never mind," Garl said. "You wouldn't understand. From what I know of the Reds the Elves have in captivity, you're years from thinking about a mate."

"I would like to meet others like me," Rynok said. "I don't think I want a mate. I just want to talk to one, and his friend."

Garl patted Rynok on his neck. "I don't know about that. You might be disappointed. All Dragons aren't like you. You know others don't have a friend like me."

"Why not?"

"It's hard to explain. Besides, we would have to go to the other side of Kerr to the Eastern oceans to find more like you. I was told that was where the clutch of eggs came from."

"One day we could go."

"Yes, one day. But not today. How long before the Elves catch the group?"

"Those on the big deer stop now and again to check the signs of those ahead moving across the fields and woods. They went the wrong way for a while and circled back. I would say, when the sun is high in the sky, they will catch them."

"Horses. They ride horses, not deer," Garl explained. "That doesn't give us much time. Now get back in the sky, but make sure you can't be seen. I need to get to the head of the trail and see what I can do to help them. We may have to fight. It's been a while since I trained with my club."

Rynok sprang into the air and beat his wings steadily. Soon he faded into the background of the sky. Garl watched for a few moments, then looked for the braided leather rope and his bag of teeth.

\* \* \*

Garl waited until the group of Humans were halfway across the glade before he stepped out. The first few saw him and stopped short, causing the others to bunch up behind them. One held an axe, the other a wooden spear. The man with the axe shouted a name.

"Nessille!"

Garl stood transfixed as an Ogre came out of the trees behind them. She was a head shorter than he was, and about his age. Her hair was pulled into a single bunch at the back of her head, long enough it came over her shoulder. She wore the typical leathers of those residing in Zar. Garl saw her necklace of stones.

"I am Garl," he said, ignoring the Humans for the moment, "of my own clan."

"I am called Nessille," she answered after a moment's hesitation. "I am...I am the last of Clan Stoneshapers." She lifted the stone hammer in her hand. A hardened wooden handle held its head.

"The last?" Garl asked. "What happened to your clan? I know it was large. Your clan feeds the young Dragons."

The Human with the axe looked back and forth at the two Ogres, unable to follow their conversation. He said, "Nessille, we must go. The Elves will be here any moment. This time we may not be able to trick them and disappear into the hills."

Garl answered him in his language, "Not go far. After hills is big water."

Nessille's hands dropped to her side, the hammer in one forgotten. "We have reached the coast. We can run no farther."

The Human had a perplexed look on his face as he tried to understand her. Garl explained, "It name sea in Human words."

Several of the women in the group pulled their children close upon hearing this. They may have been slaves in Zar, but they knew of the sea. The Elves held Humans in such contempt, they spoke freely around them.

"You can tell me what happened later," Garl said. "For now, take them to the cliffs. There is a way down to the sands by my home. You will see it."

Nessille turned to the Human. "Keep going. Go to sand. Easy to find. By clan house."

"What will you do?"

"Stay and fight."

An hour later, the first of the Elves rode out into the glade. They were met by the two Ogres on the far side. Familiar with Ogres, one spoke in passable Ogre. "Have you seen Humans?"

"Of course I have," Nessille answered. "They are my friends."

She had spent the last hour telling Garl what had happened to her clan and why. She said they'd have taken her, too, if the Human, Silas, hadn't insisted she crawl into his hut and stay there.

The two Elves spoke quietly to each other. Garl knew why they were indecisive. An Ogre waiting for you with a club in his hands was enough to make anyone hesitant. Two presented a foolish undertaking.

When six mounted soldiers came out of the trees, the Elves made their move and came galloping. Garl and Nessille eased back into the trees behind them. The first two Elves rode down the trail, only to be unhorsed by the rope tied at chest level to a rider. The weight of their armor did little to soften the blow of striking the ground. Garl made short work of them.

The two riderless horses kept moving down the trail, away from the noises behind them. Garl roared with every swing of his club, causing panic among the others. When the six Elves were down, the Ogres turned and ran through the wooded hills toward the sea.

With nowhere else to go, Garl and Nessille waited on the sands. The Elves were left with no choice. They dismounted and took the rough stairs to meet those standing between them and the Humans.

Three of the dozen readied their bows. They never got a chance to use them, as a bolt of lightning from a massive shape flying by knocked them and two more to the ground. None moved. The rest surged forward.

Garl blocked the sword with his club, a piece coming off of the sharp blade. A stone hammer slammed into the extended arm, and the sword fell. Garl finished him and turned in time to ward off another blow. He couldn't stop the Elf beside him from slashing his forearm. Garl roared in rage and swept them both aside with a mighty swing.

When Rynok landed among the remaining Elves, crushing two, Nessille stopped fighting and stared. That nearly cost her life. Garl's club handle was cut in two, blocking the two-handed sword. Rynok made short work of the rest of them.

\* \* \*

Nessille, still in awe of Rynok, asked "Do you want us to strip the armor and feed the bodies to your Dragon?"

"Disgusting," Rynok declared. "Thank you for your concern, but I don't eat meat."

Nessille stared. Finally, she managed to say, "You speak. How is this?"

"Of course I speak. Doesn't everyone?"

"But you…you speak Ogre."

"Again, doesn't everyone?"

Garl said, "No, Rynok, everyone does not. The Humans can't speak it. Not fluently. They have their own language."

"Interesting," Rynok said. He laid his big head on the ground and looked closely at the small Human crawling toward him. The child's mother snatched him up nervously. "It's the only one I know. Do you think there is a Dragon language?"

"I'm sure there is, though I've never heard the Reds attempt to speak to each other."

"That's because they're insane," Nessille said, "kept that way in isolation from the time they hatch until they are trained."

"That isn't right," Rynok declared.

"No. Not right," Silas said in halting Ogre. The tone and nuances were off slightly, but the three understood him.

"He sounds funny," Rynok said.

"He's learning," Nessille explained, "just as I'm learning the Human language.

"Will you teach me?"

"I don't see why not."

"But not today," Rynok said. "Today I go fishing."

He moved away from the children playing in the sand while the others removed armor and clothing from the Elves. One by one, the bodies were moved up the stairs and into the woods to a deep pit

Rynok had clawed out at Garl's insistence. When he was far enough away, he leapt into the air.

"Fishing?" Nessille asked.

"Yes," Garl confirmed. "He's a Blue. His kind eat fish, not meat. I discovered that a day after he hatched. I tried to feed him meat, and he got sick and refused any more. In desperation, I tried a piece of fish, and he ate it with no issues, just a huge appetite."

"That's it!" she exclaimed. "That's why the Blue Dragons never live beyond a week. We were feeding them meat, like we did the Reds."

"Years ago, half my clan were killed because we lost a clutch of Blue Dragons," Garl said. "That's why the Long Tooth clan was moved to work the warming caves and no longer feed the young."

She stared at the ground for a long time. "That's why I'm the last of my clan, and why I had to help the Humans leave Zar."

"I am sorry for your loss. I'm not sorry you came to the sea," Garl said.

She looked at him for a long moment. "I am, too. We can go no farther."

"Stay. All of you, stay," Garl said. "Unlike those in my clan, I don't mind the Humans. Their size takes getting used to—one must be careful not to hurt them—but I like the company of all of you. It's been just Rynok and me for too long."

She smiled at him and brushed a loose strand of hair from her face. "Are you sure it's not because you're looking for a mate?"

"What did he tell you?" Garl demanded. "The traitor."

\* \* \* \* \*

## Chapter 5

Four years later, Rynok stretched out, relishing the warmth of the sand. He turned his head so he could keep an eye on young Kaniss. Garl's daughter was knee deep in the water, trying to catch crabs with several Human children. Every time they caught one, they brought it to him. He didn't mind the snack, though it wasn't much of one.

One of the Human children wandered too far into the water for his liking, so he stretched his neck out and nudged the offender back toward the shoreline. "Tilnith, you know your mother doesn't want you to go that far."

"But I was chasing a big one," the boy protested in perfect Ogre.

"Tell it to your mother," Rynok said. "I won't be the reason a toothfish feeds on you instead of me feeding on one of them."

"I like toothfish," Kaniss declared.

"Me, too," Rynok said. "I'll go catch some when your parents come back down to the beach."

"What are they doing?" Kaniss asked. She stood with her hands on her hips.

"They're helping Silas and the others with the corn. It's time to harvest it," Rynok answered.

"I like corn, too," Kaniss said.

"I know," Rynok said.

He watched the little ones play for a while, and then sighed to himself. "I wonder if young Dragons play endlessly like Humans and Ogres."

"They do," a voice said beside him.

Rynok whipped his head around. He didn't recognize the voice, nor the Human standing where none had been moments before.

"Who are you?" he demanded. "If you think to harm just one of—"

"I would never consider it," the Human interrupted. He reached up and stroked his long white beard.

"You *are* a big one, aren't you?" the Human said. He nodded to himself as if answering someone. "Greetings, Rynok. I am Zeronic."

"How do you know my name? I've never met you. Do Garl and Silas know you are here on the sand?"

"They do not," Zeronic answered. He spoke sternly to one of the children. "Tilnith, that's deep enough." The boy moved back.

"Where was I? Oh yes, how do I know you?" Zeronic stroked his beard. "Let's just say, I know everyone. No matter the race. I am, after all, the God of Wind and Change."

"Garl talks of the God of Lightning. I've never heard him mention you," Rynok said.

"Ah, yes, I did speak to my brother about Garl. Rest assured, there are no hard feelings between us."

Rynok squinted at Zeronic. "How do I know you are who you say you are?"

He found himself on the balcony of a huge tower overlooking an island and the sea. "Where are we?" he demanded. "What of the children!" He bared his long teeth and drew in a deep breath.

Zeronic dismissed the attempt with a wave of his hand. "Don't be silly. They're fine. Not a heartbeat will pass before you're with them again."

"Take this back with you." He pointed to a large leather saddle.

"That looks like what Silas and the others sit on when they ride the horses," Rynok said.

"Exactly," Zeronic said. He held out a key with a blueish-green stone in it. "Now, I'm going to put this key in one of the keyholes. Make sure you point it out to Garl."

They were back on the beach, the saddle between them. "Well, that's all I have for you now," Zeronic said. "I will leave you to your task, though keeping an eye on this lot would tire even one such as myself."

Rynok's eyes widened as the old man disappeared. "Wait! That is it? Will you not explain more?"

"No, I don't believe I will," Zeronic answered. "I'll leave that to Dolner."

\* \* \*

"Who is Dolner?" asked Garl.

"You let a stranger near our children?" demanded Nessille.

"I never heard of this god," Silas said. "I know of Saint Lanae, and even Minokath, Lord of the Sea, but not Zeronic." He looked around. "Some of the words from the Book Of The One have been spoken by my father's father. I don't know where he learned it."

"Too many questions," complained Rynok. "I only know what I told you."

Garl surprised everyone as he walked away, his eyes up along the long stretch of beach. "There are our answers."

In the distance, two black dots slowly grew to become red ones. They could make out the flapping wings of Dragons. As they got closer, they saw two Humans sitting in saddles like the one on the beach beside Rynok.

The Dragons circled several times before landing softly, sand kicking up around them as they beat their wings. Their riders, a man with dirty blond hair and a woman in mail armor with short red hair unlocked the leather bracers holding their legs to the saddle with keys like the one Garl now held. They dismounted and walked over together.

The man hissed at Rynok. When he received no reply, he tried again. The largest of the Red Dragons did the same. Finally, the woman asked, "Do you understand Human language?"

"I do," Rynok said. He switched to Ogre. "But this is my language."

The woman tilted her head slightly and shook it.

To everyone's surprise, including the redhead's, the man spoke in perfect Ogre. "You don't know your own language? That's interesting. What are we speaking now? Ogre? I didn't know I could speak Ogre. This is great. Remind me to thank Zeronic in my prayers." He rubbed a leather band with a blue stone in it.

"I can speak the language of Dragons and Lythons. I may know more. Of course, I don't know if I do...oof!" He rubbed his side where he had been elbowed.

He switched back to Human. "Sorry. I'm Dolner. This is June."

The largest of the Reds said haltingly, "I'm Wryle. This is my mate, Lyna."

"I am Rynok." He studied the Reds. The largest was almost his size. "I've never seen another of my kind until today." His use of the Human language was much better than the Ogres.

"Why you come?" Garl asked.

"Hey," Dolner said. "When the God of Wind and Change says to come this way instead of going with armies over land into Zar, you do it." He shrugged his shoulders and ran his hand over his head, letting his hair fall to both sides. "Now that I see that big saddle, I know why."

"Who have you accepted as your Rider?" June asked. She looked expectantly at Silas, the closest Human.

"My Rider?" Rynok asked. "I don't have a Rider. I have Garl. He raised me from the egg."

June stared at the key in Garl's hand. Her eyes widened. "An Ogre? An Ogre as a Dragon Rider?"

Dolner laughed. "Why not?"

\* \* \* \* \*

## Kevin Steverson Biography

Kevin Steverson is a retired veteran of the U.S. Army. With several best-selling novels, including the Salvage Title Trilogy, picked up for development into feature film, he is also a published songwriter. When not at a convention or concert, he can be found in the foothills of the NE Georgia mountains, writing his next story.

- Sign up for his newsletter at www.kevin.steverson.com and receive a free short stories.
- Facebook: https://www.facebook.com/KevinSteversonAuthorPage
- Instagram: https://www.instagram.com/kevin.steverson/
- Bookbub: https://www.bookbub.com/authors/kevin-steverson
- On Amazon: https://www.amazon.com/dp/B07R68TF8P

\* \* \* \* \*

# The Empty House
# by J.T. Evans

The abandoned house terrified Harold, but Mark had used the infamous Double-Dog-Dare on him.

Now Harold stood at its crooked front door, watched by a gaggle of other kids waiting outside the rusted iron fence. He swatted at a buzzing fly and swiped away the sweat from his forehead that the early autumn heat had brought on.

The other kids made fun of his hesitation at the door and swinging hands at the annoying insect. The group pointed and laughed at Harold, though they'd stayed on the outside of the fence next to a gate hanging askew on its bent hinges.

He yanked on a loose lock of his unkempt blond hair while thinking about how to get out of this.

No one wanted to go into the house. It was once a beautiful mansion, but now stood as a massive, rotting symbol of a dead family. The house had been falling apart as long as Harold could remember seeing it at the end of the country road. It seemed as if it had remained unchanged over the course of Harold's life, but Harold had to remind himself that his ten years of age wasn't all that much to a house like this one.

Harold wished he could just race away from the house, past his so-called friends, leap onto his bike, and ride off into the sunset. He didn't need to prove anything to them. He didn't *want* to prove anything to them.

But then again, maybe he did.

Anyone caught being a chicken would have to prove their bravery twice-over on the playgrounds of Joseph A. Krankton Elementary School. The games of dodge ball, red rover, freeze tag, and wall ball would become especially brutal for anyone branded as a coward. Harold wasn't sure he could survive another year as bottom dog in the pile.

Swallowing hard, he pushed on the front door, but it was stuck firmly in the frame. The crooked door refused to budge even a hair. He turned back to the crowd of kids with a shrug.

Mark yelled, "You gotta go 'round to the back door to get in, Doofus!"

Another of the boys shouted, "Make sure you open a window so we know you went in! No crying in the back for twenty minutes and then lying to us about going inside."

Kevin, the meanest one, added, "Yeah, you little baby. Get going. No running to your mommy."

Harold stomped off the sagging porch and fought through overgrown bushes, tall grasses, and trees whipping in the wind to get to the back door. He glanced overhead to see if it might rain and drive away the other kids. He could just sit under the porch, stay dry, and not have to go into the house. The sky's cerulean blue was barely broken by a few wispy clouds that moved by at a leisurely pace. He'd hoped for gray and foreboding storm clouds, but nothing seemed to be going the way he'd hoped today.

Glaring back at Kevin for invoking his mother, Harold wanted to tell Kevin to eat sand, but he didn't dare speak back to the bully. He hated it when people called out his mom, but he couldn't do anything about it. His mom had always been overprotective, and it felt to Harold like she was always present. He didn't mind. He'd found comfort in being able to turn and quickly find her in a crowd.

Harold kicked at a rusted can at the side of the house and tried to push down panic from a memory of the first time he couldn't spot her while they'd been shopping at the mall. Thinking back on that episode, Harold wasn't sure who'd been more scared, himself or his mom.

She'd done her best since his dad had died a little over a year ago. Harold relied on her for everything, but the kids at school didn't know how strong he had to be for her.

After his dad's death, Harold's mom had seemed to let go. She no longer drove him to school every day. She no longer hovered over him while he played on the monkey bars. She didn't check up on him when he came home late after playing on the weekend. It seemed as if she'd given up on everything after his dad died, and Harold was at a loss for how to help her.

He did his best not to cry in front of her, worry her with trouble at school, ask for help with homework, about getting bullied on the playground, or any of that other "kid stuff" he dealt with on a daily basis. Harold wasn't entirely sure what his mom had left to worry about, but it seemed as if working, crying, and sleeping were all she did these days.

Harold didn't mind not getting dropped off at school anymore. He was almost eleven now, and that was plenty old enough to ride his bike to school and back home. He actually enjoyed riding his bike around their small town. Pedaling wherever he wanted to go gave him an immense sense of freedom and solitude.

The wet grass from rain the night before stained his white tennis shoes a sickly green color. Pollen and the cloying scent of disturbed plants floated through the air, aggravating his allergies. Before he made it to the back of the house, he suffered a sneezing fit, and his eyes teared up from the ever-present allergies. Glad to be out of hearing range of the rest of the boys, he sniffled hard to prevent another sneeze. He knew they'd interpret his body's reaction as crying.

When he finally arrived around back, a yawning black hole appeared where the door should have stood. A preternatural darkness exuded from the house, as if the comfort and warmth of the sun wasn't allowed to enter. Harold wondered, not for the first time, how he'd been cajoled into going into the empty house.

He took a deep breath in a vain attempt to calm his nerves. The smell of wet dog filled his senses and caused another sneezing fit. He wiped his runny nose on the sleeve of his shirt and pressed forward with small steps toward the open doorway. White paint peeked through large patches of rust on a set of metal lawn furniture. The padding on the chairs had long since rotted and fallen away. Kids' toys were scattered around the pseudo-jungle of the back yard, and only the largest were visible through the weeds and tall grass.

Rumors held that the last family to live here had been killed by the father, and he'd boiled them down to their bones. Some stories said he'd locked everyone in a different closet until they'd all starved to death. Other stories claimed they'd all drowned in different bathrooms. The most popular tale avowed the mother ran from the house covered in blood, crying about her dead children and murderous husband. She'd been locked up in the state's loony bin three counties away until the end of her days.

Harold didn't know which urban legend about the house he believed in the most. He supposed none of them were really true, but those tall tales about old country houses were usually rooted in some nugget of truth. He hoped he wouldn't find any of those nuggets while he was inside the house. The last thing he needed was nightmares about dismembered bodies and the gruesome eating habits of insane father figures.

He pushed forward through the overgrowth, and was so focused on gathering the courage necessary to enter the door, he tripped over something and fell to the ground hard with a powerful *oomph* that knocked the air out of him. In a moment of panic, he turned onto his backside and crab-crawled in a hurry away from whatever skeletal thing had burst from the tall grass and grabbed his foot. It wasn't until his back slammed into the house next to the back door that he saw his assailant.

A mop had been tossed into the back yard and left to rot along with the toys and lawn furniture. He'd tripped over the handle and fallen. Instead of the skeletal hand of the dead come back to life to exact its revenge on the living, Harold had lost his cool over a common cleaning utensil. The boy clambered back to his feet and marched over to stand above the thing that now raised his ire.

Harold glared down at the offending mop handle and stomped on it in frustration. The handle broke off from the head of the mop, which had grass and weeds growing through the cloth fibers. As he looked between the black doorway and the mop handle a few times, an idea grew in his mind.

*A weapon. People don't live in there anymore, but animals probably moved in at some point.*

He reached down and grabbed the splintery wood in one hand. Yanking it free of the grass that had wrapped around it, Harold marched with more confidence toward the house. He took a few practice swings and jabs with the stick to gain familiarity with its heft and length.

Satisfied that he had a passable weapon, Harold stopped before going through the doorway.

He smiled as he pretended to jab, slash, and club an invisible foe in the backyard. Within a few moments of pretend fighting, Harold saw in his mind a dozen ninjas crawling out of the house's darkness, and he spent the next several minutes soundly defeating each and every one of them with flourished strikes of his mop handle.

With the defeat of his final imaginary foe, he danced around the trampled grass and stepped into the house with a sense of confidence and pride he'd never felt before. Using that confidence, he crossed the threshold and stood in the gloom of the back room.

The sudden shift between the brilliance of the sun and the shadows of the house blinded him. He held the broom handle out in front of him like a sword in hopes that anything trying to bite him would hit the wood first. He blinked several times before squinting into the darkness.

Large, flowing shapes gradually became more defined. Harold extended his weapon toward the nearest and poked it. Dust and mold cascaded from the sheet covering some sort of large piece of furniture. When the dust-mold combination hit the floor, it billowed up around Harold in a cloud.

He tried to take a deep breath and hold it before the mess surrounded his face, but he reacted too slowly and got a lungful of the crud.

The combination of sneezes, coughs, and chokes sent him dancing around the room like a spastic monkey. He bounced into the sheet-covered hulks surrounding him and recoiled from each one. In order to escape the haze filling the room, Harold fled deeper into the house. He skidded to a stop on a tile floor, surrounded by dust-covered kitchen counters and utensils. Even in the dim light, the fridge, stove, counters, and pantry stood out. A large, stained stew pot sat at a crooked angle on a broken burner with a metal spoon jutting out the top.

Sneezes hammered through his body, forcing him to one knee. Despite the explosions wracking his body, he was careful to not disturb the house further. He was going to have a hard enough time explaining why he was covered in dirt and other nastiness to his mom when he got home. He didn't need to make the mess worse.

When the last sneeze finally left his body, he took a shuddering breath through his mouth and whined in pain. Stars swam through his vision, which made seeing in the strange gloom of the house even worse.

A darker shadow broke free from the depths of blackness in a corner of the kitchen. It grew in size as it approached Harold.

Hoping he was seeing things from the sneezing attack, Harold froze.

When the shade coalesced into a form with legs, arms, and a head, Harold let out a little squeak.

A deep voice cascaded down. "Well, well. What kind of mouse do we have in my house?"

Harold extended his broom stick out in what he thought was a menacing gesture.

The form slapped the stick aside and leaned closer to Harold with a growl. The smell of hot spices and wet fur filled the air. At this close proximity, the human shape resolved into a hairy man with red, glinting eyes, and a mouthful of teeth. A glob of saliva was smeared from the corner of the man's mouth into his bushy beard.

Harold had never seen such a crazed figure before in his entire life, and deep in his gut, he knew he was now face-to-face with the cannibal father from the urban legends. Cowering from the frightening countenance, he whimpered, "Sorry. So sorry. Came in on a dare. Sorry. Didn't mean anything by it."

The man chuffed and looked to the front of the house. After a moment, he broke into a laugh that shook his entire body. The laugh ended with the man throwing his head back and roaring at the ceiling.

Unsure of what the laughter or roar meant for himself, Harold stayed perfectly still and hoped the man would forget his presence. The boy didn't want to end up in the stew pot on the stove like the rest of the family that used to live here.

The man hadn't forgotten Harold. He pointed at the floor. "Stay there." Fading into the gloom, his footsteps resounded through the house as he stalked to the front of the house. A sliver of brilliant light pierced the darkness when the man parted the curtains on the front windows.

Harold watched the thick dust motes dance in the light and concentrated on not sneezing again. He sniffled and bit his bottom lip in an effort not to cry. He had no idea what the giant of a man had in store for him. Just as he thought to stand up and run out of the house, the light vanished with a swoosh of cloth.

Cowering as close to the nasty hardwood floor as he could, Harold let out a whimper and clenched his eyes shut.

Footfalls approached, and the man stood over him. "Get up, *Boy*."

Harold didn't move.

The man yanked him up from the floor. He planted Harold on his feet and held him there while he regained his balance. "I took a look at your friends out there."

In a small voice, he said, "They're not my friends."

"What? If they're not your friends, why do you let them push you around?"

Harold shrugged.

"Didn't hear you. Stand up strong. You're the one in here, not them. In my book, that makes you more brave than they are."

"If I don't do what they say, they'll pick on me at school. Maybe beat me up if the teachers aren't looking." Harold shuffled his feet around and dug the toe of his shoe into the floorboards.

With a sigh, the man crouched next to Harold and placed a hand on his shoulder.

Harold flinched again at the gentle contact.

"Wow. You certainly are a flighty little bird."

He scowled at his feet. He tried to sound angry, but knew his voice came out in a pathetic whine. "I'm not a chicken. I'm here, right?"

With a hard squeeze on Harold's shoulder, the man said, "I didn't call you chicken. You're just jumpy. That's understandable. I don't exactly have what you would call a kindly face." A minute passed in silence before the man sighed again. "How long do your *friends* expect you to be in here?"

Another shrug.

"Didn't hear you. If you want people to respect you, you have to stand up tall, use your strongest voice, and look them in the eyes." With a gentle shake, the man issued the order, "Do it. Stand up tall." He removed his hand from Harold's shoulder.

With an exercise of will, Harold forced his body to comply. He stilled his shuffling feet and planted them on the floor as he straightened his back. He didn't know why the frightening man wanted him to stand up tall. *Maybe he wants to see if my bones will fit in that stew pot.* Whatever the man had planned, Harold decided the easiest path would be to go along with it.

The man extended a giant hand. "Good. Now look me in the eye, tell me your name, and shake my hand."

Harold looked the man in the eyes and stuck out a sweaty palm. The gleam in the man's eyes seemed even more intense than when he'd first loomed over Harold. The inner light of confidence and wisdom shone from beneath bushy eyebrows. The boy wished he had a gaze like that. He wanted everything contained in that look. From what Harold could see, the man had the power to take over the world with that gaze.

Without looking at what he was doing, he missed the man's hand. He finally fumbled his sweaty, limp hand into the man's calloused grip.

The man squeezed Harold's hand, but not painfully. "Squeeze back. Firmly. Not so much as to hurt the other person, unless you're trying to drive home a point. Let them know you're there with them."

Harold returned the squeeze, and the man nodded. "Good. Now. What's your name? I'm not going to keep calling you 'boy' for the rest of the day." He released his grip.

With a stammer, he managed to say, "H-h-harold."

The man shook his head. "Say it with confidence. This is your chance to make a first impression. Let them know you're proud of your name. Your parents chose that name on purpose to give you a sense of who you are. Do them proud. Try again."

He didn't want to have to try a third time, and he certainly didn't want to let the memory of his dead father down. He worried about his mom so much that he felt saying his name with pride might do her some good. With a sense of determination, he cleared his throat and said as firmly as he could, "My name's Harold."

The man roared. "Fantastic! Well done, Harold. My name's Kurt. Nice to meet you."

One corner of Harold's mouth twitched up in a smile. With as much confidence as he could muster, Harold said, "Nice to meet you, too." Something inside Harold swelled up and took over. It was a new feeling he'd never experienced, so he didn't have a word for it. He knew it wasn't fear or doubt, but something better. It was something the opposite of those dreadful feelings that seemed to dominate his life.

Kurt broke into a snaggle-toothed smile. "Well done. Said with power and presence."

For a brief instant, Harold was certain Kurt's canines were longer than any others he'd seen before. Blinking and focusing on Kurt's teeth more closely, Harold tried to make out his elongated teeth.

Kurt's smile faded and his expression turned more serious. "Now. There are several things we need to clear the air about."

Disappointment filled the boy. He hadn't gotten a good look at Kurt's teeth. "Like what?" He was quickly becoming comfortable talking with the strange man before him, despite the worry gnawing at his gut about what Kurt might have planned for his bones.

"What's it going to take to make that group of boys outside go away?"

"I gotta open a window in the front to show them I made it through the house. Then they'll leave, and maybe leave me alone for a week. Maybe."

Kurt motioned. "Good. Get to it. Send them on their way. I don't like them here."

Harold took the order from Kurt and carefully made his way through the dim light to the front window. He threw aside the curtains and flinched at the sudden brilliance. Once his eyes adjusted enough for him to see, he looked back at Kurt. The giant of a man motioned toward the window. Harold caught a glint of gold in Kurt's left ear as a thick hoop of gold shifted in the bright sunlight.

Harold turned back to the window and waved to Mark and Kevin and the others. It looked like half the boys had grown bored, waiting for Harold to make an appearance, and had already left. At least Mark and Kevin, Harold's two main antagonists, were still there to witness that he'd bravely entered the old house through the back door and made his way to the front window.

Mark waved back.

Kevin yelled something, but he was too far away for Harold to hear.

The entire group of remaining boys gathered up their bikes, and Harold's as well, and rode away back to the suburbs.

Fuming with anger at the theft of his bike, Harold stomped his foot. He screamed through the window, "Hey! That's mine!"

From behind, Kurt asked, "What's got you upset?"

Harold bit his bottom lip again to keep from crying like a baby. "They took my bike. That was the last thing my dad got me before he died."

"You'll get it back." Kurt sounded firm and confident.

Harold turned on the man and glared. "How do you know?" He was shocked at the force of his own question.

"Because I'll teach you how. It might not be today or tomorrow, might not even be next week, but you'll get it back on your own."

Suspicious of Kurt, Harold narrowed his eyes. "How are you going to do that?"

"Just wait and see. Trust me."

Harold put his hands on his hips. "You're a stranger. Why should I trust you?"

Kurt laughed. "You're a trespasser! Why shouldn't I just eat your bones here and now?"

Harold's eyes flicked toward the kitchen. Even though he couldn't see it from this angle, he pictured the stew pot precariously balanced on top of the stove. His stomach churned at the thought of being parceled out and eaten, and he suddenly felt like he was going to throw up all over Kurt's feet.

Kurt's laugh deepened. "Relax, Harold. I'm not going to eat your bones...or any other part of you."

Sensing the joke, Harold relaxed and swallowed hard. The churning in his guts relaxed a bit, but he was still worried about what Kurt might do to him or make him do.

When Kurt recovered from his laughter, he said, "There is the matter of your trespassing. I do take that seriously. You'll owe me reparations for invading my privacy."

"What are 'reparations?'"

"Oh. Sorry. Big word. It means you have to pay me back for a wrong done to me."

Harold looked down at his grass-stained shoes and the dust-covered floor. "Oh." He wondered what kind of payback he'd have to do for Kurt. Since his dad died, they didn't have much money, and Harold didn't know how he was going to get whatever amount the big man was going to demand of him.

Kurt placed one meaty finger under Harold's chin and lifted his head. "Look me in the eye when you speak to me, or anyone else for that matter. It shows respect. It demonstrates your strength."

"Okay."

Kurt shook his head. "Not 'okay.' The proper response is 'yes, sir' or 'no, sir.' Understood?"

"Oka—I mean, ummm, yes, sir."

Clapping his hands together, Kurt exclaimed, "Fantastic! Now for your reparations. Have you ever had a job?" He waved his own question aside. "Of course not. You're too young for employment. How old are you, anyway?"

Harold focused on looking Kurt in the eye despite being uncomfortable doing so. "I'll turn eleven in two months."

"Oh. Those boys out there looked younger. Why are you hanging out with them?" Kurt narrowed his eyes and looked Harold up and down. "You also seem a bit small for your age."

Harold looked down at the floor and opened his mouth to answer. Kurt cleared his throat, and the boy snapped his eyes back up to meet the man's intense gaze. "I've always been small. I started school late, and when my dad died, I didn't do so well in school that year. They held me back a year. The rest of the kids don't know I'm almost three years older than them."

"How are you doing in school now? Better?"

Harold shook his head and shrugged at the same time. "Kinda. Well, not really. History classes are hard. I don't get science, and math is the worst. I do pretty well in English. I do okay at the rest."

"Have you ever asked for help? Gotten a tutor?"

Harold sniffled as tears escaped from his eyes. His bottom lip quivered, and he tried to keep his voice from cracking. "Can't. No money for a tutor, and Mom doesn't have time to help between her three jobs and it seems all she does at home is cry and sleep and cry some more. Dad was a good helper with my homework, but…"

Kurt chewed on one side of his mustache for a moment. "Well, then. Part of your reparations to me will be to improve your grades. I can't have someone help me around here"—he spread his arms wide— "and fail in their primary studies."

Harold stared up at Kurt. "Sir? I don't understand."

Kurt sighed. "I can tell you're a smart kid. There's something about you that screams that you're special, in a good way. Listen closely."

Locking eyes with Kurt, Harold had to remind himself to breathe and not shuffle his feet around in nervous circles. "Yes, sir."

With a broad smile, Kurt continued, "You've trespassed in my family home. To pay me back, you're going to work for me and help me clean this place up. Make it livable again. But I can't have you failing your classes on my conscience. The time you spend here will pull you from your studies, so I'm going to make sure we get your education back on track. I'm going to teach you as best I can in what you're studying in school."

Harold gaped. "You? You're going to teach me?"

Kurt exploded with a deep-bellied laugh again. "I'm going to teach you more than you can ever expect. Are we in agreement on this?" Kurt extended one hand.

With a nod and a smile, Harold shook hands with his new mentor. "Yes, sir!"

\* \* \*

Each day after school, Harold walked the two miles between Joseph A. Krankton Elementary School and the house. He always entered through the gaping back door. When he crossed the threshold into the darkness, trepidation gripped his chest, but when Kurt stepped out of the gloom, Harold couldn't help but smile.

Harold spent an hour helping Kurt clean up the living areas before they sat down at the kitchen table, now cleared of dusty clutter. Kurt walked Harold through his math homework, but never gave him the direct answer. Despite his appearance as a wild man, Kurt's mind was sharp and full of knowledge. Harold found himself grasping concepts and ideas with more clarity.

On the third day, they worked together to hang a new door on the back of the house. Once Kurt was satisfied with the door's operation, Harold asked, "How big is this house?"

Kurt shook his shaggy head. "Big enough for a family. Too big for me alone."

Harold followed up with, "Then why don't you live here with a family?"

Kurt growled deep in his throat and clenched his fists. "Let's hope you never find out."

The crazy stories of the house's history bounced around Harold's head, and he took a step back.

Kurt ground his teeth together for another moment before blowing out a hard breath. "I'm sorry, Harold. I didn't mean to startle you. There's a long story to tell there. Maybe I'll share it with you when you're older." Harold opened his mouth to say something, but Kurt waved him silent. "I know the stories people tell about this place and my family. None are true. The truth is different. Much different."

Harold could only nod and hope the truth wasn't half as horrible as the stories he'd heard.

Over the next three weeks, hard work cleared much of the detritus, dust, and clutter from the kitchen, dining room, living room, and den. The house practically sparkled, compared to the first time Harold had stepped foot inside. Harold's grades also improved, and the bullies gave him a little more space.

Harold knew his scholastic improvement came as a direct result of Kurt's tutelage, but he couldn't figure out why the bullies were giving him some much overdue peace and quiet.

One evening, after the tutoring rolled to a close, Harold told Kurt about the bullies leaving him alone.

Kurt asked, "Why do you think that is?"

Harold said, "Dunno. I'm still me."

Kurt smiled down at Harold. "No. I don't think you're the same boy that trespassed in my house those few weeks ago. It's only been a short time, but you've changed. You stand taller. You carry yourself with more confidence. The hunch-shouldered child who first walked into my house is not the same young man I see before me. You've made a wonderful transformation in yourself. I'm proud of you."

Harold choked back a sob and swiped at the tears suddenly running free down his face.

Kurt placed a gentle hand on Harold's shoulder. "What's wrong? Did I say something to upset you?" The giant man's voice was filled with concern.

With a shake of his head and a hard sniffle, Harold did his best to find his voice. When he finally spoke, his voice cracked. "No one's ever been proud of me before."

Kurt squeezed Harold's shoulder with tenderness. "I'm sure your mom is proud of you."

"She's never said so."

"What about your dad?"

Harold shrugged. "Dunno. Maybe. I don't remember him ever telling me that, either."

"I'm not trying to make excuses for your mom, but she has the three jobs. Work harder at school, and when your next report card comes in, I'm sure she'll be proud of improvements in your grades."

Harold shrugged. "Maybe. I think I should go. It's getting late, and I need to get home before Mom goes to bed."

Rising from the table with Harold, Kurt said, "Take a three-day break. You've earned it. We'll resume the cleaning and repairs here, along with your studies, on Friday."

"Really? You sure?"

"I insist. Please don't come around during the next three days. I need some alone time. Understand?"

"I guess...I mean, yes, sir."

Kurt added, "I also expect to see you riding your bike up my driveway Friday, not walking."

Harold's eyes widened. "But Kevin still has my bike!"

"By Friday, he won't have it anymore. Right?"

Something in Kurt's fatherly tone made Harold stand taller. "Right! I'll get my bike back."

It took two days for Harold to gather the courage to get his bike back. When Kurt's deadline arrived, Harold had to take action. He couldn't let Kurt down by not showing up with his beloved bicycle at the ready. Harold walked to Kevin's house after school and knocked on the door. Before anyone answered, Harold had to imagine his feet nailed to the ground to keep from running away.

Kevin's father answered and scowled. "What you want?" The man had a few tattoos on his hairy upper arms, and Harold could tell the man had once been muscular and fit, but had let his physique go to waste in recent years. The thin, white t-shirt the man wore barely covered his extended, sagging belly.

Harold focused on standing tall and hid his shaking hands behind his back. With as much confidence as he could muster, he said, "Kevin took my bike from me a few weeks ago. I'd like it back."

The man leaned over Harold and breathed out his sour whiskey stench. "You sayin' my boy stole somethin'?" Along with the smell of rotten liquor, the man smelled of stale sweat and old cigarettes.

Suddenly afraid of the man, Harold swallowed hard. He pictured Kurt standing behind him as a protector. Even the large man standing in the door would be no match for Kurt if Harold came away hurt. This imagined backup gave Harold the confidence he needed to speak. "Yes, sir. My bike. He took it from me. May I have it back?"

With a snarl, the man asked, "Wazzit look like?"

"Red, sir. With chrome handlebars and silver pinstripes."

"Yeah. Seen it. You callin' the cops on my boy?"

Harold shook his head. "No, sir. I just want my bike back."

Kevin's father clumsily waved toward the detached garage next to the house. "It's 'round back. Go get it and get outta here. I don't wanna see you here or around my boy again. Got it?"

Harold stepped off the porch. "Yes, sir. Thank you."

Kevin's father turned into the living room and bellowed, "Kevin!" Rage filled the shout.

Harold didn't want to get caught up in the impending storm of yelling and screaming, so he quickly moved around the garage and found his bicycle. In the intervening weeks, he'd pictured all sorts of abuse and damage being done to the bike, but his fears were unfounded. He found the bicycle in pristine shape.

He rode away from the house with freedom in his heart and the wind rushing past his ears. After a while riding around the neighborhood, his face ached from his unending smile. He slowly made larger and larger circles out from his neighborhood, enjoying the ride, and not caring where he ended up.

Before he realized where he was going, Harold found himself pulling to a stop at Kurt's rusted, iron fence. The sun set behind Harold and gleamed brightly on the front expanse of the house. The windows glittered and shone, the lower levels brighter than the upper levels. Harold realized he'd never been to the upper level before and made a mental note to ask Kurt about it.

A slice of the beautiful full moon rose over the house and silhouetted one of the upper-level windows. The window flung open, startling Harold enough that he jumped from his bike and almost ran away. There were no details in the window, and Harold wasn't even sure what had caused the window to swing open. All he knew was that he was frightened to his very core, worse than the first day he'd trespassed in Kurt's house.

With thoughts of what Kurt had taught him over the past few weeks, Harold decided to stand strong. He decided to be proud and show strength in the face of unknown adversity.

A gigantic wolf head jutted through the open window with a growling roar that evolved into a mournful howl into the approaching night sky. The slavering jaws of the wolf pointed at Harold with lips curled back to reveal jagged teeth.

Harold wanted to scream. He wanted to pee his pants. He wanted to run away. He wanted to crawl into a hole and hide from the beast half hanging from the house.

He did none of these.

His concern and worry for his friend took over. He scanned the lower level for signs of light shining forth in the dimming day. When he didn't see anything on the lower level, he scanned the upper level, but only saw the strange wolf-beast hanging out the window and snarling at Harold. The boy pushed his bike through the missing gate in the fence and called out, "Kurt? Are you okay?"

The snarling beast broke off its growls. The wolf lips rippled as the head shook back and forth. A golden earring swung to and fro from the thing's left ear. A harsh word finally escaped its throat. "Flee!"

Harold recognized the earring, and he hoped the strange beast in the window hadn't killed Kurt and taken the earring. The boy continued in a slow march down the overgrown pathway to the front door they'd repaired only a few days ago. He looked up at the beast. "No, sir. I will not flee. I will help my friend." Harold looked into the eyes of the wolf-beast and saw a familiar sight. Kurt's confidence, wisdom, and compassion shone forth, but it was buried beneath a mask of rage and fear.

In that moment, Harold knew what his best friend in the whole world really was. He'd discovered the truth behind the empty house. He'd found out why no one ever came around or cared for the grounds.

The wolf snarled again. "Flee!"

Harold leaned his bicycle against a pillar supporting the front porch's roof. With his back straight and chin held high, he said, "No, sir. I'm here for Kurt. I'm going to help him get through whatever trouble he's in."

Another growl. "Flee!"

Before ducking under the sagging lip of the front porch, Harold called out, "Never. Not from you."

The growl tapered off into a pathetic, high-pitched whine. "Help me."

Harold called up to the window, "Let's help each other." Kurt deserved better than to be alone in his large house, so Harold decided he would fill the huge, empty house before him with as much love and compassion as he could.

Kurt's massive wolf head nodded twice before withdrawing into the house.

Harold opened the newly repaired front door and entered with a confident stride. He turned to the stairs on the right and waited at the bottom.

Kurt's massive wolf-beast form slowly prowled down the stairs. Every few steps, Kurt's elongated muzzle twitched as it sniffed the air. Even though the words coming from Kurt were deformed by the horrific maw his face had turned into, Harold picked up the words clearly enough.

Kurt asked, "Alone?"

Harold nodded. "Yes, sir."

"Bicycle?"

"Yes, sir. I just got it back from Kevin this afternoon after school."

At first, Harold though Kurt's shift in expression was a grimace or preparation to bite his face off, but then the boy realized his mentor and friend was smiling.

Kurt said, "Proud."

Without hesitation or thought of danger, Harold met Kurt's wolf-beast form at the bottom of the stairs and gave him a hug. "Thank you, Kurt."

Harold held onto the furry form for a long time before he realized Kurt was shaking. Harold stepped back. "What's wrong?"

Kurt swiped at the tears soaking into the fur on his face. "Happy you're not afraid."

"Oh, I'm afraid. I'm really scared, but a wise man taught me to not show fear, to stand tall, to be proud, and to show confidence."

Kurt snorted. "Wise man." He sat down on the steps and stared at Harold. "Thank you."

Harold shrugged. "You've shown me kindness when I was in a bad place. I can at least do that for you. I think your bad place is worse off than the one I was in, but I don't care. I'm here for you."

The strange smile crossed Kurt's visage again. "Your words are better."

"I have a good mentor."

Kurt nuzzled his giant head into Harold's shoulder. "I have a good friend."

"We both do, Kurt. We both do."

They sat at the bottom of the stairs, leaning on each other for a long while. Finally, Kurt sat up and looked Harold in the eyes. "Time for you to go. Your mom'll be worried by now."

"How would you know?"

Kurt shrugged. "Call it instinct."

With a nod, Harold got up and headed to the front door. He turned back around with a laugh. "Thanks for not eating me."

*****

## J.T. Evans Biography

J.T. Evans arrived on this planet and developed into an adult in the desolate, desert-dominated oil fields of west Texas. After a year in San Antonio, he spent a year in the northern tundra of Montana. This year-long stint prepared him for the cold (yet mild compared to Montana) climate of the Front Range of Colorado.

He has thrived in The Centennial State since 1998 with his lovely Montana-native wife and rapidly growing son. He primarily pays the bills by keeping computers secure. Like most writers, he dreams of earning enough income via publication to drop the Day Job and prosper. His debut urban fantasy novel, *Griffin's Feather*, was released in October of 2017, and *Viper's Bane* hit the shelves in March of 2019.

J.T. rekindled his love for writing with his discovery of the Colorado Springs Fiction Writers Group in 2006. He was the president of the organization from January 2009 to January 2013. Even though he's no longer part of the CSFWG, he has continued writing and expanding his knowledge of the business and craft.

J.T. is also a member of Pikes Peak Writers, which he joined in 2008. J.T. was elected the vice president of PPW in January of 2013, and stepped into the role of president of PPW in September of the same year. In April of 2017, he resigned from the role of president.

He joined the Gnome Stew Crew in March of 2016. Since that time, he has written dozens of articles for the site and has earned three Gold ENnie awards (2016, 2017, and 2018) as part of the team at Gnome Stew.

When not flinging code at the screen or throwing words at the wall, he enjoys role-playing games, home brewing, Boy Scouts with his son, but dislikes anything related to long walks on the beach. His favorite genres to write in are fantasy and urban fantasy, but he writes the occasional science fiction or horror short story.

J.T. once held 13 different jobs in a single year, and at the age of 15, his right arm was amputated in a violent car wreck. Don't worry. He's become more stable in the job area, and the arm was successfully reattached shortly after the car crash.

\* \* \* \* \*

# Small Favors
# by Jon R. Osborne
## An Accords Universe Story

Cleod's stomach rumbled at the scent of hot food wafting on the breeze. His nose followed the wind north. Cooked food meant small folk. Small folk could mean an easy meal if they screamed and fled, or better yet, left their cooking food unattended long enough for Cleod to help himself and shuffle off. They could also mean pain, as they shot him with arrows, or brave ones got close enough with spears to jab him.

Cleod rose and sniffed again. He'd eaten a goat three days ago. Hunger warred with caution. An ogre who pilfered too much livestock or regularly menaced small folk would soon draw enough ire for them to send warriors after him. His stomach rumbled again.

The food smelled too close to be one of the farms along the river. Maybe if this meal didn't pan out, Cleod would continue north. He hadn't stolen a sheep from them for a moon. However, roast meat made his mouth water. Maybe small folk such as sidhe or hobs camped in the woods, cooking game above a fire.

He paused. Hunters had bows and fired with painful accuracy. A group of them could hurt Cleod, and once he was injured, they would finish him off. Greedy ogres became dead ogres as the promise of easy meals lured them to the territories of the small folk. Cleod wiped the drool from the corner of his mouth.

The wind shifted, and he lost the tell-tale odor. Cleod continued north, watching for the flicker of a campfire and listening for small folk. Animals scurried from his path, but birds continued singing. Birds were too small and too hard to catch to interest an ogre.

The breeze changed direction again, and Cleod picked up the scent.

*Close.*

Cleod veered northeast, and after a moment he spotted a glimpse of flames through the trees. He crept closer until he heard their crackle. No voices accompanied the fire. Small folk were seldom silent when together. Talking, laughing, singing—they gave themselves away.

A campfire burned on a small hill, with a pair of spitted rabbits sizzling over it. Cleod peered through the brush, searching for the small folk who built the fire. Had they wandered off? Stagnant water filled a ditch surrounding the hill, but the small folk preferred fresh water. Had they gone in search of a stream? The river was nearly a mile away.

Cleod shuffled to the edge of the scummy water. He wasn't worried about the depth, but if hidden small folk hadn't already heard him, splashing through the ditch would give him away. He eased his feet into the water, feeling for obstacles. A sharp stick scraped his calloused sole when his left foot slipped in mud. Cleod reached forward with his long arms and grabbed small trees on the other bank. The leaves rustled as the trees bowed when Cleod hauled himself out of the ditch.

Water and algae dripped from the hem of his tunic as Cleod surmounted the mound. The hair on the back of his neck bristled. A shimmering distortion hung in the air on the hilltop, resembling a pool of water perpendicular to the ground.

The strange ripple couldn't compete with the roasting meat for Cleod's attention. He trudged to the fire, salivating. Cleod grabbed one end of the spit, ignoring the heat singeing the hairs on his knuckles. He bit off half of a rabbit, crunching bones between his huge teeth. He might gnaw the meat off the bones of larger game, but the tiny rabbits weren't worth the effort and time.

"Good, isn't it?"

Cleod spun at the voice, snarling. *Have the small folk set a trap for me?* A lone person sat opposite him, watching him over the flames. Slender and fair, the aos sidhe smiled at Cleod.

"Don't let me interrupt your repast, my friend," the stranger said. He watched as Cleod greedily scarfed the remainder of the first rabbit.

Cleod shuffled back a few paces as he yanked the remaining rabbit off the spit. The sidhe wore no weapons, but Cleod knew they could draw them out of thin air. By now, the small person should flee or brandish a weapon, but he sat with a smug smile. Suspicion gnawed at Cleod's mind. He sniffed the remaining rabbit, but smelled nothing except sizzling meat.

"Don't worry. I'm not trying to poison you. I'm merely offering you a sample," the sidhe said.

Cleod cocked his head at the strange word. He grasped the basics of the small folk speech, but clever words eluded him. "Sample?"

"I bet those morsels barely whetted your appetite," the sidhe replied, adding, "I bet you're still hungry."

Cleod munched on the remaining rabbit. "Always hungry."

"If you crave more, it awaits on the other side of the ford." The sidhe gestured toward the shimmering distortion.

Cleod eyed the wavering mirage. "What is it?"

"Do you know about wold-fords...what is your name?"

"Cleod," the ogre replied. "Use simple words—Cleod not like fancy talk. Makes Cleod mad." He snapped the spit.

"Clod? How delightful?" The sidhe clapped once. His mirth annoyed Cleod. "I am called Feidhlim. The ford leads to the Dunwold—think of it as a door or cave entrance. If you step through, you will be in a world of soft people and plentiful food."

Cleod narrowed his beady eyes. "Why?"

Feidhlim appeared taken aback. "Why? Why what?"

"Why you want Cleod go to Dunwold?"

"You're smarter than I gave you credit for," Feidhlim said. "Without going into annoying fancy words, self-important people don't want us to go to the Dunwold. I bet they'd have trouble telling you 'No,' which would amuse me."

Cleod jabbed at the shimmer with the broken spit. Examining the wood, it appeared unchanged. "Why you not go?"

"I've been a few times. The last time, a nasty woman threatened me," Feidhlim replied, puffing up. "A common, dirt-scratching...well, it's not important. What's important is, she accosted me and denied me a chance to indulge my appetites. If she tries to do the same to you, I hope you put her in her place."

A kernel of truth at last. The puny sidhe had been bullied, so he sought a bigger bully. Cleod could grasp the concept. A handful of giants roamed the mountains far to the west. Ogres avoided tangling with their larger cousins out of self-preservation. Would the sidhe's bully await on the other side of this wold-ford?

If nothing else, he could step back through. Cleod lumbered forward. The air shimmered around him, and the air changed. The campfire with its smoke and burning fat drippings vanished. The air took on a metallic tang, and the lush green of the foliage grew muted with leaves already turning for autumn. No one accosted Cleod as he surveyed his surroundings.

The hill and its stagnant ditch remained the same. Cleod sniffed—no fresh scents, though the undergrowth was trampled. More importantly, Cleod spotted no sign of food. The smiling sidhe had fooled him. Cleod smacked a meaty fist into his open palm. *He won't smile so good with a mouth full of busted teeth.*

Cleod turned to vent his anger on the trickster, but the shimmering distortion had vanished. Cleod retraced his steps. The hilltop was too small to lose the path. Nothing happened when Cleod passed through the space the mirage had occupied. He paced back and forth across the hilltop—it had to be here! The sun grew low before Cleod plopped to the ground and beat his fists on the earth. His stomach rumbled.

Lurching to his feet, Cleod scanned the surrounding woods. The river lay to the east. Maybe he could ambush game watering along the banks. The wind shifted, and Cleod caught a whiff of cooking meat. His head snapped to the spot the campfire had occupied before, but the hilltop remained empty. No, this aroma wafted on the breeze from the west. This scent differed from the campfire—smokier, and different meat.

Cleod shuffled west, his mouth watering. Revenge against the crafty sidhe dimmed in priority compared to tracking the source of the smell. He lumbered through the undergrowth, threading his way through the woods. Both the brush and the trees seemed scrawny and feeble compared to before.

The wind shifted and Cleod lost the scent. He spied a break in the trees ahead. The woods abruptly ended at a field of grass. A small river cut through the meadow. Strange, blocky buildings sat across the river—could they be the source of the cooking aroma?

He plodded forward. Something was wrong with the waterway. The river had been turned to stone! Cleod squinted at the black ribbon of rock stretching across in front of him. It disappeared around a bend in both directions, following the perimeter of the forest. Cleod crept to the edge of the stone river and rapped his knuckles on it.

The surface remained solid. He prodded at the black stone with a thick finger, to no avail. A monster with glowing eyes roared around the bend on the left. As it bore down on Cleod, it shrieked a shrill call. Cleod fled for the safety of the trees, not slowing until the woods obscured the freak stone river.

The breeze altered again. The roasting meat was nearby. Cleod followed the trail north. Would the monster beat him to his goal? Perhaps it could only swim in the stone river; it hadn't pursued him. The trees thinned again, giving Cleod glimpses of buildings beyond them.

Another strange sight prompted Cleod to slow near the edge of the forest. A barrier blocked the path ahead. He'd encountered fences on small folk farms sufficient to keep docile animals penned, but unable to impede a hungry ogre. This fence appeared solid, a bright white structure that reached Cleod's chin.

A building rose behind the wall, different from the farmhouses Cleod had seen, or even the village Cleod had skirted around to avoid drawing a hunting party. He spied another building off to his left. A metal net surrounded it, but only as high as Cleod's belly.

Smoke laden with the scent of meat tickled his nose. It wafted from the other side of the white wall. Cleod peered over the white wooden barrier. Close-cropped grass meant goats or sheep, but he couldn't find them. A smoking metal capsule drew his attention. The prize awaited in the strange iron apparatus.

A small dog charged across the grass, yipping at Cleod. As opposed to wolves or farm dogs, this canine massed little more than the rabbits Cleod had snacked on. He tugged on the wall experimentally—it wavered under his grip, surprisingly flimsy. The yapping dog redoubled its efforts to scare him off, snapping its teeth from the base of the wall.

Cleod eyed the metal capsule, seeping delicious smoke. It remained tantalizingly out of his reach. With a tug, the white fence split open, accompanied by cracking timber. The dog immediately retreated several yards before renewing its cacophony of yips.

"Figsy!" A young boy emerged from the back of the building, yelling at the dog until he spotted Cleod. The young small folk babbled something incoherent at Cleod, trepidatious, but also curious. While some of his kindred considered young small folk a delicacy, Cleod knew better. Eating folk, especially the young, drew wrath like no other. Besides, the metal construct held the repast he sought.

Cleod peeled aside the wood fencing and shuffled to the smoking metal cylinder. He prodded the surface, only to yank back his fingers from the searing heat. The boy spoke and pointed at the side of the capsule. Cleod tried to decipher the words. He poked at the source of smoke again, only to jerk away his singed digits.

The boy approached cautiously and picked up a metal implement from a small table. He pointed at the metal structure with the tool. Cleod shuffled back a pace to encourage the boy. He plucked at the piece of wood mounted on the cylinder and a hatch swung open. Smoke and the scent of roasting meat billowed out. Racks of beef and pork filled the interior. Using the implement like a pair of fingers, he picked a slab from inside and held it out to Cleod.

Cleod gingerly took the offered meat, hanging onto his prize despite his scalded fingertips. The child clapped as Cleod tore off a mouthful of savory meat. No bones, no fur, just delicious meat. The dog continued its frantic yipping; on an impulse, Cleod tore off a tiny piece and tossed it in the dog's direction. It only took a single sniff for the creature to fall silent as it gobbled the morsel.

Another small folk emerged from the building, yelling. The new arrival stood as tall as a sidhe, but he was plump, resembling a fattened pig. Red-faced despite its otherwise pasty complexion, it shouted and brandished a strange tool, a metal stick on a wooden handle. The boy argued with the adult, the child's tone turning fearful. He set the grabbing implement on the table.

The adult waved the boy aside, pointing at Cleod with the stick. The man remained out of reach, so Cleod contently munched on his purloined slab of beef. No more people appeared, but if a village lay nearby, the noise could draw attention. Cleod decided to grab another piece of meat and retreat to the forest. Greedy ogres became dead ogres. He returned to the smoking apparatus, eliciting more noise from the adult small folk. The child had retreated behind the chubby man, who extended the long, straight tool toward Cleod.

*BOOM!* The blast startled Cleod, causing him to knock over the hot cylinder. A swarm of flies pelted his skin, tearing small holes in his tunic and pinging off the metal fire-holder. The rotund man goggled at Cleod in dismay. Annoyed, Cleod bared his teeth and snarled.

*BOOM!* Another swarm accompanied the report. Cleod flinched as a couple struck his face, but they harmlessly rebounded from his hide. Perhaps the thunder-stick was an alarm? Time to flee before the racket mustered more small folk. Cleod seized a metal leg and the handle of the open hatch. Hefting his prize, Cleod lumbered through the gap in the fence.

Another blast accompanied small bits of metal peppering the wood next to him. Did the thunder-stick spit metal flies? Cleod lacked the curiosity to remain, instead heading for the tree line. The shouting receded—the small-folk chose not to pursue him. Should he return to the hill? Perhaps the path had reopened while Cleod had sought his meal.

Cleod scanned the trees. His nose had guided him here, but he'd been so enraptured by the scent of cooking meat, he'd paid little attention to his route. Long shadows from the setting sun darkened the woods. East—the hill stood between him and the river to the east. He couldn't see it, but if he got close enough, he should recognize it.

He paused to fish out another hunk of meat, resorting to using a pointy stick. His efforts rewarded him with a slab of fatty, salty pork. Cleod bit off a delicious mouthful and resumed lugging his trophy deeper into the woods. At least the sidhe hadn't lied about the food.

\* \* \*

Luke Dahler pulled his car to the curb. The mailbox matched the address on the call—one of the upscale houses on cul-de-sacs carved into the woods surrounding the Forest Park Nature Center. The call had sounded sketchy; a giant homeless man had stolen a resident's smoker grill. Deputy Dahler didn't doubt someone had stolen the homeowner's barbecue, but the description of an 8-foot-tall man dressed in rags sounded almost as outlandish as an earlier Bigfoot report. The only reason dispatch had requested a prompt response was the neighbors had reported gunfire.

A middle-aged man emerged from the house and waited on the front porch. He bore no weapons, though Luke guessed he could hide a small arsenal in his cargo shorts. He double-checked the computer; the address and caller had no record, other than one parking ticket five years ago.

"Dispatch, Adam-Three-Seven on scene. Everything looks calm, so I'm going to collect a report and will advise, over." Luke clicked on his bodycam, though he doubted he'd need it. Better safe than sorry.

"You took your time getting here," the man called from the porch.

"Sir, are you armed?" Luke responded, walking slowly across the lawn.

"What?" The man's eyes widened, and he opened his empty hands. "No, I'm not dumb enough to greet a cop holding a shotgun. It's in the house, if you need to check it out."

"I'm Deputy Dahler. Is the perp in your house or yard?"

The man shook his head, relaxing his stance. "Naw, he ran off into the forest preserve after I peppered him with trap shot."

"You discharged your firearm?"

The man crossed his arms over his beer belly. "Damn straight. The huge freak demolished my fence and menaced my boy in our backyard."

"He was hungry," a voice pipped up from beyond the front door.

"Boy, let me talk to the police."

Luke suppressed a sigh. "Perhaps I should interview both of you, and you can show me the crime scene."

"Aren't you going to bring in the canine unit and hunt down the hobo?" the man demanded.

"Was the suspect armed? Did he attempt to attack anyone?" Luke asked.

The man frowned. "Well, no."

"Let me get some info, and dispatch can determine how to proceed. Since he doesn't pose an immediate threat, we can see if there've been other incidents…"

"And triangulate a search area! I saw that on 'Local PD Files.'" The man smiled proudly.

Luke didn't mention that he hated those shows. It took half an hour to get the story out of Ronald Perkins and his son Carson. Luke considered impounding the shotgun, but he'd found no blood or signs of injury. Despite Mr. Perkins' attestation that he'd hit the thief at least three times, Luke suspected he'd fired into the air—technically illegal within the city limits.

One nagging fact was both Mr. Perkins and his son insisted the suspect stood over eight-feet-tall and possessed a squat, hulking build. It didn't square with the occasional meth-head who raided cars or open garages for something they could pawn. The house lacked a security camera, and neither of them had thought to grab a phone and snap a picture, so Luke only had their description to type into the report.

Luke submitted the electronic form five minutes after the end of his shift. "Adam-Three-Seven to dispatch—take me off the board. I'm done for the day."

"*Roger, Adam-Three-Seven. Have a good night.*"

Luke closed his laptop and stowed his notepad. The talk of the perp stealing an entire smoker laden with meat had left Luke craving barbecue. Maybe he'd hit Riverfront Grill; he'd need to go home to change out of uniform and swap cars if he wanted to enjoy a cold beer and smoked brisket. With a plan in mind, he pulled his keys out of his pocket.

Movement caught his eye. A nosey neighbor who felt it safe to snoop now the excitement had died down? The woman peered over the fence, then followed it through the neighbor's open yard toward the side facing the preserve. Luke pocketed his keys and opened the door. Better to shoo her away in case Mr. Perkins remained twitchy.

He rounded the corner at the back of the yard. The woman knelt near the breach in the fence, examining the ground.

"Miss, this is a crime scene. You shouldn't poke around." Luke readied in case she reached for anything suspicious in her baggy hoodie.

She didn't even flinch. The woman rose slowly, keeping her hands in view as she turned to face him. "Hello, deputy. I don't suppose they reported anything unusual about the culprit."

Luke caught himself distracted. She wasn't model gorgeous, but her features combined the best of a mixed heritage. Her dark eyes regarded him, waiting for an answer. "Are you Peoria PD or something? I'm not going to discuss a case with a civilian, and if you're a journalist, you'll need to contact our press liaison."

"I'm Grace Ramirez, Deputy...Dahler. I'm kind of a consultant—a subject matter expert, if you will." Her gaze tracked the trampled grass to the brush at the edge of the woods. "Let me guess, impossibly large? Did the residents tell you anything else?"

"A good guess, especially if you listened to a scanner and caught the call. Miss Ramirez, I'd appreciate it if you vacated the scene. The homeowner has an itchy trigger finger, and I'm off duty, so I'd hate to have to fill out a report because you spooked him, and this time he was less careful with his warning shot." Luke dismissed the idea of her being city police. They'd be content to receive a copy of the report, since it was a property crime with no injury. Maybe she wrote for some online site delving into weird news?

"There's nothing to learn here, anyways." Grace paralleled the path to the edge of the undergrowth. She bent over to examine the broken branches. "You're not checking out my ass, are you, Deputy Dahler?"

Luke blushed. He hadn't intended to notice when the hoodie rose over her jeans. "It's getting dark. I doubt you're going to find anything. We'll watch for our hungry perp to pop back up, but since he didn't hurt anyone, I'm not going traipsing in the woods at sundown."

"Probably a good idea. Didn't you say you were off duty?" Grace marched into the trees without a second glance at Luke.

If the hobo still lurked in the preserve, and she stumbled across him, she could get hurt. Luke set off after her. "Wait a minute. This guy hasn't hurt anyone yet, but if he's strung out on drugs, he's not safe—assuming you find him before twisting your ankle in the dark."

"I'll be fine, Deputy Dahler. I don't need your help. Watch out for the dip."

"What?" Luke caught himself on a tree as his foot snagged in a depression. The woman stalked through the trees ahead of him, confident despite the fading light. "Wait, someone's going to get hurt."

"I don't have time to hold your hand, Deputy," Grace said, waiting for him with a half-smirk.

"My name is Luke."

She nodded. "If I'm not mistaken, this way will loop around toward where we want to go."

"Why are you doing this?" Luke asked, following Grace along the narrow path. It veered away from the direction they'd been travelling, but the footing proved less treacherous. "You should leave it to the authorities."

"Because you don't know what you're dealing with," she replied. Another trail crossed their path, and she turned left. "I don't need you to protect me—it's the other way around."

Luke caught a whiff of cooking meat. "Do you smell that?"

* * *

Grace sniffed. Deputy Dahler had a sharp nose. She strained her ears, searching for a noise beyond the birds and wind—a wet smacking noise, followed by a loud belch. She faced Luke and held a finger to her lips.

To his credit, he stopped trying to dissuade her and nodded. She studied his face, a combination of farm-grown healthy with intelligent eyes. If he'd shown up at her bar instead of on the trail of a supernatural beast, she might have given him a free drink and contemplated asking for his number.

*Focus*, she chided herself. Her abuela cajoled her for not having a boyfriend, but tracking a beastie from the otherworld in the woods wasn't the time to let her mind wander and play matchmaker. She debated drawing her weapon, but didn't want to spook the deputy, let alone explain how she kept it in an extra-dimensional pocket. Heck, *she* didn't even understand how it worked.

She crept along the path, scanning the darkening woods. Even with her heightened vision, the shadows grew murky.

There—a large form shifted among the bushes. Grace carefully picked her way through the undergrowth, avoiding stiff branches and deadfall. Rounding a large tree, she caught full sight of the ogre.

The druid hadn't exaggerated when he'd called her. The humanoid possessed arms thicker than Deputy Dahler's thighs and a hulking physique. A smoker grill lay on its side next to the ogre, smoke wisping out of the open hatch. The ogre sat on the ground, munching contently on a slab of smoked pork belly.

All she had to do was convince him to go peacefully back to the wold-ford, call the druid out to open it, and send him through. Given his stolen larder, the ogre might even prove agreeable if approached cautiously. As long as she didn't startle him.

"Holy shit!" Luke blurted at her elbow.

\* \* \*

The voice snapped Cleod out of his food-induced reverie. Two strangely dressed small folk, a man and a woman, stood watching him. He recognized neither, and they lacked any obvious weapons or a thunder-stick like the chubby man had brandished back at the house.

If they weren't hunters or warriors, scaring them off would let Cleod return to eating in peace, or he could resume his search for the hill with the ford back home. He rose to his full height—size impressed the small-folk—and bared his yellow teeth in a slobbery snarl.

The woman took a half-step back while the man scurried several paces. The male pointed threateningly at Cleod. The female turned and berated the man in the same unintelligible tongue the earlier people had spoken.

*Why didn't they flee?* Cleod waved his arms in the air and roared again.

*Pop! Pop! Pop!* Bees stung Cleod's chest, raising welts. Magic! Cleod snapped a branch off a nearby tree. While not as loud as the thunder-stick, whatever the man held had hurt Cleod, even if it didn't match a hornet. The boy from earlier popped up from behind a bush and shouted at the bee-casting man.

"Stop!" the woman yelled. "Do you understand me?"

Cleod paused. She used the same language as the sidhe, even if it sounded strange from her lips. The man called the woman, earning him an admonishment in their tongue. She pointed at the child and gave an order.

Cleod shook the branch and bellowed again. Perhaps they would retreat to protect the child. Cleod had no intention of harming the boy, but they didn't know that.

"Put down the stick," the woman commanded. She drew a wicked blade from behind her back.

A thought clicked into place as Cleod recalled Feidhlim's words earlier. He pointed the branch at the woman. "You bully woman."

Her stance eased a fraction. "Wait, what?"

Cleod swung the branch side to side. "Sidhe warned about you. You bully sidhe, you bully Cleod. You even bully man-mate."

* * *

Luke struggled to process everything. He couldn't decide what boggled him more—that the huge monster shrugged off 9mm bullets, it spoke a guttural Irish-sounding tongue, Grace could converse with it in the same language, or she'd conjured a machete out of thin air.

"Don't hurt him!" Carson Perkins cried again. Add to the list the boy had trailed them through the woods. *Great detective work!*

"Get the kid out of here!" Grace commanded. She was the only one keeping her cool, the monster included.

The hulking beast pointed its club at Grace and rumbled something accusatory. Grace's tone in response sounded confused. The creature uttered a longer accusation, swinging his weapon menacingly, ending his statement by pointing at Luke. Maybe he'd been insulted by a woman challenging him, and now he was demanding to fight Luke?

"What's going on?" Luke crept a pace closer since Grace refused to give ground. Even with her machete, how could she hope to go toe-to-toe with the brute?

"You're scaring him! He's just hungry!" the boy called.

"He…he called me a bully," Grace said, her tone wavering between confusion and amusement. "He said I even bullied you."

"You're both bullies," Carson added. "You shot at him, and she has a big knife."

"Kid, he's eight feet tall and tore off half a tree for a club," Luke retorted. To Grace, in a lowered voice, he continued, "How can you even talk to that thing?"

"He's an ogre. His Goidelc is about as good as mine. It's a patois used by the magical folk," Grace replied. She switched to the foreign language and spoke reassuringly to the ogre, lowering her machete.

The ogre eyed her suspiciously but stopped swinging the branch. They exchanged a few more sentences. Luke checked to make sure Carson remained at a safe distance only to find the kid at his elbow.

"That son of a bitch!" Grace muttered, clenching her teeth to control her volume.

"What? Did it say something..." *What would an ogre say?* "Should I shoot him?"

"No! It's not Cleod's fault. An aos sidhe named Feidhlim sent him to our world, probably hoping exactly this would happen," Grace replied.

"He hoped the ogre would steal a grill?" Luke asked.

"No. He hoped I would hear about an ogre on the loose and tangle with him. Guess his plan almost worked." Grace switched languages for another exchange with Cleod. "I think I've convinced him we were tricked."

"Who is Feidhlim, and what is an ow she?" Luke had a zillion more questions.

"Aos sidhe—but close." The ghostly man emerged from a nearby tree. If the apparition didn't slightly glow, Luke might have mistaken him for a local.

"About time, druid," Grace said.

"You were expecting a ghost?" Luke asked.

"Whoa, cool!" Carson chirped.

\*\*\*

"A bartender, a deputy, and a druid walk into the woods," Knox said. "Great, a kid to boot. This will poke some holes in the shroud of secrecy."

Grace kept Cleod in her field of view as she spoke to Knox. "Yeah, I know, not ideal. I didn't know how to shake Deputy Dahler without raising more suspicions. The kid was a bonus."

"Is he a ghost?" Luke asked. At least he didn't point his pistol at Knox's apparition.

"No, I'm a flesh and blood druid, but projecting through the spirit world was faster than traipsing through the woods. I'm physically at the wold-ford." He switched to Goidelc to address Cleod. "I am Druid Knox, First Druid of the Accords. Do you know what that means?"

"You know fancy words," Cleod replied.

Grace snickered into the back of her hand. "I like his definition."

Knox shook his head. "It means I'm in charge of magic on the Dunwold. I suspect Feidhlim tricked you into coming here, hoping you would hurt someone, starting with Grace, and cause trouble for me."

The ogre grabbed the hunk of meat he'd dropped at the beginning of the fracas and tore out a bite. "Feidhlim told Cleod about food and bully. Right about both."

"I am not a bully!" Grace retorted.

"You mean to Cleod. You mean to man-mate." Cleod nodded toward Luke.

The druid laughed. "I like his definition."

"What's he saying about me?" Luke asked.

"The ogre thinks you're her boyfriend, and she bullies you," Knox replied before Grace could interject.

"You're her boyfriend?" the kid asked. "Does she always boss you around?"

Grace took a deep breath. "Can we focus on the problem? How do we get Cleod home?"

"Get him to come to the wold-ford, and I'll open it," Knox replied.

Grace nodded. "Cleod, do you want to go home?"

Cleod licked grease off his fingers and patted the smoker. "Cleod keep food?"

"Sure. I doubt the previous owner wants it back."

\* \* \*

Cleod discarded the branch. The druid would open the path, and Cleod could return to his familiar haunt. This world proved too noisy, and the small folk panicked easier than skittish sheep. Cleod would miss the succulent meat, but at least he knew what to expect back home.

"I will wait for you at the ford." The druid's shade vanished.

Cleod hefted the meat-cooker. The surface remained hot, but not beyond what his thick hide could tolerate.

"I am Grace. I'm the local..." She seemed embarrassed to finish the sentence. "I'm the local champion."

The child stepped up next her, speaking and pointing to himself. Grace translated. "His name is Carson."

Cleod hunched over. "Greetings, Carson."

"Greetings, Cleod," the boy replied, or at least an approximation.

"I know the way to the wold-ford," Grace said.

Cleod nodded, standing.

*　*　*

Luke broke out his flashlight as they wove their way through the paths. "You know this park pretty well," he remarked.

"Cleod isn't the first visitor from the Glaswold," Grace replied.

"Glaswold?" Luke asked.

"It's another name for the otherworld. Think of it as a reflection of our world, but humanity never arose. Instead of cities and roads, they have faerie folk and ogres. I've only been there a couple of times with the druid, and not for long." Grace led them north at the next intersection.

"So magic is real, and there's another world full of monsters and supernatural folk?" Luke checked to make sure Carson was keeping pace with them. When instructed to go home, the kid had feigned fear of going through the woods by himself. Luke suspected the boy knew exactly how to get home but didn't want his adventure to end yet.

"Am I going to have to explain everything twice?" Grace asked.

"Sorry. I'm trying to wrap my head around things. I grew up in Galesburg. Even with cable television, I didn't have much time for fanciful things like dragons and wizards. Here's a new question—why did my bullets bounce off him and Mr. Perkin's shotgun blasts?" From the tattered patterns in Cleod's tunic, Mr. Perkins' warning shots hadn't been in the air.

"A lot of supernatural folk have a magical 'pact' protecting them from base metals, including copper, tin, and lead. I'm guessing your ammo is steel jacketed," she said.

"Semi-jacketed hollow points," Luke replied. He glanced back at the ogre, who plodded behind them, silent despite his bulk.

Grace nodded. "Those steel rings were the only part not covered by the magic, so they stung Cleod, but didn't have enough mass to injure him. Knox might be able to connect you with a supplier who makes rounds effective against magic."

"Assuming I remember any of this." Voicing the suspicion sent a chill down Luke's spine. He lowered his voice. "I caught his reference to a 'shroud of secrecy.' If magic and mythical creatures are real, how do you hide it? Getting rid of witnesses only raises more suspicions, so they must use magic to make people forget. Hypnotize them or something—so am I going to remember you?"

"I hate to think I wasted my time explaining this stuff to you," Grace replied. "Knox knows we can't keep this bottled up forever. Besides, what are you going to do—get on a podcast and tell everyone you saw an ogre?"

"I guess you're right," Luke admitted. Wind rustled the trees ahead, and a breeze whirled around them. A light flickered in the woods nearby.

Grace nodded toward the illumination. "We're here."

\* \* \*

Grace led them toward the hill. "Watch out for the ditch." She waited until the deputy shone his light on the stagnant moat. "There's a bridge over here."

Two logs spanned the water. Grace deftly crossed, then helped Carson. She held out her hand to Luke as he reached the halfway point. He smiled sheepishly as he grasped it and finished traversing the logs. Cleod eyed the fallen trees skeptically. One shifted under his weight, but he kept his footing and reached the other side.

Knox waited at the crest of the hill, a small lamp at his feet. His pixie girlfriend stood at his side. Grace remembered the deputy's question—would the purple-haired woman mesmerize the 'mundanes' to fog their memories?

"So you really dress like that?" Luke asked. "I was expecting something…I don't know, wizardy."

Knox looked to his girlfriend. "Am I the only one who likes this flannel?"

"You look like you walked out of the Tractor Depot Store, sweetheart," the fae replied in a musical accent.

Knox plucked at his shirt. "I live on a farm. Deputy, what's your name?"

"Luke. Are you going to wipe my mind?"

"No. Can you stay here with the boy while we take Cleod home?" the druid asked.

"My name is Carson. I want to see Cleod's home."

The druid rubbed his temple. "Of course you do. However, we don't know what's waiting on the other side."

"If it's dangerous, I should go," Luke protested.

"Between Grace and Cleod, we'll be okay," Knox said.

"Your gun won't do much good over there," Grace added. She turned to the druid. "You could lend him one of yours."

"Whose side are you on?" Knox asked. "Besides, the kid…"

"Carson."

"…needs someone to keep an eye on him."

Grace was torn. The druid made sense, but she wanted Luke alongside her. "Could there be critters lurking in the woods? I'd hate to leave them behind and have some dog monsters eat them."

"I asked the local spirits. Nothing crossed from the wold-ford since our large friend," Knox replied.

She cracked her knuckles. "It means Feidhlim is still on the other side. The bastard sent Cleod through to stir up trouble, not caring what happened to him."

"You talk about tricky sidhe?" Cleod asked in Goidelc, recognizing the name and Grace's tone.

"Yes. I'd consider it a favor if you'd punch him if I don't get the chance," Grace replied. The ogre nodded.

"Do you want me to stay with Carson?" the fae asked. Her eyes glowed purple in the fading twilight. "I'm sure I could convince him."

"I don't want to stay!" Carson protested.

"Sure you do." The purple haired woman leaned forward to get eye level with the boy. "You don't want me to be all alone in these dark woods, do you? Why don't you say good-bye to your friend?"

Luke took a step back and whispered, "Is she going to erase our brains?" Grace nudged him in the ribs with her elbow.

The boy sagged. "I guess I'll stay. How do I say good-bye so he'll understand?"

"Slan avail uh," Grace replied, simplifying the Goidelc.

Carson peered up at the ogre. "Slan avail uh, Cleod."

The ogre's face split into a crooked yellow smile. He patted the boy gingerly on the head. "*Slan abhaile*, Carson."

The fae sat on a fallen tree. "Why don't you come over and sit by me?"

The druid clasped his hands, then pulled them apart, his staff appearing out of thin air.

"Knox." Grace tipped her head to Luke.

"Right." The druid reached into his jeans pocket and drew a revolver far too large for the space. He checked the hammer before handing it to Luke. "Double-action revolver with silver-jacketed tungsten carbide loads. Don't lose it. Try not to shoot anything friendly."

\* \* \*

Cleod watched the druid sketch an opening in the air with his staff, and the shimmering distortion returned. He shifted his grip on his prize. The heat had ebbed, so he could tuck the canister of meat under his arm. He gave the child a final wave and stepped through the path between worlds.

The metallic tang vanished from the air, and the night sky became a bejeweled canopy. Feidhlim stood on the other side of the campfire, conversing with four sidhe. These bore the arms of hunters and warriors. Cleod regretted discarding his branch.

Feidhlim turned, surprise etched on his face. "Clod? I see you're alive and well. A bit of a surprise, really. I didn't open the ford, so how did you return?"

"I opened the ford," the druid stated, emerging from the path with Grace and her mate on his heels. "We have enough trouble without assholes opening the ford for random visitors."

The tricky sidhe's smile evaporated when he spied Grace. "Oh, shit. Kill them!"

Grace's mate asked a question in the stinking world's tongue and gestured toward one of the closing hunters, who brandished spears.

"Don't you idiots know who I am?" the druid asked. Wind whipped around him as he raised his staff.

Feidhlim slipped from the edge of the group, slinking down the side of the hill.

Cleod uprooted a sapling.

\* \* \*

They'd stepped through a heat mirage, and suddenly a campfire and a group of guys appeared on the hill. Luke didn't need to know the language to know the leader was a smarmy asshole, and his imperative to his armed friends left little room for doubt.

Still, Luke asked, "Are these considered friendly?"

"No," Grace replied, producing her machete from behind her back. What was it with these people and magic pockets? "These are assholes. Feel free to shoot them."

Luke sidestepped, forcing one of the spearmen to separate from the group to press an attack. Luke didn't let him close the gap. BOOM! The shot struck center mass, and the man sprawled back. Two of the men went after Grace, while the last rushed the druid.

Luke held his gun low, waiting for the combatants to separate in the flickering firelight. The druid parried a series of jabs with his staff, giving ground to his assailant. Grace's opponents flanked her and pressed their attack. One lost a quarter of his spear to Grace's machete. She twisted with the swing, the thrust of the other spearman glancing off her side. She threw her momentum into landing a solid sidekick in his gut.

The man stumbled on the slope of the hill, using his spear to arrest his momentum. Luke seized the opening and fired. The bullet hit the man in the shoulder, spinning him around and sending him stumbling into the darkness.

Facing Grace one-on-one, her remaining foe went on the defense. Grace passed up an easy opportunity to gut the man, instead splitting his remaining spear-haft. She stepped in, snapped his head back with a palm strike to his jaw, and jabbed him in the upper arm with her machete, again forgoing a fatal strike. The man staggered a pace, dropping his pieces of wood and shaking the stars from his eyes. She said something in the foreign tongue, and the man fled into the night.

The druid's attacker blinked and squinted as a gale-force wind howled in his face. The staff sprouted a metal blade, and the druid skewered his foe's foot. Knox ducked away from the reflexive counter. Before Luke could line up a shot, Grace grabbed the spearman from behind and held her blade to his throat. He got the message and dropped his weapon.

\* \* \*

"What's your deal?" Grace growled. "Why are you here?"

"Telling her the truth will hurt less than me splitting open your skull and reading your brains before I cast your spirit into the Deep Umbra," the druid added. Grace wondered if he'd used English to rattle Luke's nerves as well.

"Feidhlim plotted this!" the sidhe replied in accented English. "He sent the ogre, figuring if it didn't kill you once it caught your attention, it would at least draw you here."

"Are you okay?" Luke interrupted, reaching tentatively toward where the spear tip had struck a grazing blow.

Grace bit back annoyance. He meant well, and his concern was endearing. "I'm fine. My hoodie deflected the edge."

"What?" Luke furrowed his brow.

"My hoodie has chain mail and boar-leather woven into it. I'll explain later," Grace replied. "Meanwhile, I want this dirtbag to explain what Feidhlim offered these assholes."

The man gulped carefully with the blade still against his skin. "An opportunity to get a stake in his smuggling operation."

"Smuggling what?" the druid demanded. In the dim firelight, one of his eyes glowed blue and the other green.

"Women. Dunnie women."

Grace muttered a string of curses in Spanish.

"What does he mean by Dunnie women?" Luke asked.

Grace snorted. "Women from our world. I busted Feidhlim trying to drag off a co-worker with a magical roofie. Evidently he didn't get the message. What do we do with this *pendejo*?"

"I'm tempted to let you lop off his head so I can turn his skull into a candle holder, but we need someone to spread the word," the druid replied. "Can you do that? Get the message out that anyone caught trafficking people either direction will meet gruesome justice? I have space for a lot of candles, and I might make it a contest to see who can bring me the most sidhe poachers' heads."

"I can do that," the sidhe promised with a tiny nod.

"If not, I'll be waiting." Grace lowered the blade from his throat. "I'll make sure your skull is one of the first."

The sidhe nodded enthusiastically before fleeing into the night.

"Where did the ogre go?" Luke asked.

\* \* \*

Feidhlim slipped through the darkness. *Curse the luck!* He hadn't figured on reinforcements, let alone her turning the ogre. Better to slip away in the confusion and relocate to another wold-ford. Perhaps he could wheedle his way into the troupe working out of the dunnie city Joliet. He would need to rebuild his Dunwold assets, but transportation hadn't proven such an obstacle there.

A rustling noise caught his ear a split second before a sapling, root ball and all, slammed into his back. He pitched forward, sprawling in the undergrowth. Pain radiated through his back, and thorns scratched at his right arm as brambles snagged his sleeve.

The ogre loomed out of the darkness. "You tricked Cleod!"

"You've got it wrong! She *is* a bully! She hates the old folk like us!" Feidhlim tore his arm free of the brambles' grasp, drawing blood in the process. "People like her want to keep us trapped in this backward land."

The ogre's long arm lashed out faster than his bulk belied and snagged Feidhlim's scrambling ankle. The brute dragged him across the forest floor. Feidhlim desperately mustered *lledrith* and threw it behind his will. "Release me!"

The ogre balled his hand into a meaty fist the size of Feidhlim's head. "No."

The fist crashed down.

*   *   *

Cleod lumbered back into the firelight.

"Where'd you go?" Grace asked.

"Cleod did Grace favor. Cleod punched trickster in face." Cleod shuffled to his metal meat holder. The journey here had jumbled the contents, so Cleod had to shake charred wood and ash off the piece of beef he fished out. He skewered it on a discarded spear and held it over the campfire.

Grace's mate asked something. "Did you kill him?" Grace translated.

"He still breathed when Cleod left, but now not so pretty." Cleod pulled back the slab of meat and took a bite. He was going to miss meat free of bones and fur.

"Cleod, I have a question for you," Grace said after a moment.

"Another favor?" Cleod asked.

"More like an exchange of favors."

\* \* \*

"What's that?" Braon asked. A strange box rested near the crest of the hill. It appeared to be carved from bright red stone with a white lid.

"No clue," Dagan replied in a low voice. "Perhaps we should have sought a different ford."

Braon shook his head. "The *Gwuedd* is thicker here. I can draw *lledrith* to open the wold-ford far easier."

"I heard only those with the First Druid's blessing can cross here. Are you sure this is a good idea?" Braon scanned the surrounding forest.

"He's not here to collect a toll, is he?" Dagan retorted.

"Cleod collect toll," a deep voice rumbled. An eight-foot-tall ogre emerged from the brush. "You have token?"

"No. I told him this was a bad idea," Braon blurted. The ogre hefted a large club of polished wood.

"Fine. Let's find another ford," Dagan grumbled.

Cleod watched the two scurry off into the woods. As their footfalls faded, he shuffled over to the cooler. Cleod popped the lid long enough to confirm it had been filled with brisket and smoked pork belly. In exchange for Cleod patrolling the forest around the woldford, Grace brought him meat every moon.

It felt good to do his friend a favor. His stomach rumbled—it tasted good, as well.

\* \* \* \* \*

## Jon Osborne Biography

Jon R. Osborne turned a journalism education and a passion for role-playing games into writing science fiction and fantasy. His second book in The Milesian Accords modern fantasy trilogy, *A Tempered Warrior*, was a 2018 Dragon Awards finalist for Best Fantasy Novel. Jon is also a core author in the military science fiction Four Horseman Universe, where he was first published in 2017.

Jon resides in Indianapolis, where he plays role-playing games, writes science fiction and fantasy, and extols the virtues of beer. You can find out more at jonrosborne.com and at https://www.facebook.com/jonrosborne.

\* \* \* \* \*

# A Lesser God
# by Mark Wandrey
## A Traveling Gods Story

Even on a windy night, you can hear a branch crack if you're in constant fear for your life. Your senses become hypersensitive to anything out of the ordinary, be it smell, sight, or sound. Ever since the world went crazy, survival had replaced safety, panic had replaced calm, and death had replaced life.

Jeannie sat up on her elbow in the little tent, ears now tuned one hundred percent to any sound out of the ordinary. She reached under her pillow for the knife and pulled it up against her chest. She was fully dressed in her sleeping bag, except for her shoes, which were within easy reach, and her coat lay over her bag. She moved slowly and deliberately to avoid making any noise.

It was at least a minute later when she heard a crunching sound, like a bunch of leaves being crushed into the forest loam.

"Fuck," she cursed under her breath and slid from the bag. In seconds she had her shoes laced up, coat on, bag rolled up, and was slipping outside into the chill night air. She always underestimated how much warmer it was in the little Alpine puptent, heated by only her own body. The tent collapsed in seconds, and went last into her pack.

"You hear that?" someone said.

Jeannie guessed twenty, maybe 30 yards as she swung her pack over her shoulder and picked up the knife from where she'd placed it on the ground while packing.

"I don't hear nothing, dumbass," a man snapped back. "Ain't nothing in these woods but rabbits."

"What about that glowing yote last week?"

"You made it up, now shut up before someone hears us."

"I didn' make nuthin' up," the other complained.

"Shut up, you make tings up all the time."

Their voices faded as Jeannie moved deeper into the woods, opposite their direction. A few minutes of careful walking later, she'd put a couple hundred yards between herself and the voices. She had no idea if they meant her ill, and would never know. It didn't matter.

She passed into a small clearing, and the moon peeked out from behind the clouds. It was only a quarter moon and threw little light. She was lucky enough to be blessed with exceptional night vision. It had served her well in the last two months of running.

Jeannie stopped and listened.

Now in a place to run if necessary, she was in no hurry. She guessed she stood by the tree for fifteen minutes. Clouds passed over the moon several times and it was slowly dropping towards the trees. Finally, she decided it was safe and she sat on a deadfall to calm her breathing.

Like anything she removed from her pack, Jeannie took out her compass carefully. It was one of the only things she owned from before, a relic from when backpacking was for fun. The Proster IP65 wasn't fancy. She'd bought it on Amazon and only taken it camping twice. It had a rarity in the modern age, a tritium dial and a clinometer. It had taken her weeks to relearn how to land nav in the post smartphone age. Now it was her second most valuable possession.

She checked the dimly glowing compass dial, still shielding it with her hands, even though it shouldn't have been visible from more than a few feet away. She was starting to shiver. She closed her eyes for a moment and recalled the location of her camp, comparing it to her compass, and fixed a bearing. She couldn't risk getting too far from a road. The area of West Virginia she was in could be treacherous, for a lot of reasons.

She had to stop after a few minutes of working through trees and brambles. First to urinate, then drink from one of her water bladders. As she was drinking, she noted a growing headache. "Damnit," she cursed. Too late to summon up more piss, and she was low on pain killers. She finished her business and moved on.

Like many, she didn't have a watch or a way to tell time. She didn't even have a moon table. She was reduced to guessing based on how tired she was, and that wasn't a good barometer, either. She guessed it was around midnight. It was as good a guess as anything else.

An hour later, she climbed a slight incline to find a large, blacktop roadway which had to be Highway 250. She turned right, which would be south, and walked along the road as close to the trees as she could get. Before long the moon had dropped below the trees, and she was in near total darkness.

Jeannie walked for a short time, the headache getting worse, as well as her thirst. There was little doubt left in her mind now. She needed to find a place to get off her feet and do a test. It wouldn't be hard in a town, but towns were something she tried not to do. Ever.

Another hour of walking, and she stumbled twice, the second time landing painfully on her knees. She cursed under her breath as she got back to her feet. Only then did she detach her aluminum pole walking stick from its mounting place on her pack, something she should have done shortly after abandoning her night's camp.

A few minutes later she came to her first candidate. It was an older four-door pickup, pushed off into the ditch. But the windows were all broken out, and it smelled like someone had used it as a latrine. The odors reminded her how badly she needed to urinate again. She took a drink from her camelback and moved on. Walking helped.

A few minutes later she found an overgrown gravel drive cutting off to the left. It immediately entered dense trees. She paused by the edge of the trees, trying to see inside.

It was like a tunnel of leaves and pine needles, something right out of a fantasy novel cover. More importantly, something light colored was visible just at the edge of how far she could see.

Jeannie stood there for a long moment, considering. The unknown almost always equated to danger, anymore. She had to weigh the risks, and staying on the road just then was the greater risk, so she slowly, quietly headed down the gravel drive.

The lighter colored shape turned out to be a small delivery truck. She had no idea why it was there. Maybe on the evening of February 28th, they'd been heading for a late delivery? Or maybe they'd been moving goods between towns. She had no idea as she circled the truck. Weeds and grass had grown up in the weeks since that fateful evening. There was no sign any of it had been trampled recently. It looked good.

She gently put a hand on the driver's side door handle. After taking a couple calming breaths, she wrapped her fingers around it and pulled. *Pop.* The door swung open freely. Of course, the light didn't come on, nor the instrument panel. It had been over a month since that would have happened.

The cockpit didn't smell bad, and the windows were all intact. A water bottle sat in the driver's seat cup holder. She reached over and took it. Unopened. The driveway was angled downhill slightly from the road. Whoever had been driving must have pushed it or coasted it down here, parked it, and left. "But they didn't lock it?" she wondered aloud.

Whatever the reason was behind it being there didn't matter. It was out of the cold, intact, and out of view. She took her pack off and sat in the driver's seat. Opening the top, she removed her kit and walked to the edge of the driveway. With a quick glance around to be sure nobody was in view, she unzipped her pants, opened the kit, carefully removed a strip, squatted, and urinated on it.

A minute later she was back to the truck, and she found the lighter she was currently using and flicked it to life, holding it low so no one outside could see the flame. Through the dim light she could see the reagent strip, which was a rich shade of magenta. Jeannie had long ago memorized the matching guide. "Yeah," she said, and dropped the strip on the floor.

She closed the truck door and opened her kit once more. Cleaning a syringe liberally with a cotton wipe, she set it in the bottle, and holding the two in one hand, she lit the lighter once more. By the dim light, she filled the syringe.

"I hate doing this in the dark," she said, her voice echoing in the compartment. Exposing a thigh, she used the wipe again before sticking herself and injecting. Wiping sweat from her forehead, she had just enough presence of mind to put the kit carefully on the dashboard and pull the sleeping bag from her back to cover herself, then she fell deeply asleep.

\* \* \*

Jeannie jerked awake, sun bright on her face. It was swelteringly hot in the van. She took a moment to evaluate how she felt. No headache, clear eyesight, not overly thirsty. It had been at least four hours, and she didn't have to immediately urinate.

No need for another test strip, so she grabbed the kit off the dashboard. She hadn't cleaned the needle, so it was toast. She capped it and tossed it on the floor. Needles were never a problem, anyway.

The vial of insulin she'd used last night had one light dose left in it. There were two more vials beside it. She took them out and examined them, letting the sun shine through the bottles. Both were crystal clear. That wasn't a guarantee of their condition, but it was good enough for her. She replaced them in the kit, zipped it up, and stashed it deep in her pack. A week, no more.

"I'll starve long before that," she said and checked her pack's contents. Four packages of Mountain House freeze-dried macaroni with tomato and hamburger sauce, one sausage and eggs breakfast, and a tuna noodle casserole.

She considered carefully. Lunch the previous day had been a protein bar, her last. It was a common brand full of sugar and carbs, and also likely the reason for her high blood sugar.

Ever since she'd been diagnosed as a type 1 diabetic at the age of five, her life had been a gradual process of learning to cope. By age ten she was fully dependent on insulin. Two years ago, her physician had *almost* convinced her to get an insulin pump. "It would make your life so much simpler," she'd told Jeannie, who'd only decided against it at the last moment. She never knew why she'd decided against it, only that she'd probably be dead now if she'd said yes.

"How many diabetics are still alive?" she wondered as she rummaged through all the pockets of her pack, trying to find anything but the pasta dishes. The eggs and sausage were fine, but they were also the last ones she had. She didn't know what she was saving it for. When she was down to her last pocket, she found a large pack of cashews. "Bingo."

She pulled out her map and tried to get a better idea of where she was while chewing cashews. It was hard not to dump the whole pack in her mouth and wolf them down. The salt was wonderful on her tongue, and the flavors combined to bring back memories of better times. Times when she didn't have to constantly think about how to survive another day. Times of running water and flush toilets. Times when light appeared at the flick of a switch, and you could casually go on a twenty mile drive.

When the nuts had been devoured, she washed them down with water, then got out to take care of her morning business. As she finished burying the product, along with the nut wrapper, she turned back to the truck, only just then realizing it was a FedEx delivery truck. She hadn't looked last night, another statement to how high her blood sugar had been. She was lucky she hadn't passed out in a ditch.

The back of the truck proved to be locked, so Jeannie picked up a rock and hammered the handle until it snapped, and the door opened. Inside were dozens of undelivered packages. She suddenly felt like Tom Hanks on the beach of a desert island. What possible wonders might be found here? A couple boxes had Amazon markings on them, and she knew they delivered essentials. Was it worth the time, or more importantly, the energy she'd consume? Ultimately the answer was yes, it was.

The little knife took longer than she liked. Back in her Columbus, Ohio apartment, along with innumerable artifacts of a previous life, was a Leatherman tool, a gift from her father when she'd been a Girl Scout. The knife she used now had been salvaged from a truck stop in Chillicothe two weeks ago. As she cut open packages to examine the contents, she tried not to remember the refugee camps in Columbus, the fighting, the…

She shook her head and chased away the thoughts, looking down at a new Kindle ebook reader. She smirked and tossed it aside, opening another package and finding a spice rack—sans the spices, unfortunately. Next was a webcam, followed by an undecipherable medical device, a collection of tubes and straps called a CPM. She put it in the small pile of 'maybe' and went on.

Roughly two hours later, all the packages had been opened, even the smaller, letter-sized ones. The most interesting was a divorce decree; the most useful was a package containing a waterproof poncho, which actually fit, and a camping hammock. She was surprised to find any camping gear, since the event had happened in February, too far from spring for the build up to camping season. Overall, she decided, it had been worth the time as she got out and walked back toward the road.

The main road was just as it had been the previous night, abandoned and quiet. A cool, gentle breeze moved the trees in its passage. The smell of pine needles and loam filled her nostrils, helping make the previous night's events seem far away. As she scanned the opposite side of the road, she caught movement. It looked like a dog staring at her, only it didn't look quite right. Its face was funny shaped for a dog, and it was white. The eyes almost seemed to glow the purest white she could ever have imagined. She did a doubletake, but the dog was gone.

"Huh," she said, looking around again. Nothing else seemed out of the ordinary, so she headed southward once more, resuming her trek.

\* \* \*

Highway 250 meandered between low hills, heading generally southward. Two days later, Jeannie was coming to a decision point. She'd given up and eaten the eggs and sausage, consuming it as her midday meal. As before, the problem with the Mountain House dinners was their size. They were intended as 'meals for two,' and simply too much food to eat in one sitting. They were also difficult to keep.

She ate as much as she could, then finished the rest several hours later, hoping she wouldn't get sick from it. So far, she'd been lucky.

Eating the pasta was trickier, as anyone with diabetes knows. Pasta converted to sugar rapidly in your stomach, and sugar was bad. She ate the sauce and meat, along with about a quarter of the pasta. The rest went, regrettably, into the ditch. She had two of those left, a couple packages of corn chips—not much better than pasta—and then she was out of food. The conundrum was that a town lay just ahead.

She'd started walking just after dawn, and was now staring at a road sign; Mannington-2 miles, Fairmont-15 miles. A small dirt road to the left led into the hills. Based on her maps, it connected to a fire road that would lead around Mannington. However, a town meant food, and maybe more insulin.

She'd rummaged through a house or two since leaving Columbus. Her ingrained sense of propriety had kept her from doing it more often, and also an overwhelming sense of fear. After the camp in Columbus, people scared her like never before in her life. She'd rather die in a ditch than allow herself to be a victim again.

It was ultimately hunger that drove her to continue on to Mannington, which she reached the outskirts of in another half hour. Like most West Virginia towns in this part of the state, the first clue you'd arrived was mobile homes cut into the hills along the road. A short distance further on, stick-built houses appeared. The road went down a hill that angled left, which was where she saw her first Manningtonians.

There was a large white house with a man and a woman standing on the porch, watching Jeannie walk by. The man held a rifle; the woman held a child. *They don't know yet,* she thought. She almost yelled to them, then decided against it. Instead, she walked on around the corner and saw the town for the first time.

There was a self-storage unit on the right, near Buffalo Creek, which the road had been paralleling. A car wash was next door. She spotted several people opening storage units with bolt cutters. One stopped to stare at her, and she walked a little faster. *Welcome to Mannington*, a sign said. So far, she didn't feel terribly welcome.

At first she thought the town had fared better than the last couple of smaller towns she'd passed through. The auto parts store was untouched. Later, she realized that of course the auto parts store was fine. When she reached the IGA, it was completely wrecked. It looked like pictures of war-torn regions of the world before. Trash was everywhere; nothing looked untouched. Across the street, First Exchange Bank looked to be in better shape, though the glass doors were broken. *Were people stealing money?*

A little further on, she came to the town's main street intersection, called Market Street here. To her right was the old downtown area. Like many similar towns, the state highway skirted downtown, largely because said downtown area had been built to accommodate horse and buggy. When trucks began moving goods in the 50s, there just wasn't room. However, on the south east corner of the intersection was something of much more interest; a Rite Aid pharmacy.

She stopped and gave the area a good look. It still felt strange to just stand in the middle of the road. A lifetime of habit hadn't been washed away in a few weeks, after all. She still caught herself checking both ways when crossing a road. Over on the curb, she sat down and made a big show of removing her shoes and checking them for rocks, or whatever, all the while examining the pharmacy.

Unlike the IGA and the bank, there were no signs of looting here. There were a few cars in the parking lot, which had all been pushed to one side. A small farmer's market style trading operation was underway in the furthest corner of the lot, opposite the store itself. Maybe twenty people were either selling items or trying to barter for something. None of them took any notice of her.

By the door to the pharmacy were two men, both big guys, holding metallic baseball bats. She could see people moving inside the business, pushing shopping carts. *Organized looting?* She tried to remember if Rite Aids were franchises, or corporate stores. She didn't know the answer. What she did know was she'd found the first pharmacy in a month that hadn't been looted, burned, or both. In short, it was a lifeline for continued survival.

She was sitting, her shoes completely forgotten, and thinking about how she could go about asking for some insulin when a group of men noticed her. She didn't realize they were talking to her until one came close and spoke again.

"I said you alone, little lady?"

Her response came without fully thinking it through. "Leave me alone."

"Oh, she looks lonely," one of the others said. His voice dripped with menace.

She came back to herself with a jarring suddenness brought about by a sense of imminent fear. The four men were spread out in a semicircle as they approached her, with a clear eye to keeping her from leaving. They all had an unwelcome smirks on their faces.

"Piss off," she hissed.

"Oh, don't be that way," one of them said, grinning even bigger to show off rotted teeth. The appearance of the whole group spoke about their favorite diversion. Skinny as rails, lots of tattoos, missing teeth. *Meth, what a drug.* Before she could fully grasp the danger of her present situation, one reached down and grabbed her by the arm and, with surprising strength, yanked her to her feet.

She only knew she wanted to get out of his grasp, memories of the camp in Columbus and surprise at being manhandled in the current day and age combined, and she reacted instantly with a knee to the balls. Only, he must have been used to this reaction, because he turned his hips as fast as she attacked.

"Oh, ho!" He laughed and pushed her.

She thought she was about to crash to the ground, but another of the rednecks caught her, this time from behind, and by both arms. She tried to stomp down on his instep, and missed again. In the back of her mind she realized they were well-practiced abusers, and she was in real trouble.

"She's a little spitfire," one of them said.

"Leave me alone!" she cried and tried to kick the one in front of her. He knocked her leg out of the way in contempt.

"What's in the bag?" one of them demanded, out of her view.

"Leave my stuff alone!"

"Probably makeup and shit."

Fear of being abused was magnified a hundred-fold as she heard the pack being unzipped. Out of the corner of her eye she saw all her possessions dumped onto the sidewalk, and her insulin kit rolled away, standing out because it was in a floral pattern, a legacy of before.

"Bet that's her makeup!" one hooted.

"No, it's my—" She never finished explaining that it was her insulin before a boot heel stomped down on the kit with a *crunch!* She went limp in shock, and they let her fall to the concrete.

"Guess she really likes her CoverGirl!" one said, and they all laughed.

"Why don't you assholes leave the lady alone?"

She was only dimly aware of the new arrival. *I'm dead*, she thought over and over again as she crawled to the crushed bag and opened it.

Both bottles of insulin were broken, as she'd known they would be. She briefly entertained somehow straining or squeezing the fabric for enough to fill a syringe, only to find all the syringes damaged beyond use as well. The only thing which survived were the test strips. All they'd be good for now was telling her how close she was to dying.

Someone yelled. There was the sound of metal on metal, then a loud *thud!* Another person yelled, or yelped in pain, and then someone tripped over her and crashed to the ground. She turned her head to see one of the rednecks lying half over her, both hands holding his throat as gouts of bright red blood gushed between his desperately grabbing fingers. She screamed and tried to crawl away, only then looking around to try and understand what was happening.

In addition to the man who'd fallen over her, another was staggering around screaming, holding his right arm just below the elbow, where it ended. The other two were trying to bracket a newcomer from two sides at once, one with a machete, and the other held a wooden baseball bat that had a dozen big nails driven through it. The newcomer had a no-shit *sword* dripping in blood.

The swordsman was maybe 30 and whipcord lean. Where the meth-head rednecks were pale and gaunt, he was lean, with skin that looked like leather—a man who spent a great amount of time outdoors. A backpack was on the ground twenty feet away, an empty sheath strapped to the side. He held the sword, a good three feet of steel sharpened on both sides, the way a lumberjack held an ax. It was an extension of his arm.

"Not as easy as the movies, is it?" he asked the man with the machete, gesturing with the sword at the armless man.

Jeannie glanced down and saw the rest of the arm lying nearby, still grasping a long butcher knife. She should have been scared, but she was more amazed than anything. *Who just carries a sword around, for crying out loud?*

"Fuck you!" the machete wielder screamed. He kept switching the machete from one hand to the other, then trying to grasp it with both hands, as if trying to decide how to hold it. The other one was now behind the swordsman. Jeannie's eyes went wide, and she looked from the man to the swordsman.

He caught her eye, gave the barest of head twitches behind him, and winked at her. Fucking *winked* at her.

A part of Jeannie's being purred.

She was roughly to the side of the drama, giving her a perfect view of the final moments. At least a dozen people were running from the Rite Aid parking lot. Many also had baseball bats, crowbars, and one guy had a two-by-four. Others stayed by their merchandise or bicycles.

The eyes of the two men bracketing the swordsman met. For the barest of moments, Jeannie thought they'd do the smart thing and run. They had no chance, none. This swordsman clearly knew what he was doing and, for whatever reason, had no problem employing his skills to deadly effect.

Then she knew they wouldn't leave it. Maybe they were the local tough boys and had never lost a fight. The ground rules had changed, and they hadn't fully come to grips with it. The machete wielder nodded to his partner, who screamed and rushed in, swinging the spiked bat like the swordsman's head was a fastball.

It was all over in a blur of violence. The swordsman took a half step sideways and crouched, spinning and swinging as he moved. The bat wielding man's eyes went wide as the blade swished past his exposed abdomen. The machete wielder had also stepped in, but too far. The baseball bat caught him in the temple. The man let go of his bat as he stumbled, but the bat stayed attached to his friend's head; one of the spikes had gone through both eyes and poked out the other side, transfixing his head. He fell face-first to the ground, and the machete flew, bouncing off the pavement, drawing sparks as it cartwheeled.

The swordsman finished his pivot, coming all the way around with the blade back up, pointed at the two men, hands held low. He hadn't made so much as a grunt. He continued to watch the last man stumble a couple steps, then turn to look at him, same confused look on his face.

"I told you it wasn't like the movies."

The man took his hands away from his middle, dripping with dark red blood. At the same time slippery ropes of white intestines tumbled from a gaping wound. He fell to his knees, screaming and trying to gather up the organs. The swordsman lowered the weapon and turned to Jeannie. "Are you okay?"

"Yeah," she whispered, shaking her head. Then she repeated it louder. "Yeah, I'm fine for now. Why did you do that?"

"Huh?" He looked confused and she pointed to the man still trying to recover his guts. "Them?" She nodded. "They started it."

A woman and her young son who'd come running from somewhere at the sounds of a fight drew up short. The boy gawked, and the mother became noisily sick onto the street.

"Over me," she complained. "I'm not worth four lives."

He looked at her and she realized his eyes were a striking shade of blue. "They decided their lives were more valuable than mine. They were wrong."

"Put the weapon down!"

He turned and looked at the man yelling, a police officer leveling a shotgun at him. The swordsman laughed. "Are you kidding me?"

"Don't make me shoot you!" the country cop yelled, and the safety clicked off.

"You haven't talked to many travelers, have you? Your gun went the same way as the cars, power, and everything else over a week ago."

The cop didn't seem to even try to understand, just continued to point the gun at the swordsman's head. "I said put it down!"

The swordsman glanced at the men he'd fought. The first, with his throat cut, was still, his eyes staring up at the March sky. The second one was on his knees, his severed arm squeezed by his left hand, not entirely stopping the flow of his life's blood. He made a mewling sound every few seconds. The third was quite dead, a nail through his face, while the last had collapsed in his own intestines. She didn't know if he was alive or dead, and wasn't sure if she cared.

"You really ought to reconsider this—" the swordsman started to say, and took a step toward the cop.

"Don't fucking move!" the cop screamed. Several people in the crowd that had now gathered took steps back. One of them spoke.

"Bill, that gun don't work no more."

"Shut up, Ted," the cop snapped. "This guy just killed three people!"

"That guy with his throat dun cut tried to hit the guy with the sword!" a teenaged girl yelled.

"All of you stay out of this!" the cop screamed. "I'll arrest all of you!"

The swordsman sighed and shook his head. "This isn't a world for police anymore," he said and suddenly lurched toward the cop.

*Click!* The cop pulled the trigger. Naturally, nothing happened. He racked the slide and stroked the trigger again with identical results. This time when he worked the slide, he expertly caught the ejected shell; clearly he was an accomplished marksman. The indent in the primer was clearly visible to Jeannie.

"Beginning to understand?" the swordsman asked.

The cop cursed, dropping the gun to the sidewalk with a clatter, and drew his pistol. *Click*. Same results. "This is impossible," he said.

"Y'all mean like that?" someone yelled, and pointed to all the nearby cars, forever silent now. "Or this?" For emphasis, the man brought out a smartphone, now just a piece of plastic and metal. Jeannie would have thought it was strange that he still carried it, but she'd had a glucose meter in her backpack until a week ago, when she'd finally realized it was silly to keep carrying it. After more than a month, it was clear; the lights were never coming back on again.

There was a dawning realization on the police officer's face. "I didn't believe it was real," he said. He made a reach for the baton on his belt, and the swordsman took a step toward him, raising the blade slightly.

"That would *not* be a good move. Go home, or back to your station, and think about it. Maybe talk with your other cop buddies about setting up a town defense. Not everyone with a weapon like this would have stopped with these scumbags."

"I'm the only one," the cop said. "Everyone else left after a week. The guns still worked!"

"Stopped about ten days ago," the man with the cellphone said. "Didn't hurt like the first time."

Jeannie cringed slightly, like most people when they remembered the searing pain in their bodies when the power went off. She'd thought it was like having their world burned from their beings. Everything except very simple technology stopped working. Cellphones and powerplants were gone. Old fashioned incandescent flashlights and simple chemical batteries worked. A Tesla electric car or a new SUV stopped. An old 1950s Jeep ran just fine.

The swordsman retrieved his pack, oblivious to the carnage covering the street, and pulled out a paper towel to clean his blade. *It's all so mechanical*, Jeannie thought. He removed the sheath from his pack and hooked it to his belt via a clip that was already there. Then he turned to walk away.

"What about them?" the cop demanded. His face was a study in confusion.

"Leave them, bury them, I don't care." The one with the missing arm was wandering away down a side road, forgotten by everyone. His severed limb remained in the road.

The locals were pointing, talking, and yelling. Many seemed to want the confused cop to do something. Arrest the swordsman, or go get the sheriff, whom the cop had already said was gone. Jeannie watched the developing mayhem. None of them seemed to even notice her sitting on the street next to the dead man whose throat had been cut. The swordsman was almost out of sight. She made a snap decision.

She crammed her gear back into her backpack and zipped it closed, then on impulse, she scooped up the machete from where it had landed and ran after the swordsman. Nobody moved to stop her or question her actions.

\* \* \*

A couple blocks south of downtown, she thought she'd lost him. The swordsman walked with massive strides, far longer than hers, and he seemed tireless. Jeannie stopped at an intersection, one way heading into the hills east of Mannington, the right toward the downtown area again, and south out of town. A large brick building was to her right, many of the windows broken out, and effects strewn across the street. She thought it might have once been a thrift store. Not seeing him, she turned the other way just as a voice came out of the ruins. "Why are you following me?"

She spun around, the machete clattering out of her hand. She nervously bent and picked it back up.

"If you're thinking of using that," he said, a wry smile on his face as he nodded at the machete, "you should consider what happened to the last guy."

"Oh!" she said, looking down at the blade. "No...I just..." She shrugged, confused.

"So, if you don't want to stab me, why are you following me?"

"I hoped you could help me."

"I thought I just did."

"I didn't ask for you to cut those guys up."

"And I said I didn't do it because you asked for help, I did it because they started some shit they couldn't finish. We've been over this. Regardless, why are you asking me now?"

She felt her cheeks getting hot. Part of the truth was, she'd never seen a guy be so much of...well, *a guy!* She was deeply embarrassed to admit it had been exciting, up until the guy's guts fell out, anyway. "Because those guys broke my last insulin."

His hard features slowly lost their edge and he sighed. "I can't help you."

"Why not?"

"Because you're dead already; you just don't know it."

She felt her anger growing, which unfortunately led to tears. The swordsman scowled. "I'm not asking for much."

"Just for me to go back there, where they're probably making me out to be a one man plague on their peaceful little community, and break into the pharmacy to get you what you want. If you didn't notice, there's some organization in Mannington, and it isn't the legitimate government. There were a dozen gnarly-looking dudes checking out my incident. Likely they didn't get involved because it didn't matter to them one way or another. Shit, they probably figured the four assholes I killed would have been a problem down the road, who knows."

He stepped out of the broken doorway of the thrift store and past her. "I feel for your situation, I do, but there's nothing I can do to help you. Good luck." He walked briskly away.

"Fuck you!" she screamed after him. The swordsman waved over his head, turning up into the hills a block down the road and out of sight.

She stood there for a long time, machete stupidly hanging in her hand, staring after the man. She almost turned around and returned to the scene of the fight. Almost, until she looked back in that direction and saw the crowd had grown to 50 or more. She hadn't done anything wrong, but she also didn't want to explain that to them. Instead, she followed the swordsman again.

* * *

The night was colder than the previous night, likely because she'd climbed at least a thousand feet into the hills, following the swordsman. He hadn't tried to lose her, which was good, because her decade-old woodcraft experience wouldn't have let her track a bleeding rabbit. Instead, he almost seemed to pause in places to allow her to follow. She took it as approval and continued behind him.

Eventually he made camp on a driveway next to a burned-out house. The house had once been huge, but was now collapsed in upon itself. The stench of burning wood and plastic still hung over the area, suggesting it might have burned after everything had changed. She hung her new hammock between two trees 50 or so yards from the home's clearing. Close enough to just see his campfire, but far enough away to not be a constant reminder of her presence.

Even in her sleeping bag, the hammock was colder than she expected. She pulled the new poncho over the top as well, and while it helped, it quickly gathered dew. Besides being cold and damp, she was miserably hungry. A few crickets sang, but mercifully no mosquitoes made their presence known.

She was shivering in the dark, trying to sleep and forget about how hungry she was, when the swordsman walked over to her. He stopped a few feet away and stared. "Don't take a hint, do you?"

"Why do you care where I decide to die?" she snapped.

"Hmm," he grunted and put a metallic pan on the ground a few feet away. "I thought you might be hungry."

"I don't want anything from you," she said. The smell of food reached her nostrils, and she inhaled deeply, saliva filling her mouth.

"Suit yourself," he said, and returned to his camp. She craned her neck over the side of the hammock. The pan was still there. She extracted herself from the hammock and went to the pot. It was hot and smelled wonderful. Looked like mostly meat, with some vegetables like mushrooms and carrots. No potatoes or pasta. Not at all what she was expecting. She tasted it with the wooden spoon he'd left and sighed as the warm food made its way down. The seasoning was perfect.

"Squirrel," he said from near his fire. "Shot with a slingshot just before I came into town."

She wandered closer. "Tastes great." She took another bite. "Thank you." He grunted and nodded. The fire felt wonderful, and she found herself close enough to see his bright blue eyes again. "I'm Jeannie."

"Tanner," he said and nodded to one of two fallen logs next to the fire.

She sat gratefully and devoured the stew. "How'd you know what was the lowest risk to a diabetic?"

He reached into his leather jacket and withdrew a small case. Leaning past the fire, he sat it next to her on the log. Jeannie chased the last bit of broth with her spoon, then set the pan down by the fire to examine the case. Inside were a half dozen syringes, an electronic glucose meter, test strips, and a vial of insulin. She looked up in surprise. "Yours?"

"My sister's," he said. "We were in Wheeling, looking into a college for her freshman year, when it happened. Sixty miles wasn't all that far in a car, but it's a long damned way with a type 2 diabetic with bad feet. So we stayed there until that gang took over."

"I heard about it coming south; they're still there."

He grunted. "I figured. We left last week to come here, back home." He looked at the burned house. "Insulin ran out three days ago. It was cold that night, and she'd been cutting back for some time to stretch it. Somewhere along the line, I think her last vial froze? I don't know, but she wasn't doing well. I thought we could make it here in time. That's when *he* showed up."

"Who?"

"Said his name was Chirich. Strange enough to find a white coyote, and even stranger when they can speak."

Jeannie sat up straighter, remembering the white dog. Was it a coyote, then? That explained why it's face had looked strange. "It spoke?"

"Clearly, and with a slight British accent."

She gave a little laugh, and for the first time, she saw Tanner smile. "I'd seen some other things around Wheeling, so a talking coyote wasn't a stretch. But when the sun went down, Chirich *glowed*, too. He said he wanted to help us, if we helped him first."

"How could he talk at all?"

Tanner took a deep breath and sighed. "I don't know if I can believe anything he said, but this is what he explained. He said our world had collided with his world, and we can go back and forth at certain points. He called those 'stepping stones.' The one he came from wasn't far away, but some people were there, holding his family captive. If I helped him, he'd get me some insulin for Alice, my sister."

Jeannie didn't know what to think. *Worlds colliding? Glowing coyotes who could speak?* It all sounded like bullshit to her. "What happened to our technology?"

"Chirich said magic cancels out science; it won't work while our worlds are in contact. The collision of our worlds was what caused the pain. I wanted to know why guns stopped working later, but he didn't know."

"What'd you do?"

"I followed him. I didn't have much choice. I'd found a wheelbarrow and was using it to move Alice. She was in pretty bad shape. It took almost an entire day to get to where Chirich took us. Sure enough, there was this old mansion on a hill, and a half dozen guys inside. They looked like bikers. Whatever, the place clearly wasn't theirs.

"I let Chirich explain the layout, left him to watch Alice, and went in around midnight."

"What happened?" she asked. The warmth of the fire felt good, and the cool glass of the insulin vial in her breast pocket almost seemed to glow with promise. Another few days of life.

"I got within view, but something felt wrong. These guys were all gone. I went inside, and they'd left only a few minutes before I got there. I ran back as fast as I could, but I was too late. They'd circled around to my camp, found Alice." His face clouded over. "They'd all taken their turns with her by the time I got back."

"What did you do?" she asked, breathless.

He looked up at her, the firelight catching his eyes. The expression on his angular features was predatory. "I killed them all. Every last one of them." He was quiet for a minute. In the silence he added a log to the fire. "I didn't find Chirich, but I knew what happened. He led me there on purpose. There *were* no other glowing coyotes, and never had been. But maybe my killing all those bastards wasn't in his plan, so he took off.

"Alice died in the night. There was nothing I could do. After I buried her, I picked up Chirich's trail, and I've been tracking him ever since. I don't know why he came here, to our town. Haven't figured it out yet." He gestured at the detached garage. The door was open, a truck inside. A Humvee, it looked like. Pretty unusual for West Virginia country. "The insulin I gave you was in the truck in an insulated container. I don't think it ever froze."

Jeannie held it up to the firelight. It looked pure. The frozen bottles she'd found a week ago were all milky in color. "I'm sorry," she said. "About your sister."

"Who knows how many millions are dead?" he said with the same detachment he'd used when speaking of the men he'd killed in town. Around them, the woods were full of night sounds, crickets, the hoot of a distant owl.

She looked up at the burned home. "Anyone else in the house?"

"Just Alice and I. Our parents passed five years ago in a car crash, and I finished raising her myself. I don't know why the house burned. Maybe lightning? Without power, nobody came from town to put it out. Probably a lot of burned houses around here."

He moved to get more comfortable on the stump, and his sword's hilt glinted in the firelight. His eyes followed hers. "Oh, this?" He smirked a little. "Group called ARMA, Association of Renaissance Martial Arts. Kinda like the SCA, but crazier. Caught the bug as a kid before joining the Marines. I guess it became an obsession, but ultimately a damned useful one. I didn't even have a blade when we went to Wheeling, just my Glock." He snorted. "Found this in, of all places, a damned pawn shop in Moundsville." He took a drink from a canteen. "Since it's show and tell, your turn."

The night was split by a howl from the woods. Tanner was on his feet in a flash, the sword somehow in his hand. "Son of a bitch is right here," he said.

Jeannie spun around and saw a glimmer of light disappearing into the woods. Before she could say a thing, Tanner was up and sprinting after the apparition. She watched as he was swallowed up by the night and stared after him for long minutes before she became painfully aware that she was alone and unarmed. Her pack and gear were back by the hammock.

Quickly, before her nerve failed her, she got up and moved back to her camp. She left the hammock, just slung her pack and ran back to the driveway. The pack wasn't heavy without the sleeping bag. She'd strapped the machete to the side of the pack with one of the little bungie cords she carried with her. That was how Tanner had been carrying his sword when they'd first met.

She'd just dropped her pack next to his when the light caught her eye. A glowing, canine-like face was watching her from the garage.

"Oh, shit," she said, fumbling at the pack to get her machete.

"Don't be afraid," the creature spoke. Tanner had been right, the voice held a strange, British-sounding accent. "Is he gone?"

"H-he ran after you," she stammered. The blade came free, and she pointed it at him like a gun. "Don't come any closer, Chirich."

"He told you my name," it said, and came out of the garage completely.

It glowed like the full moon, bright enough to read by, yet it didn't seem to affect her night vision at all. The glow was ethereal and had a sort of texture to it, like she could run her eyes over the creature and *feel* the differences in the light. *Weird,* she thought.

"I said stay back!"

"What did he tell you about me? That I tricked him?"

"You led him into a trap, and people killed his sister."

"No, that's not what happened. We offered to help him, me and my mate. His sister was dying. When I took him to a place to find medicine, he ambushed us and killed my mate, for fun I imagine. He likes to kill."

Jeannie lowered the blade a little. Chirich was right about that last part. Tanner had clearly enjoyed killing the four men in town.

Chirich watched her carefully with glowing eyes, moving a little closer. "The food smells good."

She took a little of the meat on a stick near the fire and tossed it to Chirich, who caught it easily and gulped it down.

"Why are you following Tanner?"

"I'm not, he's following me." It looked around. "Do you think this is *his* place? What other lies has he been telling you?"

Suddenly everything Tanner had said came into stark relief, and its improbability as well. He'd just happened to have a sister who was diabetic, like Jeannie. He'd said he'd been tracking Chirich, but why would the creature come to his house if it was trying to get away from him? Tanner had said the only reason he'd killed those men was because they'd attacked him, not because of what they were doing to her.

The sound of brush cracking behind her indicated Tanner was coming back. She turned to face the woods.

"He's coming to kill me," Chirich said, coming completely out of the garage and looking around desperately.

She decided. "Come over here," she said to Chirich. The glowing creature leaped over to stand behind her. Tanner cleared the woods and stopped when he saw her standing, machete in hand.

"What's going on?" he asked, then his eyes dropped and he saw Chirich. He raised the sword and stepped toward her. "Move so I can kill it."

"No!" she said and raised the machete, doing her best to imitate the way he held his sword.

He stopped where he was, cocking his head.

"Think about this, Jeannie. He's tricking you the same way he tricked me."

She looked down behind her at Chirich, who looked back at her. At least, she thought he was looking at her. His eyes were tiny stars in the darkness. He suddenly walked around her to stand in front, facing Tanner. The woods grew silent, like a light switch had been flipped.

"He's using magic," Tanner said, his voice even.

"Magic? What?"

"I didn't say anything because I guessed you wouldn't believe me."

"You're right, I wouldn't."

"Jeannie," he said, pointing at Chirich. "*That* is a glowing coyote from another universe. All technology stopped working. Guns stopped working. Is it really a stretch it can do magic?"

Her eyes were drawn to the ground. A glowing pattern had begun to appear, surrounding her and Chirich. "What are you doing?"

"Trying to protect us from him."

"Why didn't you use it when he killed your family?"

"I didn't have time," Chirich replied. The pattern was more visible now, a circle with strange symbols along the inside edge. The symbols made her squint, a dull headache forming behind her eyes. Doubt was creeping back in.

"I-I don't know," she said, the machete slowly lowering. Her gaze fell back on Chirich who was still apparently staring at Tanner. He didn't seem *afraid*, so much as mad. Then she remembered what had made Tanner leave in the first place. "How did you make that light out in the woods?"

"It was a simple charm," Chirich explained. "Part of the power that makes me glow. I can teach you a lot about the new rules of your world, because they're like my old world. If you help me, I'll teach you! Believe in me." Was his glow fading slightly as her questioning grew?

"I believe you'll make the right decision," Tanner said, sliding his sword into its sheath and putting his hands in his pockets. From inside, he drew out a set of car keys. From the glow of Chirich, she could see the metallic logo on the chain, the symbol of a Humvee. Chirich laughed, and Jeannie swung.

The machete caught Chirich on the side of his neck. An explosion of light and sparks flew from the impact. Chirich screamed, a piercing sound she felt in her very soul. The pattern disappeared, and the creature fell sideways, rolling away. Behind, he left a splash of slightly glowing liquid, nothing like any blood she'd ever seen before. An electric shock ran up her hand from the machete, which she dropped in alarm.

Chirich came up on its feet, but its outline was now a blur, and the spraying blood was almost iridescent. It spun to face her, no longer a beautiful, glowing coyote, but a hideous maw spread wide, full of snapping teeth and tentacles reaching for her. She screamed, and something hit the creature, followed by a *Whack!* sound. It staggered and turned its head to the left. *Whack!* Another projectile hit it, and she saw that Tanner had a slingshot and was reloading. It stepped toward Tanner.

Jeannie scooped up the machete with her left hand and swung it as hard as she could. It went *Chunk!* as the blade nearly severed the head. There was no electric shock this time, and the...*thing* fell unmoving to the ground with the blade stuck in its neck.

She released the weapon and backed up, gasping, her vision narrowed to a point. Tanner strode over, his sword out now, and jabbed the blade into the creature's side. It didn't respond.

"Is it dead?" she asked.

Tanner walked around it, examining the body, the ground, and kneeling over a puddle of glowing 'blood.' "Was it ever alive?" he asked in reply.

"It was from another world, wasn't it?"

"I'd heard stories in the places I passed," he said, finishing his circuit. "Things that look like animals, but they glow, or walk through walls, or float like ghosts. I didn't know what to think until this bastard came along." He used his sword point to move the head so he could see the tentacle-covered mouth better. He put the sword aside and pulled out another knife, this one around a half foot long. The glow was fading as he plunged the blade into the creature's chest.

Jeannie was about to ask what he was doing, only something...some feeling...told her this was right. "Yes," she whispered.

"You feel it, too?" he said as he sawed into the central body cavity. She only nodded, not even thinking that he couldn't see her because he was fixated on his grim task. "I can't stop myself," he said, or rather growled.

"No, don't stop," she said and went to her knees to help. In a moment the body was cut from below the head to where the rear legs were attached, legs Jeannie realized had more joints than they had a right to have, and long, almost spider-like digits. She helped him pull open the body to reveal its insides.

Its insides looked like nothing she'd recognize. It looked more like a network of fibrous tissue supporting a single organ, which pulsed and glowed like the moon off a lake. Chirich's exterior glow was almost gone, but this still shone as brightly as he ever had.

"Take it," she whispered.

Tanner used the knife to deftly sever the connecting, weblike structures. As he cut the last, the remaining glow in the body instantly went out, like a light switch being flicked. Only the organ still pulsed and glowed. Even the blood was now faded.

Before a thought could form in her head, Tanner leaned over and *bit* the organ, grunting and tearing out a bite. She shook in an atavistic shock/joy at the act. "Is it good?" she asked, unsure where the words came from.

"Oh, yes," he said around a mouthful of flesh. He glanced up at her, his eyes shining preternaturally in the light of the carnal feast. Without being asked, he held up the dripping feast for her. "Eat," he said, and she did.

* * *

Jeannie awoke with the sun on her face, blinking against its brightness. She sat up, realizing she'd slept on the ground, without even a blanket. Yet she didn't feel cold, or uncomfortable.

"I tried to cover you up, but you wouldn't let me." Tanner was sitting a few feet away, stoking the fire of the night before, wrapped in a sleeping bag.

She looked down at herself and gasped to realize she was naked. "Oh!" she exclaimed, and looked up at him.

He held up his hands. "Nothing happened, you just...stripped after we ate."

She swallowed at the memory of devouring the otherworldly flesh. Instead of a feeling of disgust, she felt something akin to remembering a night of delightful sex, though those memories were years old. Examining her surroundings, she found her clothes and began dressing. Tanner had busied himself with the fire, obviously avoiding watching her. The clothes felt uncomfortable, except the leather belt, which felt like the finest silk. *What the heck?*

She moved over and helped him restart the fire. There was no sign of Chirich's body. "Did you dispose of...it?"

"No," he said. "I fell asleep, just like you, and when I woke up, it was gone." He gestured around at the driveway. "Not even a drop of blood."

"What the fuck happened?" she asked. "Did any of it really happen?"

"Something happened," he said.

"How do you know? There's no proof."

He glanced around and selected the thickest stick in reach. It was at least four inches across. He flexed his hands and snapped it like a pencil. It parted with the sound like a gunshot, proof it wasn't just rotted. "I'm in pretty good shape," he said. "Not that damned good."

Curious, she picked up a branch herself. She grunted and tried to break it, without luck. She was a little disappointed. "Was it the thing we ate that affected you?"

"Has to be," he said. He looked at her with a wry grin.

"What are you looking at?"

"You haven't really looked at your skin, have you?"

She held out her hand and stared at it. "Looks like skin."

"Put your hand on the ground."

She did, and her skin began to turn the same color as the concrete. "Holy crap!" she said and pulled it away. Immediately it returned to flesh colored.

"When you were lying there naked, you were almost invisible. You only started changing back when you woke up."

She tried the experiment several more times, with the same results.

"What are you grinning at, anyway? I'd rather be strong than some chameleon."

"You're pretty cute," he said.

She felt her cheeks getting hot and looked away from him. "Now what?" she asked, changing the subject. "You've gotten your revenge."

"Hmm," he grunted as the fire began to finally catch. "I don't know," he said. "Least I can do is help you find some more insulin. But not here—best we don't go back to town."

"Okay," she said. "I'll accept your help." She pulled her pack over and pulled out a package of the freeze dried macaroni in meat sauce, offering it to him. "Hungry?"

"Yeah," he said, getting a pot out of his pack.

She went into the woods and returned a few minutes later with an armload of various plants and mushrooms, all she somehow *knew* were edible. She'd unconsciously been munching as she foraged, her natural fear of eating plants she didn't know by name quashed by a 'knowing' inside her.

As she gave them to Tanner to add to the pot, a bird flew out of the woods and landed on her shoulder. She jumped slightly, but the animal wasn't frightened.

"Nice trick," he said.

She offered it a berry, which it took and flew away. "I guess we both have a lot to learn." He nodded as he cooked.

It was three days later when they abandoned the search for insulin. She'd used the last of the test strips. No matter what she ate, the color never wavered at all from a perfect blood sugar level. They traveled south, curious what they'd find, and what other gifts they now had in this new world.

\* \* \* \* \*

## Mark Wandrey Biography

International bestselling author of military sci-fi, space opera, and zombie apocalypse, Mark Wandrey is also the only 4 time Dragon-Con Dragon Award finalist! Military Sci-fi has always been his favorite genre, however he's recently began diverging into urban fantasy with his upcoming Traveling Gods series, a dark take on the genre. Living the full time RV lifestyle as a modern day nomad, Mark Wandrey has been writing science fiction since he was in grade school. He launched his professional career in 2004 with the release of *Earth Song - Overture*. Now, 15 years later, he has more than 25 books out, including many bestsellers, and dozens of short stories.

\* \* \* \* \*

# Through a Spyglass Darkly
## by G. Scott Huggins

Jehanne knew she was near the king when she heard the army crumbling about him.

"...should have your spurs for this, Durayne. We're in the middle of planning a battle, and you thought it was fitting to interrupt us for some addled nun's mumblings?" said a man's voice.

"Isn't it, general?" grunted another man. "Prayer could hardly make our disposition *worse* than it is now. Don't be too hard on the man."

"If our positioning is inadequate, marquis," said the general, "you haven't improved it, nor marched near the field of battle, though we outnumber the Usurper five to one!"

"I'll give battle when there's battle to be given," answered the marquis. "But I'm not volunteering my men as statuary. No need to give the Usurper and Nygurd even *better* odds."

"Courtesy, my lords," said a third man's voice. "Holy words would be better than fighting words. Show her in."

At these words, the page guiding Jehanne stepped forward too quickly. The woman deliberately stumbled, catching herself with her long staff. He muttered an apology and slowed, giving her the time to see what she could through her thick veil.

"The holy sister Lenore, my lords. Sire."

The tremble in the page's voice as he announced her alias was matched by the nervous jump in the muscles of his elbow that she held in a firm grip.

"Ye gods," muttered the thin blur that was General Desrai, folding his arms. "Are the holy sisters covering their faces entire, now?"

"For most of them, that's doing men a favor," said Marquis Dubech, his thick form shaking its head.

"Courtesy, my lords," King Michael repeated. He raised his voice and a blurred hand in welcome. "Holy Sister, Captain Durayne tells us he believes you might give us a blessing to help defend our kingdom."

"I can give you no blessing, Sire," she said huskily. "The Marquis of Nygurd and Prince Ecferth the Usurper march ever southward behind their totem, which turns men to stone if they dare to glance upon it."

"You bring intelligence, then, of Ecferth's army?" said Dubech. She could hear the hope in his voice. The clergy favored King Michael and helped where they could.

"What good is intelligence going to do us?" Desrai said with a snort.

"It's always preferable to stupidity, General," she croaked.

"Indeed? Every day the Usurper advances another fifteen miles, and we retreat fifteen. We can't even scout his rabble's progress without leaving behind a half-dozen new statues. How would a blind old woman get such intelligence?" He hesitated. "Blind?" he asked. "But then, what could you know?"

"Far from blind, General, although that would, of course, allow you to approach the Usurper's army. But before I speak further, good page, could you verify to the assembled nobles that my veil is firmly fastened down and not easily lifted?"

"Yes, sister," he said, giving a gentle tug at the woven cords that kept the dark sackcloth from flapping upward. "It is tied fast."

"And the knot is quite firm?"

"Quite firm, Sister."

"You need have no fear, Sister," said the King. "No man among us feels the need to impugn your vows of chastity in the slightest." The words were delivered courteously, but chuckles responded to it anyway.

"It's not my fear that I seek to allay," she said, straightening and stretching out her hands. Her staff clattered to the floor, and she threw back her cloak, revealing a lithe torso clad in leather armor and girt with a sword belt. "Please note that my hands are empty and unmoving," she said clearly.

"What is this?" asked Desrai, his hand moving to his sword. "Who are you?"

"I am Jehanne Dark."

The men in the room were very still.

"And do you have some proof of this..." Marquis Dubech's mouth worked as he searched for the right word. "...audacious claim?"

"You might consider that I walked right past any number of guards, in the company of Captain Durayne, without anyone penetrating my disguise as 'Sister Lenore,'" she said. "But I do have other proof. I just have to ask you not to shoot me while I provide it. And remember, my hood is secure." She concentrated.

And as slowly as she could contrive it, the heads of four of her vipers emerged from under the hood, tongues flickering languidly in their red-and-black heads.

It was difficult to tell which men gasped first and drew steel second, and which did the opposite. But all of them had backed up a step.

"Get out, Sire, and don't look! We'll cover your retreat!" shouted Desrai.

"I mean the king no harm!" cried Jehanne. "In fact," she said, "I have come to pledge fealty and offer my services to King Michael." Slowly, she sank onto her knees.

"Don't believe her, Sire! It's a trap!" snarled Desrai. "And arrest that traitor!" He pointed his sword at Durayne, who raised his hands in protest.

"Yes, by all means, waste your time arresting the poor man for being no wiser than the rest of you," Jehanne said.

"Sire, this diabolical monstrosity is the most infamous assassin on the continent! What answer do you make to that, villain?"

"Thank you?" Jehanne said.

"She cannot be trusted!" he cried.

"General, has it occurred to you that if I had wanted you killed, every man here would already be dead?"

Marquis Dubech gave a bitter laugh. "If Jehanne Dark wanted us all turned to stone, she's taken an awfully long walk when she could have just stayed home for the next week."

The king cleared his throat. "The marquis and the lady may have the right of it, Giles." He gently pushed down the general's sword and approached. "Then if you are not here to assassinate me, Jehanne Dark, why are you here, disguised as a holy sister of the Church?"

"Well, the disguise was so that I wouldn't be shot on sight by those who might be as skeptical of my intentions as General Desrai is," said Jehanne. "But the reason I'm here is that I want to deliver the Usurper to you as an ornament for your palace lawn."

"You know our situation, so you can't be coming to us for help," said Dubech. "If you could do that, why haven't you just done it?"

"I've learned after I've killed someone is a very poor time to negotiate the payment," Jehanne said.

"Ah, yes, of course," Desrai said with a sneer. "Assassins. Well, how much gold is your 'fealty' worth?"

"My price is not gold," said Jehanne.

"What then, half my kingdom?" asked King Michael. "I'm afraid hardly a third of it remains to me. What do you say to a sixth of the kingdom, Lady Dark?"

"I'll wait for half," said Jehanne. Slowly, she rose to her feet. "My price is that I wed King Michael after the Usurper is put down. He will make me his queen."

The silence in the room was absolute for the space of five seconds.

"*You* cannot be queen! You're a Medusa!" cried Desrai.

"Half-Medusa," said Jehanne.

"And you're a wanted criminal and murderess!"

"Well, the inclusion of a royal pardon was implied," she said.

"That's out of the question!" The general was practically frothing at the mouth.

"Shut up, Desrai," said the king. His voice was utterly flat.

"I think," he said, after a long silence, "that we shall have to at least consider this...proposal." He stepped forward. His features were still a dark blur, but she could tell he was staring at her. "It would be, I suppose, similar to any other marriage a king has to make. Motivated by political necessity."

"There are other ways, surely!" said a voice from the assembled nobles.

"Really, Aubron?" asked King Michael. "You think our neighbors are lining up to offer their daughters to a man in exchange for sending their armies to our aid to be turned into stone? *I* haven't received any of their ambassadors." He turned back to her. "But the Lady Jehanne and I will have to speak privately. And, ah...face-to-face."

Jehanne felt her own eyes pop.

"Sire, that would kill you," said Dubech.

"Oh, for God's sake!" snapped Michael. "Are we a royal court or a rebel camp? Do our provisions not extend to having mirrors? Then set some up so the lady and I can have a private conversation!" He turned back to Jehanne. "Assuming, of course, that the rumors we hear of your kind are true, and a man can approach you in that way?"

Jehanne nodded, momentarily flustered by the king's unexpected insight, then remembered that the gesture would be muffled. "That seems quite practical, Sire," she said as smoothly as she could manage.

"Sire, I must forbid it!" said Desrai. "There are any number of ways she could kill you when you are alone!"

The king sighed. "And the most obvious of those ways is for her to simply walk out of this camp, as we've discussed. But we shall take sensible precautions."

\* \* \*

It took the better part of an hour to set things up. Jehanne was escorted toward a black-curtained tent set up in the middle of the field by Captain Durayne and Marquis Dubech.

"This tent is surrounded by a hundred archers," the marquis said, the pleasant detachment of earlier gone from his voice. "If you come out before His Majesty, they will shoot, and I don't think you can look in all directions at once."

Durayne swept the curtain aside. After the bright daylight, the dim lanterns made all of them pause for a few moments until they could see again. The tent was split in two by thick draperies. They led her past a bench where two crossbowmen knelt, weapons pointed toward a stool, far enough apart that they each had a separate angle.

They sat her down on the stool, facing a wall covered by more curtains.

"If the king or I give the order," Durayne said from behind her, voice thick with anger, "they shoot. And that's assuming you can turn on me before I bring my sword down on your head." He drew it, the cold steel shining golden in the lamplight.

"I'm sorry about the need to deceive you, Captain," Jehanne said.

"Remove your hood before the king gives you permission," Durayne said, "and you die."

"Understood."

Jehanne heard muffled conversation to her right: King Michael entering the tent. Then he lifted his voice. "Raise the curtain."

Before her, the room brightened just a little.

"Lady," the king said, "let me see your face."

Carefully, slower than she needed to, Jehanne untied the knot that held her veil down. She lifted it and, looking down a short corridor of draperies, saw not the king, but her own face reflected at her. Her vertically-pupiled, red-orange eyes widened for a moment, then narrowed. Of course. They weren't going to risk reflecting death at the king just on her say-so. Not even if the king ordered it.

Behind her, Captain Durayne and the two crossbowmen, who remained men of living flesh, relaxed slightly from their flinch, then stared at her. The eight snakes that sprang from equidistant points around her hairline reared slowly, then settled back down to form a leathery, black-and-gold circlet, interrupted with unblinking eyes. Black patches ran down her neck and shoulders at intervals, standing out against her violet-white skin, which didn't flush, but only because Jehanne had learned to control her reflexes.

The king's voice spoke sharply. "Dubech? What's going on? Why am I seeing only drapes?"

"A little to your left, my lord," called Durayne, softly.

"Oh, of course. Sorry, Sire. Accidental misalignment," called Dubech, clearly apologetic.

"Of course it was," said King Michael, just as clearly not believing a word.

The mirror tilted left, and he snapped into clear view.

She had never seen him clearly, but Jehanne was forced to admit that the view could have been worse. The 23-year-old king was well-muscled and wore bright mail over leather, a thin gold diadem, and a thin, reddish-brown beard. He was openly staring at her.

"Well...not exactly what I expected," he muttered.

Jehanne controlled her blush again. It wasn't in her nature to get excited about looks she wouldn't see often. But what she saw hinted at a pleasant enough man to touch.

"Jehanne Dark. My father alternated between swearing that you were a myth and just swearing, especially when you managed to assassinate Sir Glamoreau of Ouestmarque. He was one of my father's best war captains."

"All I know is, he made enemies with quite a bit of money. How did he reconcile the statues if he believed I was a myth?"

"He thought you'd been invented by Church wizards as a way to cover up those among them who dabbled in forbidden magics." He sighed. "Somehow, I always thought it would be my father making my wedding arrangements, but if he were here to do it, I suppose we wouldn't be making them."

Probably not, Jehanne allowed. It was King Lawrence and Queen Judith's deaths of plague six months ago that had emboldened Ecferth the Usurper to claim that Michael's great-grandfather had been illegitimately born and seize the throne with the Marquis of Nygurd's help.

"He probably shouldn't have had Nygurd's son executed."

"Nygurd's son shouldn't have kidnapped his own liegewomen into slave-prostitution," said the king, glaring.

*What can I say to this?* Jehanne shrugged and nodded.

"Why do they call you Jehanne Dark?" the king asked. "I would have thought your gaze more potent in the light."

"Ark is a floating hamlet on a lake where my father held land near a mountain," said Jehanne. "That's all. Smaller than places like Esrai and Ubech, but there nonetheless."

The king chuckled. "Is that all?" He leaned forward. "Why do you want to help us? I've offered you no coin. Certainly you have no cause to love my line; my father would cheerfully have had you hanged."

"True," Jehanne said. "But it isn't just about helping you. Do you know why your men turn to stone as they approach Ecferth's host?"

The king's eyes sharpened. "Your name came up once or twice," he said. "Do you have a sister?"

"No," Jehanne said, watching her face harden. "I *had* a mother. They have her head. They carry it before them as they march."

"Ah," said King Michael, sitting back. "That does make sense. Now for the important question: why do you want to marry me, my lady?"

"Isn't being queen reason enough?"

"No," said the king. "If you were to turn the tide of this war for us, I could just as easily declare Nygurd attainted for treason and ennoble you in his place. You would be a duchess, and ruling queen in all but name of a duchy bigger than some kingdoms. And without marrying me."

"It never occurred to you that I might simply have fallen in love with my handsome young king?" Jehanne said, deliberately shading her voice with desire.

"No, it hasn't," King Michael said flatly. "For one thing, you're at least eight years older than I am, and we both know Desrai wasn't exaggerating your reputation. If you were that stupid or impulsive, you'd never have lasted a year in your line of work."

Jehanne blinked slowly. She hadn't expected that. Very well, if she hoped to make this work, she would have to trust him at some point. "Because I'm tired," she said. "Tired of being an assassin. Of being hunted. When you're sixteen and can literally kill with a glance, it sounds like a life of romance, daring, and power. The first year taught me it was a hard and dirty business like any other. I want rest.

I want a pardon. And I want..." She swallowed. "I will *need* protection. From my enemies. If I marry you, the kingdom protects me."

The king nodded. "I see." He rose and walked toward her. She could almost believe he was really there, though she heard his footsteps on the other side of their dividing curtain.

"How will we make it work?" he muttered, almost too soft to hear. "You are half-Medusa? Your father was human?"

She nodded. Of course she would have to bear his heirs. "We do get used to wearing veils," she said. "All the time, when necessary." Blood pounded in her ears. He was really considering it. She had hoped, but never really believed he would.

His face hardened. "If we do wed," he said, "you will turn over all the details of your contracts. Every one. And those who bought your services will face justice."

"No," she answered. "An assassin does not betray her clients."

"If you wed me, you are no longer an assassin," said the king. "You are reformed and penitent."

"If I do that, every assassin on the continent will come after me," Jehanne protested. "There will never be peace."

"I want no peace with assassins," King Michael said. "This is not a point to negotiate with me, Lady. You want the protection of the crown, and you will have it. That means you will trust in it. As surely as I must trust you never to look me in the face as long as you live."

Jehanne took a deep breath. "If I leave you now, your kingdom will crumble in a month."

"Better to see it crumble in that month," returned King Michael evenly, "than to watch it and our union crumble over a lifetime of compromise and half-measures. If we pledge ourselves to each other, let it be fully and without reservation, from the first."

Jehanne's lips parted and her hands tightened on her knees. She'd gambled on finding a weak man she might dominate. She'd more than half-expected to be killed. She had *not* expected to find a true king. She hadn't expected to find trust. She rose to her feet.

"Put down your weapons!" the king barked. The knight and soldiers froze behind her. "Now!"

Behind her, Jehanne heard the soft noise of points sheathing themselves in the grassy earth. Before her, the king extended his hand and stepped forward. She walked to meet him. At the draperies' edge, she saw her image join his in the mirror and placed her hand in his. The wondering, incredulous smiles on both their faces were astonishingly alike.

"Sir Durayne? Please hand my fiancée her veil."

\* \* \*

Outside the tent, King Michael called his council together, still hand-in-hand with Jehanne. "Gentlemen, I have agreed to the Lady Dark's proposal. After she breaks the power of the Usurper, and we disperse his army, I shall marry her and make her my queen."

There was no muttering at this, but there were some uncomfortable glances. Only General Desrai dared give voice to his feelings. "Sire, you cannot agree to this marriage!"

"Well, we're not going to have a kingdom left without it, and it is our kingdom, so we will take any chance we have left to preserve it."

"Your father would not have approved of this!" said Desrai. "What are you going to do? Wait like a princess for this adventurer to save you and carry you off in her arms?"

King Michael's face darkened, and he stepped forward. "Say that again, you old bastard, and you'll see whether my father raised a man. And you can go to your grave a regicide and a traitor *tonight*." The older man took a step back, staring at his king as though he'd never really seen him before.

Michael raised his voice. "Someday I will ask a daughter to strengthen this kingdom by welcoming a stranger to her bed." He looked around at his assembled nobles. "Should I do less to save it?" He looked at the veiled face of his bride. "At least if she has a mother like Lady Dark, I might not have to worry too much about her safety." He turned back to them. "My decision is made. Any man who doesn't like it had best hold his tongue or sneak away in the night." He turned to Jehanne. "When do you plan to leave?"

"Food and rest before I go would be welcome," she said. "I will leave before sunset."

"Is there anything we can provide you with to assist you, and do you wish an escort? My men will be delighted to see to your needs." *They'd better be,* did not need to be spoken.

"An escort would only make it easier for the Usurper to find me," Jehanne said. "But there is one more thing I will need, if you have it," Jehanne said. "I have one myself, but it is poor, and they're expensive. Do you have a spyglass?"

\* \* \*

Cloaked by the night, and more importantly, an actual cloak, Jehanne rode across the countryside for the Usurper's camp. Her mind was still reeling at how quickly King Michael had agreed to her bargain. She had expected—if she'd survived at all—to be tied up for days in negotiations.

She'd expected nothing short of revulsion to greet her, and there had been some of that, especially from the royal court.

But when he'd seen her in the mirror, the king—she'd better get used to calling him *Michael*, she supposed—certainly hadn't looked revolted. Not in the least. Her mother's words came back to her. *"Be very careful, Jehanne, of your heart. Even more careful than of your eyes. Your careless glance can kill others in an instant. Your careless heart can kill you over years."*

Jehanne had never fooled herself that her parents' marriage had been for love. They'd never fooled each other about it, either. Her mother had wanted a way to live within human society without being hunted down as a monster, and her father had wanted the freedom that comes to men who were feared. It was a kind of honesty, one Jehanne had been only too happy to run away from, and one she was now repeating. It had kept her mother alive, at least. She hadn't thought to find more than that. And had she?

She brought her mind back from its wandering. Thinking too much of the future while on a contract was a good way to end up dead.

Jehanne reined to a halt at the edge of the wood and assembled her things: shortbow, swords, provisions, and the all-important spyglass. It was time to let the horse go, though it was finer than any she'd ever owned. When it was well away, she removed the veil from her face.

The night was the most dangerous time for her, yet it was preferable to trying to approach the Usurper's camp in the day, when his own scouts and pickets would be out and might see her. Jehanne's usual trick to moving about in human society was to pretend to be a smelly, blind beggar like "Sister Lenore." No one wanted to see her *then*. But even beggars knew armies were maneuvering in south Ampyrica, and she would not be the first spy to attempt such a disguise. While she could kill any single man who inspected her, she couldn't be sure of facing only single men. Any who might get away would surely warn of her approach and cost her the surprise she would desperately need to kill the Usurper.

Night wouldn't save any man who saw her and met her eyes, but if her eyes weren't seen in the darkness, they couldn't kill. The wood she entered now could be even more dangerous. The shadows would block most of the moonlight, but Jehanne hadn't relied only on her gaze for her reputation as an assassin. The assassin who relied only on one skill died when it failed her. This was a lesson she didn't think the Usurper had learned, moving forward as he was under the invincible aura of her mother's head.

Slowly, imitating the natural sounds of the forest, she slipped between the trees.

Jehanne watched for sentries as she moved, but was unsurprised to find none. Was it possible they didn't realize the limitations of the power they'd harnessed?

The crescent moon was setting by the time she saw the orange glow ahead of her that gave her an answer. Reaching for her back, she donned her thinnest veil. This would offer no protection to anyone getting a good look at her face, but it would camouflage her pale skin from any sentries who happened to be looking her way.

The Usurper's camp was asleep for the night. Jehanne wondered if they even bothered to set sentries. They were probably there, looking carefully outward, but she doubted they needed to pay much attention, for set high on a crude wooden tower that reared at least

30 feet in the air, her mother's head stared down at her, framed by the light of a dozen torches.

Above the torch-bearing platform, mounted on a pole, her mother's head was fixed to a great, wooden shield bound with an iron rim. A corner of her mind wondered how many men were needed to lift it. Iron nails pierced the sides of her mother's throat and ears. A huge spike had been driven through her nose, and dozens of the snakes that crowned her had been fanned out and stapled above her head. The glazed orange eyes stared out, death to any human who would look upon them. Their lids had been cut off.

Jehanne had never thought her mother perfect, but she remembered those eyes looking down on her with love, and her lips pulled back from her teeth. They would pay. She would see them pay.

After savoring it for a long moment, Jehanne forced her rage downward. There would be no wage of any sort paid or collected tonight without work. She selected a tree and climbed as high as she could. Then, with her belt knife, she set quietly to work.

* * *

When the enemy extinguished their torches, Jehanne knew it was time to make her move.

From the blind she'd fashioned near the top of the tree—in truth, it was more a matter of cutting and binding some branches to make the most of the available leaf cover—Jehanne could see down into the camp, and was almost on a level with her mother's head. A figure made small by distance climbed underneath it, keeping its eyes fixed on the ground. Slowly, it extinguished each torch and rotated the shield on its pole so as to stay behind the deadly head. When it was finished, the head once again faced her. And why not? She'd approached from the south, the direction the camp would march in.

Now would come the difficult part. Carefully, she took King Michael's spyglass from its leather case. Once again, she breathed a sigh of appreciation. It was a masterwork of the glassmaker's art, with lenses pure as running water. The tube was of lacquered ebony, and both ends were adorned with worked gold filigree. That would be a problem. While this fine instrument was undoubtedly superior to her own short glass, the sun would sparkle off it. Jehanne carefully bent her archer's bracer around the far end of the glass and tied it in place with the thongs.

Then she lifted it and gazed through the eyepiece.

She first sighted on the hills beyond the camp. The images in the glass were clear and sharp as a crystal knife. Many people had wondered how Jehanne Dark had managed to petrify her victims without ever being seen or heard. A Medusa should have been easy to spot, if not easy to kill.

No one had ever realized that the invention of the spyglass and the beginning of Jehanne Dark's career had coincided. To be killed, her victims needed only to meet her gaze. And with her spyglass, her gaze was multiplied a hundredfold. How much did this magnificent device multiply it? Three-hundredfold? Five?

She would have to be careful. She couldn't afford to tip her hand by petrifying some random pikeman.

Lowering the scope, she watched the camp come to full life within its palisade walls. The cookpots belched steam as men gathered to break their fasts. Tents came down, and soldiers gathered in formations. By far the greater part of the men wore the blue-and-white tabards and light leathers of Duke Nygurd's conscripts, but there were harder men wearing plate and mail. Jehanne recognized the look of mercenaries. They were the ones on the wall, looking outward toward the horizon. Even more looked inward, watching the conscripts. It took her a moment to realize that none of the men were looking up. A smile touched her lips. Of course, her mother's head fixed above the camp served more than one purpose. While it meant that no army or scout of King Michael's could approach the camp, it also meant that any deserter had better make very sure he meant to leave and never come back. A moment of hesitation could turn him into a statue.

Feeling a little bolder, Jehanne lifted the scope to her eye again. There! A flash of shining metal. From the largest tent in the center of the camp, men in full plate stepped forth: Nygurd's knights and what vassals had joined in his rebellion, along with a smaller number of knights in the royal purple of Ampyrica's Royal Guard, which they wore to proclaim Ecferth the rightful king. And finally, the commanders. A huge man in battered but sturdy plate. That would be the mercenary commander. Then Duke Nygurd. And finally, Ecferth. Of course, none of them would look up, either. Jehanne reached in her pouch for the simple firework she kept there. It did nothing but make noise, but people instinctively looked toward a noise. That was usually enough.

Then it happened.

Duke Nygurd, having finished saying something to Ecferth, turned away and looked directly at her hiding place.

He got that look she'd come to recognize. The look on the face of every victim she'd petrified. A look of dawning horror and absolute powerlessness, begun in flesh and ending in stone.

Even from her distance, Jehanne heard the screams. Two of Ecferth's guard tackled him and hauled him bodily into the tent. The rest of the knights followed. Men were panicking, falling flat on their faces and covering their eyes. The mercenary commander was shielding his eyes and bellowing. Then he was looking at Nygurd's face.

She couldn't see the commander's face, of course, but it was clear he was thinking. Abruptly, he whirled and ran for the walls of the camp, where she couldn't see him. She could hear him yelling at his men, but of all the words, the only one she could hear was "archers."

For just a moment, Jehanne froze. If she stayed where she was…how good an idea could the mercenary commander have of her location when he dared not even look her way? But if she moved, anyone might see the motion in the trees and get a better shot. In fact, they might be looking through chinks in the palisade walls right now.

She raised the spyglass just as a ragged flight of maybe a dozen arrows arced over the wall. Jehanne swung herself behind her tree's trunk. The arrows turned toward her, falling. They were spread out, and far short of her position. Encouraged, she peered around the trunk and swept her gaze over the palisade.

Then two things happened at once.

With a roar, a large tent next to the one Ecferth had been rushed into burst open. Out of it burst a thing like a colossal statue of a man, carved out of a child's nightmares. It looked directly at her with clouded-beryl eyes and obsidian teeth. She stared at it, but it didn't turn to stone—it was more than half stone already. With a roar, it swung a great fist and smashed one of the tower's great support posts to splinters. Then it reached up and pulled down the rest of the swaying structure.

*A troll,* Jehanne thought. *They have a mountain troll.*

And the second flight of arrows arced over the wall. These were alight with flames.

Suddenly, leaving seemed like a much better decision. Clutching the spyglass, Jehanne started down the tree. Then she heard a roar. She looked up in time to see the troll pointing right at her. A third flight of arrows was in the air before she slid off the branch. She could smell smoke from below her. The rustle of arrows through the branches told her that the troll had markedly improved the shooting of her foes. A wicked buzz sounded from an arrow that stuck quivering in the branch she had just vacated. She clambered down two more branches. Three.

With an ugly *whizz,* an arrow buried itself in the trunk four inches from her nose. She looked up to see figures on the wall, shooting at her. They were daring to shoot *at* her! Professional pride rebelled and Jehanne raised the spyglass where she hung. She bracketed the bowman's face and saw it stiffen into stone just as he released the string. Leaning aside, she heard the arrow whizz by her ear, dropped a branch, and sighted on a second bowman. His arrow fell from stony fingers. She dropped two more branches and raised her glass to sight on a third figure, who was in the middle of throwing himself flat.

And a shaft of white-hot pain slammed through her left arm. Jehanne dropped the spyglass. It landed six feet down on a carpet of thick leaves, leaving Jehanne groaning and pinned to her tree. Smoke rose from the forest floor around her.

Fear washed around her, but it was a distant clamor. She looked at her arm. The arrow was a long one, and it had gone right through the skin on the inside of her upper arm, grazing the muscle. A detached part of her mind realized she'd been very lucky. If it weren't for the fact that she was pinned to the tree.

There was no time to think. With her right hand, she drew her long belt knife, and gritting her teeth against the pain, she sawed at the shaft. Arrows fell around her, none coming close. At least she'd convinced the survivors that she wasn't worth aiming at any more. After six or seven strokes, the arrow snapped. She fell to the forest floor and staggered to her knees. With a cry of pain, she slid the broken shaft of the arrow out of her arm and stumbled forward.

Just in time to see the troll smash through the palisade with an axe-blade the size of her head. Like a man stepping through reeds by a riverbank, he shouldered them aside, holding the axe in his right hand, and the shield bearing her mother's head in his left. He was marching right at her.

Jehanne stared. She was an assassin. She'd never fought in a battle. She'd won a couple of short, sharp fights with a target when everything had gone wrong, but she'd still had the advantage of surprise. Any time things had gone this wrong, she'd run away and tried again.

But Ecferth was still alive, and if she ran from this fight, she'd never have another chance. Her mother would remain unavenged. She had nowhere to go. And that was assuming the troll didn't just run her down and squash her.

Drawing her rapier, Jehanne Dark strode out to meet the troll warrior.

She could feel his footfalls through the very ground. He wasn't even bothering to use the shield. It swung at his side as if he were running a race. He was expecting her to flee, Jehanne realized. She wondered how long it had been since he'd met a foe who hadn't. Dimly, she was aware that the walls of the palisade were deserted, and with two deadly gazes dominating the battlefield, who could blame the men cowering inside? She set herself side-on to him, presenting her thin blade. The troll slowed his charge, sighting on her.

With deceptive slowness, the huge troll raised his axe.

Jehanne's left hand shot forward, flinging two heavy darts smeared with poison at the troll's face. They bounced off his craggy hide, and she sprang left toward his shield side. He flinched away, his blow slamming uselessly into the earth. Jehanne dashed forward, stabbing for his unshod foot.

The troll howled in pain at the bite of her steel, but it was a pinprick. He let go his axe and swiped at her. She ducked and struck with two of her snake-heads, instinctively. Agony from their mouths told her that she'd broken the fangs of both of them on the troll's hide. His shield-edge chopped down at her, and she danced back. Her mother's mutilated face stared out at her, and Jehanne slashed above the shield as high as she could reach.

*Never cut or stab at a shield,* her mentor's voice sounded in her head. *That's what they're for: to waste your strength, dull your blade, or at worst, trap it. You can't hurt a shield.*

But her reach was far too short to hit anything else.

Pulling up his axe, the troll swiveled toward her, and she dodged left again. His awkward blow sliced dirt, and her riposte ended well short of his massive wrist. She was forced to leap left to avoid his punch with the massive shield.

*Against a larger opponent, make him waste his energy. Wear him out.*

But she was already wearing out.

This time the troll backed a step and raised his axe high overhead. Jehanne's left hand snatched a throwing knife from her bandolier and sent it darting for his stomach. It stuck there, but the huge bulk hardly quivered, and she was forced to leap to her left again, hiding behind the troll's own shield. He batted at her with it, and she leapt away. Fear clawed at her. The shield was the only thing she could hit. She was going to be killed by the dead mother she'd come to avenge. *Never fight,* the chief of her guild had told her once. *Kill your target and disappear. Never allow yourself to be distracted from the target.* Why hadn't she run? Why hadn't she listened? Why hadn't she just come back to try killing Ecferth later?

And then it was almost as though he'd clipped her across the head for being a slow pupil.

She'd mistaken her target. And it was right in front of her.

The troll wasn't stupid. He'd realized Jehanne was using his own shield against him. This time he swung it at her, edge-on. She backed, then bore straight in at the shield, stabbing.

Into her mother's left eye. It exploded in blood and fluid.

But she'd come too close. The troll thrust the shield straight out, shoving her back. Off balance and gasping for breath, Jehanne fell back on the ground. She clawed at the earth, trying to shove herself back to her feet. The axe rose.

And a crossbow bolt slammed in under the troll's armpit. He howled, dropping the huge weapon.

"Ampyrica!!"

The thunder of hoofbeats sounded in her ears. Jehanne sprang to her feet. Only a lifetime of discipline kept her from looking around, but she didn't have to. She knew that voice. *What does the fool think he's doing?* He was going to throw everything away!

Roaring, the troll brought the shield around and raised it high. Jehanne heard a horse's high scream as it was crushed under the burden of a man suddenly becoming 500 pounds of stone. With no time to hesitate, she leaped forward, stabbing for the troll's heel. He screamed, and this time she stepped to her left, drawing the cut and slicing through whatever a troll used for its Achilles tendon. The thing staggered and shrieked, and two more bolts slammed into its back. In her peripheral vision, Jehanne could see horses sweeping around from her left and right, and she cursed, losing precious seconds as she pulled her veil down over her face.

King Michael and a dozen horsemen were circling the troll and…looking away from it? Every one of them was looking at the insides of their own shields, which had been polished to mirror brightness.

The huge troll had his axe again now. He limped forward and lunged at the riders to his left, but they spurred their mounts and rode on. The riders to his left raised crossbows and fired. Three more bolts slammed into the behemoth, but he spread his arms wide, and the shield was facing backward. Two more horses collapsed screaming under riders who hadn't looked away in time. This had to be stopped now.

Jehanne charged.

The troll turned again, dragging the foot she'd lamed. She feinted for it again, and the troll dropped its shield in pure reflex. Her rapier point stabbed forward into her mother's remaining eye.

Rolling backward, she screamed, "Look now! Look at him!"

For a moment, nothing changed. Then she saw the troll brandish the shield at the knights. A puzzled look came over its face. One by one, the knights dismounted, drawing long swords.

With an almost comical look on its broad face, the troll tilted the shield toward itself. Then it howled in rage and swept up its axe. The king and his knights charged. The troll swung his axe through one of the king's companions, then the rest were on it, swords flashing, taking it down.

Jehanne stared through her veil at the man she'd sworn to rescue as he turned to her. Well, and hadn't she done just that?

And he had come for her anyway.

Yanking her veil down, assuring herself it was still there, she advanced on him. "You mortal-blooded, half-witted *idiot!*" she shouted. He turned to face her. It was hard to read his expression beneath the helmet, but she hoped he was taken aback. "You almost ruined *everything!*"

He stepped toward her. "So did you," he said softly. "You almost got yourself killed. I couldn't allow that."

The vision of the troll raising his axe to strike flashed before her, but she pressed stubbornly on. "What good would saving me have done if the king had gotten himself petrified?"

"And what good would your death have done him at the cost of the kingdom?" he asked. "But that question alone tells me we could have no better queen. Gentlemen!" he shouted. "Are there any more who doubt my choice? Let him raise steel now!"

One by one, King Michael's knights dropped to their knees before her.

She couldn't take this in. She raised her eyes to the palisade beyond. "We're not finished here," she said. "Stay behind me."

King Michael opened his mouth to object, then nodded. "Indeed, Lady."

Jehanne removed her veil and marched forward.

A commotion sounded within the palisade, then a rending crack. "Mount!" she heard the king order behind her. "Ecferth must not escape." His knights obeyed, but he continued to trail in her wake.

Jehanne paused at the hole the troll had torn through the wall. "Any man who would surrender, cover your face with your hands!" She stepped inside.

The camp was in shambles. Not a tent still stood. The far gate stood wide open, and the mercenaries were in full rout, with King Michael's companions giving chase. Perhaps half a thousand men wearing Nygurd's livery sat amid the wreckage, faces buried in their hands under the stony, horrified gaze of their former lord.

They found Ecferth in the wreckage of his command tent, pinned under the remains of the observation tower, hands clapped over his eyes. He whimpered when King Michael hauled him to his feet and turned him to face Jehanne.

"Well, Ecferth?" the king said, his voice devoid of tone. "What do you have to say?"

The broken man could scarcely force words out. "I...surrender. Mercy. Mercy, Sire."

Michael seemed to consider this. "You plunged Ampyrica into war for no better reason than that you saw the opportunity," he said. "And but for the Lady Jehanne, I think you would have had it. So ask her for the mercy you seek."

"Lady Jehanne?" he said. "Who—who is she?"

"You've heard of her," the king went on. "The daughter of your weapon. Jehanne Dark."

If possible, Ecferth trembled even harder. "No! No!" he howled. "Please! Please, mercy. I didn't know!"

Jehanne's blood ran cold in disgust. "You didn't *know*?" she said. "You didn't know you were murdering her?"

"I didn't. I didn't!" he whimpered. "It was Nygurd. He killed your mother! You've already killed him for it. He gave it to me. A gift, he said, to his king! You have your revenge! You have it!"

Jehanne nodded. "It so happens that I, too, promised my king a gift." She placed her rapier beneath the point of his breastbone. "A statue. Commemorating his victory."

"No!"

"The only question," Jehanne said, "is how much pain it will cost you." She slid the blade forward. With a cry of agony, Ecferth's eyes popped open, and it was over. She let the rapier go, buried six inches deep in the stone.

She replaced her veil. "There, my lord," she said. "You can look now. How do you like your wedding present?"

King Michael gazed at it. "I think it will be the most effective work of art I will ever own. A present I will find hard to match."

She took his hand. "What about half the kingdom?" she said.

"Done." Hand-in-hand, they walked out of the camp.

\* \* \* \* \*

## G. Scott Huggins Biography

G. Scott Huggins, the first ever winner of both Baen Short Story contests, secures the future of the world by teaching its past to teenagers, many of whom learn things before going to college. He loves high fantasy, space opera, and their numerous parodies. He has been writing since the late 20$^{th}$ Century. He enjoys swords, venison, whiskey, and pie. Huggins currently lives in Wisconsin with his wife, three children, and two cats.

\* \* \* \* \*

# Fortune's Expensive Smile
## by Julie Frost

"You fail at everything, don't you, Wolfy?" The voice grated in my ear like a backhoe over asphalt. "You can't even drink yourself to death properly."

I hunched over my eighth whiskey. A shiver ran through my shoulders, and I tried to remember a time before I'd learned to flinch. I didn't know if the voice was an inner one fueled by survivor's guilt, or an outer one hissed by some invisible tormenter, but maybe it didn't matter. The deep ache in the breadbasket of my soul didn't care who dealt the words.

Which weren't wrong, neither. Werewolf metabolism meant getting actually sloshed was pretty dang difficult, and I was barely tipsy. I decided to drink faster, drained the glass, and signaled for another.

The bartender lifted an eyebrow, but poured after giving me a good, long once-over. "You okay, man?"

"Not really, but I ain't gonna dump my hurt all over a stranger, neither."

Everyone was dead. I couldn't tell him that.

"Woman trouble?"

"If by 'woman trouble' you mean some asshole killed my wife and all my friends while he was at it, and I wasn't there to stop him, I guess you could say, yeah, I got woman trouble." Whoops. Told him anyway. In whiskey, *veritas*. There I went, sharing the pain only I deserved to carry. I drank the whiskey down.

The bartender's face twisted with sympathy as he filled my glass yet again. "I'm sorry. Maybe I shouldn't have pried."

"Prob'ly better if you didn't, yeah," I answered, draining that shot and nodding for another. He reluctantly poured me one and moved down to someone waving at him from the other end of the bar before I repeated the process.

That voice started up again. "Even if you'd been there, you'd have just died, too, slaughtered like the sheep you've become. Big, bad wolf...ha, more like scared little lam—*urk*."

The voice abruptly stopped mid-word, and a stranger I hadn't noticed slid onto the stool beside me. A dark-skinned guy in his mid-30s with his hair tied in a tail much like my own, only his was black, and mine was blond. He wore jeans and a pale-blue button-down that failed to hide how muscular he was. He smelled...weird. Not human, not vampire, not wolf, nor any other creature I knew about. I couldn't rightly tell. Cinnamon and vanilla, and hope, and *home*. So comforting, it frightened me.

"He will not trouble you again, Dan'l."

I rested my chin on my hand and looked at him sideways. I put that hint of a scent out of my mind, because I couldn't understand it or hope to articulate how it shook me. I like to imagine I kept it all off my face. Probably didn't. "I know you?"

"Not as yet. I hope to change that." The stranger's voice sounded like a song from a Heaven I didn't deserve.

"I don't swing that way, *hombre*, and anyways, I just lost my wife and ain't lookin' for a hookup." I twisted my wedding ring around my finger.

"I know. I am sorry for your loss."

It hadn't made the news, not deemed worthy of even a 30-second mention. Hunter-wolf business—if hunters decided a wolf needed to die, no trial was needed. They had unilateral power to slaughter us out of hand. Mostly we kept our heads down, mowed our lawns, and paid our bills. It didn't always work. Humanity's methods of protecting themselves could be rough on those of us regarded as scary monsters. Even if, like Karita, we'd never hurt a human in our lives.

"What do you know about my loss?" I asked instead, a touch belligerently. This was my business, not some stranger's.

"I know you were driving your 18-wheeler three states away when you got the call. I know the authorities will do nothing, and you will get neither justice nor answers from them. I know your pack was innocent of wrongdoing." He paused with my full attention on him. "And I know why they were slaughtered."

I straightened, and my brow lowered. "Be real careful with what you say next."

"You wear a pendant." It lay hidden under my shirt. How'd he know? "Your wife Karita gave it to you, an heirloom in her family for generations. A sort of good-luck charm."

I pulled it out. It didn't really look like much—a smooth but irregular black stone with veins of white wrapped in gold wire. Certainly nothing to kill over. "This?" I whispered. How'd my glass get empty? My vision blurred, and my heartbeat thundered in my ears.

"Is an *actual* good-luck charm." He stuck out his hand. "My name is Tigraciel."

I shook it automatically. "There's no such thing as good-luck charms. That's just folks hoping for power they ain't got, grace they ain't earned."

"Have you ever received a speeding ticket or failed a roadside inspection? Had a breakdown or an accident? In all your years of driving that large and unwieldy vehicle back and forth across this vast nation in all kinds of weather?"

"Well, no, but…" I rubbed my thumb across the stone. I was law-abiding in general, but not always in particular, especially if I got in a hurry. I didn't take *stupid* chances, but I took some that weren't always bright, because an accident wouldn't kill me, right? And other drivers could be remarkable idiots around the big rigs, but none of them had ever been so dumb as to get me in a wreck.

The bartender filled my glass again. He asked Tigraciel what he'd like.

"Honeyed mead?"

That request earned him an exasperated look. "Does this look like the kind of place that would have something like that?"

It was a honky-tonk on the rougher side of town. Sawdust on the floor and a jukebox full of country tunes twenty and sometimes 40 years out of date.

"No?" Tigger—I decided that "Tigraciel" was too much of a mouthful, especially in my finally-inebriated state—sighed. "Then the raspberry wheat beer." The barkeep went to pull it for him.

"But all that don't necessarily signify," I argued. "Maybe I'm just lu—" I stopped and pointed at him. "I see what you done there, Tigger, and I ain't sure I like it."

A corner of his mouth turned up. "I did naught but make a suggestion. Your own mind supplied the logical conclusion."

"Not sure logic's a thing, shape I'm in." I sipped the whiskey this time instead of slamming it down. My brain had finally, finally started fuzzing out. Just, perhaps, when it ought not have.

"Nevertheless. You are a werewolf. You know vampires. You live the supernatural every day. Is it such a stretch to believe in other aspects of it?"

"Mebbe. Oughta keep an open mind, I guess." My nostrils worked. "So what're you?"

He sipped his raspberry beer with equanimity. "I am an angel of the Lord, Dan'l. And I have a job offer for you."

\* \* \*

I woke up in my own bed, still wearing my jeans and undershirt, though my boots were lined up beside my dresser. Karita's spot was empty, and then I remembered why and pulled her pillow to my face, inhaling deeply and letting out a stifled sob. My eyes leaked for a while before I got myself under a semblance of control.

I didn't remember getting home. I wanted a shower and a tooth brushing in the worst way, not necessarily in that order. I heaved myself upright and took care of the necessaries before wandering into my living room, following the aroma of fresh coffee.

Tigraciel slouched on my sofa, one ankle resting on his knee, and comfortable with it. I'd convinced myself I'd dreamed him, but there he sat, large as life.

I blinked rapidly and sputtered. "What are you—what did we—I thought I said—"

"You were quite intoxicated by the end of our conversation. I thought it best to see you safely home." He raised a hand. "Nothing happened, Dan'l. My Father has strict rules about, hn, *relations* between angels and humans. I made coffee when I heard you up and about."

"I don't care how weird you smell, you ain't an angel. Angels are just stories."

"Rather than pointless and tiresome arguing…." He stood up. I wasn't tiny—six foot or so, and a solid coupla hundred pounds—but he overtopped me by about four inches of height and 30 pounds of pure muscle.

I took a step back. "What—"

A pair of enormous white wings expanded from his back and fanned out. But not all the way, because my living room was too small. The flight feathers were gold-tipped, with a glow to them, and his odd scent intensified, honey and vanilla with a hint of cinnamon and jasmine. Like a baker's shop window on the first sweet day of summer, the finest day of the year. Something in my knees didn't want to hold me up, but I grasped at the wall and kept my feet.

"Now do you believe me?" he asked.

I had to be dreaming or hallucinating. I'd drunk a lot last night. "Holy—"

He grinned and gave his wings a little flap, causing my hair to fly back. "Yes, that's rather the point. You may touch them if you like."

I reached out, and he stretched one toward me. Wonderingly, I ran my fingers through the coverts and then down between the yard-long flight feathers. "They're real. You're real." Our previous conversation bubbled to the surface, and I pulled on the chain around my neck. "And this is *really* a lucky charm." My hand tightened around the stone. "Maybe if Karita had it, she'd still be alive."

"We cannot know that, Dan'l. You can kill yourself with what-ifs and wherefores." He hid the wings away. "Make yourself a cup of coffee, and let us talk."

"Sure. You want one, too? Do angels eat and drink?"

"We have no need, but we are equipped to, if necessary, and I enjoy the flavor. Yes, please. Cream and two sugars, if you don't mind."

I didn't, and came back out with a pair of steaming cups. Handing him one and sitting down, I said, "I remember something about a job offer?"

"My assignment is to work with a werewolf partner, keeping esoteric artifacts safe from demons and humans who would use them for nefarious purposes."

"Demons," I said flatly. Once that door opened, I guess angels weren't the only things to walk through. A question I'd been trying to form, answered.

"My family has its evil side, unfortunately." For a fleeting moment, sorrow lined his face, but if I hadn't been watching him, I would've missed it. "But they mostly just egg people on, rather than directly hurting individuals. You might remember a voice in your ear last night?"

I shivered and nodded. "Weren't sure if it was real or not."

"Quite real. And they would like nothing better than to get hold of that pendant or your soul. Preferably both." He took a breath I wondered if he needed. "He was part of a group working with the hunter who slaughtered your pack. The same hunter murdered my previous partner and stole from him a pair of glasses that allows the wearer to see supernatural auras."

I sipped my coffee and watched him over the rim of the cup. "So it's personal for you, too."

His jaw bunched. "It is not supposed to be. My partner Connor is safe in Heaven. But one does not simply dismiss a bond built over decades. I was on patrol while he slept, and the hunter struck before

I realized anything could be wrong. Perhaps if I had been there..." He shook his head. "Angels are not permitted to harm humans except under direct orders. I could not have physically defended him, but surely I could have given him warning. Taken him away. Something."

Tigger was on the same guilt trip as me. That probably wasn't good for either of us, so I decided to point something out. "Or might be the demon hangers-on woulda taken you out permanent-like and left these artifacts with no guardian at all. Which would mean I'd get no warning and have no idea what's really going on." I paused, because I didn't actually know, and it seemed important. "Can angels die?"

"It takes some doing, but yes. We can. I have never heard of a human accomplishing it, however. No matter how cursed, your weaponry doesn't have enough power to inflict anything but a grievous injury."

That was something, anyway. "And just how scrupulous are demons about delivering a death blow?" I asked.

"Most of the time, we are not actively trying to kill each other." He took several swallows of his coffee. "Most of the time. The Final Battle still lies far in the future, and we are none too sanguine to rush it along, on either side. Some of these artifacts make them greedy beyond all reason, however."

So it could happen. I shivered. Werewolves didn't do so hot by ourselves, but I wondered if being alone would be better than making a new friend and then losing him to literal demons. "I'm not s'sure I want this job, Tigger. It seems risky."

"It is," he acknowledged. "And if you like, you can just give the pendant to me, and I'll keep it safe and find another partner." His lips tightened. "Or you can hold on to the pendant, I can leave you, and you can take your chances alone with this hunter. I cannot thwart Free Will."

None of those options appealed. I set my coffee aside and leaned forward, elbows on knees, and scrubbed a hand over my face. "Losin' people hurts, Tigger. I know I don't gotta tell you that, but I ain't sure I'm strong enough to do it again."

"Lone-wolf it?" I caught his frown out of the corner of my eye. "This, of all the choices, strikes me as the worst one."

Me, too, but I was bone-deep afraid. Question was, was I more afraid of being alone, or more afraid of someone else dying on my watch?

"Dan'l." He waited until I looked at him. "Angels do not die easily and I would feel better in my heart if you had some protection against my fallen brethren. While angels are not permitted to harm humans, or mostly-human creatures such as werewolves, demons operate under no such strictures, though Lucifer gets somewhat cranky if they outright kill you. Something about 'the greatest trick the devil ever pulled' or something."

I nodded, a jerky movement that probably betrayed how unsettled I felt. "So how does it work? You move in?"

"I can move in, in the body, as I am. Or I can be an invisible roommate. Whatever you prefer. I require neither sleep nor food."

Something inside me shattered, like a glass wall I'd been caught behind since...since I'd gotten *That Call*. I was suddenly very sure I didn't want to be alone. "I've got a guest room you're more'n welcome to. We can load it up with the doo-dads so you can keep a closer eye on 'em. I'm guessin' we oughta get 'em from your partner's place to here, if this is gonna be a thing."

Tigger took a breath, let it out slowly, and nodded. "'Tis a good idea. Connor's house is warded against demons, but that doesn't help if the demons have human accomplices. Best to get the artifacts moved as soon as may be."

I had a pickup with a topper I used for camping. He directed me to his partner's old home, and we parked outside for a minute while he steeled himself to go in. "I apologize, Dan'l. Many good memories overlay this place, but they are haunted by the final bad one, where I discovered Connor's body far too late to do anything constructive about it."

"You don't gotta explain anything to me, Tigger. I know where you're comin' from. Take your time." I remembered coming home to an empty house, echoing with scents and sounds I'd never have again, after identifying Karita's body at the morgue, along with the rest of my pack.

His knuckles were pale where he gripped his knees, but after a minute or so, he opened the door of the truck and stalked determinedly to the house. I followed on after a second and found him standing in the living room over a huge bloodstain on the carpet that I could smell came from a werewolf. Not just death. Slow death, with pain and fear still sharp on the air. I didn't know what to say, so I just put my hand on his shoulder. Strange how we were broken the same way. Like someone planned it.

"Silver and wolfsbane. The hunter took his time," he choked out. His fists clenched and unclenched, and his wings spread wide and bristling. "Fortunately, I suppose, he was after the glasses and nothing else."

He led me to a set of stairs going up. The attic we ended up in was filled with hundreds of carefully-labeled boxes. I gawked. "We're responsible for all this?"

"It is a small subset of North America." His forehead creased. "If you do not feel up to the burden..."

"Naw, it's fine." This was nearly a lie, and I wondered if I sinned thereby—and decided not to ask. Instead, I grabbed a couple of boxes and started transferring the treasure trove to my truck.

Tigger's method was much more direct. He picked the boxes up and disappeared. Lather, rinse, repeat, and I found he was reappearing inside the truck bed and playing a stack-the-boxes version of Tetris.

"Can't you just take them right to my house?" I asked. What did he even need me for?

"I can, but it takes more energy. I am not a limitless font."

That made sense, and I walked the boxes down to the truck with less complaining and more doing. Midway between the house and my pickup, something hit me square between the shoulder blades and drove me to my knees. I kept my grip on the three boxes I carried, for a wonder.

A demon that looked just like I'd expect—curly horns, goat legs, bat wings—appeared in front of me, armed with a warhammer already in motion. It clocked me across the chin and sent me flying and boxes scattering across the lawn. I shook the stars outta my vision and scrambled to my feet, careful to keep myself between the demon and the artifacts.

"Now that was completely uncalled for," I said. I had no holy weaponry, and thought wildly that maybe I oughta hit Tigger up for some, when he appeared beside me, shining like the sun and angry with it. A longsword glowed in his right hand.

"Do not touch the Lord's anointed, Hellspawn," he growled.

"I thought the house was warded," I said.

"The house, yes. The grounds, not so much."

"That strikes me as a hole in your security."

"I'll have that pendant, wolf." The demon held his massive hand out. "Unless you want me to hit you again and let my pet hunter know there's a new Hound of God in town."

"You must be feeling particularly weak if you want *human* luck, Jalus," Tigger said with a somewhat nasty grin, while I took a step back.

"We're outnumbered two to one," the demon answered, lifting the hammer. "We'll take what we can get."

"Dan'l," Tigger said, pointing his sword at the demon's throat, "you may find something useful in that long box you were carrying."

I backed up, keeping a wary eye on the demon, who took half a step forward before Tigger made a warning noise. The box was taped shut, but I popped claws and made short work of it. My breath caught.

It was a gorgeous antique double-barreled side-by-side shotgun. The stock was dark polished wood, and the metal was etched with a floral pattern. I picked it up and broke it open to check if it was loaded—it was, and more rounds peeked out of a half-open plastic container inside the box.

"The weapon is blessed," Tigger said. "Do you know how to use it?"

"I surely do," I answered. "May not be rightly human, but I'm damn sure a red-blooded American male." I suddenly felt much better as I thumbed both hammers back. "So maybe Ugly here oughta get hisself gone before things turn unpleasant for him. Seein' as how he's outnumbered two to one."

"We're outnumbered two to one *most* of the time," the demon said, with a smile I didn't like. "Not necessarily always."

Five more popped into being in mid-leap, various weapons swinging. I had time to wonder what the neighbors would think before I pulled the trigger. The buckshot blew a huge hole in a demon chest from point-blank range, and he shrieked and disappeared with a detonation of smelly black tar.

But enemies only come at you one at a time in the movies, and something walloped me across the back, knocking me to the ground, and the breath from my lungs. I only kept myself from a stress-induced shift via an act of sheer will. The wolf wouldn't help in this situation.

The demon hit me again. Some kind of multi-chained whip, I realized. It burned like—well, Hell, on reflection, and I really didn't want to suffer another blow. I rolled over onto my back, which wasn't the best idea I'd ever had, and fired the second round at the demon. His head disappeared, and the rest of him blew up with another satisfying explosion of black tar.

My roll brought me auspiciously close to the box holding the ammo. My hand scrambled inside and came out with a pair of shells, and I slammed them home. Another roll brought me up to my knees and then my feet, hunting another target. Two demons beset Tigger, who was sore wounded and bloody-winged, and two more were headed my way with intent.

The breath froze in my lungs. Without regard for my own threat, I fired both barrels, one-two, at the demons fighting Tigger. They blew up—

And Jalus's sword took me through the guts.

Vivid agony burst through my body, and I stumbled back. The demon cackled and yanked his blade out. I managed to barely parry his next thrust with the shotgun, but barely was enough. My follow-through clocked the other demon across his snoot, and black blood streamed from his nose like a waterfall. He stumbled backward right into Tigger's sword and disappeared.

That left Jalus, who was wounded, too. He sketched off a salute and said ominously, "Until we meet again, little brother." Then he vanished.

I dropped to one knee, winded and bleeding, bracing myself on one hand. Tigger knelt beside me with a hand on my shoulder. "That was well done, Dan'l."

"Was it?" The pendant felt warm against my chest. "I'm thinkin' we oughta get home and heal up our hurts before we try something like that again."

"This was the last load, fortuitously. Can you drive?"

"Won't be the most comfy I've ever driven, but yeah." I slid into the seat and got us going. "Fortuitously?" I pulled the pendant out from under my shirt. It glowed.

"Never have I had such an easy battle with such terrible odds."

"That was *easy*?" I turned to face him with my mouth open.

"Six of them, two of us, and your first demonic fight. Think on it, Dan'l. You knew exactly what to do, and each of your shells hit precisely what you aimed at."

"We didn't escape unscathed, though."

"No, but we are not nearly so wounded as one would expect from such an encounter."

I chewed on that for the rest of the ride while we healed, slower than usual for me. When I pulled the truck into the garage, Tigger said, "We should ward your house, and probably your vehicles as well."

Warding meant holy water, chalk, and salt, turned out. I filled up a spray bottle and grabbed a fresh canister of Morton's, and Tigger blessed the ingredients and showed me how to sew the place up tight against demonic riff-raff. "Wish the place had been warded sooner," I muttered, drawing runes and spraying windowsills and doorways.

"Jalus used a human to do his dirty work, so I'm afraid warding the house wouldn't have—" His head jerked up. "Speaking of which, I've had a couple of incognito brothers keeping watch. We have an unwanted visitor."

No sooner had he got that sentence out than someone kicked my door open and came in shouting. A shot rang out. I caught a glimpse of an angry face.

"Not again." Tigger grabbed me—

And we disappeared.

It was the weirdest sensation of being everywhere and nowhere at once. A heartbeat of forever in the blink of an eye. A shudder in the middle that didn't feel quite right. We stumbled back into the world in a clearing in the forest, and I rolled to my knees and looked for Tigger, just in time to see him collapse to the ground with a wet cough and shredded wings.

"Tigger!" I rushed over to him and grasped his shoulder. Bright blood painted his lips as he coughed again. A long-ago memory bubbled up, Mama taking me to church, laying on of hands for a healing prayer. I didn't know if such as Tigger could be healed by such as me, or if it would even help, but I couldn't stand by and lose someone else without at least trying to do something about it.

Just. Couldn't.

My lips moved, no words coming out, but my heart knew what it wanted even if I weren't over-articulate with it. My hands took on a glow that surprised me enough to twitch, but not enough to take them away. Tigger's wounds faded, and he let out a relieved gasp *not* filled with blood. The stains dwindled from his shirt and feathers, and he lay there breathing for a few seconds before he pushed himself upright, wings fanned out and whole.

"Dan'l. You can stop now." A worried frown creased his brow. "Dan'l?"

It had taken more energy than I'd've credited, and I huffed out some tired breaths. "You okay, Tigger?"

He gave me a sunny grin. "T'was well done. I am glad to see the teachings of your youth have not completely departed. They will stand us in good stead going forward, though perhaps some studying would be in order."

My eyes mighta been leaking. Maybe. "I couldn't watch you die." My voice was low and broken.

"Oh, Dan'l." He embraced me, wings and all. "I would not have died from that. 'Tis not often they interfere with a move, but they appear to be determined. They did not escape unscathed themselves."

"That hunter asshole broke into my house," I said furiously. "That ain't on the free list, and I would *dearly* like to know who he is."

"I do not have the information you seek; I never got a name. But I'm thinking *you* may have it at your fingertips on your computer."

"Think he's gone? It ain't like he was gettin' the lucky charm, since I'm wearing it."

"If he be not gone, he might get a nasty shock when we come in loaded for bear." Tigger's smile was not at all nice. "This time, we will be ready for him."

I felt a bit uneasy. "Are the demons gonna come at you like that again?"

"There are no guarantees. But now I know what they are about, I can prepare and shield better."

"All righty." I popped claws. "We'll see if he's there. Ready?"

"I am." He grabbed my shoulder and swept his wings forward, and that same sensation followed us home, but without the shudder this time.

My house was empty, and I gazed sourly at my broken front door. "He's gonna pay for that, one way or another."

"First you must find him."

"I have the technology." Deciding to leave the door as it was for the moment, I fired up my computer and did an image search for werewolf hunters in my town. Wasn't long before I found his face. He was proud of hisself, no doubt. That got me a name—Boone Walken—and five dollars later I had his home address and phone number, along with several possible relations in the same locality.

"Welp. I know where he lives. Maybe I oughta pay him the same sorta visit he just paid me." Walken had murdered my pack. Slaughtered my wife.

"Dan'l." Tigger tipped his head, with one eyebrow lowered. "Is this a good idea?"

I shrugged. "Prob'ly not. But I got his address and I don't need your help if you think you need to sit it out. This ain't angel business, Tigger. I'm endin' it, here and now."

"Then I will accompany you and hope that the still small voice in your ear will stay your hand if need be."

I couldn't guarantee him that. A clamorous inner voice bellered that Boone Walken needed to die, and die slow, for what he'd done. But I welcomed the company. I grabbed the keys to my truck, and we headed out.

\* \* \*

Of course, it don't ever go smooth. I pulled up in front of Walken's house and hopped out, only to be immediately immobilized by a net of wolfsbane fired from a weird-ass gun. It wrapped me up and sent me crashing to the ground before I got twenty feet into Walken's front yard.

But Tigger backed me up. He grabbed the net and yanked it away before it paralyzed me longer than a few seconds. Then he had his own issues as demons popped into existence and laid into him.

I'd managed to walk us right into a friggin' ambush. Lucky charms apparently didn't cover being a damned fool.

Way more than one hunter, and too many demons for Tigger to take on by himself. I shouted at him to get gone, but he was in it for the long haul and refused to leave me. A dart filled with aconite smacked into my thigh, and I clenched my teeth around a pained grunt as I hit the ground again, unable to move. Tigger couldn't do nothin' for that, but he had his own issues.

In the end, we wound up bound on our knees in the front yard of Walken's house, surrounded by enemies that'd just as soon see us dead. Three hunters besides Walken and a passel of demons. Walken, wearing the glasses I assumed he'd stolen from Connor that let him see supernatural auras, stalked up to me, grabbed hold of the pendant chain, and ripped it off my neck.

"You should've just given it over, Danny." He got down in my face, holding a semi-auto nine-mil loaded with silver down beside his leg. "But now you get to die, just like the rest of your pack. Only good wolf is a dead one anyhow. You all turn to murderous beasts in the end. Best to just stop you before it ever gets that far." Something in his past had damaged him, right enough, set him on this black-and-white path where he was wrong and didn't even know it. Nor would he care.

"My mate never hurt a human in her life," I retorted. "You had no reason to kill her."

"She was a werewolf. I had *every* reason to kill her, especially since she held something I wanted."

"Except she gave that to me."

He dangled it from his fingers. "And now it's mine." Jalus, riding him like a pony, gave us a toothy grin.

Demons started going invisible. I wasn't sure if this was a hopeful sign or not. "Tigger?" I asked.

"They seem to have found urgent business elsewhere, now that 'tis all over but the shouting," he said. "Interesting."

Cell phones rang in hunter pockets. The one who'd shot me with the net said, "I have to go. My wife just got in a car accident."

"It's okay, I've got this." Walken waved a dismissive hand.

My fingers flexed behind my back as the paralysis faded, but the hunter behind me was glued to his phone and didn't notice. "I, uh, gotta go, too," he said and didn't wait for permission before he booked it outta there.

Jalus stood over Tigger. He had a grating laugh I was sure got him all the girls at parties. Not. He didn't seem to realize he was the only demon left. I twisted my wrists behind my back, and the rope wasn't as tight as it should have been. The third hunter muttered something about his kid's school and left, smoking his tires.

So it was down to the four of us.

Glancing at Tigger, I worked my wrists. He gave me a nod I'da missed if I hadn't been looking right at him. A cursed rope couldn't hold him if it just fell off. Which it did. He was already in motion with his sword in his hand before the rope hit the lawn. His blade thunked home, center mass up to the hilt, before Jalus even knew he was in danger. The demon let out a scream and exploded into black tar.

Walken's gun hand came up, but my own bonds had also come loose. Now that I didn't have to worry about dislocating my shoulders, I shifted and leaped, shaking out of my shredded clothes. A bullet fanned my fur. How had he missed at this range?

I hit him like a Hell-bound express train, all fangs and fur and fury, hearing the gun click without quite realizing that it'd jammed until I had Walken pinned on the ground with an audible crunch of broken bones. My dripping fangs hovered an inch over his tempting throat.

A hand rested on my shoulder. "You should not sully yourself on the likes of this." Tigger's voice was far too calm for the circumstances. "Not for his sake, but your own. Empty vengeance will not bring back Karita or anyone else in your pack."

I glanced sideways at him. His words might've been calm, but his eyes burned with fury. This was the hunter who'd killed his own partner, Connor. I wondered how much being the voice of reason was taking out of him.

I shifted to human, naked as the day I was born, and wrapped a clawed hand around Walken's throat. "If'n I let him live, we've got an even more dangerous enemy than before. This guy won't see mercy as anything but a weakness, Tigger, and you know that as well as I do. He'll just keep coming until someone dies."

"Self-defense is one thing. Cold-blooded murder is quite another. There is a line, Dan'l. I would not have you cross it."

I eyed Walken. Hate smoldered from his every pore as he glared at me through the glasses. I stripped them from his face and handed them to Tigger, who stuffed them into his jeans pocket with a nod.

"I dunno, Tigger. Maybe it ain't self-defense in the heat of the moment, but it's sure as shootin' self-defense in the long run. Just on a purely practical level. Somethin's broke up inside him, and it ain't gonna knit. He's lost out there in the tall grass, and he won't come back." My chin lifted. "Besides, didn't you just kill Jalus?"

He shook his head minutely. "As I said, killing one of us is not so easy to accomplish. That was not a death-blow, though he'll feel it for a good long while." His lips tightened. "Dan'l. I myself would like nothing more than to see Boone Walken burning in Hell for his crimes. I do not claim to be a perfect angel, and I cannot forgive as Father can. But I have no wish to see you burning beside this man."

"He ain't strictly a man anymore, though, is he? He's absorbed a lotta power by killin' wolves." I leaned into Walken's face. "By killin' my wife, and my pack. And he might be down and helpless now, but he won't be later. You know as well as I he'll come after us again, Tigger. Maybe next time we won't be so lucky."

"So where is the line, Dan'l? When do you get to decide who lives and who dies? Thou shalt not murder."

"This fella is a threat to everything I hold dear. Everything you hold dear too. You sayin' he don't deserve to die? The law ain't gonna touch him, 'cause he just killed *wolves*. We ain't 'people,' so he gets to walk free. That's some bullshit right there, and we all know it. A hunter knows what he's gettin' into when he starts plyin' his trade. We both know he's guilty. That should be enough."

"Judge, jury, and executioner? Is this what it's come to, where a single person chooses life or death for another?"

"What's the alternative? We just cut him loose, pat him on the head, and tell him to be a good boy from here on out? How many second chances does someone like this get? Lookit him. Hate seething off him in waves. He won't be grateful if I let him live, he'll just come after me worse than ever because he'll take it as a sign I'm soft, not that I'm better'n him. Which I am," I growled at Walken.

Tigger nodded. "You are. This is not in question. What is in question is whether violence is the answer here."

"I've heard, frequent-like, that violence don't solve nothin', but it's been my experience that the judicial application of violence often fixes all manner of problems." Walken squirmed under me, and my hand tightened around his throat, claws pricking enough to draw blood. "Quit that, or you'll die sooner."

"Don't I get a say?" he whined.

"No. No, you do not. Did my pack get a say before you slaughtered 'em?"

He closed his eyes. "No," he muttered.

"Then you can just hush while I decide your fate. So far, it ain't looking so hot."

His throat vibrated under my hand when he made an inarticulate animal noise. I wanted nothing more than to rip my claws through it and leave him bleeding out on his front lawn.

I glanced up at Tigger. Worry knitted his brow. He spread his wings over me, a comforting canopy in a damn comfortless situation.

Could I bear the disappointment I'd see in his eyes if I went through with an admitted cold-blooded murder? Oh, I could argue self-defense, or justice, or all kinds of high-falutin' concepts, but at the end of the day we all knew it was vengeance, pure and simple, stripped down to its bare bones.

I wanted it, though, wanted it so much it made my spirit ache. My knuckles were white from the effort of not tearing his throat out. But I couldn't let him walk away.

*Ah. There's my solution*, I thought.

I grabbed his wrist and got off him before flipping him to his stomach with no effort at all. He let out an "oof" and a "what" and then a scream when my claws flashed down. They weren't razor-sharp, because nothing organic really is, but they did the job pretty as you please, ripping through his vertebrae in four places.

Severing his spine.

Tigger flinched.

I leaned down and growled in Walken's ear. "Walk away from that, asshole."

His breath came in short, sharp gasps. "I. You. What."

"This is the mercy you get from me. You live. I'll allow that much. But you live in a wheelchair. And if I ever find out you've so much as looked at a wolf sideways—*and I will*—then I will hunt you down like the vermin you are and *exterminate* you."

"I–I need an ambulance."

"Call one your-damn-self. Your hands still work."

Grabbing the pendant, I shoved to my feet and stalked away, scooping up my boots and manfully refraining from kicking Walken in the ribs on my way past. Tigger followed and wrapped a wing around me before I climbed into my truck. He materialized, sitting on the passenger seat.

"I cannot say it was well done, Dan'l. But you showed far more restraint than I would have credited, under the circumstances."

I didn't look at him, instead staring out the windshield with my elbows resting on the steering wheel. "If you wanna find some other wolf to team up with, I won't blame you. I know I'm rough around the edges. There's baggage that ain't gonna go away in a day or even a year."

The wing reappeared around my shoulders. "I would never. Father has put us together for a reason. It is not for me to gainsay."

"Well, then, partner. I guess we oughta go home and get all those artifacts squirreled away." I glanced at the pendant, dangling from my fist. "How come this thing didn't work for Walken?"

"Because he stole it, rather than having it freely given. The luck turned bad for him, and good fortune rebounded to us, loosening the ropes on our wrists and calling his allies away."

"Huh." Good to know. Maybe lucky charms did work. Or maybe there was a Providence far greater than the stone around my neck. But those were questions for a different day.

"I am in a shocking state of nekkidness," I said. Fortunately, my truck carried a backpack with extra clothes for just such wardrobe malfunctions. I'd learned to plan for these things after a couple of disasters. "I reckon I oughta get dressed."

Tigger smiled. "I reckon you oughta, partner."

\* \* \* \* \*

## Julie Frost Biography

Julie Frost is an award-winning author of every shade of speculative fiction. She lives in Utah with a herd of guinea pigs, her husband, and a "kitten" who thinks she's a warrior princess.

Her short fiction has appeared in *Straight Outta Dodge City*, *Monster Hunter Files*, *Writers of the Future*, *The District of Wonders*, *StoryHack*, *Stupefying Stories*, and many other venues. Her werewolf PI novel series, "Pack Dynamics," is published by WordFire Press, and a novel that takes place in Hell, *Dark Day, Bright Hour*, is published by Ring of Fire Press. Visit her on Facebook at https://www.facebook.com/julie.frost.7967/.

\* \* \* \* \*

# Cold Hands, Warm Heart
# by Benjamin Tyler Smith
## A Necrolopolis Story

I gripped the armrests on the copilot's seat and hung on for dear life as turbulence buffeted the gyrocopter I found myself trapped in. *Mortus, how in the Eighteen Hells did my day end up like this?*

I'd been perfectly content at being discontent with the day's labor: resolving yet another territorial dispute between the incendiary ashlings and the combustible mummies. Of all the factions of undead in the city of Necrolopolis, why were those the ones who fought the most? They both stored their remains in jars, sort of. Couldn't they unite on that and get along?

Next thing I'd known, I'd found myself in my boss's personal gyrocopter, on a mission out of the city, with its pilot and her goblin crew.

"So there we was," a gravelly voice said, bringing me back to the present unpleasantness. I turned to look into the gyrocopter's cramped passenger compartment. Boltchucker, one of the bird's two gunners, held out his small green hands. "Flyin' through the inky fog of a shoal of sky squid, so black we couldn't see past the bird's nose. It's so dark, I know we're flyin' blind, and I says to the boss, 'Uh,

Boss Ezella, you sure this is a good idea?' An' do you know what she says, Mr. Adelvell?"

"What's that?" I asked.

"'Aw, come on, Bolty!'" Boltchucker affected a higher pitch. "'At least when the end comes, you won't see it, right?'"

Next to me the pilot, Ezella Airslicer, laughed. She was dressed in the leathers of a member of the Goblinoid Air Korps, complete with fur-trimmed cap that covered all but her pointed ears. A pair of goggles hung about her neck alongside a crystal ball necklace. "Boltchucker, I did *not* say that."

Skyglider, the other gunner, said, "It was more like, 'Oi, Bolty, ye coward, show some backbone or a dark end will be the least of yer worries.'"

Ezella shook her head, her tusks protruding from her mouth as her lower lip pulled back in a smile. "Didn't say that, either."

I shook my head. *Mina's not paying me enough for this.* I'd been hired to be the assistant of Grimina, director of the undead city of Necrolopolis. It was her job to manage its four million denizens until they could meet with her father Mortus—the god of death—at his courthouse and resolve the issues that tied them to this mortal coil. I had so much work waiting for me that it was a wonder the desk in my office-apartment didn't collapse from the weight of the paperwork piled on it.

Now I was being sent out of the city to a remote mining village deep in the Misty Blue Mountains. I had nothing more than my shovel, a letter from Mina explaining the treaty between Necrolopolis and the king whose territory included the mountain range, and my undead beast Asheater, a doglike creature whose spiritual essence had grown from crematory residue. Oh, and also a message from Mortus:

"An undead child has awoken in the land. Find her and bring her back. Then it's pint time at Mad Molly's!"

Mina hadn't approved of the last instruction. She hated it when her father was away from the courthouse for a single minute, and with the 70-something-year delay between arrival at the city and winding up on the courthouse docket, it was little wonder. Still, she'd agreed to the Mad Molly's meet-up on the condition that I bring this child back unharmed. "It is a dangerous world out there for the undead, Addy," she told me, her red eyes serious for once. "You know that more than anyone."

I did, though I hated to think about it. I touched the skull brooch that held my robes closed. "A necromancer's life isn't easy," I muttered.

"What was that?" Ezella asked. The noise of the gyrocopter made it hard to hear anything that wasn't a shout.

Rather than repeat myself, I asked, "How much fuel does this bird hold?" I asked.

Ezella tapped the full fuel gauge on her instrument panel. "Enough to get us to Ikatz and back, with some to spare." She paused. "Barring complications, anyway."

My stomach twisted. This is why I hated flying. "What kind of complications?"

"The usual kinds: headwinds, engine trouble, severe storms, aerial combat." Her green lips peeled back in a snaggletooth grin. "Haven't had a good sortie in a while."

"Let's hope it stays that way!"

Skyglider snorted. "Where's your sense of adventure, Mr. Adelvell?"

A sharp crosswind buffeted the gyrocopter with enough force to rattle my teeth. "Occupying a barstool at Mad Molly's."

"Two thousand feet below, and 50 miles behind us, then." Ezella's purple eyes sparkled with mischief as she reached back to scratch Asheater's ears. "Good to know!"

Boltchucker and Skyglider laughed. Asheater stuck her head into the cockpit, tongue lolled out as she looked at me. I stroked the bridge of her dry, gritty nose. "You, too, girl?"

She barked an affirmative, which only increased the others' merriment.

Clear skies soon gave way to thick clouds that obscured the early morning sun. Snow blanketed the treetops and fields below us, thin enough that fresh wagon tracks were visible along dirt roads. The closer to the Misty Blue Mountains we drew, the thicker the accumulation became. We passed over a large town where people the size of ants shoveled snow off roofs and dug trenches door to door along the streets. Skyglider whistled as he peered out his window. "Looks like they've got their work cut out fer them."

"Their fault for livin' there!" Boltchucker shrugged. "No one forced them to, so who cares if they're complainin'?"

"Who said anything about them complaining?" Skyglider took a swipe at Boltchucker, who leaned back in a dodge. "Besides, no one forces you to live in Necrolopolis. Should we care about you whining about the winter and summer stenches?"

"You complain about that more than me!"

"Maybe, but I'm not the one heapin' crap on others' misery, now am I?"

Boltchucker tried to kick his friend, but a sudden jolt of turbulence sent his boot into the corner of one of the two repeating ballistae turrets that were folded up in the passenger space. He cursed and pulled his foot back to rub at his injured toes.

Skyglider laughed. "Serves you right!"

Ezella chuckled as she lit up a cigar. It'd have been tiny in my hands, but it fit her stature perfectly. "Boys," she said, exhaling a cloud of sweet-scented smoke.

The argument continued for quite some time after that. I idly patted Asheater's warm head while I gazed out the window. Each community we passed over was smaller and more buried in snow than the last. By the time we reached the foot of the mountain range, all that was left was snow.

*Mortus, how does anyone live like this?* I originally hail from a southern kingdom, with heavy snows occurring once in a generation. Necrolopolis had been an adjustment with its four seasons, but I couldn't imagine living like *this*.

Ezella pointed. "Ikatz is right up ahead, before that fog bank." She frowned. "Where'd all the fog come from, anyway? I saw clear skies up to this point."

"Maybe that's where the 'misty' in Misty Blue Mountains comes from." I pulled a brass spyglass from the leather sheath fastened to the door and held it up to my eye. The ground suddenly grew very large, and it took a moment of shifting my gaze around for it to fall on Ikatz Village, with its peak-roofed homes and long streams of chimney smoke. In a clearing beyond the village, a group of villagers surrounded something small in the snow; something small, crouched, and distinctly *undead* by the aura emanating from it.

My stomach lurched. Mina had warned me that a new undead was in dire straits, and she hadn't been joking. As Ezella drew closer, I could make out the rocks and spears many of the villagers held, as well as the long black hair on the undead figure—the undead *girl*—who crouched in the snow. No matter how she'd died, these villagers intended to finish the job. I clenched the spyglass so hard I feared the brass would bend. "Take us down," I ordered.

Next to me, Asheater growled.

"Where?" Ezella stared through a spyglass of her own, her expression grim.

"Right on top of them."

"I was hoping you'd say that."

"Should we break out the Reapers?" Boltchucker patted one of the repeating ballistae in the passenger compartment. If they slid those out either door, it would give the gyrocopter a fair amount of offensive capacity.

Ezella looked at me and shrugged. "Your mission, your call."

I shook my head. "Not yet. Our mission is to rescue the undead, not wipe out the village."

"Roger."

"Besides, I doubt these people see too many gyrocopters. You come in low enough, it'll spook 'em."

She grinned. "Oh, I can manage that."

I returned to the spyglass. In the short conversation, we'd moved close enough for me to make out distinct features of the mob. Each person, young or old, was clad in furs or woolen clothing. A stoop-backed old man leaned on a cane as he shouted orders to the rest.

A few of the villagers looked up and pointed at us. "We've been made," Ezella said. "Time to drop!"

She pushed her control stick forward, and the gyrocopter dove. I nearly dropped the spyglass in my haste to grab my seat's armrests. Boltchucker and Skyglider whooped. Asheater howled with excitement. I kept silent, teeth clenched to keep my stomach contents inside.

Have I mentioned how much I hate flying?

True to Ezella's word, she came in low. *Very* low. The gyrocopter brushed past the canopies of evergreens and sailed over peaked thatch roofs as we flew toward the crowd. She pulled back on the stick when we reached the clearing above the village. The wash from the rotor blades kicked up a tremendous cloud of freshly fallen snow.

Boltchucker threw open the door on his side and looked down. "Another 30 feet or so, Mr. Adelvell—"

With a snarl, Asheater dove out. Her body contorted in the gale whipped up by the gyrocopter's blades, but she maintained her form and hit the ground running. Snow instantly turned to steam as she charged into the crowd. People screamed and ran from her, their desire to hurt the undead girl gone.

One of the villagers, a stout man with what looked like a boar spear, stood his ground and attempted to impale Asheater on the end of the weapon. Asheater leapt onto the weapon, her body opening up to absorb the blade. She chomped down on the spear shaft, biting it in two and setting both ends of the wood on fire at the same time. The man dropped his ruined weapon and fled with the others.

Cigar smoke poured out of Ezella's mouth as she laughed. "That's one way of dealing with things!"

*Tell me about it*, I thought. I bent over the armrest and scooped up my shovel. It didn't look like much of a weapon, but the blade was made from the tooth of a sky whale, strong enough to punch through stone if need be. Its shaft was made from one of the majestic creature's rib bones, and served as a great focus for my magic.

I opened the right-hand cockpit door and jumped out. As I dropped the last five feet or so, a strangely warm breeze tickled my cheeks. Then I was on the ground, trudging through knee-deep snow.

Asheater circled the undead girl, and it was clear even at a distance she was no ordinary zombie. She was a shiver, a zombie whose body had become infused with ice magic after suffering a cold death. She couldn't have been more than eleven or twelve, with long, black hair and eyes that would've been ice blue, even if they weren't frosty. Her skin was a pale, translucent blue everywhere except her hands and arms. These extremities were the blackish purple of frostbite, a condition she'd be permanently afflicted with from here on. Her blouse and skirt—which looked like the best clothes one would either be married or buried in—were dirty from being pelted with muddy rocks, but otherwise she looked no worse for wear.

She was still crouched in the snow, but she'd looked up when it became apparent no more rocks would be thrown at her. She looked between Asheater, the now-rising gyrocopter, and me, her mouth agape. "Who are you?" she asked.

"My name is Adelvell. I work for Director Grimina of Necrolopolis. I'm here to take you back with me."

"Necro-what?" Her blue lips twisted in a frown. "What's that?"

Well, that was new. I'd never encountered someone who hadn't at least heard of Necrolopolis. "It's a city for people…" I hesitated, not sure if this girl truly knew what she was. It wasn't uncommon for the recently risen to think they'd woken up from a dream or a coma.

Given how the villagers had been treating her, though, I decided she probably knew. "It's a city for people like you. What's your name?"

"Edurne." She cocked her head to the side. "What do you mean, people like me?" She hopped to her feet. "Never mind that. You have to help us!"

"Us?" I frowned. Mina had only mentioned there being one undead. That had been several hours ago, so maybe someone else had risen? "Who's 'us?'"

"My fellow villagers, of course!" Edurne placed a hand on her chest. "I'm from Ikatz Village, and all of us are in grave danger. I can't leave until everyone's safe! Especially Papa!"

*Papa? What happened to him?*

Angry shouts from the villagers stopped me from asking. They'd once again reformed around their stoop-backed elder. The man who'd lost his spear to Asheater hung behind the old man, hand gripping the hilt of a sheathed knife. The others wielded some kind of makeshift weapons, too, from kitchen knives to woodcutter's axes, to pickaxes. They outnumbered us 30 to one, but made no move to attack. I straightened my posture and made a show of planting my shovel's butt into the ground. Who knew I could be so intimidating?

Asheater growled, and most of the villagers jumped. I suppressed a sigh. So much for my ability to intimidate with raw physical strength.

The elder stepped forward. Though he looked frail, his voice was that of a deep-throated orator as he demanded, "Who are you? What do you and your monster want?"

Asheater growled, but quieted at my touch. "I'm Necromancer Adelvell, assistant to Director Grimina of Necrolopolis. I'm taking this undead child with me back to the city."

"A necromancer!" someone cried. Several villagers made warding gestures.

Now *that's* the type of reaction I'm used to.

"I am Zuzen, the headman of this village." He leveled his staff at Edurne. "That monster is our problem—one of many, it seems—and we'll deal with her on our own."

She shrank back from Zuzen's glare.

"I don't think so." I reached into my robe for the letter. "Your king—"

"Our village has no king!" the stout man next to Zuzen shouted.

"Enough, Bakar." Zuzen raised a gnarled hand to silence the man. "You'll have to forgive my son. He lost his own boy the other day, no thanks to that creature behind you."

I glanced back at Edurne, who huddled close to Asheater. A veil of mist had surrounded them, as Asheater melted the snow and frost her body generated. Her blue-eyed gaze caught mine, but she quickly lowered it. "This *girl*—" I emphasized the word, "has a name. Edurne."

"She *had* a name." Zuzen's expression was sad. "She stopped being Edurne when she died in the avalanche. Now she's just a monster in the shell of a girl named Edurne."

That wasn't how it worked, not unless demons or necromancers were reanimating soulless flesh. It was misunderstandings like this that caused a lot of my problems. "She's not a monster."

"She killed my son!" Bakar took a step forward, his hand going to his knife.

Asheater was instantly at my side, lips peeled back in a snarl. Bakar stopped dead in his tracks. He may have been afraid of Asheater, but his eyes were still full of hate as he glared past her and focused on Edurne. "She killed my boy, and she brought the wrath of the mountain down upon us all."

A woman shouted, "It's because of her my son is dead, too!"

"Bakar, Nekane, enough!" Zuzen barked.

"Mama, no," Edurne whispered, a hand pressed to her mouth. "It wasn't like that."

*That* was Edurne's mother? I studied the irate woman. If I looked past the disheveled hair, I could see the physical resemblance, but there was nothing but hot-blooded anger in her blue eyes, whereas Edurne's contained a warmth that belied her shivery condition.

*Angering the mountain?* What were these people talking about? All I knew of Ikatz Village was that it was a coal mining community, and had been for centuries. I didn't know of any deities or demigods or powerful spirits who'd made a home in the Misty Blue.

A deep rumbling sounded from further up the mountain. Tremors reverberated through the frozen soil beneath my booted feet, and I had to spread my legs to keep from falling over. *Mortus, what was that?*

The miniature crystal ball I wore about my neck—the twin to Ezella's—hummed softly. *"Addy, you gotta see this. Can you hear me?"*

She sounded like she was in a cave, but that's how the smaller crystals were. "Yes, I hear you. What's going on?"

*"Remember that fog bank we saw coming in? It's not fog."*

An explosion followed her words. Gouts of flame and plumes of black smoke rose from the mountain. I looked from Edurne to Zuzen and scratched my head. "Does anyone want to fill me in on this?"

"We've been trying to tell you." Zuzen pointed with his staff. "The mountain is angry."

"There's a fire in the mines," Bakar said by way of explanation. His baleful gaze never left Edurne, who huddled close behind me. "A fire she and her friends started when they angered the spirit of the mountain."

I looked back at Edurne. "Do you have any idea what he's talking about?"

Edurne said nothing, but the expression on her face told me she did. I tapped the crystal ball to activate it. "Ezella, you wouldn't happen to see some sort of angry mountain spirit, would you?"

"*All I see is a lot of fire and smoke. Wait, there's something—Bolt, Sky, hold on!*"

Her gyrocopter banked hard to the left, tilting the bird almost completely sideways. Even with such a sudden maneuver, she barely avoided being struck by a flaming chunk of black rock that sailed through the air. The rock—coal, I assumed—plummeted to the ground and exploded in the village green.

More fiery debris rained down all around us. The mob of villagers scattered, some throwing themselves in the snow, others taking cover in the trees. Bakar and another man of the village shielded Zuzen's frail form with their bodies and attempted to pull him back toward the village. I reached back to take Edurne's hand, but she wasn't there.

"The monster's getting away!" a woman with hair as black as Edurne screamed.

"Someone stop her!" Bakar shouted.

Edurne ran, not away from the village, but toward it. I cursed and took off after her, but the knee-deep snow was a problem. "Asheater, stay close to her!"

With a bark, Asheater took off, melting a path through the snow that I could follow. *Good girl!* I'd have to adorn the old crematory oven she slept in with asphodel flowers when we got back to the city. They were her favorite.

A flaming chunk of coal exploded next to me, and I beat at the embers that struck my thick robe. *If we get back to the city*, I corrected.

Edurne was quite far ahead of me, and she reached the village green well before I did. By this time two of the homes had caught fire, their thatched roofs burning despite the dampness from melted snow. She scrambled up onto the roof of the closest one with the speed that comes with familiarity. Without hesitation, she beat at the flames with her hands.

My heart caught in my throat, but only for a moment. A mortal or even a regular ghoul would be severely burned, but a shiver...

The fire sputtered and extinguished at her touch, the glowing embers soon replaced with the sheen of frozen water. She ran to the next piece of blackened thatch and put it out, then leaped to the roof of the adjacent home and started to beat out the flames there, too.

Asheater circled the home, but made no move to climb. She certainly could, but she must have been worried about interfering with Edurne's magic.

The door to the home opened, and an old woman came out and shook her fist up at Edurne. "Get off my roof!"

"Grandma Chloe, I'm just trying to help!" Edurne shouted. "I'm being careful—"

"I don't want help from a monster!" Chloe scooped a rock off the ground and hurled it at Edurne. "Get off my roof!"

The rock struck Edurne on the shoulder, but she continued working. Chloe reached for another stone, but stopped at Asheater's low growl. She took one look at the imposing beast and ran back into her house, far faster than I expected of her. Then again, I'd been on the receiving end of Asheater's tender mercies back when she was terrorizing the ashlings of Necrolopolis by gobbling them up, urns and all. I knew full well how…motivating her presence could be to someone on the wrong side of those teeth.

Asheater twisted her neck to look back at me. Her gaze drifted upward, and she barked. I threw myself to the side and heard something strike the ground I'd been standing on. Hot debris rained down on my head. I rolled around to shake the bits of burning coal off me. Embers popped and sizzled in the snow. *Mortus, what a pain.*

When I sat up a moment later, a shadow fell over me. I looked up and saw a huge fireball hurtling my way, much too large for me to scramble out of the way of. I raised my hands to ward it off, but knew my magic wouldn't work against flames.

"Mr. Necromancer!" Edurne threw herself in front of me, her blackened hands held up toward the fireball. Tendrils of ice spread from her fingertips and coalesced into a round shield several feet wide. "Please work," she whispered, her voice almost lost in the chaos around us.

The giant fireball exploded against the ice shield with an ear-splitting shriek. A spiderweb of cracks formed along the shield's surface, and the impact threw Edurne into me. I pushed on her to keep her from falling. The cold from her body pierced my leather gloves and bit into flesh. I grimaced, but held on as she sank to the ground. The shield shattered into ice crystals as her power waned.

"Are…are you all right, Mr. Necromancer?" she asked in a weary tone.

"I am, thanks to you." I was impressed. I'd never seen a shiver with that kind of magical power before, certainly not a newly made one. There was a school of thought among necromancers that the powers imbued to an undead—if any—were directly tied to two things: the type of elemental power that either resulted in their death or consumed their body afterwards, and the depth of the desire that tied the spirit to the mortal coil.

"Are *you* all right?" I asked her. "You expended a lot of magic there."

"Is that what that was?" Edurne hugged herself. "Ever since the avalanche, I've been so cold, and nothing warms me up. Worse, I suck the warmth from those around me." She looked up, as if now realizing our proximity. "I'm sorry. You're probably freezing."

"I'm fine," I lied, and hoped she couldn't see me shivering through my thick robe. I stood, dusted myself off, and extended a hand. "Let me help you up." When she hesitated, I added, "I deal with people far colder than you on a daily basis, Edurne." That was true, even if the context wasn't quite what she imagined.

She reached out with one of her blackened hands, and I grabbed it. The ice in her veins lanced into my own, but I kept my face neutral as I lifted her to her feet. I had to contend with so many weird sensations around the undead—from tingling numbness when a spirit passed through, to stinging burns when handling ashlings, to slimy skin when too close to a well-ripened ghoul—that this was another uncomfortable part of the job.

A knot of villagers trudged through the snow in our direction, led by Elder Zuzen and Bakar. I sighed. It was time to deal with another uncomfortable part of the job. Edurne saw them coming and tensed up. "It'll be all right," I assured her.

Asheater chose that moment to trot over and place herself right in front of Edurne. Both girl and beast studied one another, their heads cocked to the side. Tentatively, Edurne held out a hand. Asheater raised her nose and sniffed the extended fingertips before she licked them with her dry, ashy tongue.

Edurne giggled. "It tickles, but I'm not feeling much warmth." She looked around at the melted snow. "Despite how hot you appear to be. Why is that?"

"Your elemental abilities are at odds with one another," I explained. "In a way, you cancel each other out, although others will feel the heat she generates and the cold you radiate." I know I did. One half of me was sweating, while the other was chilled to the bone.

She chewed her lower lip and stared at the ground. "I see," she said in a flat tone.

I wanted to say more, but my crystal ball buzzed. *"Addy, Ezella here. You ready for extraction yet?"*

There was nothing I wanted more than to be away from this village, but I couldn't take Edurne against her will. Not only would Mina highly frown on that, I doubted we could make it far if she wanted to freeze us out. Considering how powerful she was, I doubted if even Asheater could protect us from her cold magic, not unless she attacked. Seeing how she'd already become friends with the girl, I doubted we'd get any help from that corner. *"Not yet. Stay close and keep an eye on that mine. I fear we're going to need to do something about that before we can leave."*

"Who are you talking to?"

I jumped. Edurne still stood next to me, a quizzical expression on her pale face. I had forgotten she was there. "I'm talking with the goblin lady who came with me on the gyrocopter." I pointed up. "See?"

She looked up. "Oh! I didn't realize anyone else was on it. I assumed it was your pet dragon."

Just how backwoods was this village? "No, no pet dragons. Asheater's enough trouble for me as it is."

Asheater thumped her tail against the ground.

Edurne's firefighting efforts earned us a tense parley with Elder Zuzen and his cantankerous son, Bakar. Zuzen invited us into his home, but I declined for two reasons. The first was that Edurne's innate coldness would likely suck any heat from the house and make it miserable for those of us there, unless we built one hell of a roaring fire to combat it. The second was that I didn't trust these people as far as I could throw them, and I'd rather be outside so we could run.

Some of the villagers who'd been hounding us moments ago hovered close by in small groups, but most had returned to their homes to inspect for damage and to gather supplies in case they needed to evacuate. I wasn't the only one concerned about having to run, although my reasons were quite different than theirs.

Elder Zuzen read over the letter from Mina and signed by their nation's king. He grunted. "It appears to be legitimate." He handed it back to me. "You wanted to talk, necromancer, so talk. What do you want?"

*For you to have a better attitude?* "I've already stated it: I'm taking Edurne with me." I glanced in her direction. "For some reason, though, she feels obligated to help you resolve your problem with the mine, so we're stuck here." I surveyed the charred buildings. "It's looking like we'll have to work together to see this through."

"You intend to help us?"

"In spite of my better judgment, yes." I placed a hand on the skull brooch that held my robe closed. "To do that, I need information. What's going on in your mine?"

Zuzen and Bakar shared a glance. "There was a collapse about three days ago." Bakar crossed his powerful arms and stared at the snow-covered ground. "A partial one, but bad enough that it trapped thirteen miners."

I shuddered. The threat of being buried alive was a very real one in Necrolopolis, especially in certain neighborhoods. "Have you gotten them out?"

Bakar shook his head. "We managed to extract three of them, but the other ten are a lot deeper in. Getting to them will be difficult, with our aether lamps gone, and with that creature—"

"Bakar!" Zuzen snapped.

Bakar shut his mouth with an audible click. I looked from one to the other. "You're not still talking about Edurne, are you?"

Both of them refused to look at me. "All right," I said, "let's try a different question. Does this have something to do with the explosion that nearly burned your village down just now?"

"That's our fault," Edurne said in a small voice. Ice crystals formed around her eyes, the shiver equivalent of tears. "No, it's *my* fault, and because of that, they're both dead."

"You're damn right it's your fault—" Bakar began.

"Let her speak," Zuzen said in a weary tone. I wondered how often he had to do that with his hotheaded son.

Edurne took a deep breath and exhaled a crystalline mist. "Papa Hodei is one of the ten still trapped in the mine. Falgur—"

"Don't you dare blame my boy!" Bakar took a step forward.

Asheater snarled, ears back and teeth bared like the wolf she resembled.

"Bakar, enough!" Zuzen barked, even as I said, "Asheater, down!"

Bakar and Asheater continued to glare, but they made no move toward one another. "Go on," I urged Edurne.

"Falgur didn't think we could get to them from the main entrance, but no one would listen to him. I remembered there might be another way in, and when I told him, Igon wanted to tag along. Igon is—*was* my brother." She clutched at the hem of her skirt with her blackened hands. "I was to be buried next to him, and then...."

*And then you reanimated.* I didn't voice the thought. "What did you, Falgur, and Igon set out to do?"

That shook her out of her reverie. "There's an old ventilation shaft that was sealed up decades before we were born." She pointed to the far side of the mountain. "I came across it while picking herbs one spring."

Zuzen sucked in a breath, but said nothing. Before I could prompt him, Ezella asked, *"Was this old shaft on the north side of the mountain? Say, a hundred or so feet higher than the mine's entrance?"*

Zuzen jumped, as did a few other villagers. "Where did that come from?" Zuzen demanded. "Who are you talking to?"

"Yes, that's right," Edurne said, ignoring Zuzen.

*"We saw a lot of fire and smoke coming from there."*

"We didn't mean to start a fire. We—" Edurne's voice caught in her throat. "*I* don't know how it happened. One moment Falgur and Igon were tearing away at this old paper covering the wood planks blocking the entrance, and the next moment the planks burst into flames and exploded." She pressed her face into her hands. "They were both engulfed! I tried to reach them to put out the flames, to protect them! But the avalanche hit, and then I woke up like this."

She wept for a moment, and no one said anything. Zuzen looked away, as did Bakar. Edurne's mother, Nekane, hovered close by, a look of revulsion on her face. I shook my head. Mortus, I knew prejudice against the undead was a real thing, and even warranted in some cases, but this was beyond the pale. *That's your daughter!* I wanted to scream at her, but I knew it wouldn't do any good. If a mother could be turned against her child like this, words alone wouldn't bring her back. Personal experience had taught me that, when I was born into a family of famous life mages. That they'd brought a necromancer into the world was still a stain on the family honor to this day.

Something in Edurne's testimony brought me out of my brooding. "Paper covering? That sounds like a ward."

Edurne and Bakar both stared at me blankly, but Zuzen had understanding in his grim expression. "Does that ring any bells?" I asked him.

"It was…a long time ago." Zuzen closed his eyes. "Back when I was still a swaddled babe, when my grandpa served as Ikatz's headman. In those days, so the story goes, our coal veins ran dry. We could subsist on charcoal production for a while, but without the mine, the village would inevitably die. Grandpa and a select few men dug deeper and deeper, searching for something, anything that could replace the exhausted coal veins.

"What they unearthed was something beyond our ken: living fire. What you magician types call…emelentals?"

"Elementals," I corrected. My stomach twisted. That was *not* what I wanted to hear.

"*That's not what I want to hear,*" Ezella said, echoing my thoughts.

"Can you fight it?"

"*If I'd known that was what we'd be up against, we could've come properly equipped. It'll be rough with what we've got. Wooden ballista bolts would only be a snack to this thing.*"

"How did your ancestors seal away a fire elemental, and why?" I asked. "If it had been a threat, it'd have been easier to call a mage in to destroy it."

Zuzen looked uncomfortable. "As Grandpa explained it, the king depended on our coal mine for its quality and production capacity. When rumors began to spread that it was exhausted, he sent a team of court mages to assist us. They arrived at the same time the elemental was discovered." He shrugged. "The king's court...took care of it for us, in a way that benefited everyone."

"That still doesn't explain why you didn't destroy it."

"The embers of fire elementals yield the highest quality coal, and in great quantities, enough to recharge a vein whenever one perishes." Zuzen shrugged. "Our mine was exhausted, and now it is full once more. So it would have remained, so long as that monster was producing for us."

Producing? My knowledge of elemental spirits was limited, but from what I knew, fire elementals didn't produce anything except—my eyes widened. "You mean all this time you were using its *offspring* to fuel your mine?"

Edurne gasped, as did a couple of the other villagers. The rest looked grim-faced, but resolved. To them, it was similar to raising cattle for slaughter. They didn't know that elemental spirits were on a different level than simple animals. Not quite sentient, like Humans and Elves and Orcs, but close enough that forced captivity of one was revolting to me.

The more I learned about Ikatz, the more I wondered that Edurne had a heart at all.

A deep rumbling echoed from the mountain, and a pillar of fire shot up into the sky. *"Contact!"* Ezella called. *"Addy, the elemental has left the mine, and it is angry!"*

A shining light appeared amid the trees between Ikatz village and the mine entrance. I pulled the spyglass from my robe and put it to my eye. Even in broad daylight, the fire elemental burned so bright that it hurt my eyes to look directly at it. I don't know much about elemental magic, other than what little I've seen from my days at the academy and from magicians who visit Necrolopolis. The elementals they summoned ranged in shape, size, and power based on the talent of the magician in question. Wild elementals, however, tended to be more powerful the older they got.

As fire never quite stayed the same from moment to moment, so it was with the elemental. One moment it was a giant fireball hovering over the ground, the next it looked like a woman wreathed in flames. When it reached out to touch a tree, shrub, or something combustible, hands and arms would appear out of the mass, and the bulbous flames would melt back into a distinctly feminine form.

As it touched a stout evergreen, the bark around its fingers began to char. The elemental stared down the hill toward Ikatz Village, and the hatred in its orange-eyed gaze was palpable, enough that more than one villager staggered from the weight of it. I grimaced. *This thing means to kill everyone here, and who can blame it, after the way it was treated?*

Ezella brought her gyrocopter around until she faced the fire elemental, on roughly the same level as the mine entrance looming above and behind the creature. The two auto-ballistae now hung outside the doors on either side of the vehicle. Boltchucker manned one, Skyglider the other. They aimed their weapons at the fire elemental and shot. Within seconds, two dozen ballista bolts had been launched. To my surprise, all the bolts went too high, each one sailing over the head of its target.

To make things more confusing, Boltchucker and Skyglider seemed happy with themselves over the crystal ball.

Another booming rumble sounded, then an avalanche of snow and rock tumbled down the mountainside and crashed into the fire elemental. I ran my spyglass over the mountain and saw what was left of a huge pile of rocks and boulders that had been cleft from the mountain face, likely when the mine was built. They'd somehow managed to strike all the points needed to destabilize the pile and cause an avalanche of rock.

The victory was short-lived, however. Fire burst through the gaps in the rock as the whole pile exploded. The fire elemental surged out of the hole, hand raised high, and pointed at Ezella's gyrocopter. A lance of fire shot out of its palm and seared the right side of the craft.

Ezella evaded the next three strikes and disappeared over the tree line.

Several of the villagers cried out in shock. I gaped. *How in the name of Mortus are we supposed to defeat* that?

"It's all right," Edurne whispered to herself, her voice barely audible. Her hands were clenched at her sides as she stared up at the fire elemental. "It's all right. Don't be afraid. Don't be afraid."

The fire elemental turned toward the village, but it jumped sideways and looked up. I followed its gaze and saw water dripping from the uppermost branches of an evergreen it had been standing beneath. The elemental had generated so much fire and heat that the snow around and above it was melting. It danced to the side a few more times until it stood out in the open.

*Oh ho ho.* I knelt next to Edurne. "There is a way we can defeat it."

Edurne looked at me, a surge of hope in her frosted eyes. "What can you do?"

"Not just me. *We.* Together." I pointed at the skull brooch. "I'm a necromancer. One of my jobs is to support the undead in battle. If you form a contract with me, you can share my power."

Edurne cocked her head to the side. "I don't understand."

"Remember how you felt drained after creating that ice shield? Also, good job on that." I patted her on the shoulder. "Not many people could pull that off, especially considering how new to this you are."

"I didn't do anything special," Edurne said. "I did what I thought was right."

"You imagined what might work, then you made it happen." I tapped my head and my chest. "That takes both mind and heart working in concert, something most can't handle, at least not without extensive meditation and training. And even with that, you will quickly grow exhausted until you learn to better control it."

"That makes sense." Edurne paused. "I think."

I smiled. "That's where I come in. Forming a contract with me means I can help you. Where you might grow fatigued from using a little magic, with my power, you'd be capable of many more spells before you ran dry. By combining our abilities, we should be able to defeat this thing."

"Let's do it!" Edurne demanded.

"Not so fast," I said, and my words were almost lost in a shriek from the fire elemental. I removed my left glove and pulled a small dagger from my robe. I pricked my index finger with the blade and showed her the bead of blood. "You need to understand two things: the first is that the contract is irreversible. We will forever be linked, so long as you're tied to this mortal coil, and I am alive. I will never compel you to do anything against your will. Mina—that's what I call my boss—would do worse than kill me if I did."

"Thank you for that," Edurne said impatiently. "What's the second thing?"

I used my dagger to point at the fire elemental and the fully engulfed tree. "We'll need to get close to that thing. Your ice magic is critical to our victory, but it's got to be a close, in-your-face kind of plan."

Edurne bit her blue lower lip, her eyes shifting from me to the rampaging fire elemental. She watched as it reached out and engulfed a sizable shrub in a giant hand made of flames. She shuddered, but nodded. "I'll do what I must. Do I need to prick my finger, too?"

"No, only the necromancer needs to do that." I took her hand and held my bloody finger over her. "Will you entrust your soul to me, Edurne?"

"Yes."

I dabbed my blood on her palm. The drop of crimson quickly disappeared, absorbed into her frostbitten skin. "It is done."

"I don't feel any different." She frowned at her hand.

I closed my eyes and opened up the well of my magic. As I did, I reached out and touched the blue core of Edurne's power. She had a tremendous reserve, but it was partly depleted from her earlier adventures. I imagined myself taking a bucket of black liquid from my magic well and pouring it over her core. Black mixed with blue, discoloring her core for a moment. Then the blue returned, pure and bright. I opened my eyes. "Do you feel that?"

"Yes." Edurne's expression was a mixture of shock and excitement. She looked at her hands. "I feel like I can do anything now."

"Good girl." I looked at Asheater. "I'm going to need your help, too. You ready?"

Asheater thumped her tail.

"Also a good girl." I patted them both on the head, then tapped the crystal ball hanging from my neck. "Ezella, how're you holding up?"

*"Some scorching on the fuselage, but nothing that can't be buffed out."* There was a pause. *"Oh, and Skyglider got burned."*

*"Hey! Don't treat me like an afterthought!"*

Boltchucker laughed. *"But you* are *an afterthought, my friend! Now, hold still while I treat that."*

*"Ow, ow, ow ow ow!"*

*"What do you need, Addy?"* Ezella said, her voice serious despite the antics going on behind her.

I smiled at Edurne. "Our little shiver lady could use a lift."

\* \* \*

Wind whipped about my face, and it was all I could do to keep from screaming in terror. *Mortus, how in the Eighteen Hells did my day end up like this?*

Edurne and I both hung *suspended* from Ezella's gyrocopter. Boltchucker had lashed stout rope to an anchor post in the passenger cabin that he then wrapped around my torso and shoulders. He rigged a similar harness for Edurne and attached it to my harness. She dangled from my chest, her eyes closed as she focused on her magic. I wanted to close my eyes, but for different reasons. I kept them open and focused on my shovel's white blade to keep from looking down at the ground far, far below.

I'm sure I've mentioned this before now, but if not, let me say I really don't like flying.

I felt lightheaded, and not just from the height and the wind buffeting me so hard it made breathing difficult. Edurne had been using her magic since we boarded the gyrocopter, and she was drawing on my reserves to fuel her spells. I kept my shovel pressed tight against my body and trie—

A wave of nausea hit me, and I closed my eyes to keep from getting sick.

Through my crystal ball, Boltchucker kept me updated on the movements down below.

"*Elemental's on the move! Asheater's got its attention. Hoo, boy, is it mad now! What did she do to it?*"

Since I was afraid to look, I assumed Asheater had sucked up a bit of the fire elemental's essence. "Where are they?"

"*Still running through the trees at the moment. The elemental's shooting at Asheater...Oh, Asheater tore into its flank! Now she's running.*"

"And the villagers?" I asked Skyglider. It was his job to keep an eye on them.

"They've made a break for the mine. The fires have guttered out now that the elemental's distracted. Looks like they've split into two groups, one headed to the main entrance, the other to the old ventilation shaft."

Good. I wasn't sure how much of the blaze in and around the mine was under the elemental's control, but I was glad to see most of it was. Elemental magic was strange that way. The instant the power fueling it disappeared, so too would the magic. Like the shield Edurne had made. It didn't matter that there was plenty of wood and other combustibles for the fire to consume.

"Asheater's out in the open!" Boltchucker reported. "The elemental's hot on her heels."

"Get ready," I murmured to Edurne.

"The elemental cleared the tree line," Boltchucker reported. "It's almost where we need it to be...It's here!"

I fought back the nausea and the fear and forced myself to look down. "Drop it, Edurne!"

With a grunt, Edurne released the giant ice dome she'd constructed. It crashed down on top of the fire elemental, totally trapping it. "Lower us!" I shouted into the crystal ball.

"Woah, Addy." I could hear the grimace in Ezella's voice as she complied with my instructions. "Not so loud. These pointy ears of mine are pretty sensitive, you know."

She lowered the gyrocopter. At the same time, Boltchucker extended the rope. Within seconds, we hovered mere inches over the ice dome. Already it was cracking and melting from the intense heat of the trapped fire elemental. Through the transparent ice, I could see the elemental's form writhing and twisting as runoff from the dome poured over it. It screamed, the noise muffled beneath the thick barrier surrounding it.

I cut the line connecting us to the gyrocopter, and we dropped the last couple inches onto the dome. I slipped, stabbed the point of my shovel into the ice, and went to one knee. Edurne dropped to her knees and pressed her hands against the dome's surface. Power surged through us both, and the dome solidified, and even grew thicker than it had been before.

Asheater circled the dome, whining deep in her throat. She wanted to help, but didn't want to interfere with Edurne's magic. I silently urged her to stay back. Mortus willing, she'd be needed in a few minutes, but that was only if we pulled this off.

The ice groaned and trembled as it melted, cracked, and reformed over and over again beneath our kneeling forms. I held Edurne tight against me, more to support my own waning strength than to stabilize her. She kept her hands pressed flat against the top of the dome, frostbitten skin glowing with aethereal blue light. I could feel my power passing through her and into the ice as she kept up the pressure. "Please work," she whispered.

Underneath the dome, the fire elemental shrieked and hammered against the melting ice surrounding it. Arms and legs made of sizzling, sputtering fire lashed out in every direction. A fiery fist struck the top of the dome. The impact popped my shovel free of the dome and nearly shook us from our position. I spread my left foot far from my right knee to keep my balance as Edurne poured more of our collective magic into the dome. Within seconds, the crack the fire elemental had made in the ice resealed.

"Please work," Edurne said, louder this time.

The fire elemental's form had once glowed a bright orange, but now that color had dulled and darkened across huge parts of its body. The constant rain of ice melt had weakened it significantly, but

I knew it was far too early to celebrate. A wounded animal was a most dangerous one, after all.

As if it had read my thoughts, the fire elemental's body ballooned outward, swelling to fill the space of the dome. The whole dome shook as the elemental slammed into it. It shrank down to a tiny, white-hot ball, then blew outward. Again, the dome trembled, and we were nearly unseated.

The glow in Edurne's hands grew brighter, and I felt the tug of energy increase. My vision blurred, and I struggled to keep my head up. "Please work!" she shouted, though it sounded far away in my ears.

The third time the elemental slammed its body against the dome, cracks formed all through the ice. The fourth time, large splits appeared. Edurne tried to keep up with it, but the desperate elemental had increased its tempo and continued to batter at the dome from all directions. Edurne groaned and pressed her hands so hard against the dome that her skin fused with the ice. "It has to work. It has to work! It can't end like this! Not after Falgur and Igon died! Not after I lost everything!"

With a shriek, the fire elemental pressed itself against the fracturing dome and pushed with all its might. New cracks formed, and existing ones grew larger and larger. The ice groaned and squealed.

Edurne's magic faded as my reserves ran dry. She sucked in a deep breath and shouted, "Don't let our deaths be in vain, Miss Ezella!"

The dome shattered. Edurne and I were launched clear of the wounded fire elemental. I pulled Edurne close, and we struck the ground and rolled several yards downhill before the piled snow halted our descent. The elemental loomed over us, its swollen form sputtering with wet, smoky flame.

Ezella's gyrocopter loomed overhead. *"You heard the lady!"* she said through the crystal ball. *"Light it up!"*

*"Get some!"* Boltchucker shouted. *"Get some, get some!"* Skyglider echoed.

The goblin gunners loosed their ballista bolts, one after the other. A volley of glimmering lances sailed through the air, some crashing into trees or snow, but most finding their mark. The ammunition wasn't made of wood like the ones they'd expended in the failed attempt to bury and smother the elemental. These ice bolts had been made by Edurne before she set about crafting the dome. They pierced the fire elemental's weakened body and drove solid ice straight into whatever passed for a heart.

The elemental screamed in pain, and its body expanded to twice the size I'd seen it. I pulled Edurne close, sure it would explode, but instead its form crumbled. The flames disappeared into puffs of smoke, leaving a smoldering ember that pulsed with a light that hurt to look at. "Now, Asheater," I ordered.

Asheater ran forward, opened her maw wider than a real dog ever could, and swallowed the ember in one gulp. Yellow-orange light emanated from her eyes and nostrils as her body expanded to ridiculous proportions. Then she belched out a wave of heat and returned to her normal size. She turned toward me, her tongue lolling out of her mouth. "Did I do good?" her expression seemed to ask.

"Good girl." I held out my hand to her, and she walked over and butted her head against my fingers.

The villagers cheered and whooped for joy. Husbands and wives hugged and kissed, brothers and friends clapped each other on the back, and more than a few dropped to their knees to pray. Some of Ikatz's children joined in the celebration, while the rest stared in amazement at the raw display of emotion from the usually taciturn adults.

"We did it, Mr. Necromancer!" Edurne spun in a circle, her frostbitten arms thrown wide as she laughed. "We did it!"

I couldn't help but smile. She was right. We had done it, by the grace of Mortus, and any other god who was watching.

The celebration continued for several minutes. Ezella landed her gyrocopter close by so she and Boltchucker could tend to Skyglider's wounds. From where I was standing, he appeared to have been burned on his right side, but not too badly. Goblins were not nearly so regenerative as trolls, but they still healed faster than humans. He would be fine. I just prayed the gyrocopter didn't stink of burnt goblin flesh the whole way home.

Edurne's laughter caught in her throat, and I turned to see what she was staring at. The rescue team had returned, and with them came the ten miners who'd been trapped. Nekane and some of the other village women ran forward to greet them, some carrying canteens and skins of water, others lugging baskets of food and bandages. Nekane embraced a tall man with Edurne's light complexion. "Looks like your father made it," I said.

Edurne nodded, but said nothing. Her blue eyes glimmered as she watched her father and mother's reunion. *So, the woman actually is capable of love*, I thought but didn't voice. Edurne had been through enough on account of her mother. While Nekane spoke with her husband and pointed our way, I only hoped her father proved to be more loving. What had Edurne called him? Hodei?

Nekane must have also shared the news of Igon's passing, for Hodei looked grief-stricken even from here. I had no offspring, but I'd counseled many in Necrolopolis who had, and it wasn't easy, nor did it get easier with the passage of time. Still, he had a daughter, if he would only accept her in her current state.

Edurne must have been thinking the same thing, for her expression alternated between elated smiles at her father's rescue and pensive frowns at what his reaction to her would be. Without thinking, I found myself holding her hand. The fingers were cold even through my gloves, but our link made it where it no longer hurt.

After a few minutes, Hodei left Nekane and started toward us. Edurne squeezed my hand, and I squeezed back. "It'll be all right," I murmured.

"Edurne, my girl!" Hodei called. He held out his arms as if expecting an embrace, though he was so far away. "I hear we have you to thank for our escape, and for the village's safety. That's my girl."

"Papa, it's good to see you." Edurne scrubbed at her eyes, then grinned. "We were so worried when the mine collapsed."

"It was a tough thing, girl." Hodei grinned, too. "You came through for us. You and Falgur and—" His voice caught. "And Igon, too."

Edurne's face scrunched up. "We just wanted you and the others to be safe."

"I know." He was about twenty paces from us now, and now he stopped. "I know, girl. You did good."

Hodei's expression bothered me. He was all smiles for his daughter, but there was something about his red-rimmed eyes…then it clicked like the tumblers on my office door lock. He wasn't looking at Edurne or me. He was looking *behind* us.

I spun on my heel, dragging Edurne behind me as I brought my shovel around. The flat of the blade struck an arm with a jarring crunch. Something dropped into the snow, and the man—one of Zuzen's bodyguards—screamed and clutched at his broken arm.

"What in Mortus's name is this?" Ezella looked up from tending to Skyglider, her green face full of fury. She pointed. "Addy, get down!"

I shouldered Edurne to the ground and placed myself on top of her as a soft *twang* filled the air, followed by a dull *thunk*. A crossbow quarrel had buried itself in a tree stump nearby, directly in front of where we'd stood an instant before. I looked up and saw the shooter in the doorway of the closest home. He cranked back the winch on his crossbow so he could load the next shot.

Two crossbow bolts sailed through the air in the man's direction. One shattered the window, while the other embedded itself in the doorjamb. He ran into his home and slammed the door behind him.

I looked at the gyrocopter. Boltchucker had retrieved crossbows for himself and Skyglider, who sat propped in his gunner's seat. Both were reloading their crossbows with great haste. "Mr. Adelvell, Miss Edurne, get back here!" Boltchucker called. "Boss lady's gettin' the gyro spun up!"

Asheater hopped out of the passenger compartment and started to run, but her movements were sluggish, and had been ever since she ate the fire elemental's ember core. I had no idea how a beast like her digested stuff, but I knew it'd be awhile before she was back in top form. "Stay there, Asheater!" I ordered. "Back in the gyrocopter!"

I climbed to my feet and pulled Edurne up. "Come on, time to go." Well past time.

Edurne didn't move. She stared at Hodei, anguish in her piercing blue eyes. "Papa, why?"

Hodei looked equally pained, but that look was tempered with another emotion: revulsion. He wasn't sad over what he'd just been party to. He was mourning the loss of his children. *Both* his children, including the one right in front of him.

"Get them!" Zuzen shouted, his booming voice at odds with his frail body. He pointed at Edurne and me. "We can't let word get out that a filthy undead came from our village! It would ruin us with our neighbors!"

Four men charged at us, with Bakar leading the way. "Kill the monster!" one of the bystanders shouted, while Nekane screamed, "Kill it! My family's suffered enough!"

Anger I hadn't felt in a long time burned within me, and the fatigue that had weighed me down faded. I pushed Edurne toward the gyrocopter, then rushed to meet our attackers. One of the men hadn't expected that, and he faltered. A second man slammed into him, and the two went down in a heap. Bakar and the fourth man kept running. The fourth man reached me first and swung a pickaxe at my head. I ducked and kicked him in the exposed midsection. He doubled over, breath gone from his lungs. A quick rap across the forehead with the flat of my shovel knocked him out.

Bakar charged headlong at me, hunting knife thrusting. I dodged, but Bakar followed. He slashed and thrust again and again, staying close enough that I couldn't easily swing my shovel. I deflected and blocked as best I could while we worked our way through the thick snow. Pain lanced along my cheek, arm, and side, and I gritted my teeth against what I hoped were minor wounds.

He attempted to thrust his knife into my chest again, but he stumbled on something in the snow. Seizing the opportunity, I tripped him with the haft of my shovel. He stumbled past me, then one of his other companions lunged at me. I swung my shovel and cracked him in the face with it. The final companion tried to strike me with an axe, but I caught the blow on the shovel blade. The force of the strike reverberated up my arms, and I almost dropped my shovel. I kicked him in the knee and struck his chin with an underhand blow from the shovel's butt. He fell flat on his back, stunned.

I whirled around as Bakar tried to stab me in the back. My return strike sent his knife flying. My second swept his legs out from under him again. When he landed on his back, I stomped my boot into his stomach and raised my shovel to deliver a killing blow. He deserved it. They all deserved it. This whole Mortus-forsaken village deserved—

Icy arms encircled my waist. "Mr. Necromancer, *stop!*"

At the last instant, I shifted and drove the shovel several inches into the hard-packed ground next to Bakar's head. His eyes bulged out of his head as he looked from me to the razor-sharp blade. He held his hands close to his face, palms open in a pleading gesture. "Please," he begged.

"After all she's done for you," I snapped, "*this* is how you repay her?"

Edurne's arms tightened around my midsection. "Please, Mr. Necromancer," she repeated. "It's all right."

"Listen to the girl, Mr. Adelvell!" Zuzen called. He stood about 30 feet away, crooked body leaning against an equally crooked staff. He held out a shaking hand. "Please don't harm my son. Haven't we suffered enough?"

"Oh, so *now* she's a girl to you?" I snarled. "Before, she was a monster, but now she's a girl." And suffered? They were the reason they suffered! Their ancestors had trapped a fire elemental and tortured it to fill and refill the coal veins running through their misbegotten mine. Now they were tormenting an innocent girl for the crime of refusing to stay dead so she could help them.

Edurne's arms continued to grip me, reminding me of my true purpose here. I ground my teeth in frustration, but lifted my shovel and stepped away from Bakar. "Get out of my sight," I told him in a voice as icy as Edurne's limbs.

Bakar scrambled to his feet and hurried back to his father's side. The other three picked themselves up and limped back toward the village. One by one, the villagers disappeared into their homes. Silence descended on Ikatz, but for the slow turning of the gyrocopter's rotors as it spun up to full speed.

Even after Zuzen and Bakar retreated indoors, Hodei showed no signs of leaving. He alternated between looking at Edurne and staring at his feet, his coal-dusted face red with what I hoped was shame. Finally, Nekane pulled him back toward their home deep inside the village. She never once looked our way, never once tried to catch a last glimpse of her daughter. To her, Edurne was well and truly dead.

At last Edurne pulled away from me. She took a few steps toward the waiting gyrocopter. "Mr. Necromancer, am I truly dead?" she asked, pitching her voice to be heard over the spinning blades.

"In a sense." I wondered what had brought this on. "You've died, but your soul has yet to cross over. That makes you undead. Certainly not alive, but not quite dead."

"I see." She clasped her hands behind her back. "And the dead don't feel pain, do they?"

The patch of skin between my shoulder blades itched as I thought about the one villager's crossbow. We were very vulnerable, standing still out here, and me most of all. "No, not in the way the living do." Certainly spirits and skeletons didn't, and neither did ashlings and mummies. I could go on about how some ghouls and zombies reported pain-like sensations from time to time, but even that was limited.

"If that's the case—" Edurne paused, her clasped hands tightening into fists. At last she turned around to face me, frost rimming her eyes. She placed a hand over her heart. "If that's the case, then why does my chest hurt so much?"

She threw her arms around me and wept. Ice crystals fell from her eyes and bounced on the snow or shattered on the exposed earth. I patted her back and tried to think of something comforting to say, but all I managed was, "There, there. There, there."

Edurne's hands were so cold, yet her heart was so warm. Why couldn't they see that? I blinked away sudden tears. *Mortus, why couldn't her own parents see it?*

After a moment, I steered her toward the gyrocopter. "Come on," I whispered. "Let's be rid of this place."

She deserved far better, and they didn't deserve her at all.

\* \* \* \* \*

## Benjamin Tyler Smith Biography

Benjamin spends his days creating maps for cemeteries and his evenings herding the undead and battling aliens. He is a writer of fantasy and science fiction, with two novels published in Blood Moon Press' Fallen World universe and numerous short stories in anthologies, magazines, and floating about the internet. Many of these short stories are set in his Necrolopolis universe, a dark fantasy world where a necromancer protagonist must keep the peace in a city of the undead. He is currently writing the first set of novels in that universe, as well as working on projects in the shared universes of his fellow travelers of the writing path.

He lives in an area of rural Pennsylvania with more cows than humans as neighbors, ruled over by a benevolent Calico Countess and her feline knight, the Earl of Grey. Helping him maintain this noble estate is a saint of a wife and a beautiful baby girl who absorbs way too much of his productive time.

Follow him at BenjaminTylerSmith.com and join his mailing list for free short stories!

\* \* \* \* \*

# Widow's Feast
# by Casey Moores
## A Deathmage War Story

I strolled through the dark, mangled trees with a hint of a spring in my step. The encounter with my suitor hadn't been mind-blowing, but it had been satisfactory. He certainly hadn't been any kind of conversationalist, but he'd been a fine specimen. A delicious specimen, in fact, who'd been thoroughly entranced by me. He'd gotten the job done, and I was pleased to have met him.

It had been a long time since I'd met another of my kind. Ever since I'd left my own family and all their infighting, I'd remained a very solitary individual. Anyone raised in those conditions would be. This recent encounter had made me contemplative in a way I'd never been. The meeting had given me purpose. Perhaps there was more to life than hiding in a hole and collecting food out of a web.

For now, however, I was still hungry. Insatiable might be a better word. Without much deliberation, I decided to wander by the nearest Human village to pick up a snack on the way home. Odds were, my web would be filled with treats, but I just couldn't wait that long. Besides, Humans were tasty. I'd ponder my future once I'd fed some more.

Thunder echoed across the sky, heralding a storm. For now, it was distant and in the opposite direction from my forest, but it would be best to grab the snack as quickly as possible and get home before it hit.

Picking up the pace, I found myself at a quiet village in a valley well before the thunder got any closer. Truth be told, it didn't seem the thunder had moved at all. Either way, I slowed and kept to the shadows as I approached the town. I hadn't hunted here in a long time, as it was a small village, and a little too close to home. If one such as I made myself too obvious, the lesser creatures were known to form large bands of warriors, and I would become the prey. I hadn't survived as long as I had by drawing attention to myself.

The sun was low and scattered shadows through the trees as I crept toward a stream where two Humans drew water. Long ago, I'd trained myself not to click my mandibles with glee in anticipation of such scrumptious delicacies. The instinct was always there, but it'd be a dead giveaway to my prey. Silent as the wind, I slid up a large tree one leg at a time. Humans were particularly bad at looking up. As soon as I'd approached as close as possible overhead, I'd pounce.

"So you're telling me that's not a storm coming?" asked one of the Humans, a female by the scent.

"Not at all," the other, a male, replied. "It's the start of a war. Lutetia's up in arms again, it seems, and our soldiers have gone out to meet them."

A war? That wasn't good news. I resolved to abandon my web and move far away. Wherever Humans and the other lesser creatures fought wars, the land would be flooded by warriors. The chance of being discovered and hunted increased greatly.

"If they're so close, shouldn't we move away until it's over?" she asked. Her face had flushed with blood. I could practically taste her already. "I know armies of either side are known to take what they want wherever they go. I'd rather not be here when they do."

"Oh, they're not that close at all," the male said. "The cannons have just gotten so much louder. The rider who came through yesterday said that the fighting is happening at Vilseck."

"What?" she replied. "No, I don't believe it! Vilseck is quite a ways away. If the guns are *that* big, so many would die, would they not? I can't even imagine."

"Oh, yes," the male said and smiled, as if he enjoyed speaking of such death. Perhaps he enjoyed the response he was getting from the female, considering his blood had warmed as well. Humans only got this delectable when they were fighting or mating. "The bloodshed will be immense. Whole fields will be covered with the dead."

*Whole fields covered with the dead?*

As a rule, I avoided the lesser creatures when they fought, but I was ravenous. The thought of fields covered in food…

The female gasped and bowed her head to concentrate on her water bucket.

"They won't call you up, will they?" she asked.

The male bowed his as well, let out a long breath, and put an arm around her.

"Hard to say," he said. "For now, I'm too old. But if too many of the able-bodied boys die, they'll call everyone up."

They turned to face each other, and the female tilted her chin up. Both were so flush I could feel their hearts beating. Humans were very vulnerable when mating, but the females were most likely to scream and attract attention. The males would usually try to fight at first, which would leave me the opportunity to dispatch the female and move on to the male before he'd try to shout.

As their lips pressed together, I launched myself from the branches and latched my mandibles onto the female's head. I curled my left legs around the male, who grunted and struggled.

When I felt the female's head crack, I released her and latched onto the male's. The sound of the bones crunching and the feel of the juices splashing into my mandibles was divine. Both were dead within moments.

I could have bitten them a little softer and injected them with venom, so they'd remain alive and fresh. However, this might have given either one the opportunity to shout for help before they died, as the venom took a few seconds to take effect. I also had no interest in keeping them alive—these, I would eat immediately. I wrapped them in silk and carried them deeper into the forest. It was the sweetest meal I'd had in as long as I could remember.

With a full belly, I wandered a little until I found a nice spot to rest. A tree had fallen, leaving a hole in the ground with some roots hanging in the air for good cover. I relaxed as night fell, lulled to sleep by the rhythmic reverberation of what the male Human had called cannons. I'd heard them before and always moved away as quickly as I could. This time, the male's words returned to me.

*Fields of the dead.*

In and of itself, the idea was revolting. Rotting corpses were not only unfulfilling, but made me sick. On the other leg, when Humans and similar creatures battled, the bodies were usually pretty fresh that night. Even better, there was a chance of wounded being left scattered about. It didn't get any fresher than that.

Someone shouted from far away. Another answered them. More shouting slowly grew in a chorus all around. The light of torches illuminated the trees, matched by a dance of shadows as the torch carriers moved about.

There'd been a time when the Humans wouldn't have dared to chase those such as I into dark forests, but the thunder sticks they now carried had made them more and more brazen. A cluster of angry Humans, with torches and thunder sticks, was not my idea of a good time. Home, if I were to go there, was directly through the encroaching Humans. I'd have to go around in a long, circuitous route. Anything caught in my web might be dead and rotting by the time I got there. Meanwhile, there was the promise of a bountiful feast, if only I would disregard my survival instinct and head toward the sounds of the lesser creatures' storm.

Even though I'd just fed, and for the second time that day, my stomach still growled. I was famished.

Toward the storm it would be.

\* \* \*

Just as the male had said, the trek to the source of the thunder was a long way. After that last meal, I remained unfed for most of the distance. Night had fallen by the time I left the forest and entered low, rolling hills. Keeping to the shadows in the valleys, I paralleled the Human roads as best as I could. That way, I would be near any villages on the way. I desperately wished to find another meal in one of them.

However, for some reason, the first town I came to was full of activity. Though most homes were shuttered and locked up, the streets were full of males of all races. They drank and sang late into the evening, yet kept a solid guard on all the roads.

Once, and only once, did I find a short, hairy-footed male who'd wandered away from the well-lit areas. He smelled horrible, his blood tasted bitter, and he was too small to make much of a meal, but it was better than nothing.

As the glow of dawn came over the horizon, I found a low overhang in a hill to reside in for the day. It overlooked the road, but was far enough out that I didn't think any would venture my way. My stomach rumbled and ached, but there was nothing I could do for it.

Not long after the sun had risen, a stream of black-uniformed Humans, half-sized Humans, Dwarves, and Orcs marched by in a seemingly never-ending procession. It was odd to see Dwarves and Orcs in the same army, but I didn't think too hard on the matter. I had a strong desire to rush out, snatch up a few tasty morsels, and run off before any could react. Unfortunately, almost all the beings who passed by were armed with those vicious thunder sticks. They'd blast me to pieces in no time.

A few animals, fleeing the mass of soldiers, wandered up to my little cave several times during the day. Sadly, all seemed to sense me before they got too close and scampered off. Animals were, on average, much more intelligent than the Humans and similar races. When the land darkened, the last of the soldiers stomped away and disappeared into the distance.

By the time the sun set once again, I was dizzy and almost insane with hunger. I crawled out and skittered after the army as fast as my eight legs would take me. A light rain pattered down, which suited me just fine. It was easier to sneak up on the lesser races with sound and visibility diminished by rain.

When I saw torches dancing along the horizon, I shifted further away from the road and worked to circumvent the enormous group. I slowed and became more cautious. Such a large group of soldiers would post scouts and guards around their fringes, as they had in the town. However, from experience, I knew there was a strong chance I could find a small, inattentive group.

Find one, I did. I passed by three such groups in which at least one of the soldiers looked alert, with their thunder sticks held at the ready. While passing those, I remained low and slow. The fourth group, however, consisted of just two soldiers, both of whom sat on the ground with their heads down. I could see one fumbling with some sort of food in a little metal box. I scuttled up to the pair, pressed against the ground, moving a single leg at a time to shift ever closer.

Over the gentle tapping of rain, I heard one of them snoring as I approached.

*Perfect.*

No more than a few feet away, I stretched up, lunged forward, and snatched at the one who was still awake. His skull cracked open, and the insides dribbled into my mandibles. As I wrapped that one in silk to drag away, the other opened his eyes, shouted a warning, and lifted his thunder stick before I could dispatch it. Before he died, his thunder stick made a loud *crack*. I recoiled at the sound, but then realized it had missed me entirely. That was a minor miracle, as my abdomen alone is the size of a pony, but the noise set off a chorus of shouts from all around.

In a hurry, I wrapped just enough silk around the second one to drag him clear, and I carried my food straight away from the soldiers' encampments.

The soldiers were a little soggy from the rain, but they tasted far better than the drunken short one from the village. Even so, it was not enough to satisfy me.

When I tried to return, I found all the army's guards active and vigilant. There would be no sneaking up on any of these groups. Dejected, I backed away from the army and moved on in the direction of the never-ending thunder. This time, when dawn arrived, I made my way into a decent-sized barn. There was no livestock, but it was dry and had an ample attic to hide in. It would do until the next nightfall.

\* \* \*

Fortune smiled upon me well before the next evening. After the shadows had shifted from one side of the barn to the other, I heard the creak and groan of the doors opening at one end. Moments later, they slammed shut again. Curious, I eased my way along the opening in the attic and peered down.

"That's it, we can hide here until the rest of them pass by," someone said. When I leaned far enough forward, I saw a soldier searching the barn. He looked nervous and afraid.

"Are you sure they won't find us here?" another one said. "This isn't too far from the main roads. Besides, what if they have a scrying mage with them?"

"If they have a scrying mage with them, there's no use worrying," the first said. "They'll find us no matter where we go. We'll just rest here until it's dark. In fact—look! There's an attic. If it makes you feel better, we can hide up there until night. Then we'll get as far away from that open graveyard they call the Front as we can."

"But if we go up there, it'll be harder to run if they come looking."

"You can't have it both ways. And stop being so hopeless about everything. We got away from that meat grinder hell. You should be happy. But…your happiness is not my concern. My concern is only that we remain hidden until we can escape farther away. I'm going up there to take a look, at least. Follow me, or not; it's up to you."

*Open graveyard. Meat grinder.* This Front of theirs sounded delightful.

I heard footfalls, followed by the creaking of the ladder. I shrank back and waited. Quiet as a mouse, I moved forward, snatched him off the ladder, and dragged him back before he could make a sound.

"Fritz?" the other one called. "Fritz?"

The ladder creaked again. Moments later, the other one came far enough up the ladder that I could grab him as well. The second one was able to release an earth-rending shriek before I crushed his jaws. While I devoured him, I wondered if the shriek might have alerted more soldiers, but none came for some time afterward.

Later on, just before the sky went dark, one more soldier came into the barn. As he was alone, I had no reservations about crawling down into the barn to gobble him up as well.

Not long after the arrival of the third soldier, and just as I was preparing to leave, I heard angry shouts and the stomp of many boots. A large group of soldiers threw the door aside and stormed into the barn with lanterns and thunder sticks.

"Search the whole building!" one shouted. I assumed that to be the leader. "They can't have gone far, and this is the perfect sort of place to hide if they needed to rest."

Stomping, pounding, and tapping noises permeated the barn as the soldiers spread around. I knew I could've taken out the first one or two that came up, but then the others would be on me. Hungry as I might be, I knew my limitations. Before the team climbed the ladder, I eased my way out a window and scampered quietly down the side. As I moved off, I heard the ladder to the attic groan under the strain of too much weight.

"Oh, milord!" someone said. A gagging sound and a splashing noise followed. Then a putrid scent, sharper and more bitter than that of my victim's voided bowels, drifted through the air.

"Ah!" the leader said. "It seems someone has done our work for us. These poor souls chose the wrong hiding place after they deserted."

"Poor souls, Captain?" someone else said. "Sir, don't you mean no good, craven cowards?"

"Well, yes, of course, Sergeant," the leader answered. "That they were, but I imagine they would've preferred a bullet to the head over this. That said, it might do some good to let this story get around."

"It would make a good warning, sir," another said. "But, sir, where's the beast that did this?"

"Let's hope it's far from here by now," the leader replied. "I wouldn't want to run into it in the dark on the way back to camp. Stick together as you search around, just in case. I don't need to tell you all to maintain high vigilance, do I?"

*I should be so lucky.*

As the sounds of their investigation continued, I crept into an overgrown field of wheat and hurried away.

After another long night of scuttling toward the sound of thunder, I crested a ridge to discover an endless sea of small, white structures. The lesser creatures had erected a massive encampment of soldiers that was larger than anything I'd ever witnessed. My stomach roared at the sight of so much food, yet I knew I couldn't just walk in and take what I wanted.

Looking further out, flashes of light popped up in a sporadic pattern all along the horizon. *That* was where the fighting was. *That* was where all the fresh bodies would be. I wasn't quite sure how I would get to the fields of dying soldiers. When I did, however, I knew I would feast until my belly burst.

\* \* \*

Even more so than when I'd circled the marching soldiers, I had to be extra cautious to avoid the sentries and patrols along the great encampment. These were all far more alert than any I'd come across during the trip. As always, I stayed low, slow, and well clear of the sentries while trying to find a way through.

I didn't soon find a way, but I did find the source of the constant thunder. Evenly spaced along the back of the lesser creatures' army, but unfortunately well-protected, were enormous thunder sticks. They were more like giant thunder trees. Explosions burst out the tops of the trees in a continuous barrage that kept my leg hairs vibrating so hard, I feared they might fall out.

In the same manner as the thunder sticks, I couldn't see anything come out of them, but there were subsequent explosions all around. At first, it seemed strange that the thunder trees would shoot something into the air only to have it land among those who'd fired it.

After a little bit of thought, I concluded that these closer thunder trees must be launching their explosions at the other army, wherever it was, and that other army was similarly launching their own explosions at this army. It was such an odd, yet horrifyingly destructive way to conduct a battle. The lesser creatures could be vicious and barbaric when they chose to be, and they'd only gotten worse over time.

The entire Front, as the soldier in the barn had called it, was a realm of sensory overload. The sounds of the thunder trees and their explosions echoed across the land in a haphazard cacophony. Beneath and around it all were shouts, screams, and cries of all the lesser creatures. These were further interspersed by whistles, drums, and the popping of the thunder sticks. Bursts of light appeared in the sky in a steady rhythm. I couldn't guess at the source.

The stench of the dead wafted through with every gust of wind. The bulk of the scent was revolting— rotting flesh, carrion, feces, and smoke. Every so often, an unusual smell, such as something metallic or wholly unnatural, would drift by. Buried among all those other scents, however, my legs would always detect a hint of fresh blood. There was at least some truth to the rumors that had brought me here.

The sun was returning yet again before I could find a way through the never-ending mass of soldiers. As usual, I searched for a place to spend the day. This close to the great army, however, there didn't seem to be any good options. There were no forests here— only splinters and burned trunks where forests had once been. Every hill and depression was either occupied or surrounded by soldiers. In fact, there were a great number of channels and ditches that it seemed the soldiers had dug themselves.

In desperation, I found myself crouched in a strange, debris-strewn circular depression that was clear of soldiers. I considered they did so because of the torn apart, half-buried dead bodies in the depression. They were old and decayed, so they wouldn't make any sort of meal. I could only hope I'd remain secluded. I nestled against a large metallic canister and rested.

To take my mind off my desperate hunger, I revisited the thoughts I'd begun and forgotten when I'd first set out on this journey. Never before had I had any sort of desire to leave my nest until a few days prior. With no true understanding of why, I'd wandered out into areas I'd never before explored. As if due to some previously undeveloped sense, I'd gone straight to where that male had maintained his nest. I hadn't even known he'd existed, yet I'd found him nonetheless. The purpose of my wanderlust was now obvious.

Ever since that encounter, my stomach had screamed for more sustenance in a way I'd never experienced. Normally, one Human-sized meal would sustain me for several days. In my nest, I'd kept several different animals or creatures alive for days until I became hungry again and chose one to devour. Now, I was always hungry.

I also realized I'd gotten a good deal larger as well. *Heavier*, to be more precise. There was more strain on my legs than usual, and it got worse every day.

I headed toward the source of the greatest danger in perhaps the entire country. However, the fact it was so dangerous also meant that food might be abundant, as the Human in that small town had said. Such a strange turn of events, that the action that seemed most dangerous would give me the greatest chance of survival.

A rock tumbled down the side of my depression, and someone gasped. I twisted in a quick scurry and spotted a soldier standing at the edge. We stared at each other for a long moment. It never aimed its thunder stick at me. The soldier probably contemplated whether or not the thunder stick would be enough to kill me. It would not be.

From my perspective, he looked succulent and delicious, and I was starving. The problem with killing him was that he would probably shoot if I tried. Though he wouldn't cause much damage, the sound would draw more. A lot of thunder sticks *would* bring me down.

The soldier took a step backward, keeping his eyes locked on me. He took another step backward, and soon disappeared from view. I wondered if I should rush out of the hole and find another. Surely, this soldier was heading off to collect more to come back and kill me. That's what they did. On the other leg, if I left the shallow hole, even more soldiers would see me. In the end, I stayed in place. For hours until darkness, I remained vigilant for an attack that never came.

The need to feed overrode everything by the time I crept out into the night.

* * *

Frenzied and impatient, I searched for the dimmest lit stretch of soldiers and stalked toward it. My pace quickened until I was almost tripping over myself to get there. The further I scrambled, the more my legs tingled with the scent of fresh meat. My sight resolved upon two Humans huddled behind a small, curved wall beside a complex-looking thunder stick. Thankfully, their attention was toward the wasteland in front of them.

Though I could hear others talking, there didn't seem to be any other soldiers nearby. Excitement got the best of me as I closed in, and I clicked my mandibles in anticipation. Just before I struck, my front legs slid over loose dirt into a deep ditch between me and my quarry. My back legs splayed out along the edge. Momentum carried me forward, and my front legs barely reached across.

On the far side, I crunched into the nearest one and kicked at the other. With two legs, I pinned the soldier down and dug my fangs deep into my first kill.

Beautiful, delicious blood pumped up into my mandibles. Euphoria washed through me. My jaws barreled into him, and I worked to squeeze every last drop out.

The second soldier screamed, and I jabbed a free leg into his face. As soon as I'd finished draining the first, I jabbed my fangs into the second and doused him with venom. He stopped struggling, and I wrapped him in silk.

Someone shouted, and a thunder stick cracked. Pain shot through my abdomen. In a fury, I twisted about and found the offender down in the ditch a dozen yards away. I launched myself at him. One of my fangs caught in his throat, and I felt his neck snap. Behind him, more soldiers were shouting and pointing. I tossed a loop of silk around my newest kill and backed away along the ditch, dragging both bodies.

Frantic, I tried to work myself up one side, but the dirt and rocks gave way, and I slid back in. The other side was a wall made of some kind of cloth. My legs punched right through it and revealed more dirt. Confused, I continued backward. Several more *cracks* rang out, and one of my eyes burst apart. I bucked in agony. Then I tightened my legs and focused on rushing backward as fast as I could.

My back left leg sensed an opening in the wall. Without any consideration for what might lie within, I squeezed into a narrow tunnel dug into the ground. It only went a dozen feet into the ground before the walls fell away. I spun about to examine my surroundings and came face to face with a shocked and confused soldier. It raised a particularly small thunder stick toward me, but I latched onto its face before it could fire.

Something sharp jabbed into my side. Reflexively, I kicked out with a leg and felt another soldier on that side. After releasing my fangs, I rotated until I could grab onto this new attacker. It fell backward, and a thunder stick with a sharpened piece of metal at the end fell from its grasp. It screamed as I bore down on it.

With a final snap of my mandibles, it was dead. The little room I'd found went quiet. Distant shouts echoed from outside. As I had no better ideas, I went back into the tunnel and draped silk back and forth in an intricate pattern until it was full of web. Then I scuttled to one side to remain clear of any thunder sticks they might fire into the tunnel.

While trying to determine a way out of my predicament, I gorged myself on my kills. Over the past several days, I hadn't fed on more than two lesser creatures at a time. Including the one up above, I'd had five by the time I was done.

For the first time since I'd started my journey, I felt satiated.

\* \* \*

My abdomen was in pain, but the shredded remains of my eye was excruciating. I had seven more, but that didn't make it hurt any less. While I nursed my wounds, I evaluated my surroundings.

A hint of light made its way through the webs by the time I'd sucked all the life I could out of my prey. The explosions resonated in infrequent intervals, as they always had. Each one knocked a little bit of dirt down from the ceiling. Quieter pops and rattles of smaller weapons echoed down the tunnel as well. All of it kept me on edge.

I felt in greater danger in that underground room than I had in the shallow hole out in the open. They could do just about anything to me if they chose.

It seemed it would be quite simple for them to move up one of those thunder trees and fire it into the tunnel. I would be splattered all over the walls like those strange canvases the lesser creatures called art. Down in this tunnel with only one exit, I'd have no way out.

Perhaps they would bring in one of the crazy ones who wore robes, mumbled to themselves, and fired fire or lightning out of their fingertips. One of those had once tried to kill me, but I'd been too quick for it. I would have to remain vigilant for them. If I heard any sort of mumbling, I'd have to scurry out and kill it before it had the chance to shoot fire at me. However, if I did that, the others would have a chance to shoot those thunder sticks at me.

"In there, you say?" someone said. The voice sounded familiar.

"Yes, Captain. It killed the sergeant and Private Riechers, then it tumbled into the trench, where it killed poor Stefan. It dragged them all in there, sir. We can only presume it has now eaten Captain Müller and Sergeant Weber as well. We've thought we might toss in some grenades, but I doubt we could get them through the webs. For all we know, it might just make it angry."

"No, no, you did the right thing," the original voice said. It was the voice from the barn, several days ago. It was the one who'd seemed impressed with my work. He sounded very intelligent—for a lesser creature, of course. Sadly, that meant he would probably come up with a good way to kill me.

"So, what do we do, sir?" the other voice asked. "How do we kill it?"

"How, indeed," the smart one, the *captain*, replied.

Neither spoke for some time, but I heard someone let out several loud breaths.

"I think I might have a solution," he said. "We may not have to kill it. I think, perhaps, we could make this monster work for us."

"Excuse me, sir? What do you mean? Do you mean to capture it?"

*Capture me? Over their dead bodies! Delicious, succulent dead bodies. Has it already been so long since I've fed?*

"Oh, of course not!" the captain said. "That would be insane."

"Then what, sir? Do you mean to speak to it, to recruit it somehow? Like the Ogres? How could we possibly do that? We can't speak to a monster such as this."

*Yet I understand you completely. Do they think I'm stupid or something?*

"Leave this to me," the captain said.

\* \* \*

Without any thunder trees or mumbling crazy ones approaching the tunnel, the world went dark once more. No one had spoken nearby in a long time. All the sounds of fighting were far away. Not even the smart captain returned.

There was a soft *thump* outside the tunnel. A scent of blood tingled up my legs. Cautious, I shifted forward until I could see out. There were no thunder sticks, thunder trees, or mumblers waiting. The only thing I could see was the gorgeous-looking carcass of a freshly murdered cow.

It was a trap, of course. An obvious means of drawing me out where they might kill me.

*Except...*

The smart Human *had* said he might have a different sort of plan. It might *not* be a trap, after all. Besides, there was so much more blood and meat in a cow than most of the other lesser creatures. I normally avoided them because Humans became more outraged at having one of their cows stolen than they did when one of *them* was stolen. This cow, however, had clearly been left for me. There was no harm in taking a look. After all, they could have killed me by now with a thunder tree or a mumbler.

Maybe they'd recognized me as a superior creature and now afforded me the respect I deserved. It had never happened before, but I knew the lesser creatures spent most of their time idolizing greater beings.

Most of all, it had been a whole day since I'd last eaten, even if I had devoured five entire Humans.

One small step at a time, I eased forward. There were no whispers. No quiet words passed in the belief I couldn't hear them. My legs didn't smell their sweat or grime. By all measures, they'd dumped the cow and moved away.

Reaching the end of the tunnel, I scanned all around. There was not a single soldier in sight. As a test, I crawled to and sank my fangs into the juicy cow, then immediately sprang back up in case it *was* a trap. No one jumped out and shot at me. Tentatively, I stepped forward and dug back in. I remained undisturbed as I devoured every ounce of blood and meat my mandibles could claim.

As I scraped away at the bones, I picked up a slightly different scent of blood wafting in from behind me. Curious and still hungry, I stepped atop the wall of cloth and dirt and edged into the scarred expanse beyond the army's front line. A few dozen yards in, I spotted a freshly killed deer. With just a little less caution than I'd used on the cow, I crept up to it.

A few steps along, I scraped my front right leg against something and recoiled in anger. Looking down, I discovered a skinny thread of metal with sharp thorns. In fact, there were several strands of the wire wound up around each other further down, like a poorly made web of thorny metal. I followed it with my seven eyes and traced it to an intersection with several other strands. These had a better vertical spread, clearly meant to slow down or ensnare enemy soldiers. Now that I knew to look for it, I realized that the metal thorn webs were laced in zigzags all over the empty, torn up field.

While adapting to this new danger, I took slow, measured steps to ensure I didn't snag my legs on anything. Not long after, I arrived at the deer carcass, examined it, and dug in. As I ate, I took a more comprehensive look at the landscape.

Not a single tree stood taller than a couple feet, and none had any remaining branches. The thorn webs were everywhere. Once in a while, I spied a Human-sized corpse caught up in the stuff. I could tell they were dead because they didn't struggle. Lesser creatures *always* struggled when captured.

The terrain was covered in the same sort of shallow depressions I'd hid in a couple days back. The bursts of light continued as they had on my approach to the area. Cries of terror and pleas for help erupted at random from places unseen. Some cried out in the language of the black-uniformed soldiers—the language of my home. Others, the blue-uniformed soldiers, cried and shouted in some unfamiliar language. Every so often, there was a bark from a thunder stick or the chattering of the more complex-looking ones.

A week prior, I'd have concluded I'd found hell and run as far from it as I could. Now, however, as I surveyed the abundant food caught up in thorn webs or calling out in distress, my mandibles clacked and drooled at the prospect.

Even though the cow and deer had filled my belly more than the five lesser creatures had, I knew I'd crave more soon enough. Just as the Humans in that distant town had promised, I'd reached a version of paradise. As long as I could remain undetected, here was a place where I could feast to my heart's content.

\* \* \*

I lost track of time over the next few days—or possibly weeks. Everything became a blur of feeding bliss. Bodies were strewn everywhere. Some were rotten, of course, but plenty enough were fresh. Some were even still alive and struggling in the thorn webs. Of those struggling, some were accompanied by others who were attempting to free them. In their frustrated state, they never saw me coming.

The width between the two armies changed a great deal as I moved about. In some places, it was several hundred yards across. In others, it wasn't too far at all. I quickly learned it was best to stick to the wider swathes of wasteland. It was safer in general, and more likely to have soldiers who'd been abandoned by their comrades.

Here and there, I encountered small groups of blue-uniformed soldiers who were surprisingly easy to sneak up on. One in the group might notice me before I struck, but I simply took them out first.

Even when a soldier got a shot off with a thunder stick, it didn't seem to attract any attention in the wasteland.

The biggest problem was the small ones. Not only did they have little meat, they were also pretty nimble. They consistently noticed me sooner than all the other races, and they wriggled their way through the thorn webs and other impediments rather well. I always caught them, of course, because sooner or later something would slow them down just enough.

At night, I reigned supreme. By day, places to rest were abundant. If, on the off chance I was disturbed during the day, I always succeeded in snatching up those who happened across me. It went on like this for many days.

One day, the thunder from the massive metal trees ceased. It was the first time they'd gone quiet since I'd made my way into the wasteland. Whistles blew up and down the lines from the direction of the blue-uniformed army. Moments later, a flood of countless blue-uniformed soldiers surged out from their ditches and stormed across the wasteland. Thunder sticks erupted from the black-uniformed lines in such numbers that all other sounds were washed out. The chattering of the complex thunder sticks continued, even as the initial eruption of firing broke down into sporadic *pops* and *cracks* up and down the lines.

Blue-uniformed soldiers fell by the dozens. The flood that washed over the battlefield broke down into smaller and smaller groups of furious soldiers.

I knew the flood of soldiers would wash over me at some point. I could only kill so many of them at once and, since they all carried those thunder sticks, there was no way I'd avoid getting shot up. The idea of taking a hit to my abdomen filled me with a combination of fear and rage.

I shuffled about in the shallow depression I'd chosen that day. It occurred to me that I might escape by rushing one way or the other, perpendicular to the advancing wall of soldiers. It wouldn't work—I'd be a big target for those on both sides. Moreover, I had no idea which direction would be better, or if I'd be able to get far enough away in either direction. As I poked my eyes up just enough to see the oncoming horde, I couldn't see an end to it.

While contemplating a way out, my fears were realized by the arrival of a cluster of soldiers in my hole. Being much faster and more prepared, I was able to jab venomous fangs into one before the rest brought their sticks to bear. I kicked two of them and bit another as the rest fired. I felt something graze the top of my abdomen, and my thorax erupted in pain. Another eye went blind.

Frantic, I brought my jaws down hard on another and kicked around at the rest. I fired silk around aimlessly while focusing on stabbing my fangs into one after the other. Another projectile bit into my side. I kicked two legs into the offender and sprayed him with a line of silk. Something sharp jabbed into my other side, so I twisted and bit hard into the soldier who'd stabbed me until bones popped and he stopped moving. Scanning about, I found no more soldiers standing, so I turned and bit into the one who'd shot me. I proceeded to wrap them in silk to save for later. If I survived, I'd eat well that night.

Another cluster, this one much larger, ran up to the edge of my depression. The first to see me threw a hand up and shouted a word of warning. The rest formed an arc around me with their thunder sticks raised. Time froze as I contemplated how many metal stones would hit me before I could kill them. Too many?

"Protect the Widow!" someone shouted from behind me. It was the familiar voice of the black-uniformed captain.

An unseen force tore into the blue-uniformed soldiers with a fury. Tiny stones ripped through the entire line. Only a single soldier was able to shoot, and it went high over my head. Confused at my great fortune, but not wishing to expose myself further, I contented myself with tugging the dead soldiers down with my front legs. As leaving the depression seemed an even worse idea now that I knew there were more soldiers behind me, I hunkered down and ate.

"Eat well, Widow!" the captain shouted.

"Widow!" was shouted in chorus by a great number of soldiers. "Widow! Widow!"

Curiosity overcame me. Without dropping my food, I shifted around in a circle and scooted up to peek out at my saviors. A collection of black-uniformed soldiers crawled away from me, as low to the ground as they could manage. One soldier, with fur across the top of his mouth, knelt low but stared at me from a dozen yards away. Instead of the hard metal hats the other soldiers wore, this one wore a flat, floppy hat. It carried one of the smaller thunder sticks, like the one had carried in that small underground room. The corners of his mouth curled upward.

"Happy hunting, Widow," he said. He tapped the end of the stick against the top of his hat. Then he lowered and crawled away after the others.

*Widow? It was speaking to me. Is that what they call me? And if so, why did they call for me?*

\* \* \*

In the aftermath of the great battle among the lesser creatures, food was everywhere. While the sun still shone, I stayed in my low depression and feasted. First, I laid into the freshly dead. Once those were nothing but bones, I moved on to the ones I'd incapacitated with my venom. By the time I'd finished those, night had fallen. I chanced a trip out to collect what others I could find.

Climbing out of the shallow hole was something of a feat in and of itself. For one thing, I'd sustained a lot of wounds. One of my legs was weak and near useless. Pain flared all the way down the segments of my body. I didn't have too many more eyes to spare.

For another, my abdomen had grown larger than I'd thought possible. My legs did their best to carry me out and along, but I could barely keep it off the ground. Wherever I hit a stretch without any of the thorn webs, I gave up and just let it drag.

I didn't have to go far at all to find more soldiers to gorge myself on. They were everywhere. Dead, alive, crawling, trapped, crying, or silent, they were all around in such abundance, I wondered if I might burst open if I even attempted to eat all I could reach. Yet try I did. No matter how many I devoured, I remained ravenous. *Insatiable.*

The great hunger, which had begun weeks prior as a whisper in the back of my mind, had developed over time into an overwhelming imperative. It screamed inside my mind at all times. Even while my mandibles clicked away on the freshly slain, the hunger told me to eat more, to eat faster, to never, ever stop. It possessed all my faculties and became the soul focus of my existence.

For several days, I spent the evenings consuming all I could find. When the glow of dawn encroached on the horizon, I'd collect all I could and drag it into my next resting spot.

On one particular night, I dragged myself across the ground and followed the scent of the nearest meat, as I'd done every other night. On this night, however, I got a sudden sense of danger.

A rock tumbled nearby. Something clicked not far from the first sound. A whisper carried on the wind.

I froze and peered all around.

The scent of soldiers drifted in. By now, I was well familiar with the scent of sweat, urine, and their horrible breath. Based on the strength of the scent, I could guess at how many there were. There were two dozen if there was one.

Nervous, I pushed myself back. My abdomen had dug a small channel as I'd dragged myself along, and now it served to give me a way back to my last hiding spot.

A great light burst over my head and illuminated everything around me. Blinded, I cringed and tried to push harder.

"*Avance!*" someone cried.

All at once, a series of shouts went up all around me. A dozen feet away, a blue soldier leapt to their feet and fired a thunder stick into me. Another of my eyes exploded. More figures emerged from the ground and fired as well. One of my legs went out. Several stones went into my thorax. A few more bounced across my abdomen, while one more cut deep inside it.

As slow as I was going, I knew I'd never get away. So I charged the nearest one and snapped my fangs over his head. The skull cracked and he dropped. Another stone struck my right side. A blade sliced through my front left leg, and I tumbled.

In no time, I'd regained my footing and lunged to another soldier.

The battle became a blur of fangs, stones, and blades. For each one I killed, two stones flew into me, a blade cut across a leg, or stabbed into an eye. I killed many, but I knew I was losing.

"*Dispersez!*" someone shouted in that strange language of theirs.

I released my latest kill and discovered all the soldiers around me had backed several steps away.

Fire flew out of the fingertips of a robed figure I hadn't noticed. Heat washed over my back, and a wracking pain followed. I screeched.

*Damn mumblers.*

Weak, scorched, tired, and injured, I strained to charge forward, but it was more like a stagger. Only three or four legs still worked, and they could barely draw my tremendous weight along. Death would come for me soon, but it wouldn't come without a fight.

"For the Widow!"

The captain's arrival shocked me. Thunder sticks barked, and blue soldiers fell. The mumbler cursed and stepped sideways before spraying more fire from her hands. This time, the fire bypassed me and swept in the direction of the captain's voice.

The torrent of stones pouring into me alleviated as the blue soldiers shifted their fire. Black soldiers charged around my sides and met the blue soldiers in a furious melee. The mumbler stepped backward and tossed more fire out. Then her head snapped up. A dab of red blossomed in her throat, and she crumpled.

"*Retraite!*" a blue soldier shouted. Fear overtook the expressions of the blue soldiers. A few staggered backward and continued to fire their thunder sticks as they went, but most spun about and broke into sprints.

The captain appeared at my side. With only a few eyes remaining, it was hard to see, but I could tell it was him by his voice and scent.

"Come along, my great Widow," he said. He waved a hand forward toward the fleeing soldiers. "Let's finish this."

I had no clue what he meant, but I followed him nonetheless.

"Help her!" the captain cried. "Carry her!"

Hands grabbed at my abdomen and lifted it off the ground. Feeling lighter, I staggered forward just a little faster. Wherever the captain was leading me, I hoped they would get there soon. I needed to rest. I hurt so much, and I was so tired.

"Chain gun!" the captain shouted. He dropped. The other soldiers must have dropped as well, because my abdomen fell to the ground. A chattering noise erupted from ahead. Stones riddled me, but I already hurt so much from all the others that they felt like taps against my body. I lost all but one eye, and another leg splintered.

The captain howled in agony. He fell against me and cursed. Several of the other soldiers grunted.

"This is as far as we go, my great Widow," he said. "I'm sorry I couldn't get you further."

Weak and slow, he raised his small thunder stick and popped stones at the blue soldiers.

*Where were we going?*

Whatever it was he'd meant, it no longer mattered. He was correct in that this was as far as we would go.

"I feared it might end this way," he said. "Let's hope it was worth it. Let's hope your children fill their trenches and feed to their heart's content."

*Children?*

Another pain shot through the bottom of my abdomen, then I felt a tickle. Another sharp pain, followed by more tickles. Pain cascaded across my belly until it burst open altogether. Tiny, black, beautiful babies skittered out in front of me and rolled out like a wave.

All at once, everything became clear. The meeting with the male, the insatiable hunger, the tremendous growth in my belly. I was giving birth to hundreds of baby spiders.

Screams grew in a delicious chorus all around me, and I understood what the captain had done. He and his men had positioned us where food for my babies would be bountiful. My children would not have to fight each other, as my siblings and I had.

As the captain said, they would eat well, indeed.

\* \* \* \* \*

## Casey Moores Biography

Casey Moores was a USAF rescue/special ops C-130 pilot for over 17 years—airdropping, air refueling, and flying into tiny blacked-out dirt airstrips in bad places using night vision goggles. He's been to *those* places and done *those* things with *those* people. Now he lives a quieter life, translating those experiences to fiction.

He has written in the Four Horsemen universe with stories in numerous anthologies, his debut novel, *These Things We Do*, and much more to come. In the near future, he will be expanding in the Salvage System and Fallen World universes, as well. He was also a finalist in the FantaSci fantasy story contest with his short story "A Quaint Pastime."

A Colorado native and Air Force Academy graduate, he is now a naturalized Burqueño, retired in New Mexico.

\* \* \* \* \*

# A Gift For Mother
# by Melissa Olthoff
## A Scourge of the Angels Story

"Stop in the name of the duke!"

I tucked my head low and kept running. I mean, honestly, did yelling that ever work? The penalty for thievery was the loss of a hand, carried out instantly and without remorse. Repeat offenders were executed on the spot.

I'd never been caught. I certainly didn't intend to start tonight.

The shouts of the city guards soon faded behind me as I sprinted deeper into the Atoka slums. A smirk stretched my lips, and I slowed to a confident walk, navigating the tangled warren with the ease of a born street rat.

The City Guard to a man were overweight, out of shape, and supremely overconfident their magic was enough to stop any criminal in their tracks. To be fair, a direct hit from one of their staffs was more than enough to kill an adult male, let alone a small female. The trick was to evade the power blasts and outrun the fat bastards.

My smirk faded into a scowl. An even better trick was to not get noticed in the first place.

Lord Anderson's palatial clifftop home should have been empty tonight, with anyone who was anyone attending Duke Blevins' annual Summer Solstice Ball. *How was I supposed to know Lady Anderson would beg off to spend a little quality time with her bodyguard* and *her maid. I don't know whether to be annoyed, or impressed.*

The street ahead was obscured by heavily burdened clothing lines crisscrossing in a seemingly endless array. The fabrics were all washed-out browns and grays, with the occasional pop of color that was all the more depressing for the comparison. I pushed aside a particularly dingy sheet and ducked into a hidden alley that was little more than a crack between rundown tenements. The night sky disappeared, completely blocked out by the precarious lean of the building to the right, held up by its companion like a drunk after a long night of indulging.

Suppressing a shudder—because no self-respecting thief is claustrophobic—I hurried my steps until I finally popped out into a new street like a cork from a wine bottle and *listened*. Hearing not even the faintest echo of the guards, I patted the pouch on my hip, fat with stolen jewelry and a few precious gold coins, and grinned. Mateo wouldn't be happy I'd drawn attention, but he couldn't complain about the results.

I tugged the tight black silk scarf off my face and sucked in a triumphant breath—only to choke on the putrid air. The slums were bordered by the tanneries and slaughterhouses on one side, the sewage basin on another, and dead-ended in the fisheries of the harbor. The flavor of stench changed with the wind, but regardless, it always stank. Spending two days skulking around the clifftop estates had ruined my nose. It would take some time for my sense of smell to die from self-preservation again.

It didn't help in the least that it was high summer and the dry season. With that thought in mind, I gave a highly suspicious puddle a wide berth and set off for The Lair.

I made it one street over before I caught the barest whisper of sound behind me. Without looking back, I broke into a sprint, only to be pulled up short by a beefy hand on the back of my right shoulder. I spun toward my attacker, ducking low and turning my momentum into a solid strike below his ribcage. Looking up at the massive Human, I'm not sure he even felt the blow, but I did succeed in dislodging his hold.

I sidestepped rapidly to put some distance between us, deftly avoiding a pile of refuse without taking my focus off my attacker. My eyes locked on the Thieves Guild mark on the back of his hand. Relief swamped me, and I flung up empty hands.

"I'm on official business for Mateo!"

I wasn't really part of the Thieves Guild, but nobody with any sense claimed to be working for Mateo if it weren't true. His only response was to tug loose a baton the length of my forearm, capped with steel, capable of channeling non-lethal magical attacks and somewhat more lethal blunt trauma.

An Enforcer's weapon.

I gritted my teeth and halted my instinctive grab for my dagger. Attacking an Enforcer of the Thieves Guild was tantamount to signing your own death warrant. I checked my escape routes and felt my heart hit my toes. A second Enforcer had already cut off the other end of the street, nearly as large as the first, and armed with two batons. *Great, just freaking perfect.*

A stack of crates against a building presented an opportunity, but only if I could get past man mountain number one. I gave him my most winning smile. "Can we not piss off Mateo tonight? I'm late enough as it is."

My attacker's face remained expressionless. A hum drifted on the air, nearly inaudible even to my ears, and the baton crackled with the Human's Angel-gifted power. *Demon hells.* The hair on the back of my neck stood straight up, and I ducked on instinct alone. A crackling blast of power shot over my head and splashed against the wall, leaving blackened brick in its wake. Fear shot through me, and my hands shook. The second Enforcer had nearly caught me flat-footed. Movement was life in a fight, and I was squandering my greatest strength.

I lunged straight for the first Enforcer; the only indication my speed surprised him came from the slight widening of his eyes. I feinted to the left, spun down and under the expected blow—which passed close enough to tug at the cap that hid the tips of my ears—and sprinted past on his right. As fast as I was, I wasn't quite fast enough to escape the follow-on strike.

With the wall to my right, I couldn't dodge the blow. I could only tuck my head low and brace for the pain. The steel end of the baton caught my shoulder with a thud and a sizzle. I staggered but kept moving. Throbbing pain spread like wildfire, and I flexed my shoulder as I ran. No broken bones, and while I smelled burned leather, the skin beneath my jerkin felt unharmed.

I gave a savage grin at the cursing behind me and bounded up the stack of crates as if they were a flight of stairs. From there, gaps in the bricks presented easy handholds to the roof. I was halfway up when a power blast slammed into the wall next to my head. Chips of brick sprayed out and nicked my cheek and neck. I tensed the muscles in my legs and leaped to the next handhold, narrowly avoiding a second blast. That was when my shoulder decided to spasm.

So there I was, dangling by one hand from the side of a building, while two Enforcers took potshots at me from below. I glanced down. The thought of falling didn't bother me in the least—it was the sudden stop at the end I'd rather avoid. That and the power blasts. I swung to one side, fingers white-knuckled and arm trembling from the strain, to dodge another hit. This one barely blackened the wall. *Nearly out of their range.*

My feet scrambled for purchase, finally catching on a jagged brick. I flexed my abused muscles, regained my grip, and scampered up the rest of the wall. One final shot kissed my hip, barely strong enough to sting. I opened my mouth to taunt them and screamed in frustration instead when I felt my pouch tear free.

There was no time to grab for it. Days of work, gone in an instant. I pulled myself onto the roof and glared down at the Enforcers. The shorter of the two waved my pouch at me. "Thanks, Elf girl."

My hand flew to my hat, but all I felt was hair. I snarled and yanked the scarf from around my neck. It would work well enough to hide my pointed ears. I cast one last glare at the Enforcers, but they were already gone. No doubt they would try to beat me back to The Lair. *We'll see about that.*

I dashed along the rooftops, traveling the thieves' road. I made it in record time, sweat-soaked and more than a little winded.

Tonight, of all nights, the Guardian of The Lair was a new guy with more muscle than brains. "No mark, no entrance, little girl."

And just like that, my frayed temper shattered into a million pieces.

I drew my dagger in a blur of speed and had it nestled under his chin before he could blink. "I'm a *thief*, not a little girl. I work directly for Mateo. Now, are you going to get somebody who knows what they're doing, or do I get to carve a new smile in your throat?"

Shortly thereafter, I was escorted directly into Mateo's office. The Master Thief waited within, seated behind an ornate mahogany desk, fingers steepled in front of his face. His graying hair and short stature led many to underestimate him, but the observant took note of his whipcord frame packed with the sort of lean muscle that promised deadly speed despite his age. His sharp eyes pinned me in place, and I fought the urge to fidget.

"My dear Kessira, you've had quite the night, haven't you? First you bungle the Anderson job, then you threaten the Guardian, and now here you are. Empty handed."

I felt my face flush. "That last bit wasn't my fault—"

I choked on my next words as the two Enforcers sauntered into the office and tossed my stolen pouch onto Mateo's desk. The wordless exchange between the Master Thief and his men wasn't lost on me.

"You bastard," I breathed. "You set me up."

"I always knew there was something different about you, Kessira. Throwbacks like me are rare, but you, you're not a magic-less Human at all, are you?" The pleased smile that crossed Mateo's face chilled my blood. "Elves are outlawed in Atoka. I could make a substantial amount of gold, turning you in. But I think instead, I'll do you a favor and just call in my debt marker."

I froze. "All of it?"

"Paid in full, plus interest. Or take the mark of the Thieves Guild and work it off."

I ground my teeth in building fury. "Isn't that what I'm already doing? Paying off my *debt* to you for throwing me scraps of bread as a child?"

Mateo sat back in his chair with the air of a man who knew he held all the cards. "It's a shame you're too old to train as an assassin. You wouldn't happen to know anyone young enough, would you, Kessira? Or should I say, *Kessi?*"

Everything stopped. My heart thundered in my ears, and I nearly gave in to the violent surge of nausea. *He knows about the twins.* Rage followed swiftly on the heels of my shock, and I barely restrained the urge to leap across the desk and stab the bastard right through his black, shriveled excuse for a heart.

Knowing I'd never survive the attempt, I asked, "How much?"

"Five thousand."

I gaped at him like a fish fresh from the water. "That's insane."

"I fed you, clothed you, educated you, *trained* you. And look how you turned out. My best thief."

I struggled to breathe as I felt the trap close around me. "Why *now?*"

Mateo just smiled. "That's none of your concern. Either you pay your debt, and I'm five thousand richer, or you become a full member of the Thieves Guild, and I gain an indentured Elf. Either way, I win. You have two days."

My mind raced. The amount of jobs I'd have to pull off to get even close to that amount was impossible. Nobody had that amount of gold just lying around. Not even the duke. Not anymore, anyway.

I sucked in a sharp breath. "You're after the Twilight Star."

"Don't be ridiculous. How would I ever move something that recognizable?" Like an idiot, I started to relax. "No, I want the rest of the treasure that went down with the *Azure Wind.* You're the only one of my thieves who has a chance of getting to that gold. Elves can hold their breath longer than Humans, correct?"

I just stared at him for a moment. "That's...not really what I'm worried about."

He waved away my concern with an elegant hand. "Two days, five thousand gold. Or you belong to me. Forever."

I trembled with a churning mix of fear and rage.

"And Kessira?" he said.

I blew out a slow breath and met his eyes, waiting for the axe to fall.

"The duke may rule the city, but I *own* the streets. We'll be watching," he finished.

\* \* \*

Later that night—bruised, battered, and sore—I crept into the tiny one-room "rat hole" I called home. "Anybody home? Desmond, Bernard?"

"He's at it again."

Despite myself, I jumped like a spooked cat. "*Angel turds*, Des, don't sneak up on me like that."

I was as stealthy as the next Elf, but this kid put me to shame. She melted out of a shadowy corner I would have sworn on my father's blade was empty and gave me a disapproving frown. "You shouldn't swear, Kessi."

I blew out a slow breath. It'd been a long night, and I was about at the end of my rope. Through gritted teeth I asked, "What did Bernard find this time?"

Instead of answering, Des led me back out of the rat hole and into the shadows of an alley, where a familiar shape sat next to a trash heap. A smelly trash heap. Breathing carefully through my mouth and avoiding puddles of questionable origin, I stopped next to the boy.

"We have to help her." Bernard looked up at me with huge eyes, a tiny bird cradled in his cupped hands. "She's too small to survive on her own."

"She's also too small to eat," Des added dryly.

And that right there was the twins in an oyster shell. Des was practical down to her bones, while Bernard was compassionate to a fault. Together they made a great team, and at ten years of age, were capable of surviving the streets on their own. Which they might have to if I didn't make it back from this. I swallowed hard and knelt down.

After carefully examining the tiny thing, I said, "She's too young to fly, but too big for the nest. If she's to have any chance at all, she has to stay out here."

Bernard looked stricken. "The cats'll get her. I already saved her once from Shadow!"

I groaned, but I was a sucker for his sad face. I straightened up with a wince. "Let's head to the park, then. We can let her go there."

Once Bernard was satisfied the fledgling was as safe as could be, we went home. Des passed me a slightly bruised apple and a crusty slab of bread. "Here, we saved you dinner."

I made a face and tossed her a silver coin. "Buy more food tomorrow."

The identical sly grins on their faces didn't escape my notice, even with an apple crammed in my mouth. I hastily wiped away a trail of juice from my chin and scowled at the twins. "I said *buy* the food, not steal it and pocket the money."

"Same thing," Bernard said impishly.

Des tugged absently at her shirt and frowned. She wouldn't be able to pretend to be a boy much longer. The streets would become more dangerous for her once that happened. "Something's bothering you. Tell us."

I debated briefly, but there really was no point in putting them off. Des would badger, and Bernard would cajole until I told them everything, anyway. So, I did. Mostly.

"If I don't come back, don't wait. Take the coin I've got stashed away and find someplace better. You remember how to get to it, Des?"

The girl's face hardened. "We don't care about the money—"

"We care about you!" Bernard finished for her. "Let us help. You know we can."

Des nodded firmly. "We've done it before; we can do it again."

I shook my head. "This one is too dangerous. Stay here and stay safe."

"But–"

"No," I replied, fear sharpening my voice. "Not this time."

Their mulish expressions didn't fill me with any confidence they planned to listen. I waited until I was sure they were asleep and crept out in the middle of the night like a coward. A coward who wanted her friends to live. I'd left a few key details out of my story. Hopefully it would be enough to keep them away from Bloodmoon Bay.

Shaped like a near-perfect crescent of aquamarine water, cliffs encircled the bay and a narrow strip of sandy beach ringed it. The tail end of the cliffs jutted out into the water at the mouth of the bay, leaving only a narrow stretch leading to open water.

Morning light found me crouched on top of the cliffs, cold and uncomfortable on the unforgiving rock, using the height to study my target.

The *Azure Wind* was near the mouth of the bay, where the green of the shallows reluctantly gave way to the darker blue of the deeps. It was only visible at low tide, and even then, most of the galleon was underwater. Still, the duke could have easily recovered his lost treasure last year when it first sank, if it weren't for one very large problem.

I'd spoken with the old fishermen at the docks before the fishing fleet left the harbor in the dark hours of the morning and gotten some advice. The wooden bucket at my feet, filled to the brim with chum bought from those same fishermen, wasn't the worst thing I'd ever smelled. Or rather, it didn't smell any worse than home on a bad day. Even so, I positioned myself upwind as I stretched out cold muscles in preparation.

The mournful cry of a seabird distracted me. I tilted my face to the sky and smiled at the bird's graceful flight as it circled overhead.

*What I wouldn't give for wings like an Angel, to soar through the clouds, far above all my problems and worries.*

A gust of wind blasted the scent of the chum right into my face. I gagged at the stench, and my eyes watered, breaking me out of my fantasy.

I grabbed the bucket, spun around in a circle to pick up momentum, and flung it out over the cliff as hard as I could. Chum flew in a shining arc of scales and offal over the water, landing a respectable distance from the shore.

I crouched back on my heels and waited.

I scanned methodically, watching as the seabird and its brethren dove at the water. My breath caught when a muscular body broke the surface, coil after coil of gray scales topped with a narrow head larger than a wagon and full of needle-sharp teeth perfect for rending fish. Or small Elf girls.

"*Angel turds.* I was really hoping it was gone."

I spent the rest of the day coming up with useless plan after suicidal plan. With the sea serpent making its home in the bay, anyone diving down to the ship would be easy prey, even at low tide. The seafloor was littered with the remains of those foolish—or desperate—enough to try.

I made a cold camp on the leeward side of a couple of boulders, and quickly choked down a miserable meal of cheese and hardtack as the sun set. Afterward, I leaned back against the sun-warmed rock and considered my options.

"What I need is a distraction," I muttered.

"You know, I was thinking the same thing."

I leaped to my feet, dagger in hand. "Who's there?"

Nothing but silence answered me for several drawn-out moments. "You...you can *hear* me?"

"Of course I can," I snapped. My fingers tightened on the hilt of my dagger. "Come out where I can see you."

"I'd rather not. I'm not as pretty as an Elf."

My free hand flew up to my head, but in my haste to sneak out last night, I'd forgotten a hat. I was lucky it had been dark when I'd spoken to those fishermen, otherwise I might have found myself on the wrong end of a boat hook. I pulled a scarf out of my pack to wrap around my ears, but paused when I saw the deep green color instead of the expected black. Once again, haste had worked against me.

I hesitated, one hand gripping my dagger, and the other a swath of green silk. There was no way I could tie the scarf with one hand, not that it mattered anymore.

The owner of the distinctly male voice seemed to pick up on my distress. "I'm sorry, was I not supposed to call you pretty?"

I gritted my teeth. "You weren't supposed to call me an Elf."

"Why not?"

I gestured with my dagger. "These are Human lands. My kind aren't welcome."

A snort. "Neither are mine."

So not a Human, and not an Elf. "What are you?" I asked bluntly.

"I couldn't help but notice you scouting the bay today," he replied evasively, a hint of aggression in his tone. "Are you after the Twilight Star, too?"

I tensed. "I'm after the gold. Nothing more."

A rumble echoed off the cliffs and fear skittered up my spine. *What in the demon hells are you?*

"You can have the gold, but the Twilight Star is mine. I need a gift for my mother."

Fear generally pissed me off. I opened my mouth to say something scathing and possibly suicidal, but glanced at the scarf in my hand. The words died unborn. I barely remembered my mother. The only thing time hadn't taken was the feel of her arms when she'd hugged me, but that too was being edged out by other things. Unbidden, my fingers tightened on the scarf, my grip threatening to crush the fragile silk. I gently pushed it back into my pack where it wouldn't be damaged further.

"Like I said, I only want the gold."

"Sounds like we're not competition, then," he replied, sounding pleased. "I propose an alliance."

"People who hide in the dark rarely make good allies." I panned my gaze over the rocks, but saw nothing and no one in the deepening shadows. "Ironic coming from me, considering my profession, but here we are. Come out and we can talk about an alliance. Otherwise, shove off."

The silence stretched out long enough, I started to wonder if he really had just up and left as silently as he'd arrived. Then he sighed. "Are you sure?"

Exasperation won out over caution, and I snapped, "Show yourself!"

"Be careful what you ask for."

He strode out into the open, movements oddly graceful for such a large creature. The fading light glimmered off a lithe body covered in scales of dark blue and dusky purple. Wings fanned out, reaching for the stars, so large they blocked half the sky. I pressed back against the rocks, nowhere to go and with only a puny dagger for defense. My heartbeat thundered in my ears and my breath shook.

"Dragon," I said with a gasp, filled with a strange mix of fear and awe.

"Last time I checked," he replied with a snort. His mouth didn't move. Nevertheless, I heard his words. His voice was a rough baritone tinged with...amusement? He was the most beautiful, terrifying creature I'd ever seen. And I was fairly certain he was laughing at me.

I scowled, caught between fear and annoyance. "I didn't know Dragons could talk."

"We talk all the time, it's just that nobody ever hears us." His head tilted, yellow eyes narrowed as he studied me. "In fact, no Elf has heard us since the Angels brought us all to this miserable realm. What are you called?"

I stared at him for another moment, the awe winning out over the fear when he made no move to devour me. "Kessira."

"Kessira," he repeated, drawing out the syllables as if he were tasting the word. "I am called Adair-Rhys. You can put away your tiny fang. I promise I won't bite."

I glanced down at the dagger still clenched in a white-knuckled grip. I eyed the Dragon, massive against the sunset sky, armored with scales I couldn't hope to pierce. "You promise not to kill me?"

"I swear on my mother's wings, I will not kill you…" I let out a short breath and relaxed. Because I was an idiot. "I never said I wouldn't hurt you, though."

Adair-Rhys opened his maw, revealing fangs as long as my dagger, and roared. I shrieked and raised my useless blade, prepared to go down fighting—only to see the damn Dragon rolling on the ground. Laughing. I stood there, chest heaving, and barely restrained myself from attempting to stab him. But only because I didn't want to break my favorite dagger on those scales. Even his belly was armored.

"I'm sorry, I couldn't help myself," he said around snorts of laughter. "Never mind, I'm not sorry. The look on your face!"

"That wasn't funny!" I glared at him as I sheathed my blade. It took three tries due to the shaking in my hands.

"It was hilarious," he replied, snickering as he tucked his wings against his back. His nostrils flared, and he leaned closer to me, drawing in my scent. I squeezed my eyes shut, and his laughter cut off. "You truly are afraid of me."

There was shock and hurt in his voice. I opened my eyes, but couldn't read the expression on his scaled face. "Have you Elves forgotten so much, you really think I could ever hurt you? You can *hear* me."

"I was raised by Humans," I replied shortly. "And what does *hearing* you have to do with anything?"

"It's something potential mindmates can do."

Everything screeched to a halt. "Are you crazy? I can't mate with you!"

His laughter echoed in my head, much like his roar echoed off the rocks. "Get your mind out of the gutter. Not that kind of mate. I'm talking about a mental bond."

"A bond," I repeated dumbly. A mage light went off in my head. "You're talking about Dragon riders. That's a children's fairy tale!"

"No. It's how Dragons and Elves used to be." Adair-Rhys' yellow eyes regarded me reproachfully. "I can't believe you thought I would hurt you."

"Well, you *are* a Dragon. You eat people!"

He snorted again. "We do not! That's disgusting."

"Fine, you kill people."

He looked at me as if I were stupid. "Wouldn't you kill to protect yourself? To protect your family?"

My hands tightened into fists as I remembered wanting to kill Mateo for threatening the twins. If he ever realized how powerful their magic was, he would stop at nothing to acquire them.

And I would stop at nothing to protect them.

"Point taken," I said quietly. Then I scowled. "It still wasn't funny."

The Dragon grinned, showing off fangs meant for rending prey. "Yes, it was. You made the cutest little squeaking noise!"

"It wasn't cute," I replied through gritted teeth.

"I think I'll call you Squeaks from now on."

"You most certainly will not!"

The Dragon curled up in front of me, spiked tail tip wrapping around his front legs as if he were an overgrown cat. "So, how about that alliance, Squeaks? We can work together to get the treasure."

I ignored the obnoxious nickname as a nagging doubt coalesced in my mind. "Why would you want to ally with me? What can I possibly do that you can't?"

Adair-Rhys regarded me with a seriousness I hadn't been sure he possessed until now. "The sea serpent is too big for me to fight, but if we work together, maybe we won't have to fight it at all."

I hesitated, but really, what choice did I have? Either I got Mateo his gold, or I would spend the rest of my days trapped in the Thieves Guild, living a life I hated. Worse, it would be impossible to keep the twins beneath his notice. I'd have to send them away before they were ready. Before *I* was ready.

I'd be alone. Again.

I straightened my spine and nodded firmly. "Allies, then. If you can provide a distraction, I can dive for the treasure."

The Dragon gave me a toothy smile. "I think I can manage something."

\* \* \*

I crouched at the tail end of the natural breakwater, as close as I could get to the sunken ship and still be on dry land. A wave crashed into the rocks, the chilly spray shooting high into the air and falling like rain. I wiped salt water from my face and cast a worried glance at the threatening skies, the clouds heavy with the promise of actual rain.

*Angels, please hold back the storm. We have to do this today, or not at all.*

My father taught me to swim, but it had been years since I'd had the chance to put the lessons to good use. At least I'd remembered to strip down to tight-fitting clothes that wouldn't drag in the water. Everything else was hidden at my campsite. I'd either go back for it later—or it wouldn't matter.

Adair-Rhys and I had spent half the night devising a plan. In the end, we kept it as simple as possible. He'd draw the serpent to the other end of the bay with a few choice deer carcasses, and I'd dive for the treasure and secure it to the mast. Once I was clear, Adair-Rhys would swoop down and grab it all. *Simple, right.*

Simple as trusting a *Dragon*, one of the most feared predators in the entire realm. A Dragon who claimed we were potential mindmates. I snorted. Dragon riders were a fantasy, nothing more.

If it weren't for the dusky purple scale I'd found when I woke this morning, I might have thought I'd dreamt the whole thing. Stress could do strange things to a person, and I hadn't slept well. But no, Adair-Rhys was real, and I was going to have to trust him to hold up his end of the deal.

I shook my head at my foolishness. Still, I glanced wistfully up at a soaring seabird and wondered again what it would be like to fly. A distant roar jerked my head to the south. My breath caught at my first sight of a Dragon in flight. He was magnificent...and terrifying.

"I prefer magnificent. But I will accept magnificently terrifying," Adair-Rhys said haughtily. He was on the other end of the bay, yet I heard him as clearly as if he stood before me.

"How did you...can you read my mind?" I demanded, more than a little concerned.

"I can't read your mind, but we can talk to each other, even if we're apart," he replied cheerfully. I could actually *feel* his happiness and excitement. "If we decide to bond —"

"Why would you even *want* to?" I demanded, suspicion sinking sharp claws into my heart. "I get why Elves would, but what do Dragons get out of it?"

"It's not a matter of want, not for Dragons. We need the bond to feel whole." Sorrow and longing rose up within him, drowning his excitement. "When the Angels and Demons brought their war to our realm, they brought death, destruction, and misery with it. The Angels might have saved the remnants of our people by bringing us here, but they left us broken, Squeaks."

"So it's just about the bond itself?" My heart hit my toes at the unexpected disappointment. For just a moment, I'd thought…"It really has nothing to do with *me*."

"No, Kessira. It has *everything* to do with you. We can only bond with a kindred spirit. Can't you feel it?"

I tensed in alarm.

I *could* feel it. It was like a phantom tug deep in my mind, gently pulling me closer to the Dragon. But I was already struggling to get free of the Thieves Guild, and it seemed like just another set of chains. I shuddered and fought off a panic attack.

"What if I don't *want* to bond with you?"

Adair-Rhys was silent for a moment. When he spoke, his voice was gentle and held no hint of the hurt I knew he was feeling. "Don't fret, Squeaks, you have to want to bond for it to happen. Nobody can force it on you."

Shame bubbled up. I'd hurt a Dragon's feelings. Maybe I could kick a puppy for an encore. "I—I didn't mean it like that. It's just this is…it's…"

"Scary?"

"Yes, that!" I forced myself to take a deep breath. "I'm not saying no, I'm just saying maybe we can talk about this bond thing later. After we get the job done."

I shook off all thoughts of mental bonds and Dragon riders, and began to stretch.

"I don't know. That storm isn't going to hold off much longer. Maybe we should try again tomorrow," he said.

"No! We've got time."

I tried to stay calm as I waited for his decision, but desperation cracked the reins, and my heartbeat raced in response. If I lost Adair-Rhys' support, I'd have no choice but to try on my own.

"Ah, demon hells," he finally said. "You only live once. Here we go. Oh, and Kessira? Whatever you do, don't scream. Or move. Or breathe…you know what, just pretend there's a giant sea serpent wrapped around that ship and hold very still."

I froze mid-stretch. The rocks blocked my line-of-sight to the ship, but that didn't mean the serpent couldn't see me. Adair-Rhys soared overhead, a deer carcass clutched in each hind foot, and offal dangling from his front claws.

"Here fishy, fishy, fishy," he sang softly. "She's on the move. Alright, mindmate, your turn."

Despite the danger, I rolled my eyes. "Don't call me that."

"You prefer Squeaks?"

"I prefer Kessira! You know, my actual name."

I crept over the rocks and to the shore. The ship was only about a hundred feet out, maybe less. It hadn't seemed that far when I'd scouted it from the clifftop, but from down here, it looked a lot further. I eased into the cool water and paused. The rocky bottom was sharp on my bare feet and quickly disappeared from sight in the murky green water. There was no telling what swam beneath the choppy waves, and I really didn't want to find out.

I didn't want to belong to the Thieves' Guild more.

I strode into the water and swam. To my relief, I hadn't completely forgotten my father's lessons, and I quickly gained confidence—right up until salt water went up my nose. My eyes burned, and I hacked up half the ocean, but I kept going, valiantly ignoring Adair-Rhys' snorting laughter.

The jagged mast became my beacon, as my muscles burned from the unaccustomed activity, and I focused on it to the exclusion of all else. It was only when I was able to cling to the mast that I turned my attention to the rest of the ship.

With the tide as low as it was going to get, there was a small section of the stern above water. Any treasure should be in the captain's quarters just below the deck—which, while slimy with algae, was surprisingly intact. I'd have to dive down to the door.

Knowing it would be dark below, I hung on to the mast with one arm and tugged open the small pouch on my hip with the other. I smirked down at the small mage stone shining faintly in the overcast daylight. I could only hope the Enforcer I'd snitched it from got in trouble for losing the valuable tool.

I drew several deep breaths into my lungs and dove beneath the waves. I forced my eyes open and held the shining mage stone in front of me as I kicked my way deeper. The door to the captain's quarters was still closed, but the giant hole told me someone—or something—had gotten here before me. Careful of the ragged edges, I pulled myself through. Then I screamed, and all my precious air escaped in giant bubbles. I kicked for the surface, too panicked to even consider whether there *was* a surface in the mostly-submerged cabin.

"What happened?" Adair-Rhys demanded, concern a sharp edge that sliced through my panic. "Are you all right?"

My head broke the surface and hit the ceiling nearly simultaneously. I tilted my face back and gulped in huge breaths of rank, stale, wonderful air.

"I'm fine, I'm fine," I gasped as I treaded water. I glanced at the dark shape trapped below and shuddered. "I just found another would-be thief. Or what's left of him."

"Pleasant," he quipped.

Since the ship had sunk at an angle, the air pocket was deepest near the far wall. If I'd come up any closer to the door, I wouldn't have hit air at all. "Not the first time I've seen a dead body," I replied absently.

I used the mage stone to illuminate the submerged cabin floor as I swam deeper into the room. I blew out a sigh of relief at the glimmer of gold in a busted strongbox. Evidently, my new friend had gotten it open, but hadn't managed to get any of the treasure.

"I found the gold."

"You better hurry, Squeaks. She's going through the meat faster than I thought, and the storm is rolling in."

I felt the urgency in his voice as if it were my own, and it was an effort to keep my movements slow and steady. Haste only led to mistakes. I pulled the first of six sturdy sacks from my belt, drew in a deep breath, and dove. I hooked a foot under the rotting desk to anchor myself and filled the sack. Mateo had gotten one thing right. Elves *could* hold their breath longer than Humans, and I was able to not only fill the sack, but bring it out of the cabin and up to the surface with only minimal strain.

The sea was getting rough as the storm drew closer, and I choked on salt water twice before I managed to secure the sack to the mast. I caught my breath, prepped the next sack, and swam back to the gold. This time when I surfaced, the wind had risen, and the waves were worse. It took longer to catch my breath. I dove again and secured the next sack. Then the next. By the sixth, a light drizzle fell from the gray skies, and my arms trembled from hauling roughly three hundred pounds of gold to the surface.

Worse, there was no sign of the Twilight Star in the strongbox.

I dove back under one more time, but found nothing. I treaded water in the air pocket as my mind raced. I'd searched the desk as well as the captain's storage chest. I'd even checked under the bunk. I was running out of places to search.

"I can't hold her attention much longer, Squeaks. You need to get out."

My anxiety spiked to new levels. If I didn't hold up my end of the bargain, Adair-Rhys wouldn't hold up his. I wouldn't get the gold. I *needed* the gold. I panted desperately, but the stale air wasn't enough for my starved lungs. I could almost feel the branding iron against my flesh, imagined how my skin would sizzle and burn. I stared at my hand, and for just a moment I could actually see it—the permanent mark that would bind me to the Thieves Guild as surely as iron chains.

I would never escape.

"Get out now!" Adair-Rhys roared.

An image flashed in my mind. I saw the bay as if I were standing on the cliffs above. The sea serpent was coming back!

I hesitated. "But I haven't found the Twilight Star yet."

"It's not worth your life!"

"Without the gold, I'll have no life!"

He snarled, but I could feel the fear under his anger. "I'll still get your demons-damned gold, Kessira. I swear it on my mother's wings."

"That's not how it works! Nobody does anything for free!"

Adair-Rhys was silent for a beat. Then I felt his fear and anger morph into steely determination. "Friends do. Now get off that ship."

A roar split the air, so loud I could hear it through the thick wood. That idiot Dragon had attacked the sea serpent to buy me time to get out. We weren't even bonded—might never *be* bonded—but he hadn't thought twice.

"You're crazy," I whispered.

But…was it really any different than what I'd done when I found the twins? Two tiny thieves in the making who'd tried to steal from the market and gotten caught. I hadn't hesitated to save them from the guards. It was a split-second decision I'd never regretted.

Now I had to ensure he didn't regret his.

I sculled along the air pocket as fast as I could before diving for the exit. I was tired, though, and veered way too close to the body for my comfort level. I wrinkled my nose and began to turn when the mage stone reflected off something clutched in the man's bony hand. I squinted through salt-irritated eyes and kicked closer, careful to stay clear of the splintered boards jutting from the wall. One had snagged the man's belt and trapped him in a watery grave. I had no intention of suffering the same fate. *Sorry about this, but there really is no honor among thieves.*

I pried open his hand and stared in girlish wonder. *So beautiful.* The Twilight Star really did shine like a diamond bathed in the colors of sunset, and was expertly fashioned in a distinctive star pattern. I could see why Mateo didn't think he could move it.

Elation surged, but I clamped down on the emotion and tucked the gemstone into my pouch. Escape now, celebrate later.

I kicked my way out of the cabin and into a nightmare. The storm had arrived.

I clung to the mast and coughed miserably, but wave after wave slapped me in the face, and I was unable to get a clear breath. An eerie moan cut through the howl of the wind and was answered by an echoing roar.

I didn't want to look, but I wiped the rain from my eyes and forced my head up. And up. Fear shriveled my guts as I beheld a true titan of the sea, and I hugged that mast as if it were my new best friend.

Adair-Rhys harassed the larger monster much like a starling would a hawk, striking and darting away, baiting and barely avoiding the return strike. Watching the battle, I realized I was wrong. This was so much worse than eluding a pair of overweight guards in a crowded market.

This was suicide.

And he was risking his life…for me.

"Why are you doing this?" I cried out, my voice lost to the howl of the wind and sea. He heard me anyway.

"No Dragon…has found a mindmate…in centuries," Adair-Rhys gasped into my mind. I could feel his growing fatigue, an ache that matched my own as the waves battered my tired body. "And you don't get to die…before we figure out if that's what we want to be. Now swim!"

I pried my hands off the mast and swam.

Try as I might, the rising fury of the wind and the waves pushed me deeper into the bay, away from the rocks. Away from safety.

A giant wave overtook me, and I went under. I fought my way back to the surface and realized I was perilously close to the battle. Close enough to see the serpent finally catch my friend with a mighty blow of its bony skull. I felt his pain as he tumbled from the air and hit the water with stunning force. I screamed, both from the phantom pain and in fear for my friend.

Fortunately, the serpent had no interest in continuing the battle and turned away from the stunned Dragon in favor of its home. I entertained a brief hope it wouldn't spot me struggling against the rising seas, but I was right in its path, and I felt the weight of its gaze like a blow. Its jaw dropped open, and that eerie moan rose again. *Demon hells.*

I stopped fighting to get to the rocks. The current was too strong, and they were no protection from the sea serpent's wrath, now that it knew I was here. I did the only thing I could think to do and turned back for the ship. I searched for the mast, my beacon of hope, only to realize I'd already been pushed too far into the bay.

"Kessira!" Adair-Rhys screamed. I twisted back around. I could see him beyond the fast-approaching serpent, wings thrashing as he struggled to break free of the water. He couldn't help me.

All of a sudden, a life in the Thieves Guild didn't seem so bad. I could have found a way out. I could have tried, anyway. Instead, I'd gambled everything on this foolish venture…and lost.

With no way to fight, no way to run, I did the only thing left to me and stared my death in the face. The serpent's jaws opened wide in preparation to strike. It rose higher, backlit by lightning, neck frills drifting in the wind like colorful seaweed. An oddly beautiful last sight, at least.

A power blast slammed into the side of its head, knocking it sideways. *What?*

The serpent shook its head, dazed from the blow. Adair-Rhys rose up behind it, wings spread like an avenging Angel, and tore its throat out. Blood sprayed, and the Dragon roared in triumph as the serpent fell.

The resultant wave did its utmost to drown me, and nearly succeeded. I kicked hard for the surface and broke through just as my lungs begged for air. I swiped at my eyes and realized the wave had carried me to the center of the bay. It wasn't until a fin cut through the water, racing past for the blood feast ahead, that I remembered the other reason the fishing fleets avoided the bay.

Adair-Rhys laughed wildly. "That overgrown snake wasn't so tough after all!"

Something large brushed past my legs. Terror constricted my heart and I spun wildly, but the sea was too churned up by the storm to see more than a few feet in any direction.

"Shark!" I gasped, then choked as a wave pummeled me. I fought my way back up and sucked in a breath. Another fin cut past, then circled back. I turned with it, desperate to keep it in in my sights. Then the fin disappeared.

"Adair-Rhys, a little help!"

I filled my lungs and dropped below the waves, searching. A dark shape rushed me, and I kicked frantically, trying to escape. It was still playing, though, and merely scraped along my side, its rough skin abrading my exposed flesh and tearing my clothes.

*Adair-Rhys! Help me!* I shouted in my mind.

"Where are you?"

*I'm here!*

I spun in the water, tired lungs already aching from the strain of holding my breath yet again. I caught a glimpse of the beast, but it faded into the shadows. Out of sight but not gone. I could feel it circling, growing ever closer.

"I can't see you," Adair-Rhys cried, fear replacing his earlier triumph. "I can find you if you accept the bond!"

Lightning flashed, illuminating the stormy seas…and the shark charging right for me. I screamed and lashed out with my fist. I hit it right in the snout, but the blow lacked power. All I managed to do was startle it and lose all my air.

The shark retreated, and I surfaced, lungs heaving. I searched for Adair-Rhys, but the storm had turned day into night. If I couldn't see a flying Dragon, there was no way he could see a half-drowned Elf. *Not without a beacon.* Hope surged, and I reached for my pouch. It was dark enough for the mage stone to shine. Adair-Rhys would find me. I wouldn't have to shackle myself to a bond.

The pouch was gone.

*No!*

I clawed at my hip, but the pouch was truly lost. It must have torn away when the shark scraped my side. I could feel the beast circling again, drawing the noose ever tighter, and I ducked beneath the waves once more. If I could have, I would have sobbed, but the water stole even that from me.

*Adair-Rhys, please!*

"You have to let me in," he snarled back. I could feel his rage, his terror. All for me.

The bond called to me, a siren's song of hope. I tentatively reached for it, then faltered. My mother's tales of Dragon riders were full of Elven royalty, heroes, and knights of the realm. I was just a thief.

*Why would you want me?* I screamed.

Adair-Rhys roared in frustration. "Because I don't feel broken when I'm with you!"

The emotion behind his words slammed home like a well-aimed dagger to the heart, leaving no room for doubt.

"Please, Squeaks!"

I knew that ache of loneliness, those echoes of grief.

"I promise you won't regret it."

It was never the bond calling to me—it was *him*.

"Kessira!"

A kindred spirit whose jagged pieces were a perfect fit to my own.

The shark charged.

I closed my eyes…and gave the Dragon a piece of my soul.

Lightning flashed again, and thunder rumbled.

No.

Not thunder. A Dragon's enraged roar. Talons flashed and pierced the surface, snatching several hundred pounds of startled shark right out of the water.

I didn't see what happened to the shark after that. I just let the waves push my exhausted body to the shore like I was nothing more than flotsam. I felt like it, too, as I crawled up the beach until I was beyond the water's reach.

I collapsed on the sand and concentrated on breathing. Anything more seemed like too much to ask at that point.

Faint cheers barely audible even to my ears drifted down from the cliffs above and told me who had power-blasted the serpent. I huffed a tired laugh. I hadn't given the twins enough credit if they'd figured out where to find me that easily.

Adair-Rhys landed on the beach and galloped over to me. I glared at him as I dragged my tired body upright and tried to wipe the wet sand he'd liberally pelted me with out of my eyes.

"Why did you grab the shark instead of me? I had to swim the rest of the way in!"

The Dragon reared his head back and gave me an offended glare of his own. "I was afraid I'd snap your neck!"

My righteous anger deflated. "Oh."

"Yeah, oh," replied Adair-Rhys angrily. "Are you hurt?"

"No." I cleared my throat, nervously running a hand over where my pouch used to hang. A lump rose in my throat, and I had to rush the words out past memories of failing Mateo, and what had followed. "I lost the Twilight Star. I'm sorry."

Adair-Rhys shrugged his wings. "The gold's gone, too. The serpent took out the ship in its death throes. But who cares about that?"

Despair slammed into me. I'd come so close—so close to freedom, so close to death. It was too much. My knees buckled, but he caught me in his front claws before I could fall. He leaned in close, eyes bright with concern.

"Kessira? Are you alright?"

"Not really." Unable to reach anything else, I awkwardly hugged his snout. "Thank you for saving me."

He quickly set me back down, and I feared I'd crossed a line with my impromptu hug. But the Dragon scooped me closer, right against his chest, and angled a wing to block the worst of the rain. I didn't realize just how cold I was until I felt the heat coming off his scales, and I pressed closer, shivering.

He rested his head on top of mine and sighed. "I was afraid I'd lost you, Squeaks."

I could feel the truth of his words. More than that, I could feel *him*, curled up in a corner of my mind like a contented housecat. Oddly enough, he didn't feel intrusive. A new emotion welled up inside me, one I hadn't felt in so long, I didn't immediately recognize it.

I felt…safe.

I let out a shuddering breath and a few tears. After a sorely-needed moment, I regained control and pulled back so I could see his face. "So we're bonded now?"

"Yes. Do…do you regret it?" Adair-Rhys asked tentatively.

"Not yet." I smirked up at him and arched a brow. "Am I going to?"

"Probably," he replied with a snort. "Just wait until you meet my mother."

"Your mother?"

"I apologize in advance," he replied dryly. "Actually, I'm just going to go ahead and apologize for most of my clan. They're all loud, opinionated, bossy…"

They sounded wonderful. But Mateo had enough magic users under his thumb to threaten even a Dragon, and he was vindictive enough to send them after me, no matter how far I ran. Or flew.

"You are coming with me, aren't you?" Adair-Rhys asked, concern radiating from him like heat from a bonfire. "I can't stay in Atoka; I don't think I'd be welcome here. I think you'd really like my home."

I swallowed hard, tears threatening once more. "I'd love to, but without that gold…I can't."

"Why do you need the gold?"

I told him.

Adair-Rhys grinned with all his teeth. "I think I can take care of that little problem."

\* \* \*

I loved flying with every bit of my heart and soul. My body didn't agree. It turned out Dragon riding was *hard*, especially without a proper harness. The single leather strap around Adair-Rhys' neck just wasn't cutting it. The twins, carried in his front claws, had it easier. All they had to do was sit back and enjoy the ride, whereas my thighs were aching, and my rear end was no longer on speaking terms with me.

To distract me from my discomfort, I pictured the look on Mateo's face when a Dragon had come calling on him late last night and snickered. "You know, when you said you'd take care of my problem, I didn't think you meant you'd literally pay him off."

Adair-Rhys snorted and cast an offended look over his shoulder. "I told you, Dragons aren't monsters. We don't always solve our problems with violence."

My eyes popped in disbelief. "Says the Dragon who had enough gold to pay off my debt, but still chose to steal from a *sea serpent* rather than buy a gift."

"You know what they say—you only live once," he replied with an evil chuckle before abruptly tilting his wings. I shrieked like a little girl as we plummeted toward the unforgiving ground. The twins whooped in delight, and Adair-Rhys roared with laughter as he leveled out again.

I fought back a grin. "That wasn't funny."

"It was hilarious, *Squeaks*."

Bernard's voice drifted up to us. "Hey, look! Elves!"

I steeled myself and peered over the Dragon's shoulder, hands white-knuckled on the leather strap. I caught a glimpse of a pair of horses running full tilt between the trees, but no Elves.

"I would never let you fall," Adair-Rhys assured me. "And he's right."

"Aw, they ran away," said Bernard.

"Maybe because we're on a Dragon," Des said bitingly. "They left some things behind. We should see if there's anything worth stealing."

"Kessi said we're not supposed to do that anymore."

"It doesn't hurt to look."

Adair-Rhys circled the wagon the Elves had abandoned. It probably wasn't anything important. I shrugged. "Old habits die hard. I need to stretch my legs, anyway."

We landed in a thunder of wingbeats and a cloud of dust. I slid to the ground and groaned. Definitely needed that harness sooner rather than later.

The twins wasted no time and raced each other for the wagon. Des proved herself the more ruthless sibling once again by tripping her brother. She hopped up in the wagon and reached for the lone strongbox, but her hand stopped short as a blue barrier flashed. Bernard jumped up into the wagon and pulled her back in alarm.

"Elven magic. Allow me," Adair-Rhys said with a rumbling laugh. He flipped open the box with a flourish and laughed again when we all stared at him. "Dragons are immune to Elven magic. Ancient pacts between our two races, and all that."

I told the twins what he'd said, since they couldn't hear him. Des shrugged, unimpressed, and elbowed her brother into letting her go. She reached inside and withdrew an angular gemstone.

Bernard looked over her shoulder and groaned. "Aww, that's it?"

I raised a hand to stop him from closing the box. "We're honest thieves now, kids. That means we need to pay for what we take."

Adair-Rhys snorted a laugh. "Don't look at me, I spent everything I had freeing you."

I considered for a moment, tapping my chin in thought, then grinned. I dug through my pack and pulled free the loose scale Adair-Rhys had dropped in my campsite. In the darkness of night and storm, I had thought him a dark blue and dusky purple. In the sunlight, his scales shone as bright as any gem.

I placed the amethyst scale in the strongbox, and Adair-Rhys sealed it shut again.

Des passed me the gemstone. Nearly translucent, it shone with the faintest of lilac wisps that seemed to curl and twist in the brilliant sunlight. It was almost as beautiful as the Twilight Star.

I raised an eyebrow and looked up at Adair-Rhys. "Think your mother will like it?"

"She'll love it."

\* \* \* \* \*

## Melissa Olthoff Biography

Melissa Olthoff spent her youth daydreaming about riding dragons and slaying monsters. After joining the United States Air Force, she spent years having real adventures before becoming a responsible adult. Sort of. She now works as an accountant (seriously) and is back to daydreaming of adventure. Sometimes those daydreams even make decent stories.

\* \* \* \* \*

# The Time of the Dragon
## by Rick Partlow

The kid had one of those turned-up noses just made for punching.

Only two things kept my hands at my side and a smile on my face: the purple sash across his waist, and the bag of gold on the table between us. One promised death for anyone who touched a member of the nobility, even as tangential as this kid's connection might be, while the other was the solution to every one of my current problems.

Well…*three* things, if you counted the bruiser hovering over the kid's shoulder like a guardian angel in polished chain mail. His features were smashed and scarred from injuries that should have killed him, yet they hadn't. I *thought* I could take him, but why find out? He'd reached his fourth decade by being too tough to kill, and I'd reached mine by outgrowing the need to test myself against warriors who were too tough to kill.

"They say you're the best tracker in all of Helvetia, Master Brennos." The kid was trying to sound confident and grown-up, but he had to raise his voice to be heard over the buzz of conversation in the great room of Grafton's Inn, and his manner struck me more as a child playing at war. "I have need of the best."

"Your lordship wants something killed?" I asked him, getting to the point, but careful not to push past the line of disrespect because of the big, honking mace in the meaty hands of Sir Scarface. "I'm your man, then. There ain't the animal born I haven't brought down." I leaned forward just an inch, as if I was sharing a secret with him. "I been known to take on bounties, as well, if there's an outlaw's head you'd like brought back lacking a body...if you take my meaning."

His lip curled, maybe disdain, maybe disgust. I didn't try to guess.

"I am the heir to Count Cerethrios," the boy reminded me, arching an eyebrow. "If I or my father wished to hunt a man, we have many who could take care of such things." He nodded toward his bodyguard, and the point was well-taken. "I don't want something killed, I want it tracked down and located so I may kill it myself."

I couldn't restrain the grimace, even with a couple decades of practice. It wasn't as if I'd never guided a hunt before. Pampered nobles got bored deciding which jewel-encrusted cloak to wear, or which courtesan to bed that night, and decided to spice up their life with a "hunt," which usually meant I herded an elk or a bison at them while their guards pumped arrows into it, and they "finished" it with an ineffective thrust from their spear. Then they made a show of eating the heart and bragged of their prowess at royal feasts.

Still, it was easy money. I plastered an ingratiating smile on my face and pressed on. "Of course, my lord. I would be happy to be the master of your hunt. Do you have any particular game in mind?"

The kid hesitated just a beat, as if the words didn't want to come.

"A dragon."

The laugh wouldn't be suppressed, and if I'd tried, I think I might have ruptured something. Sir Scarface didn't like it and leaned over, the flanges of his mace growing too close to my face.

"I told you this was a mistake, Lord Allucius." The bodyguard's voice was a boulder rolling across a field of broken glass. "Your father wouldna' approve."

"That is between the count and myself, Morgan," Allucius snapped, not even sparing the big man a glare.

"Your pardon, lord," I said hastily, still chuckling, "but I have seen dragons...from afar, which is why I'm here to talk t'ye. They can swallow your man here whole." I nodded toward Scarface. "And were you High King Senecius himself, still I would not throw my life away hunting a dragon for a bag of gold twice that size." I motioned toward the untouched pouch on the table, some of the luster gone from its contents. "If I could even find one," I added. "The nearest anyone has ever seen one is in the Alps on the borderlands with the Rasenna, and that land is full of outlaws and deserters, and even, I've heard tell, men and women who worship the dragons as gods. Such a journey could take weeks, and the costs alone would be..."

"I know the cost," Allucius snapped, though I doubt he knew the cost of anything, even of the mugs of ale his guard had brought for us to the table. "My father will cover it. And this bag is a down payment. An advance. If you agree to the job, you may take it with you." His voice hardened, and for the first time, I took him halfway seriously. "Though you would be foolish to think you could flee the city with it. The count has men patrolling the gates."

I didn't know if the pure greed had been so obvious on my face as to warrant the threat, but it was surely in my heart. It had been my first instinct. Say yes, take the coins, and travel south or east. The Rasenna or the Carthaginians surely needed hunt masters as well, and gold spent anywhere...

"And if I take the job," I said, running a finger over the edge of the gold piece jutting out the top of the bulging pouch, "how much?"

"If you find me a dragon...another pouch equal to this one." There was something about his smile, something older and less entitled than I'd seen from him since he'd sat down at my table. "And if I kill it, you get a third."

"Shite." The word stumbled out of my mouth of its own accord, but I paid it no mind, my thoughts afire with ideas of what I could spend that much money on. A title. I could buy a title with that, a minor barony anyhow. Maybe not in Helvetia, but somewhere where they were less touchy about who they let into the nobility. My wife would be a baroness. My sons would have an inheritance no one could take from them. At least not without sparking a small war.

I sighed. The brat had known what the answer would be. He had to know, unless he was a complete idiot.

*No, Brennos,* you're *the complete idiot.*

"All right," I sighed. "I'll need time to put together the expedition…and letters of credit from your lordship."

"You'll have it, hunter," he assured me. "As long as we leave from the count's palace in a fortnight. At dawn."

I weighed the pouch in my hand.

"Aye, my lord. I'll be there."

\* \* \*

"Is this," Count Cerethrios demanded, speaking down his nose at me, "the best you could do?"

Now I knew where Junior had gotten that punchable face. The count's fortress was a lot like his features: ugly, pockmarked, gap-toothed, round in the middle, and probably bigger than it had a right to be. The guards at the gate were still shooting me dirty looks for bringing so many horses and questionable characters into their courtyard, and I hoped the crew was smart enough not to mouth off. A crossbow bolt fired in anger meant I'd spend hours or even days trying to convince a fresh, new idiot that hunting a dragon was a brilliant idea that was sure not to end in horror and tragedy.

"Your Excellency," I assured the fancy-dressed, overstuffed boob, "I have hunted all across the five kingdoms, and even once in the Carthaginian Empire. I've never come back empty-handed."

Which wasn't to say I'd never had any of my hunters die in the process, but I really needed that damned gold.

The count sniffed at me, as if speaking to me outright would be beneath him…which, I suppose, it was. I was a commoner, a former man-at-arms still wearing the leather armor they'd issued me in the King's Levy, and I'd never spent one night in a palace.

"Allucius," the count said to his son, turning away from me as if he'd already forgotten I existed, "I expect you to do our family name proud." The old man's eyes were sunken and piggish, but they grew even uglier for a moment. "If you bring disgrace to our legacy, don't expect to be allowed to bring your shame to our bloodline."

"I understand, father," Allucius said, not meeting the count's glare. He was looking at me, though I didn't know why, and I could have sworn there was a pleading tilt to his eyes.

"I will accompany the young lord, of course," Scarface, the one he'd called Morgan, spoke up, one hand grasping the hilt of his falchion, the other filled with the handle of his mace. I was beginning to wonder if he put the thing down to bathe or have sex. "I may not be able to do the lad's duty for him, but I can keep him alive until the time comes."

"He should go alone," the count declared, arms crossed over his chest. "*I* went alone. As did my father before me."

"You traveled three days' journey to the Pyrenees by boat, Father. The dragons were cleaned out of those mountains 30 years ago. Master Brennos says we must go to the Alps."

"And pretty damned far from anything," I added, trying to be helpful. "It'd be a chancy go even without the dragons." I stopped, mostly because I didn't want to give the men I'd hired any reason to ask for a raise.

"Will Mother be saying goodbye?" The boy's voice was nearly a whisper.

His father's lip curled into a sneer.

"She isn't feeling well. She'll be waiting, should you return."

"We should ride," I suggested, hoping to just get away from the awkward scene. "We need to put some miles under our feet before we break for the night."

It was fairly weak as excuses went, but the kid took it gratefully, grabbing the reins of his horse and leading it to the front of our train, nearly out the gate. Paranoia struck that the count might shut the gate on us and send his son out alone in some perverse, stubborn impulse, so I bowed to the man, then jogged to my own steed, ready to be shut of the place.

I looked around, saw Morgan still cinching the saddle tighter on his horse, and took advantage of our separation from the count and his people to speak softly to Allucius.

"That's some kind of family you got there." I scowled. "I think t'were I to send one of our boys off without letting my wife give them her blessings, she'd likely slice off my balls with a rusty knife." I shrugged. "But then, we ain't noble blood, of course, so maybe we just wouldn't understand."

"If you ever do understand, Master Brennos," the boy murmured, swinging into his saddle, "maybe you can explain it to me."

\* \* \*

I moaned as I slid off my horse, limping as I led the gelding to the small clearing where we'd decided to make camp.

"It's been too long," I complained, "since I spent a day in the saddle. I'm starting to feel my bloody age."

"I thought you did this for a living, *Master* Huntsman," Morgan rumbled, sounding indecently fresh for a man of like years who'd worn chain mail all damned day in the summer heat.

"I've hired out apprentices since my sons were aborning," I allowed. "My wife prefers me closer to home."

"Then why are you off chasing a dragon?" Allucius wondered. Those were the first words he'd said to me or anyone else since we'd left his family's estate, and it was a more perceptive question than I would've expected from the boy.

I glanced around to make sure the hirelings were doing their job, setting up a rope corral for the horses and pulling off their gear, rather than eavesdropping on their betters.

"Because I've come into a debt I couldn't pay," I admitted, "and if I hadn't taken your gold, the creditors would have taken our farm."

"*You* have a *farm*?" Morgan asked, not trying to hide his scornful laugh. "Your pardon, huntsman, but you don't strike me as a man given to toiling at the land."

"Work's work," I said, maybe a bit defensive, if I'm being honest. "It was what my wife wanted. A place of our own me boys could work when I'm gone." I swatted at a maddening cloud of mosquitos, longing for the higher altitude that would take us out of their reach. It wasn't quite dusk, though, and for the night, they were only going to get worse. "What about you, Morgan? You have a little woman at home, taking care of a few burly little tykes running around with wooden maces, pretending to brain each other?"

The man-at-arms snorted humorlessly as he stripped the saddle off his warhorse, pulling out a brush and going to work on the burrs tangled in the horse's hair.

"Family is for farmers and nobles. I'm naught but a man-at-arms, and damned good at it. There'll be no titles or properties for my get, nor any lass higher than a scullery maid happy to have me." His voice softened as he focused on the task before him, working out a particularly knotted tangle. "'Sides, lads shouldn't have to grow up without their father, and I'm like as not to have my guts dripping on the ground somewhere afore their beards grow."

I didn't have an answer for that. It was why I hadn't gone into the King's Guard from the Levy when I was offered the chance. Being a hunter was risky enough. I left Morgan to his task and set about making sure the rest of this lot wasn't buggering things up too badly setting up the camp. I knew most of them, and wouldn't have hired them for a job like this if they didn't know their arse from a hole in the ground, but friends had brought friends, and you never knew when someone was going to go on one drunken bender too many and suddenly lose the brains the gods gave them.

After I was satisfied none of the shitbirds was about to set fire to the woods or collapse a widowmaker tree on top of the camp, I laid out my own bedroll, laying my boar spear beside it. I was so busy at my task, I didn't notice the kid coming up behind me, carrying his own saddle and roll, until he was almost on top of me.

"Are there dangerous animals this close to the city?" Allucius asked, hand clenching around the sword sheathed at his side as he stared at my spear.

I bit down on the first answer that came to me, knowing that insulting the customer wasn't a good policy.

"Boars are everywhere, and not a damned thing you can do to wipe them out. Not like bears or wolves—they're just too tough. But it's not boars that worry me, your lordship. It's the two-legged sort of animals that are the danger here close to the road."

Which was why we'd moved a fair way off it before we camped, despite the bugs and tanglefoot.

The kid hesitated, then threw his saddle down a man's height from mine and began laying out his gear. I sighed. If he was sleeping here, that meant his man, Morgan, would be as well, and that bugger had the look of a snorer.

"Pardon me for asking what's none of my affair, your lordship," I said, trying to be quiet enough not to attract Morgan's attention, "but what the hell sort of business is this, anyway?" The lad frowned as if he didn't understand the question, and I pressed on, heedless of the hornet's nest I might be stepping into. "There's a reason dragons were hunted out of the ten kingdoms, there's a reason they're still up in the Alps and the north country, and it's the same gods-damned reason. They're huge, and they're deadly, and they can kill a warhorse with a single chomp. Why in the name of the Horned Lord is the son of a count riding all the way to the trackless mountains just to kill a beast that's nae harming anyone except some bison?"

Allucius didn't look up from straightening his bedroll, but his mouth became a hard line. "It's a family tradition. The designated heir must slay a dragon to prove their worth."

"A family tradition going back how long?" I blurted, unable to keep the disbelief out of my tone.

"To the days of my great-grandfather." The lad hesitated, glancing up at me before looking down again. "Though he died in the attempt. Then my grandfather's two brothers both died as well. And my father's brother." His voice grew even softer. "And my older brother, Attalus."

"Sweet Lady," I hissed, staring at the boy in disbelief. "So you lot just send one son after another into the mountains to kill a dragon? What happens if they all fail? Does your line just *end*?"

Allucius shrugged, blinking rapidly in a way I thought meant he was trying hard not to cry in front of me. I hoped it was sadness from the loss of his brother rather than fear, because this was about the least scary thing we'd do on this trip.

"I don't know. It hasn't happened yet."

"And what proof do y'be needing to bring home to your father, lad?" I was so flummoxed, I didn't even remember to address him politely. "'Cause we ain't going to be hauling a whole dead dragon out of those mountains!"

"Father wants the head, but…." He frowned. "He didn't bring back the whole head himself, just a jawbone. And his father, just a single claw. But he told me to bring back the head."

"The damned head," I repeated, collapsing down on my bedroll, thoughts of supper suddenly forgotten. "Your da' doesn't really like you all that much, does he?"

"Attalus was to be the heir." He almost whispered the words. "He was the oldest. I wanted to serve the gods as a druid."

"This money, lad…." I broke off, biting down on the words. He was staring at me, expectant. "I need this gold. But if I were a just man, I'd turn you down, throw the bag at your father, the count, and return to face me wife."

"You're not a just man?"

"No. I'm just a man." I waved at the fire, where Caracalla had stew going in a pot. "Get yourself something to eat, lad, then get some rest. Tomorrow's ride will be a long one."

* * *

They were all long ones, day after day. We pushed the horses harder than I would have liked, but there was plenty of grass and water to be had, and I wanted badly to beat the rains. They'd be coming in less than a month—could come at any time—and when they hit, those mountain passes would be death traps where landslides could bury us in seconds.

The mountains were perpetually on the horizon, illusions put there by the gods to torment us, and the only thing that changed on our ride was the accents of the villagers we passed. My people almost rebelled and left for home when Morgan declared we wouldn't be availing ourselves of the inns at Salodrum, but I could understand his worry. It was a larger city, filled with possible thieves and cutpurses, and I couldn't have, in good conscience, given assurance that my men wouldn't use the coins I'd advanced them to go a'whoring and get roaring drunk in the process.

"We don't have the time nor the spare gold to be bribing the city guards to get you lot out of the city lockup," Morgan had growled, rolling the words around in a grinder before he'd spat them out. "We'll stay in an inn when we come to one that doesn't come complete with brothels and ruffians."

Given that none of the workers and huntsmen I'd brought along were willing to challenge Morgan without my help or leave, that was that. I'd secretly been glad. Salodrum was overly clean and overly policed, and not a city given to looking the other way when strangers disturbed their peace. Not to mention, I was fairly certain there was still a bounty on my head there for breaking the legs of the son of a local baron. Long story.

But the men and I, and I think even Morgan, were all happy when we came to Limenos.

Well, maybe not Morgan.

"I don't like having to hire a boat," he complained as we led our horses through the streets. Not mud yet, thank the Horned Lord and the Lady. We were still ahead of the rains. "We should just ride around."

"Are you insane?" I blurted, then withered under his glare…just a little. After a week on the road, even Morgan's menace had quailed. "That would add another *week* to the journey! The rains would be on us in the mountain passes! You know what that means, right?"

"Aye, you've said it often enough, huntsman," he snapped. But he shook his head. "I know it has to be done. But I don't like boats."

"I've never been on anything larger than a rowboat," Allucius said, staring out at the mountains. They were much closer now, close enough to touch, and we might have even found a dragon in the closer foothills, but that would have meant more time. I knew the passes where they laired in the summer, and they were far afield from the cities. They were across that lake.

We found Captain Proteus at an inn called the Baleful Moon, in one of the seedier parts of Limenos, near the harbor. Proteus was a Greek, of course, because all the best sailors were.

"I trace my ancestry to the men who steered the ships of Alexander the Great!" Proteus declared, slamming a not-quite-empty mug of beer onto the scored and stained tabletop, sending droplets flying. One hit me on the cheek, but I refused to wipe it off.

"And I'm sure Great-grandaddy Pissantius would be so proud of you," I assured him, not having to put on too much of an act to seem unimpressed. "But my question still stands. How much to take our party across the gods-damned lake?"

Proteus's features wiggled and twisted, and seemed to try to find new ways to make his pockmarked, scarred face even uglier as he fought to focus on my eyes, but couldn't quite win that battle. The beer, I was sure, wasn't his first, or even his tenth. The man I took for his first mate was passed out cold on the seat beside him, drool dripping down his waxed beard to further stain his tunic, not contributing to this sterling conversation.

"There's a stiff headwind these mornings," Proteus warned. "More oar time for my rowers. They'll want more coin for the passage."

"Give me," I said, beginning to lose patience, "a number. A number you'll stick by. Or I'll go find the second-best ship and the second-best captain on this lake and give *him* my damned coin."

And thank all the gods that Morgan and Allucius had gone off to find a bath, because I was sure the man-at-arms would have bashed Proteus's brains in by now. I'd brought Lucien with me, instead, because he was old enough to avoid a fight, and Rasenna by birth, exotic enough for people to underestimate him...and the dagger concealed under his jacket.

"Ten gold drachmas," he declared, slamming down the mug again.

"Stop doing that, you drunken sod," Lucien murmured, wiping beer off his chin.

"*Ten?*" I stared at him in disbelief. "D'you think we wish to *buy* your gods-forsaken boat, man? Three and not a coin more!"

"You filthy thief!" It should have been full of outrage for the proper effect, but Proteus was too drunk for that, so it sounded more like he'd discovered a dog licking up the last of his beer. "You think I should provide whores for your passage, too? You think I should wash your feet as you board? Eight! And I'm dishonoring my ancestors to accept such an insulting amount!"

"Enough!" I cried, jumping to my feet, throwing up my hands as if beseeching the gods. "I would sooner *swim* across the lake with a horse under each arm than pay you more than four golden drachmas!"

"Then swim away, and may the cold freeze your balls off so that no more of your line will trouble any more of mine! And if I take less than seven drachmas, may mine fall off right beside yours!"

"This," Lucien declared, rubbing at his temples, "is making my head hurt." He reached into his pouch and pulled out four golden coins and smacked them down on the table. "Here. Four now, and two more once we reach the eastern shore. Is it a deal?"

Proteus looked at Lucien sidelong, as if trying to judge whether the Rasenna would be more or less likely to cheat him than a Gaul, but his hand snaked out with deceptive speed for one so large and drunk and snatched up the coins.

"Be at the docks by dawn, ready to board. If you're late, I'll leave without you and keep your damned money!" Proteus lurched to his feet, kicking at the man beside him. "Up, you drunken dog! We've work to do!"

Lucien waited until both men were gone, then shot me a grin.

"Did I do well, Brennos?"

"You did *very* well," I assured him. "I would have paid him seven." A smile spread across my face. "Let's put that extra coin to good use." I waved at the chubby wench hauling a keg to a table of greasy little Carthaginians. "Barmaid! Bring us your best wine!"

\* \* \*

I knew now the real reason Morgan didn't like boats. The big man hung over the railing, retching pitifully, so vulnerable and strengthless, so unlike the intimidating warrior I was used to. I can't say there wasn't just a *little* secret glee running around like a child inside my chest, happy to see the big man taken down a peg. But Allucius seemed worried about him, staying at his side the whole time, bringing him water and caring for him like he was the big man's servant rather than his lord.

I didn't *quite* feel the urge to push the big arsehole right over the railing, but it was a near thing.

"Not a bad passage," Captain Proteus declared, sniffing the cool lake air, riding the swell and heave of the waves with remarkable agility for a man of his bulk. He must have considered the occasional spray of lake water over the railing to be cleansing, because he hadn't bothered with a bath before leaving the inn, and in fact still wore the same clothes. At least the wind was carrying away his stench. Proteus grinned at Morgan's discomfort, clapping the man on the arm. "This is nothing, good sir! You should try crossing the North Sea if you want some real sailing!"

"I ain't no bleedin' 'sir.' I work for a living." Morgan was somehow able to squeeze the words out between heaves. "And I been on the bleedin' ocean. I don't like it any more than this."

I didn't know how anyone couldn't like *this*. The Alps were hell to ride through, double hell to walk through, but rising up above Lake Limenos, they were pure heaven, the most beautiful thing I'd ever seen.

"I'd almost forgotten," I murmured.

"You've been here before, huntsman?" Allucius asked, his voice breaking slightly as he tried to pitch it to carry over the waves. I half-expected him to be skeptical of the claim, but the look in his eyes was, instead, envious.

*Why the hell would a lordling set to be a count envy me?*

"Once, your lordship. When I was part of the King's Levy, they sent us as far as Taurini to ally with the Rasenna and drive out the Carthaginians." I laughed softly, without much humor. "The battle, I do not have such pleasant memories from, but the Alps..." I shook my head. "Back then, I dreamed of living here. With the gold you and your father, the count, are giving me for this hunt, I may yet."

Then I winced, cursing myself, for Proteus was still behind me, and when I glanced his way, I saw his eyes growing wider. And being a Greek sailor, the man lacked the tact to pretend he hadn't heard.

"What would you be hunting worth so much gold?"

I was about to lie, but Allucius blurted the truth in that way that only ignorant youth can.

"A dragon."

"A *what?*" From the look on his face, the boy might as well have said he intended to kill his father and marry his mother. "What in the name of the All-Father would you do that for?"

"It's none of your concern, sailor," Morgan snapped, wiping vomitus out of his beard. "See to your ship, and we'll see to our business." When Proteus walked away, still glowering back at us, Morgan turned to his young charge, looking no less angry at the lordling than he had at the sailor. "My lord, you need to learn to keep your teeth together. This is not the place nor the company to be sharing your secrets."

Allucius reddened, and I thought he might talk back to Morgan, but he merely nodded.

"How much longer till we hit shore?" Morgan asked.

I cast a critical eye at the sails, stretched to their limits, the oars secured to make the most of the favorable wind, then to the shore drawing ever closer. The rooftops of Tor Dacha were just visible above the swell of the waves, and when they tossed the boat up a few feet, I could see the storehouses at the harbor.

"Another hour or so, I'd judge."

"Good. When we arrive, pay this damned pirate and then we ride straight out of the city." He scowled, though he was careful not to aim it at Allucius. "Now that Proteus knows why we're here, I don't want to be the target of every would-be guide and supposed wizard within a dozen miles of Tor Dacha."

I wanted to argue with Morgan, but I had to admit he was right.

I *hated* that.

\* \* \*

"**B**lood of the Lady," Allucius moaned, nearly toppling over the edge of the switchback as a gust of wind hit him, barely catching himself on the reins of his horse, "is the entire trail like this?"

"No, your lordship," I said, eyes on my footing. "Just through this pass, and we'll be back on level ground."

I tried to sound more confident than I felt, because I was getting nervous for the horses, and more nervous about the way back. We'd ascended a good two thousand feet, and I hadn't remembered the trail being this narrow this early. If it turned to mud while we were up above the tree line, we'd be hard pressed to get through ourselves, and we'd have to leave our mounts behind. Which meant either a damned long walk back to Helvetia, or I'd be buying new mounts out of my own pocket.

At least the pure fear was keeping me warm, despite the best efforts of the wind ripping through the mountain pass. I could see straight down that switchback, down the boulder-strewn slopes, every bit of the way to the bottom.

"Shouldn't we be roped together?" Lucien called from behind Morgan, fourth in our narrow file. He was the steadiest of the crew I'd hired, and even he looked pale, eyes constantly flickering toward the edge. He was leading his horse, the same as the rest of us, since I wouldn't have trusted a mule up here, and the animal seemed even more worried than he was.

"If we're roped together," Morgan answered for me, "and one of us goes, then all of us go."

He was right, but I wouldn't have been quite that honest.

"Just around the bend!" I promised everyone, pointing up ahead.

When the trail bent inward, through a narrow gap in the rocks and past it into a clearing, I nearly bent the knee and kissed the ground, but it would have been rude with so many waiting behind me. I did allow myself a relieved hiss of breath and a moment to stare up at the jagged peaks rising naked above the trees ahead.

"There," I turned and said to Allucius, "we should be through the worst of it."

Damn me for a fool, I should have known better than to tempt the gods that way.

I've been a hunter for twenty years, and I know better than anyone what it is to stalk, but I'm not much of a soldier anymore, and I'd forgotten what it's like to *be* stalked. When we walked into the clearing, surrounded by thick clusters of fir and aspen, I should've been looking near the ground, should've been checking for movement. If I had, I would have seen the bowstring pull back before the arrow snapped across the 70 yards and into Lucien's neck.

His eyes went wide, hands clutching at his throat, and when he coughed, gouts of blood poured down his chin and soaked his sheepskin vest. Everyone who saw it froze...except Morgan. And me.

I might not have had a soldier's instincts anymore, but I did have the memories, and the sight of a man dying beside me was high among them. There was nowhere to run, nowhere to hide, and that meant charging straight into their teeth, which might be suicide, but was at least a better way to go out than sitting around and letting our attackers pick us off at leisure. I swung into the saddle almost synchronously with Morgan, as if we'd practiced the motion together, and I snatched my boar spear from its mount down the side of my saddle, couching it under my right arm. I wished I had a shield, but if wishes were horses...well, then, I'd have a big enough herd that I wouldn't need the count's money to retire.

"Charge the arseholes!" I yelled, hoping *someone* would listen, because Morgan and I were going to feel pretty damn silly attacking all by ourselves.

I dug my heels in, and Dancer leapt into the fray as if he were a warhorse born. He wasn't, but he'd faced down lions and bears and boars beyond counting, and what were a few humans beside that? I tucked my head down close to his neck and prayed to all the gods that he wouldn't take an arrow…and that I wouldn't, either. Because the two of us were the point of the spear.

As it happened, the enemy didn't waste time sitting back and shooting arrows at moving targets. They had an ambush to run, and they were seeing to it with a laudable enthusiasm, running out of the trees with the sun flashing off axe-heads and spear points. No swords. Swords were for nobles, and by the look of these people, not one of them had been close enough to nobility to smell the perfume. Those who had armor wore boiled leather or stiff, quilted arming jackets, but most of the two dozen or so of them had just the shirts or vests or jackets they would've worn working the docks or tending to their beasts.

Bandits, then, which was better than someone's army only because they wouldn't be as well trained. A couple more arrows passed overhead, though I couldn't take the time to look back and see if they hit home. I wouldn't have heard the screams, not over the yells coming from the bandits, the rumble of Dancer's hooves on the tightly-packed dirt, and Morgan's basso war cry as he gained on me, his stallion's hooves ripping up chunks of sod.

Then I tried to shut out all the sound, all the frantic action, all the fear, and focus on one man, on a tall, broad-shouldered man with a bit of gray in his beard out in front of the others. He wore an arming jack and carried his long-handled axe easily in one meaty hand, his mouth open as he yelled a battle cry, crooked teeth bared to the sun. I put the point of my boar spear over his heart and stood up in the stirrups.

When the impact came, it nearly threw me out of the saddle—would have if I hadn't let go of the spear. It had plunged through his chest, and with the boar guards, I wouldn't be getting it out unless I put a boot on his belly and yanked. He was a powerful man. He tried to stand for a moment, the heavy spear pulling him off-balance, but in the end, he went down as we all do, and someone screamed, keening in woe.

Better them than us, I figured. But that left me with empty hands, and that wouldn't do. I ducked behind Dancer's neck, one leg draped across his back the only thing holding me to him, as a throwing axe passed through where my head had been a breath before. The woman who'd thrown it screamed frustration, and I ended her scream with a boot to the face. I felt the blow all the way up my heel to my hip, reminding me I wasn't as young as I used to be, but she went down, her face a mass of blood. I was past the bulk of the charge, surrounded by a handful of bodies left by Morgan's mace. I'd missed the blows, but the aftermath was a bloody, gruesome mess.

One of them had held a long-handled axe, and I jumped off of Dancer's back, holding his reins with one hand, snagging the weapon with the other, then vaulting back into the saddle. When I turned back to find more of the bandits to fight, my heart fell down through my stomach and just about out my arsehole. The bandits had melted before Morgan and myself, and Allucius had been smart enough to stick close to his protector, though I saw no hint of blood on the blade of his sword. But the rest of us...we'd been a dozen in all.

"Shite."

Now we were three. They hadn't been warriors, hadn't been much more than laborers, stable hands who knew their way about the woods. They'd carried knives or axes, a couple of spears, and I doubt a one of them had ever seen a man dead at their hands. And they hadn't had the instinct to mount the horses. That was what had killed them. There was no doubt they were dead...one of the bandits was hacking at them with a hatchet, and the rest were turning back toward the three of us, pulling out their bows again. Had they been my friends, I might have forgotten my family and my vows to my wife and charged into them, bent on revenge.

But they were hired men, handy and trustworthy, but mostly strangers to me. And I ran.

"This way!" I yelled to Morgan and Allucius, spurring Dancer toward the trail leading through the trees.

There might be more of the bandits through there, but I didn't think so. Two dozen was a good size for a band of brigands, and if anything was left this way, it would likely be the nursing mothers and children, left behind with the wagons while they did the dirty work.

But I didn't see even that. The trail was empty, veiled in shadows, like a gateway to the nether world, not even a rabbit or squirrel to be seen, much less one of the bandits. I slowed my steed to a walk, looking behind us for signs of pursuit. Dancer's chest heaved, and he snorted, as scared as I was, but better at hiding it.

"We should go back!" Allucius cried, breathless. "Those men...."

"Those men are dead, lord," Morgan declared. His voice sounded strained, and I risked a look back. Red stained the hide of his riding breeches.

"You've taken an arrow," I said, spotting the stub where he'd broken it off in his upper thigh.

"I've taken worse." His mouth was a hard line. "Keep riding. Those lot didn't have horses, but there might be more ahead."

"What's ahead is more mountains," I told him. "More switchbacks. We need to head down."

"We can't take them all on by ourselves." It wasn't what I expected to hear from the man-at-arms, and I thought it reflected how bad his wound was rather than his estimation of the bandits.

"There has to be another way down. They didn't come up here the way we did...we would have seen them." I pointed. "There has to be a fork in the trail ahead."

I tried to picture the terrain as we trotted through the forest, imagine where another path down could be...and all I could imagine was that it was on the other side of the peak we'd ascended. It would be steep, and it would have to come out miles past Tor Dacha, but it was the only place there could be another trail.

"There it is!" I said, pointing to a fork heading to the right. I didn't recall it from my last trek through the Alps, but that had been long ago, and I'd mostly been following the man in front of me. And the hell with it, it was a way out, and I badly wanted out. "Let's go!"

The path was narrow and rough, and ungodly silent. No birds, no squirrels, not even the whistle of the breeze, just the clop of the horses' hooves, the rasp of their labored breathing...and my own. The walls closed in on us, granite, dirt, and way too many boulders strewn along the path, buried in clay...evidence of landslides from last summer. There was way too much of a chance that this path would be blocked by the slides if I was wrong about the bandits coming up this way.

"Tracks," Morgan said, nodding ahead of us.

"Damn right they are," I agreed, sighing in relief I didn't bother to hide. Footprints. They *had* come from this way.

"I don't hear anything behind us." Allucius sounded hopeful, which was, I supposed, better than panicked.

"They don't have horses," Morgan reminded him. "It bothers me. How would they expect to get the food and gear they stole from us back down the mountain without horses?"

"They could use ours," I suggested, bitterness grinding my teeth together.

"Aye, they well could, but d'ye think they knew that beforehand?" He shook his head. "This is a damned strange place for bandits to hit. I'd have wagered they'd hit us down at the foot of the mountain, not after we'd half-climbed it."

"Maybe you're right, but so what? So, they're *stupid* bandits. I don't recall ever meeting one who impressed me with his intelligence. What's your point?"

The curve in the path was nothing special, much like any other, except I sensed a bit more light coming from around it, which could mean another flat spot, another clearing. Maybe someplace we could rest and take a look at Morgan's wound. I spurred Dancer around the corner, hoping for the best.

And found a dragon.

I know it's hard to believe, but I didn't see him at first. There was a rock shelf beside the path, looking down on a pool coming out of a spring, then trickling down beside the path, down the mountain toward the lake. And up on that shelf, the dragon blended into the grays and browns of the rock, its wings folded over its body, only one golden eye staring out at us. It was easy to underestimate its size, hidden as it was, easy to think it was close, maybe 30 or 40 feet away instead of nearly 50 yards.

But I knew. I'd seen one before, from far away, but I'd seen what it had done to a warrior ahorse. Standing on its hind legs, the thing was over twenty feet at the shoulder, probably another ten feet between the neck and the head, 30 more just of that sinuous, barbed tail, and when those wings spread, they could block out the sun. And they were fast, as fast as a striking snake, which was why I didn't scream, didn't yell, didn't swing Dancer around and run the second I noticed the thing.

"Morgan," I said softly, calmly, even though my heart was fit to beat right out of my chest. "Allucius. Very slowly, begin walking your horses backward. Do *not* run, do not turn. Just begin backing up your gods-damned horses."

"What in the nine hells are you...." Morgan trailed off, and his eyes went wide. He wasn't a man who scared, but he was scared now. Allucius followed his gaze, and his face went slack with horror, even though he, of all of us, should have expected it. Seeing it with his own eyes was something else.

And worse, the damned horses saw it...or smelled it.

Dancer tossed his head and snorted, but he was trained not to run at the scent of a predator. Morgan and Allucius' mounts were warhorses, conditioned to ignore the clash of battle...but this wasn't a warrior in armor. Allucius' horse reared up, screaming like it'd already been gutted, and tried to run.

And the dragon moved. It didn't leap so much as it unfolded, the wings sweeping outward, the neck uncoiling, legs the size of a hundred-year-old oak propelling it off the rock face and across the 50 yards in the space of a second. The rock creaked with the movement, and the air thundered from the motion of the wings, but the thing was amazingly silent for its tons of bulk.

If I hadn't shat my breeches just yet, it wasn't for lack of trying, but this was another dangerous animal, and I had twenty years of hunting them...and having them hunt me back. I wheeled Dancer, knowing what was coming.

The only reason I reached Allucius before the dragon was that it went after Morgan first. Morgan's horse was a charger, seventeen hands tall, and powerful enough to bowl through an armored man, but the dragon ripped its head off its neck with a single swipe of its talons, spraying blood in a fan that splattered the both of us.

Morgan fell, and Allucius' horse went mad, throwing him off the saddle, flat onto his back. I leaned out of the saddle and yanked him up by his collar, nearly falling out myself, but he helped, scrambling back to his feet and jumping on behind me. Dancer shied at the added weight, but I just needed him to get us back around that corner, back to where it would be too narrow for the beast.

I gave no thought to Morgan, not because I disliked the man, but because he was dead. Though he was on his feet, his giant mace in his hand, shouting a war cry despite the fear I'd seen earlier, he was a dead man, and nothing I could do would save him. I just wish Allucius had known that, because he jumped off the back of my horse, grabbed his fallen sword, and rushed at the monster, yelling a high-pitched war cry.

"Oh, you bloody twit!" I screamed, and still wouldn't have been heard, because the dragon opened its mouth and roared.

There's nothing I've ever heard in my life comparable to the roar of a dragon. It was as if a lion had been given the voice of a howling wind, resonating in my chest, my sinuses, my very bones, in the Earth itself. The temperature rose by ten degrees, promising fire.

That was too much even for faithful Dancer. He spooked and bucked, and I was still half out of my stirrup, reaching for the kid. I slid out of the saddle, barely kicking free of the stirrups, and landed hard on my shoulder, the breath going out of me in a *whoosh*, the flaring lights of pain exploding in my vision. The axe was gone from my hand, and I couldn't even see where it had landed, couldn't see anything. I struggled to get up, to get to my feet, though I wasn't sure why I was bothering.

*Get away. I can still get away.* The dragon would be occupied with those two fools, and I could get down the mountain, get back to my wife and sons. Dirt under my hands, the coolness of a rock. I pushed against it, and my vision cleared as I turned away from the dragon, back to the narrow passage between cliff faces…and the bandits.

They stood across the path, axes and spears at the ready, just waiting. Watching. Not with fear or horror, but with religious awe. That was why this attack hadn't made sense to Morgan. They *weren't* bandits, hadn't ever intended to rob us. They were dragon worshippers.

Their mouths worked in unison in a chant I couldn't hear over the roar of the beast, the scratch of its claws on the rock. I knew what it was, though. I'd heard it before.

*Drakon.*

I almost charged into them anyway, knowing I had a better chance against them than I did the beast. I didn't owe Allucius anything, surely not more than I did my family...

I cursed loud and long, enough to drown out the roar and the chant, and I found that gods-damned axe and ran at the dragon. It had brushed Morgan aside with a sweep of its wing, throwing the big man twenty feet backward, where he lay motionless, though I thought I saw his chest still rising. Still alive for the moment.

Allucius was circling the dragon, holding his bastard sword in both hands with better technique than I would've thought for a stripling who'd wanted to be a druid. Maybe the count had insisted on fighting lessons. The dragon stared at him, shifting its upright, two-legged stance on the rock, its forelegs clutched into its massive chest, coiled for a blow. Its teeth were the size of short-swords, its tongue forked and flickering over them, snakelike, narrow curls of smoke coming out of its nostrils, and I knew the lad had seconds to live.

And yet, those eyes.

The dragon's eyes were golden, and I'd seen many golden eyes in my day. Wolves, raccoons, deer...but these were different. There was something behind them, an intelligence I hadn't seen even in the canniest of wolves.

"I would not kill you, princeling."

I spun, thinking the voice had come from one of the cultists, but they stood stock-still, even their chanting ceased, faces slack in a look I'd only seen during sex. I turned back, and Allucius had straightened, sword hanging at his side, eyes wide with disbelief, and I *knew*.

"If I kill you," the dragon said, though its mouth didn't move and no sound came from it, "then your father will simply send his next son, or his nephew. And if his line died out entirely, another of your foolish little lordlings would get the idea, and back they'd come until my mountain was filled with their armies. Their hired hunters."

Those golden eyes settled on me, disgust and disdain pouring off them. The dragon...it was as a man. It could speak, and yet how in the nine hells could it speak my language?

"Because I'm not *speaking*, you brainless ape. I'm projecting my thoughts at you...and reading yours."

Horror was a trickle of ice-cold water down my back. The thing could read my thoughts. Gods above and below...could *all* the animals I'd hunted think? Were they all as smart as humans?

"Of course not, you dolt." Puffs of flame sputtered out of the dragon's nostrils...a laugh? "If all the animals you've killed could think as well as you, one of them would surely have killed you instead. Some of them are smarter than others, but you hairless apes are the very pinnacle of evolution on this world."

"What the hell is evolution?" I blurted.

The dragon lurched forward, and Allucius and I both jumped back, but it was going down on all fours, pacing across the rock slowly, deliberately.

"You should be grateful, you know? You wouldn't exist if it weren't for us. Before we arrived, you were destined to be conquered, to be wiped from the face of history when the Romans marched north."

"Wh...what's a Roman?" I was beginning to sound like a toddler, but the words tumbled out of their own accord, my tongue loosened right alongside my bowels from sheer terror.

The dragon grinned. "You'll never know, because my kind landed in the northern reaches of the Rasenna first and *ate* them. But they would have become nasty, pushy bastards intent on conquering the world. Every kingdom, every people you know—the Rasenna, who they would call the Etruscans, the Greeks, the Persians, would all be subservient to them. You Gauls would have disappeared entirely, and there would be nothing left of Carthage except charred ruins."

"How do you know this?" Allucius asked, managing finally to make his mouth work. "How do you know what might have been?"

"It's our curse, stripling." I'm not sure how a 60-foot-long dragon managed to sound bitter, but it did. "It's the nature of our existence to see how things may be…and then, when we try to change them, to generally make them worse. When we saw our world was dying, we made a portal through reality to come to yours, using up all the magic left in us, leaving us to live as beasts, hunting bison and horses, and yes, sometimes *you*, to survive. When we saw that the hunger for power and control at the heart of the Romans would unite a whole continent against us, we put an end to them while they were still aborning, burned down their wattle huts, and scattered them to the winds."

The huge head twisted to the side, regarding first the boy, then me. Its scales glittered in the sun like quartz.

"No Rome, no Roman Church, no Holy Roman Empire…no Crusades, no jihad, no Reconquista." The words were meaningless to me, whether the dragon spoke them with its mouth or in my mind. "No New World, no Reformation, no Renaissance, no Industrial Revolution. No steam engines, no gunpowder. Just dragons and magic. And you'd think you would have been grateful for the respite, yet you still come to hunt us, leaving us only these high peaks for refuge…for the moment."

I slugged my brain into motion, which was no easy thing when a beast the size of a castle wall was staring down at us, its eyes as large as dinner plates.

"You're talking to us. You must want something from us, or we'd be strips of meat in your belly."

"I want something from *him*." The head settled in front of Allucius, the hot breath pushing back his hair, blowing dust off his clothes. "Your father sent you for my head, as he did your brother before you."

"You…" the boy stuttered, his jaw firming up as he continued. "You killed Attalus."

"And if I had not," the dragon said, quite reasonably I thought, "he would have killed me. But this grows tiresome. There are only a few of us left, and I would not have my children constantly fighting yours. I have a gift for you."

The beast's wings beat down like a sandstorm in one of the Iberian deserts, the wind knocking Allucius and me down on our asses, hot wind beating at my face, grit trying to find its way into my eyes, and the dragon was gone.

"Drakon! Drakon! Drakon!"

The chant of the cultists filled the sudden silence, and now they were on their knees, except for the ones holding Dancer and Allucius' horse. I had a wild thought of rushing them while the beast was gone, grabbing our horses and running. But fear kept me rooted to the rock. We weren't going to outrun that gods-damned dragon.

The wind returned with the beast, appearing as if through a door in the mountain, though I knew it had just come around the other side of the rock face. It lit like a hawk, light as a feather, and in its arms was a skull. A dragon skull, gleaming white, teeth still meshed together like a wall of knives. The beast laid its burden down at Allucius' feet.

"I give you my brother in exchange for yours."

Allucius' gaze flickered back and forth from the dragon to the skull, disbelief strong in his expression.

"Your father killed him," the dragon went on. "He brought two dozen soldiers with him, armed with crossbows, the bolts poisoned."

"Two dozen…" Allucius hissed, remembering, no doubt, the same thing I was, the same thing the dragon repeated, reading the boy's thoughts.

"And he told you he went alone, big hero that he is." Foot-long teeth parted in a grin. "Take this to him. Tell him you killed your dragon and take his seat."

"Why would you do this?"

"It's a trade, boy, and your part of it is to *end this*. To end this idiotic family tradition. I expect you to pledge to your gods you'll do everything you can to protect us." The dragon's head turned sideways, as if it was eyeing the boy from a different direction. "After all, you did wish to become a druid, did you not? To protect the creation of your gods?"

Allucius said nothing for far too long, and I wanted to scream at him to agree to it, because there was no other way we were getting off this mountain alive. But that wouldn't work, either. If he was lying, the dragon would know.

"Yes, I would," the thing told me, and I winced, trying to shut down my thoughts, be a blank.

"I'll do it," Allucius said, kneeling to pick up the skull. He grunted with strain, using both hands and putting his back into it. "I'll end this madness. I would have, anyway. But as count, I'll do what I can to keep your kind safe." He eyed the dragon suspiciously. "*If* you keep yours from hunting us."

"Of course." The dragon spoke so smoothly, I wanted to feel for my purse.

"And what of me?" I asked, my voice hoarse. I should have said "us," for Morgan was still alive, from what I could tell, though he hadn't moved much, and was likely nursing a few broken bones.

"You could go back to your family with my gold, hunter," Allucius suggested. "Or, when I am count, you could come work for me…as the warden of my lands. To control what is and isn't hunted."

"Would your wife approve, huntsman?" the dragon teased.

"I believe she would." I bowed to the new count. *She'll approve of anything that keeps me from insane adventures like this.*

But even as the cultists brought us our horses and tended to Morgan, I couldn't help but ponder this other world the dragon had spoken of. It seemed to hold untold marvels, unfinished stories, and I wondered if we'd ever see its like.

"Don't fret on it, huntsman," the dragon told me, reading my thoughts again. "You wouldn't like it." He rolled his eyes. "Reality is boring."

\* \* \* \* \*

## Rick Partlow Biography

Rick Partlow is that rarest of species, a native Floridian. Born in Tampa, he attended Florida Southern College and graduated with a degree in History and a commission in the US Army as an Infantry officer.

He has written over 40 books in a dozen different series, including *Drop Trooper*, *Holy War* and *Earth at War*, and his short stories have been included in twelve different anthologies.

He lives in central Florida with his wife, two children, and two lovable mutts. Besides writing and reading science fiction and fantasy, he enjoys outdoor photography, hiking, and camping.

To subscribe to Rick's newsletter, go to this link: https://www.subscribepage.com/o1m0u1.

\* \* \* \* \*

# A Song of Mercy
# by Josh Hayes

### One

*"I would become the Shield of the World. I would show no mercy."*

Warden Jasson Rainlight let the rushing stream wash over his fingers, watching as it carried away the blood crusted on his skin. The frigid water stung his hand, but he held it under nonetheless, relishing the cold and pain.

Beneath the clear surface, a fish flicked away from him and then turned, as if considering the intrusion into its realm. Jasson had fished these waters as a boy, though the yellow scales of the animal beneath the waters today were much duller than he remembered.

*Another sign*, he thought. If there had been just one, his convictions might not be so strong, but this was but the most recent in a long line of signs which had led him along this path. A path he knew had but one destination. Death.

"Your path ends at the Tomb, Warden," the Seer had said. "The Fallen King awaits."

*But will it be my death, or his?* The fish heeded him not, swimming just hard enough to hang in the current like a kestrel in the sky.

It called to him again. A deep, reverberating voice the Warden felt rather than heard. *Mercy*.

*You are becoming desperate*, the Warden thought. He did not know if the voice heard him or not. In the months since his journey began, the voice had never engaged with him, never acknowledged him, only begged for mercy. Mercy which the Warden would not give it.

Jasson rubbed his hands together, washing the last of the blood from his fingers, and the fish darted away. His hands clean, he stood and left the bank, drying them on his black woolen cloak.

Challenger, his armored stallion, snorted at his approach.

"Easy," Jasson told him, running a damp hand down the bridge of Challenger's muzzle. "Trouble's gone for now."

He pulled a strip of cloth from a pouch on his saddle and bound the wound on his forearm. The slash wasn't deep. He'd suffered worse.

"You should heal yourself, Master," his squire said.

Yul, dressed in brown woolen breeches and shirt, stood beside a brown and white mare. The han'jani had filed his eyeteeth—just the hint of a nub showed between his lips. Most han'jani—or trolls, as some called them—prided themselves on the length of their teeth, a symbol of dominance and power among the tribes. Yul did not, and he had never explained why he'd done this. A braid held his black hair away from his olive-colored, brown-freckled face.

Jasson shook his head. "Unnecessary."

"They might have killed you."

The Warden considered the dead. "They perished as soon as they decided to attack. Tell me, do you not mourn for them?"

The four han'jani were carrion now, mangled and bloody. Only one had managed to get away. Jasson had briefly considered running the brigand down, but ultimately decided against it. Too much blood had already been spilled, and he knew there was an ocean still to come.

"I mourn their passing, Master. They were not the wisest, especially to challenge a Warden." Yul offered Jasson his horse's reins. "But I do not understand why they were so far east. They were well beyond the border."

The eagerness Yul had shown to serve had surprised Jasson. No han'jani had ever served the Wardens, and certainly no being had ever chosen to serve as readily and as fervently as Yul had. But over these last few years, Yul had become more than a mere servant to the Warden; he had become a friend.

Jasson patted the horse's neck, brushing flecks of blood from his mane. The midnight-black stallion lowered his head, nudging his master. "I expect they were lost. As you said, they weren't the wisest."

Sunset painted the sky orange and purple. Clouds grew on the horizon. The air was damp, and Jasson could feel the coming chill in his bones.

"Storms will be here soon," he said, swinging himself up into the saddle.

"Aye, the elves say the rains will be the harshest in a thousand years."

"The elves say every season will be the harshest."

Jasson turned Challenger away from the stream toward the path leading into the mountains. The stallion obeyed without hesitation, seemingly oblivious to the carnage that littered the rocky bank.

"We will reach the Tomb soon," Jasson told his squire.

"Of course, Master."

*Mercy*, the voice said again.

The Warden put a hand on the pommel of his sword, his Retribution. *I bring no mercy, demon. I bring death.*

# Two

*"To hold back the Tide, there must always be a King, the price of which is high."*

On the eleventh day, Jasson felt the evil. Ethera the Destroyer was near. It was unmistakable and, even for the seasoned Warden, the power of it gave him pause. Spira, God of the World, would give him strength, this Jasson knew without reservation, but there were limits, even to her power. The dark energy touching him now was far greater than anything he had ever encountered before.

Shadows played across the path and through the trees around them, dancing in the light of Yul's torch. The light swayed and flickered with the mare's stride, giving the impression the forest was alive. The trees seemed to converge tighter and tighter as their journey continued.

On the trail ahead, Yul reined in his mare, soothing her with gentle words and a pat. He glanced over his shoulder, the orange firelight from his torch illuminating his concerned expression. "The mist, Master."

Jasson pulled up next to his squire. Challenger snorted and stamped the ground with a forehoof. The Warden ran his gloved fingers through the horse's mane, soothing him.

A slate-colored mist crept toward them through the trees, tendrils of gray seeking to envelop everything around them. As it neared the travelers, it seemed almost to hesitate, as if unsure how to proceed. Slender arms reached out, then pulled away, growing progressively braver until one finally touched Challenger's near forehoof.

The stallion stamped again, snorting and shaking his head.

"Easy, my friend," Jasson said, rubbing a hand on Challenger's neck. "Steady."

"The horses sense the evil, Master."

Jasson nodded. "They sense a great many things, Yul. Much more than you or I."

Yul touched his chest. "Perhaps we should listen…"

"We will leave the horses here."

"Yes, Master."

Yul dismounted and secured his mare to a nearby tree. Jasson slid off and led Challenger over, looping the reins loosely over a branch.

The Warden made his way to the edge of the mist, his hand on Retribution, regarding the swirling mass of gray. The scriptures spoke of the mists with reverence; they were the demon Ethera's very judgment upon the land.

*Mercy.*

He stepped closer. As his foot neared the mist, it parted, pulling away from the Warden as if refusing to be touched by one such as he. As Jasson moved further in, the mist closed behind him.

After a few steps, Jasson called to his servant, "Spira will protect you."

The han'jani rubbed the back of his hand against his protruding, flattened eyetooth, considering the mist, then straightened and followed his master. As promised, the mist parted, as if it knew what these two represented. Jasson nodded, pleased at Yul's courage, then pressed on.

As they moved deeper into the forest, the mist became thicker, its presence growing more and more pervasive. Jasson could feel Ethera's power raging against him, feel the darkness and anger demanding freedom. Not for the first time, he considered the implications of what he had set out to accomplish, wondering if he did indeed possess the strength to fulfill his task.

They found the entrance an hour later in a rock face at the base of a towering cliff that disappeared into the night sky. An archway cut from the rock, marked with glyphs that, even with his years of study, the Warden had difficulty interpreting. These writings were beyond ancient. They pulsed with a pale blue light, and Jasson could feel them when he moved near.

Jasson placed a palm against one, and the glyph's curving double lines flickered as its power flowed into him. The energy contained within the glyph was not unlike his connection to Spira, which did more to terrify the Warden than it did to comfort him. He held his hand firm to the glyph, feeling its power pulsing within.

"You are weakening," Jasson told the glyph.

Anger burned within him as he took in the power, contemplating the perversion of Spira's sacred energy. A Warden must have scribed these glyphs, but who would have done so? Who would have blasphemed in such a manner? It was a desecration. One Jasson Rainlight could not abide. He took one last look at the glyphs around the archway and entered the Tomb.

As he crossed the threshold, a scream, raw and bestial, echoed from deep within, rattling his soul.

*MERCY!*

# Three

*"I can feel it now. The power is pulsing within, and I hate it."*

"Master?" Yul said, jumping back.

"Do not be afraid, my friend," Jasson said absently.

The han'jani eyed the glowing glyphs with trepidation. "I felt something."

"You feel Ethera's Power." Jasson motioned for him to follow. "Come."

The tunnel led them deep into the mountain—its slope suggested they were going down, but the Warden was uncertain as to their depth. The air was cold and stale, undisturbed by mortals in millennia, perhaps longer. Yul's torch provided the only light. Neither spoke as they descended into oblivion.

After what seemed like hours, they came to a vast, domed chamber. The torchlight didn't reach the far wall, nor the ceiling above. A curved rock platform extended from their side of the chamber, at the end of which a wide, stone bridge arched away into the darkness.

Jasson held out his hand. "Your light."

Yul handed him the torch, and the Warden touched it to a stone outcropping at the entrance. Fire burst from a bowl, igniting a trough that stretched down the wall. The flames raced around the perimeter of the room, branching up and out in all directions. In less than a minute, fire illuminated the entire chamber.

The bridge spanned a hundred yards, crossing a chasm of darkness. The ethereal smoke rolled over the stone from a tunnel on the far side of the chamber. The gray mist seemed to pulse as it poured over the edge of the chasm, like a cursed waterfall.

The smoke curled away from Jasson as he neared the bridge. Wide enough for two horse drawn carts to cross abreast, the edifice was enveloped by the mist, as if the etheric cloud was protecting it somehow.

A deep, bestial growl echoed from somewhere in the distance, causing the mist to pulse and ripple.

*Mercy.*

*You are frightened,* Jasson thought. *As well you should be.*

He stepped onto the bridge and felt the rage around him growing. A guttural roar challenged from deep inside the Tomb. Ethera did not want him here.

"I am coming for you," Jasson said with finality.

As he reached the apex of the bridge, a chest-rattling *boom* echoed from the depths, reverberating through the chamber, shaking the very stone he stood upon. Another roar shook the air, followed this time by a chorus of high-pitched screams that seemed to reach through Jasson's skull, piercing his brain.

*Leave this place. You will fall.*

"You will not turn me from my task, Evil One," Jasson said, gripping Retribution tighter.

*You do not understand. You will not leave this place alive.*

"I will gladly sacrifice myself to destroy you, demon."

The smoke at his feet drew back at a pulse of energy from the source. It began to rotate, now a vortex of etheric energy. The spinning mist coalesced into a vaguely human form. Two oversized eyes blinked open, glowing green; two curved horns twisted from its skull. Lines of green energy swirled just below the surface of the seething form; Ethera's power made manifest. A bastard sword grew in the creature's hand, easily twice the size of Jasson's own longsword.

Jasson drew Retribution, holding it above his head, blade pointing behind him. He could still feel Spira's power in his veins, a gift he would not squander.

"I will cleanse you, abomination," he said.

The ethereal uttered a high-pitched scream and charged, a trail of smoke in its wake. It swung its blade in a sweeping arc upward. Jasson brought his own blade to meet his enemy's, and the two weapons slammed together. Yellow light exploded from the point of impact.

Surprised at the force of the blow, Jasson pulled back, presenting his weak side, allowing his momentum to carry his sword down and behind him. The ethereal, already bringing its sword around again, pressed its attack. The Warden grunted as he brought his blade up to parry the powerful blow. He drew on Spira, using her to enhance his swing.

The weapons collided with a resounding *crack*. A ring of energy exploded from the blow, throwing the ethereal into the air. The energy rippled through the thin layer of smoke still covering the bridge. A pained cry rang in Jasson's ears as the ethereal flipped over, its sword evaporating into nothing. The demon landed on all fours twenty feet away.

The ethereal rose, its bright green eyes locked on Jasson. It unhinged its mouth, stretching it unnaturally wide, and roared.

"Your fate is here, monster!" he shouted at the foul being.

With a burst of inhuman speed, the ethereal launched itself, the sword blossoming from its hand.

This time Jasson didn't wait for the creature. He struck, using Spira's power to bolster his speed, and met the ethereal head on, swinging his sword across the creature's chest. Unprepared for the Warden's charge, the ethereal couldn't block the attack, and Jasson's blade sliced through the swirling mass of gray-green smoke.

The ethereal burst, sword vanishing as smoky fingers vaporized, leaving thin wisps of green hanging in the air.

The stone under Jasson's feet shuddered in the wake of a terrible roar, and the smoke swiftly retracted to its source.

The Warden took a breath, then turned to Yul. "Come. Let's finish this."

# Four

*"The most important thing to remember about this text is: I was wrong."*

Blood pounded in Jasson's ears as he approached the Tomb. A line of glyphs unfamiliar to him marked the threshold. He gripped his sword tighter. Much of Spira's strength had left him. The Warden wondered if Her power could reach this desolate, evil place.

"Master, I—I—" Yul said behind him.

"You may wait here, my friend," Jasson said to his squire. "However, if I call upon you, you will come. Do you understand?"

"Are you sure it will work?" Yul asked.

"I don't know."

After a slight hesitation, Yul nodded. "Yes, Master."

The magic Jasson had bonded to Yul, a form of Spira spoken of only in secret, had been ancient when this world was still waking. The agony Yul had endured during the process had been great, but the han'jani had held strong, showing more courage than any being Jasson had met before. Yul was brave, he'd proven himself among his peers, but this evil would test anyone's heart.

Even the Warden's.

Jasson felt Ethera's power touch him as he stepped across the threshold. His hair stood on end, and his skin tingled. Somewhere in the back of his mind, his fortitude wavered as the glyphs at his feet glowed to life.

*Stand firm*, he told himself.

The Tomb was vast, three or four times as big as the cavern of the bridge. Glyph light illuminated a rocky plinth in the center. Steps, cut into the living rock itself, climbed seemingly endlessly to a mammoth throne at the peak.

The being on the throne said nothing as Jasson approached.

The figure's armor was grand, its matte black finish seeming to absorb all the light in the cavern. A misty, emerald glow emanated between the plates and through the angled eye slits on the full-face, horned helm. Gauntleted hands rested on armrests adorned with demon heads.

Hundreds of ethereal demons danced in place at the base of the throne, their glowing eyes fixed on the Warden. They snarled and snapped, but they didn't engage him.

"My salvation comes," said the throned figure. The emerald light emanating from his armor pulsed with each word. His voice was deep and slow—a voice Jasson knew all too well.

The Warden drew his sword. "I have come for you, demon. The scourge you bring upon these lands ends today. Ethera's reign ends here."

"Your understanding of the world is flawed, mortal. The power Ethera controls is everlasting, relentless, unstoppable. It is inevitable."

"Your lies will not sway me from my task," Jasson said. "You will end here and now."

"A mercy," the Fallen King said.

The Warden's retort died on his lips.

"The Seer was correct, Jasson Rainlight," the King said. "Your path ends here."

Jasson steeled himself. "My path ends at your corpse."

"You speak the truth." The King stood, his armor plates clinking. "I, too, have seen the visions of what is to come, Warden. I have seen Ethera's evil sweep across the land, devouring all. And soon I will be free."

Jasson raised his blade. "You will never leave this place, demon."

The King drew his sword, a massive, black-steel nightmare. Wisps of emerald smoke curled from the edge and trailed in its wake.

"I can feel your power, Warden. It is strong, more powerful than I have felt in an age. But it will not save you."

"Enough talk, monster."

Jasson crouched slightly, balancing his weight on the balls of his feet. He felt Yul behind him and said a quick prayer, asking Spira to protect them both. If the Bond wasn't enough to end this vile creature, their lives would be forfeit.

Then, with a roar, Jasson attacked.

The King's emerald light flared bright as he gave voice to his own battle cry. He leaped, the rocky plinth shaking as he pushed off, sending waves of power rippling out from its base.

The King landed between Jasson and his squire, his knee smashing a crater into the stone. The impact shook the ground, sending out a ring of smoke. The King brought his eyes up to the Warden, trails of smoke curling away from the glowing slits.

Without a word, the two warriors joined battle. Jasson brought his blade over his head, meeting the King's. The weapons slammed together in a resounding clang. Jasson continued forward, pushing his blade high, trying to throw his opponent off balance. The King moved with the attack, letting Jasson's momentum carry them back.

The Warden swung, then stepped back, creating room to work. The two heavy weapons were not short swords to thrust and parry; these were massive destroyers of men, and they needed space in which to kill.

Jasson swung his weapon around in an arc at the King's waist. The demon blocked the blow, then countered with an upward thrust, barely missing the Warden's chin. Despite it being twice the size of Jasson's, the King wielded his blade as if it were merely a dagger. Jasson spun to attack the demon's flank.

Something slammed into his back mid-turn. The impact lifted him off his feet, sending him sprawling. The Warden's armor clanged on the stone as he slid for several feet before righting himself, coming up on one knee. He ignored the pain coursing through him and searched for his opponent.

The King pressed his attack, his sabatons fracturing the stone with every step. He held his sword to the side in a one-handed grip.

Jasson sprang to his feet, heaving his sword around. Again the blades met, steel sang, etheric energy flashed. The impact knocked both combatants back a full step, each taking a moment to compose before attacking again.

The King fought with a ruthless ferocity. Swing after swing Jasson deflected, following up with his own attack. His hands ached, his muscles screaming for rest with every blow. Still they danced, seemingly deadlocked.

Jasson knocked another attack aside, but the angle pushed him off balance. The King didn't hesitate. He slammed an obsidian boot into the Warden's chest plate, sending him backward with a flash of green. Jasson landed hard, his helmet bouncing off the uneven rock.

"Master!" Yul appeared at the Warden's side, his face a rictus of terror. "The Bond!"

Jasson pushed himself up on his elbow. The King waited, but the light leaking through his armor was dimmer, less brilliant than before. It was time.

The Warden got to one knee. "Spira, grant me your power."

Jasson reached out and drew Spira's power free. Yul gritted his teeth as tendrils of light streamed from his body. The power Jasson had stored within Yul flowed into the Warden's fingers. Energy flowed over his hand and down his arm, the power of Spira filling him with rage.

"Yes," the King's voice said, the word rumbling through the stone. "Mercy."

"You will receive no mercy from me, demon. Today, I will destroy you."

The King rested his massive sword point on the stone. His cadre of ethereal warriors materialized out of the smoke, flowing around him, their glowing green eyes on the Warden. They seemed to dance with excitement—no, with anticipation.

The Warden leveled Retribution at the demon. Wisps of light curled from the blade. "This is my calling."

The ethereals screamed. Several broke off in a flanking move, clawing across the stone like galloping beasts. Their high-pitched wails echoed around the vast throne room. Shadows of dull green smoke followed them, afterimages chasing the creatures.

Jasson attacked, streamers of light in his wake: the power of Spira manifested. The King brought up his sword, widening his stance, holding the blade in front of him. Jasson roared, bringing his sword down in a Bond-powered overhead blow. Steel sang a song of devastation as light smashed against green. Holy against evil. Life against death.

Jasson spun, letting his momentum carry him around the King. He pulled his sword in, blade up, then lashed out again. The edge bit into the demon's armored thigh, and the King cried out as green light spilled from the wound. He brought an arm back, knocking Jasson aside with a powerful blow to the face.

The Warden stumbled, briefly dazed, but recovered, letting more of the Bond flow into his veins. A rivulet of blood flowed down his chin. He ignored the pain, gritted his teeth, and went back into the fray.

The King's blade rose to meet Jasson's. The Warden knocked the sword aside with a quick two-handed swing, then released the pommel with one hand. He gathered Spira's power within his fist, then lunged, throwing his open hand forward and releasing a burst of energy.

A blast of light threw the King backward through the air. Ethereals shrieked as their master crashed against the wall of the chamber, cracking stone. Emerald light flared from the King's armor, pulsed briefly, then faded. He slid to the floor, and his sword fell from limp fingers, clanging to the stone.

A blinding light glowed around the Warden as if he was burning, illuminating the area like a bonfire. Jasson walked toward the King with deliberation, fighting to keep the rage from taking him.

The King's helm turned toward him, the light from the eye slits now the color of moss. "A mercy."

Jasson held Retribution out, tip pointing at the King. Tendrils of light curled off the blade. "I told you, demon, you shall receive no mercy from me. Your reign has ended."

Coughing, the King said, "A thousand years. That is the span of my reign—my curse." The demon pulled the horned helm from his head. "I can bear it no longer."

Jasson's breath caught in his throat.

Dull, tired eyes sunken into a weathered face regarded the Warden, their light dimming. Scars marked his flesh, as if he'd endured years of excruciating torture. Long, white hair grew in patches atop his skull, clumps matted together with sweat. His lips were drawn tight, his teeth yellow and rotting.

This was no demon; it was a man.

# Five

*"Even now, only moments after gaining the Throne, I feel its anger, its hate."*

Ethereals snarled and gnashed their teeth, appearing in a ring around them, not daring to come closer. The old man threw a hand out, voice booming commands in a tongue Jasson did not recognize. A wall of energy spread out from his open palm, pushing the demons back. Some lashed out, long, spindly arms clawing at the shimmering wall; others launched themselves through the air, slamming into the barrier. Emerald energy rippled from each blow, repelling any demon with the courage to charge. The cacophony of their cries filled the air as they melded with their brethren, then reformed to try again.

"I cannot hold them," the King said. His voice was frail: gone was the commanding authority he'd spoken with only minutes before. "But I could not simply surrender the Throne."

Jasson flinched as another ethereal threw himself against the invisible wall. "You were a Warden."

The King nodded.

"Then why?"

"Ethera's evil comes for all," the King said. "It does not discriminate."

"And yet you sit here, commanding it?" Jasson pointed his sword at the throne.

The King coughed, grimacing in pain, struggling to control the spasm. Blood sprayed from his lips. "No...I have held it back."

A loud *crack* as another ethereal slammed into the barrier. Lines of emerald drew themselves in the air like lightning across a dark sky. Seeing the weakness, several more joined the attack, throwing themselves relentlessly at the wall. Energy flashed and cracked, a spiderweb of glowing lines fracturing the gloom.

"Be gone!" the King shouted, waving a hand. A burst of wind blasted through the ethereals, vaporizing some, blowing others away. A few retreated, cowering at the King's display of power.

"Our time is short," the King said, hand falling to his side. "Your time is near."

"My time?"

"I have been calling for you. I have felt my weakness growing, and I have long feared I wouldn't have the strength to hold them back long enough."

"Hold them back?"

The King nodded at the ethereals, slinking back to the barrier. "Ethera's demons. Desolation made manifest. The end of the world. I have struggled and fought against its power for centuries, so long that I cannot remember my life before the Throne. It has consumed me, as it will consume you."

"I will be consumed by nothing," Jasson said, anger swelling in his chest. "I have come to defeat this evil. I will rid the world of Ethera's scourge. Your words, your…lies will not deter me from my task."

"Your quest is righteous and just, but you cannot defeat Ethera, you can only hold him back. I have searched the depths of the world for means and have found none. For centuries, I have held to the hope that I would find an answer, but alas, my crusade was for naught. The Evil is coming, and I cannot hold it back any longer." The King turned his tired eyes on the Warden. "But you can."

Jasson shook his head. "I don't understand."

"I can feel the power of Spira within you. Your control of the Bond is beyond anything I've ever experienced. You are powerful, Warden Jasson Rainlight. Even more powerful than I. Is it possible that you are the Shield of lore and myth? Would you accept your charge?"

Jasson raised his sword. He could feel the Bond beginning to fade. Retribution's glow dwindled.

"We do not have much time," the King said, pulling off his obsidian gauntlets.

"I will fight them back," Jasson said, unable to keep the trepidation from his voice. He called upon his remaining reserves of Spira, pushing the power through Retribution. "You speak of charges, demon? You speak of destiny? Well, this is mine. I will defeat you and all the rest of them."

"You cannot defeat this evil with your Bond alone. You must protect the world from desolation. You must become the Shield."

The King extended his bare hand, his spotted, wrinkled fingers reaching.

"You must sit upon the Throne. That is your destiny."

Emerald lightning flashed around them. Ethereals clawed and punched and kicked at the barrier. They climbed over each other, shoving each other out of the way, all scrambling to get through the barrier. Cracks began to grow on the shimmering wall of energy, and the snarling, bestial screams intensified.

The King extended a hand, fingers spread. Jasson stepped back as emerald light began to flow from his fingers, crossing the distance between them in a lazy, winding arc, like a stream down a mountain. Tendrils of emerald energy reached for the Warden, then recoiled at his hesitation.

"It is the only way," the King said. "You must control the Evil. If you do not, this world will fall. I no longer have the strength."

To Jasson's right, a single ethereal forced its way through the barrier. It dropped to the ground, rolling and screaming in pain as the barrier closed behind it, trapping a second demon. The trapped ethereal screamed, writhing in pain, talons clawing against both sides of the barrier, frantically trying to free itself.

The first ethereal staggered to all fours, bringing its glowing eyes up to the Warden. Lips pulled back, revealing razor-sharp fangs. It snarled and began to stalk its chosen prey.

Jasson kept his sword pointed at the demon, the power of the Bond barely evident.

The ethereal launched itself through the air. Jasson brought his sword up to block the attack. The demon slammed into him, clawing against his armor. Jasson grabbed one of its arms and threw it aside. The ethereal flailed as it spun through the air, slamming into the barrier and crashing to the stone floor.

The second ethereal pulled itself through and struck without hesitation. Jasson swung Retribution, slicing the demon in half. The two halves vanished in puffs of smoke, cutting off the monster's screams.

A third pushed its way through the barrier, then a fourth. The first righted itself, and they came at him as a pack. Jasson cut down a monster with a one-handed horizontal blow, then pulled his short sword with his free hand and jabbed it into the chest of the second. The third slammed into his chest. He dropped the short sword and yanked the demon off, throwing it backward as the other two vaporized.

"Warden!" the King shouted.

Four more ethereals were through, hesitating, apparently waiting for their brother to get to his feet.

"Accept your destiny! Become the Fallen King!"

The five were upon him.

Jasson roared, feeling the King's power sustaining him. He pulled the energy in. Green smoke billowed around him, extending his perception to everything the emerald cloud touched: the stone ground, the walls, the very air around him. Energy filled his body with a power he'd never felt before.

He lashed out, throwing a stream of energy into the advancing ethereals. Gusting air crackling with power battered the demons, vaporizing them. The Warden slammed his sword on the ground, rending the stone. He reached out with both hands, feeling the power of Ethera, letting it fill him completely.

The barrier fell. Ethereals dropped to the ground. He felt their drive, their need to consume. Felt the rage. The feeling burgeoned until the demons themselves were but an extension of him, and he felt their compulsion in the back of his mind. *Devour.*

"No!"

He pushed the urge down, burying it deep within himself. At a wave of his hand, the teeming mass of ethereals quieted, cowering before him. A few snapped and snarled, but none made any further attempts to attack him.

An understanding of things he'd never even imagined rose inside him, and in that moment, he understood his new charge. He turned back to the dying king, understanding now that the mercy he asked for was not his life. It was his death.

"Go," the Warden said, his voice reverberating through the chamber.

The ethereals vanished, disappearing in puffs of green smoke.

Jasson knelt beside the dying king and put a hand on the old man's shoulder. "You are free of your burden. Be at peace."

The King looked into the Warden's eyes and smiled, the emerald glow behind his eyes dimming. "Thank you," he said with his final breath. And the light behind his eyes went out.

## Six

*"The Throne does not want a king; it yearns to be free.
I will not let it, for which it hates me."*

The Warden—no, the King—found Yul near the entrance of the Throne Room, his back against the stone, trembling. The glow of the energy pulsing within him reflected off the walls and bathed his squire's face in an emerald hue. The han'jani's eyes were wide with fear.

Yul lifted a hand as the King approached. "Please, don't..."

"Do not be afraid." His voice had changed somehow, deeper now than before.

A compulsion to devour swelled within him, and he pushed it back, feeling a crashing wave of agony. His mind screamed at him to release the evil, to leave Ethera's minions to their work, but he refused, and in doing so invited torment to flourish within him. The pain filled his mind, and it was everything the King could do to hold back Ethera's power.

"Master, I—I don't understand."

"Nor do I, completely. The King has shown me much, my friend. However, my time with you is short."

"I have sworn my life to you, Master Warden."

"Indeed," Jasson said, nodding. "But my journey is not the same one we started all those years ago. I did not fully understand the task set before me, and it has cost me dearly. I have become the Shield of the World, but in destroying the King, I have sealed my own fate."

"Master..."

"The world thrives on the power, Spira and Ethera's both. I am but a dyke set against it, holding back the inexorable waves of change. This is my calling, and my curse."

The King raised a hand, fingers spread. Yul flinched as several thin lines of energy flowed from the King's fingertips. The power touched the squire, and immediately his terrified expression became calm understanding.

"A new Bond?"

"No, my friend. This gift is so much more."

"Thank you, Master."

"Do not thank me, Yul, for our story is not one of glory, but of pain. Already, I can feel the torment growing, but despite it, I must take my place on the Cursed Throne. The ultimate achievement of a Warden is to protect life, even if that means he must sacrifice his own."

Yul frowned. "But the world hates you."

"It is an uncommon thing for a person to give so much for those who care so little, but it is our calling. A Warden's life is not glamorous, nor do we seek fortune or fame. My duty here is the epitome of a Warden's charge. I will serve Spira and sit upon the Throne to hold back Ethera's evil."

Yul stood. "I will return and help you, Master."

"No," the King said, a little too harshly. "You will never return here. I will not subject another to this burden. It is mine, and mine alone, and I will seek no mercy."

\* \* \* \* \*

## Josh Hayes Biography

Website: www.joshhayeswriter.com

Amazon Author Page:
https://www.amazon.com/Josh-Hayes/e/B00O4VA2YK

A retired police officer, Josh Hayes is the author of the Valor Trilogy, Stryker's War (Galaxy's Edge), The Terra Nova Chronicles w/ Richard Fox, and Tranquility w/ Devon C Ford, along with numerous short stories.

His debut solo novel, *Edge of Valor*, was nominated for the 2020 Dragon Award for Best Military Science Fiction or Fantasy Novel.

He grew up a military brat, affording him the opportunity to meet several different types of people, in multiple states and foreign countries. After graduating high school, he joined the United States Air Force and served for six years, before leaving military life to work in law enforcement. During his time with the Wichita Police Department, Josh served as a patrol officer, bicycle officer, community policing officer, and was an assistant bomb technician on the Bomb Squad.

His experiences in both his military life and police life have given him unique glimpses into the lives of people around him and it shows through in the characters he creates.

Josh is also the creator and president of Keystroke Medium, a popular YouTube show and podcast focused on the craft of writing.

\* \* \* \* \*

# Mythical Creatures
# by Kevin J. Anderson

The prow of the *Compass* cut the rough gray waters like a knife carving a Landing Day roast. Prester Ormun closed his eyes and drove away all his pleasant memories of the traditional holiday…or any other family memories, for that matter. Those were behind him now; only bleak settlements on the scattered Soeland Islands lay ahead. The prester had a difficult path to follow, even if he did not understand God's reasoning behind it.

The ship's damp sails creaked and sighed, and he felt the cold spray on his face, blown by the coming storm. Dobri, the bright-eyed cabin boy, came up beside him, leaning over the bow to peer down into the choppy waves. "Are you looking for *sylkas*, Prester? They say sometimes you can see them in the whitecaps just before a squall."

"I do not believe in *sylkas*. And neither should you." Prester Ormun knew that for a young man like this, the world was filled with mysteries and wonders, but also ignorance. It was his appointed task to enlighten the people of the islands.

The cabin boy squinted at the sea, which looked leaden under the thick sky. "They're real, Prester—beautiful women with golden hair or seaweed all over their bodies. Other sailors have seen them."

"I don't care what other sailors say. *Sylkas* do not exist. It is written in the Book of Aiden that God created the peoples of the land, but only fish, seals, whales, and sea serpents inhabit the sea—no intelligent creatures. I can show you the Scriptures, if you like." Since Ormun knew the cabin boy couldn't read, the proof would be lost on him.

Dobri was both disappointed and skeptical to hear the prester's pronouncement. He had grown up in a small fishing village, and this was his first voyage away from home; he wanted to believe all the wondrous, imaginative stories, whether or not they were true. Now the boy gazed ahead, intent on spotting one of the imaginary *sylkas* so he could point out the creature to Ormun.

With a pang, the prester realized that his own son Aleo would have been about Dobri's age now…

A large wave gushed over the *Compass*'s bow, and the cabin boy scuttled away, but the prester did not try to avoid the splash; instead, he let it wash away his past again. His family was gone, and nothing remained for him in the city of Calay. That was why he'd been sent across the rough waters to the bleak Soeland Islands. A new chance…a last chance.

The church's prester-marshall had sent Ormun to preach among the roughshod and hardy islanders; he would bring them the Book of Aiden to comfort the people in their storms and cold northerly winds. Ormun accepted his first mission with neither enthusiasm nor complaint. He was humble enough not to expect redemption, but he did hope to achieve something positive with whatever remained of his life. That was all he asked God for….

Back in Calay, before he became a prester, Ormun was a shoemaker with a wife and two children, a home, friends—a lifetime ago, or a year ago, depending on whether he measured time by a calendar or the gulf in his heart.

The gray plague had swept through the Craftsmen's District, as it did every few years. Shops closed their doors and latched the window shutters. But Ormun had his family to feed: his son, his daughter, and his wife, a dark-haired, tan-skinned beauty named Risula. And so he kept working, while others hid.

He never knew which customer exposed him to the plague. Ormun lay shivering in bed for days while his family tended him: Aleo, only twelve years old, acting as the man of the house, Risula giving him salty broth to drink; even little Essa brought him flowers that she'd picked outside.

Ormun gained strength day by day, then suffered a relapse, falling back into a deep fever, sleeping like the dead, drenched in cold sweat. His last murky memory was of Risula shushing their daughter and leading her away, telling her to let her father sleep. And then his wife had started coughing....

When his fever broke, Ormun emerged from his coma, very weak, and he could barely open his crusted eyes. His throat was parched, and he called out for water, but heard nothing. The house seemed quiet, much too quiet. After he gained enough strength to crawl out of bed, he found his family huddled together, dead, victims of the fever that he had somehow survived.

Ormun had walked away from his home, wandering the streets in a daze, until he finally came upon the kirk. He stumbled inside, and the local prester cared for him, read to him from the Book of Aiden. It was then Ormun decided what his mission in life must be. The gray plague had left him with an empty heart, no laughter and no love. He clutched onto his service to the church like an anchor of hope, read the Book several times through, and debated with great fervor. When the kindly local prester could no longer answer his questions, he sent the gaunt and intense Ormun to the main kirk in Calay, where he met with the prester-marshall himself.

Cast adrift in life, Ormun begged the church leader for a new course to set. The prester-marshall did not try to explain God's personal message for Ormun, didn't pretend to reveal the purpose behind all the pain he had suffered. "I know a place where you can be of service. The Soelanders need you, and I think you belong there." He anointed Ormun a prester and presented him with the Book and the fishhook pendant that was a symbol of their faith.

No one called Soeland a pleasant place to live, but that mattered not a whit to Ormun. He took his Book and his letters of passage, and begged a bunk on the *Compass*, which was ready to sail back for the islands....

Now the sea grew rough, and waves rocked the vessel. Captain Endre Stillen came to join the prester, looking troubled. He was a red-bearded man with a muscular chest and potbelly as hard as a wine cask. "Your cabin would be more comfortable, Prester. No sense staying out here in the storm—the weather is going to get worse."

"Discomfort doesn't bother me, Captain," Ormun said.

Stillen shot an uncertain glance to the anxious cabin boy who hovered nearby. "Dobri says that you don't believe in the mysteries of the sea." He raised his bushy eyebrows.

"I do not."

"The ocean is vast and uncharted, and we've all seen things we can't explain. I'm as inclined to believe in *sylkas* as in anything else. If nothing else, it gives me hope to know that those dark waters might contain benevolent creatures, should anything happen to my ship."

"I don't need mythical creatures to give me hope, Captain. The Book of Aiden says that *sylkas* don't exist, so therefore they don't exist. It doesn't matter what tales you've heard or what you think you've seen."

The conversation reminded Ormun of a recent outspoken stargazer who had adapted a seaman's spyglass so he could stare at the stars and planets in the night sky. The astronomer convinced himself that he saw tiny satellites circling one of the planets—an impossible idea. To prove his assertion, the stargazer had asked the prester-marshall to observe for himself; but the church leader refused to raise the spyglass to his eye. "The Book of Aiden tells us that God made the world as the center of all things, so therefore other satellites *cannot* circle one of the tiny planets in the sky. I have no need to look, when I already know." He handed the telescope back to the baffled astronomer. Ormun thought it was an amazingly profound demonstration of the prester-marshall's unshakable faith. He only hoped he could be as worthy someday.

Seeing that the prester's mind was set, Captain Stillen chose not to pursue the argument. "Those legends are a vital part of Soelander life and folklore, Prester. You'll be in for some lively discussions when you get to the fishing towns, that's for certain."

"I'm not afraid of debate."

The captain ordered the sails trimmed against the squall. As the winds picked up, waves hammered the side of the ship. Most of the crew hurried belowdecks before the rain started to sheet down.

Dobri yelped, pointing off to starboard. "I saw one! Look, Prester—it's a *sylka!*"

Ormun froze, wanting not to look, *almost* strong enough to refuse, but he couldn't help himself. He turned to where the boy pointed—and that was his weakness, his failure.

While he looked in the other direction, a rogue wave swamped the bow and gushed over the rails with enough force to knock him overboard. He reached out, grabbed for anything, and his fingers caught the slick wood, but couldn't get hold. Then the rush of curling foam bore him overboard into the wide gulf of the sea.

Prester Ormun sucked in a breath to shout for help, but he swallowed a mouthful of salt water instead. Flailing, sinking, he coughed and retched as the wave crest bore him upward, then plunged him under again. He clawed at the water with his hands, seeing grayish light above. His face burst from the waves again, and he drew in a deep breath. He rose and sank, completely lost, adrift. His heavy woolen shift pulled him down.

In the pouring rain he spotted Dobri and Captain Stillen struggling to their feet on the deck. He caught a glimpse of the cabin boy, his mouth open in dismay as he saw the prester in the water. Dobri waved and shouted.

Ormun raised his hands to signal, but the seas were too rough. Currents whisked him farther from the ship. The *Compass* could never send out a boat to rescue him.

He tried to stay afloat, but his arms and legs felt leaden. His shoes—good leather boots that he had made in his own cobbler shop long ago in that other life—filled with water. He was going to drown out here.

Oddly, he didn't view the thought with any particular terror, but he did feel a heavy confusion. God's course for him had been so clear—to spread the word out in the Soeland Islands. What was the purpose of saving Ormun from the gray plague only to let him be swept away by a capricious wave, drowning before he even had a chance to preach to his new charges?

He went under again, struggled to the surface, caught another breath. Letting go, he let himself be flung about by the waves. Barely able to think, he experienced a paradoxical sense of calm and peace.

Then clammy hands grasped him from below. A firm grip took his woolen shift, cradled his head, buoyed him up to where he could breathe. But Ormun didn't want to breathe. He struggled and fought against the strange figure below, but he was too weak.

In the end, he simply surrendered to the water and the mythical savior that his imagination had created in his last moments of life. Prester Ormun sank into the darkness, trying to remember a prayer.

\* \* \*

When Prester Ormun awoke, he smelled fish in the dank and cold air around him. Dried saltwater plastered his hair to his head, and he had to pry open his crusted eyes. Before his vision adjusted, he rolled over onto his knees and retched, puking up foul-tasting saltwater.

He saw that he was in an empty cave at the waterline, which looked out upon the open sea. Outside, the waves sounded like drumbeats against the algae-encrusted rocks that he could see beyond the cave opening. With a start, the prester realized he was naked, his woolen shift spread on a rock nearby. The cloth was stiff and salt-encrusted, but reasonably dry. He shivered and pulled his clothes back on, hiding his nakedness.

He noticed four gutted fish on a flat rock next to him, along with a pile of oysters and clams, all of which had been pried open, ready for him to eat. Weak and starving, Ormun devoured the food without thinking, without tasting, and he felt reborn, as when he'd emerged from his fever after the gray plague. Now, however, questions clamored in his mind, and he looked around, trying to understand what had happened to him.

A figure swam in the sea outside the cave. It seemed human at first—until the creature hauled itself onto the rocks and climbed dripping into the cave. Covered with luxurious locks of golden fur, it was obviously female, with rounded breasts covered by matted weeds. The face was narrow and ethereal, with large brown eyes—soulful eyes, like those of a sea lion. She smelled of salt from the sea. Her lips curved in what was an unmistakable smile as she saw him awake and looking at her.

Ormun squeezed his eyes shut and felt for his fishhook pendant in a protective instinct, but the religious symbol was gone. Perhaps it had washed away when he'd been swept overboard, or perhaps this *thing*—this *sylka?*—had stolen it, fearing the sign of Aiden.

Ormun opened his eyes again, but the creature was still there; he had expected her to vanish like a mirage-shadow. She came forward to squat near him, briny water trickling from her fur, and he struggled away. The *sylka* picked up the empty oyster and clam shells and cast them out of the cave, then she turned back to scrutinize him, like a raven fascinated by a shiny object…or a predator deciding how best to devour its prey. A thrumming sound echoed from her throat, a call that was at once mysterious, mournful, and hypnotic.

When the creature edged closer, Prester Ormun backed away until his shoulders struck the cave wall. "You're not real!"

The *sylka* trilled at him. Her eyes showed a yearning to communicate. She repeated the sound and chirruped with a higher note at the end, like a question.

"You're not real." Though he could see the *sylka's* form as if she had been sketched from the logbook of a delusional sea captain, could smell her musky iodine odor, and hear the sound she made, Ormun clung to what the Book of Aiden taught: That God had blessed *mankind* with intelligence, giving only His *chosen children* the minds to understand and worship Him. All other creatures of the land and sea were lowly animals. In another verse, the Book specifically denounced mermaids and *sylkas* as distractions for a devout man, superstitions unworthy of a true follower of God.

But now Ormun found himself faced with the contradiction. The Book of Aiden stated plainly that this *sylka* could not be here. Ormun had read those words of scripture with his own eyes…yet those same eyes showed him this impossible creature. Right here.

Back in Calay, the prester-marshall had instructed him in the use of rational thought. If this *sylka* truly existed, then the statement in the Book was in error. A small error, perhaps—and how could anyone know all the mysteries and all the creatures in the vast sea?

Yet one error in one verse was as bad as a thousand errors, for either way it proved that the Book of Aiden was flawed.

And because it was the word of God, the Book of Aiden could *not* be flawed. Therefore, that one verse, and all verses, had to be correct. By definition.

Hence, the *sylka* could not exist, and she was not there. He stared hard at her, willing the illusion to go away.

The *sylka* hunkered down and continued to gaze at him with mournful eyes. She let out a series of complex musical trills, but Prester Ormun closed his eyes and covered his ears.

* * *

The *sylka* left the cave several times throughout the day, diving into the sea and swimming away. She always returned with fresh fish, oysters, or abalones for him, all of which he ate suspiciously. Ormun used the empty abalone shells to capture dripping water that trickled from the moist rocks of the cave. It tasted gritty and dirty, but soothed his parched throat.

Each time the mythical creature went away, Ormun tried to convince himself that she was only an illusion brought about by delirium, perhaps a relapse of the gray fever. Then the *sylka* returned, and they would stare at each other again....

He feared she might bring back others of her kind to show them the strange captive she had hauled from the stormy seas—but, again, the prester knew that couldn't happen, because *sylkas* did not exist. There were no others. Each time she came to him, she was alone...and so was he.

When he felt strong enough, and desperate enough, Ormun made his plans and waited for the *sylka* to swim away again. The creature slipped out of the cave one afternoon, and Ormun decided it was time to escape—if he could. He ventured out of the opening and climbed up on the rocks, hoping to find some landmark that would tell him where he was.

If this was one of the Soeland Islands, Ormun could make his way inland, where he might find people—a fishing village, a shack, or a boat dock. But when he scrambled up the algae-covered boulders above the tide line, he saw that this island was merely a tiny patch of land, an elbow of reef that barely rose above the waterline—a few acres of forlorn boulders and tufts of misplaced grass. He could see the full swatch of land from end to end, side to side. The island was empty. He was alone.

Staring at the watery horizon with tears burning in his eyes, he discerned the gray hummocks of other islands in the distance, larger shores that might be inhabited...but they were much too far away. He could never swim that far, and if he tried to escape, he was sure the *sylka* would come after him, grab his legs, and drag him beneath the water. He still didn't understand why she had saved him in the first place.

As he stood there in empty dismay, the *sylka* rose out of the surf and climbed onto dry land on the other side of the islet. Silhouetted in daylight, she looked like a seductress, her form voluptuous, the golden kelplike fur haloed by the sun. Ormun had looked at women once, had found Risula so lovely that she made him dizzy with desire...but he had been a different man before the gray fever—someone without the same convictions, without the same priorities. He averted his eyes.

The *sylka* came toward him, clearly alarmed to see him out of the cave. On land, her movements were ungainly, like a seal's, although he had seen how sleek and lissome she was in the water. When the creature urged him back to the cave that was his prison, he recoiled at her touch, but could not resist. He saw no point to it; he had nowhere else to go.

Back in her lair, the *sylka* was intent on showing him something. She trilled, inducing him to come to a dank alcove in the rear of the small cave. Under a weed-covered overhang, she had piled rocks to create a protective barrier, a sort of nest. The *sylka* looked at him with great wonder in her eyes as she grasped the rocks with her webbed hands and lifted them away one by one.

Beneath the protective barrier rested a group of pulsating, grayish spheres, pearlescent objects, each one larger than a ripe melon. Ormun counted five of them grouped together with loving care, moist with a filmy membrane—a clutch of eggs! The creature's young. She was reproducing, about to unleash five more of her kind into the world!

Obviously the *sylka* wasn't entirely alone out there in the waters. Ormun imagined her out in the gray cold sea, at night, letting out her trilling song, calling a mate from across the waves. Did she lay her eggs here in the cave and wait for a male to spray his milt on the clutch like a frog? The very idea made him shudder with disgust.

The *sylka* inhaled and exhaled wet burbling breaths, and she crouched closer, cooing. The creature extended a pale finger and stroked the nearest egg. Her touch activated something within, a sparkle in the air accompanied by the smell of ozone, and Prester Ormun felt an overwhelming sense of importance and hope—a magical, unnatural connection.

On the egg's shifting metallic surface, he saw distorted images, like memories seen through the fever fog. The *sylka* touched a second egg, and a third, and more images formed on their reflective shells...the prester's hopes and possibilities from the lost part of his life, things she could not possibly know about him.

Ormun saw the blurry, uncertain features of his son Aleo, laughing, full of tales of fish he had caught or beetles he had collected. The second eggshell displayed sweet, doe-eyed Essa, who loved to pick the flowers that grew in meadows just outside the city. And exotic, beautiful Risula.

But the last time Ormun had seen his family, they were dead, plague-ridden, their bodies huddled on the floor of their home, while he shivered in a coma on the narrow bed. Now, he gasped a quick, perfunctory prayer, but he continued to look. He knew he should turn away, even though those faces made his heart ache.

Sensing his reaction, the *sylka* trilled with happiness.

Then Ormun realized these visions were not just memories, for he saw Aleo as a young man, standing with a thin and pretty redhaired woman. They held each other, kissed—Aleo's wife-to-be? Ormun saw another maiden with fresh-picked flowers in her hair, unmistakably Essa, just at the edge of growing up. He saw Risula cradling another baby—her own, or a grandchild?

The eggs held possibilities, a wellspring of the future.

"No," Ormun whispered, drawing away. "No, this never happened! This can't be." He covered his eyes. The *sylka* was distraught, not understanding his reaction, but Ormun clung to strength within.

The images that pooled on the shells of her eggs did not represent the path that God had chosen for him. He had endured the pain. He had read the Book. He had fought for understanding and acceptance, like a pathfinder hacking through persistent underbrush, rather than taking a simple and easy trail that did not lead where he wanted to go. These illusive memories were not *his* memories, and that future did not belong to him.

"No," he said again.

With obvious disappointment, the *sylka* piled the rocks again over her eggs.

\* \* \*

Even though the prester understood his mission now, he feared he wouldn't have the necessary strength. As he shivered through the cold, damp night while wrestling with his thoughts, Ormun once again told himself that none of this was *real*. Maybe he had actually drowned when the wave swept him overboard, and this was his test before God let him enter Heaven. The only thing that had kept him alive after the plague, the purpose that allowed him to get through one day, then the next, was the anchor of his faith, his dogged belief in what the prester-marshall had taught him. If he abandoned that, then he would be abandoning everything he had left.

The eerie, tempting images he'd seen in the *sylka's* eggs—his family, his happiness, a bright future—none of that was true. How he longed for what he saw in those illusions, wanted that reality more than anything else he could ever imagine. But that, in itself, was what warned him. *His* wishes did not matter: It was about what God wanted. Ormun had to be strong, and his only strength was his faith.

On the fourth morning after being washed overboard, Ormun watched the *sylka* return to the cave, climbing out of the water. As the creature sloshed toward him, she looked excited, gesturing with a webbed hand. When the prester didn't follow, she hurried back to the cave opening and stared out to sea, then trilled a sharper sound, more urgent than her soothing music. Ormun felt compelled to look out upon the sun-washed waters.

In the channel between the islands, close enough that he could see the sails and rigging, a two-masted vessel cruised in from the north. He even recognized the lines, the look of the hull, the cut of the sails. It was the *Compass*! Maybe Captain Stillen had come back to look for him, or maybe this was just the ship's regular return route through the archipelago.

Thrumming, the *sylka* looked at him with her limpid eyes. Ormun's heart lurched, and he knew the time had come. This was the crux, and he clung to the truth like a man grasping a lifeline. He had not dared to pray for a chance at redemption, to demonstrate his devotion and his acceptance—and now the sailing ship had returned! The *Compass* would rescue him.

He lurched to his feet, uttering a prayer of thanksgiving. The *sylka* gestured for him to hurry, and by her demeanor and bright expression he guessed that she intended to swim out to the *Compass*, draw the attention of the sailors, and get Captain Stillen to change course to the islet. This creature had already rescued him from drowning, and now she would save him from being marooned on the small island. She turned away, looking out to sea.

Ormun picked up one of the melon-sized reef rocks, held it in both hands, and brought it down with all of his strength on the back of the *sylka's* head. He bashed as hard as he could, and her skull was much softer than the rock. The *sylka* collapsed, letting out a mournful hooting sound, and Ormun struck again.

He stood tall and dropped the rock on the floor of the cave. "You don't exist." If the captain, the cabin boy, and the rest of the crew saw her, they would not have the strength to cling to their faith. Ormun had no other choice but to save them from their own gullibility.

He went to the back alcove, pulled away the rocks piled over the clutch of eggs, and gazed down at the quicksilver pooling—the reflections that were mocking echoes of a past that was already gone and a future he would never have. Useless and dangerous, a mocking temptation. Prester Ormun was strong enough to avoid fantasies, no matter how attractive they might be. He knew his life's course.

Ormun picked up another rock and smashed the first *sylka* egg, obliterating the illusions of things that might have been. Then he destroyed the rest of the clutch, one by one, until he felt safe again.

When he was finished, he was surprised to discover that the *sylka's* body still lay on the cave floor; the dripping slimy fragments of broken eggs remained strewn about their nest. Now that he had passed his test of faith, Ormun expected them to vanish instantly, but he didn't search for, or want, explanations. It was time for him to be rescued, to return to his role as a prester preaching the Book of Aiden. The Soelanders needed him.

Ormun carried one of the abalone shells as he scrambled out of the cave and onto the high point of the small islet. There, he jumped and waved, seesawing his hands in the air, trying to get the attention of the *Compass*. He caught the bright sunlight with the shiny interior of the shell, flashing a signal. He yelled until his throat was raw.

And finally—finally—he saw pennants raised on the mainmast, and the ship turned toward the rocky island. Someone had seen him.

When the *Compass* anchored at a safe distance from the islet, Prester Ormun watched the ship's boat lowered, saw men rowing toward him. Though he was not a good swimmer, he dove into the water and struck out to meet the boat partway. He recognized the boy Dobri at the front of the boat, and two sturdy Soeland sailors pulling at the oars. The prester flailed in the waves, swimming as far from the islet as he could.

He needed to be away from the persistent imaginary remnants of the *sylka* and her eggs. He didn't want any of these men from the

*Compass* to see the evidence, otherwise they would be deceived by what they wanted to believe.

Gasping and exhausted, Ormun reached the boat, and his heart swelled with joy. Dobri leaned over to catch his hand. "Prester, we thought you were dead!"

"I thought I was, too," he said as they helped to haul him aboard. "But I survived, and now I know that God still has more work for me to do."

The cabin boy laughed, and the sailors rowed back toward the *Compass*. Ormun was too tired and shaken to tell his story, and he still had much to think about before he revealed anything.

When they tied up to the sailing ship, he climbed aboard to congratulations from Captain Stillen. "We couldn't believe it, Prester! No man ever survives out here. How did you make it to that small island? We were just continuing our passage among the islands, but Dobri spotted the flashing light."

"An abalone shell," the prester said.

The captain admired his cleverness, and Dobri added, "I was at the bow looking for *sylkas* when I saw it."

"*Sylkas* don't exist, boy," Prester Ormun said, more convinced now than he had ever been.

But while the crewmen took him to change into dry clothes, the prester watched Dobri hurry back to the bow with a spyglass in hand. Seeing the boy's eager willingness to believe, he felt only sadness and disappointment. He had to teach these people the truth, no matter how difficult it was.

Nevertheless, Dobri continued to scan the waves, always looking, always hopeful.

\* \* \* \* \*

## Kevin J. Anderson Biography

Kevin J. Anderson has published more than 170 books, 58 of which have been national or international bestsellers. He has written numerous novels in the Star Wars, X-Files, and Dune universes, as well as unique steampunk fantasy novels *Clockwork Angels* and *Clockwork Lives*, written with legendary rock drummer Neil Peart. His original works include the Saga of Seven Suns series, the Wake the Dragon and Terra Incognita fantasy trilogies, the Saga of Shadows trilogy, and his humorous horror series featuring Dan Shamble, Zombie PI. He has edited numerous anthologies, written comics and games, and the lyrics to two rock CDs. Anderson is the director of the graduate program on Publishing at Western Colorado University. Anderson and his wife Rebecca Moesta are the publishers of WordFire Press. His most recent novels are *Vengewar*, *Dune: The Duke of Caladan* (with Brian Herbert), *Stake*, *Kill Zone* (with Doug Beason), and *Spine of the Dragon*.

\* \* \* \* \*

# The Name of the Monster
## by D.J. Butler
A Tales of Indrajit & Fix Story

"**M**y daughter is a poet." As the green-skinned shipowner spoke, the mass of thin tentacles hanging off the front of his face beneath his nose danced. The voice emerging from the worm-like strands was deep and monotone.

Indrajit cocked his head. "Poet?"

"Oh, now Indrajit is listening," Fix said.

"I was listening before." Indrajit snorted. "I am very concerned for Melitzanda's safety."

They stood in the shipowner's office, a single wooden room whose walls were lined with shelves. The shelves sagged under the weight of ledgers, boxes, and stacks of paper. The office crouched at the head of a long wharf in the Shelf. Outside, Indrajit heard the crying of seagulls and a squeaking sound that he thought was made by the Sobelian Lamprey. That made sense; autumn was arriving, and the lamprey's migration patterns meant it should now be starting to swim around the rocky beaches of Kish. Soon, it would swim south, toward the Free Cities.

"Oritria." The face-tentacles circled slightly and flexed. The shipowner's golden eyes flared wide open and his nose flattened into his face, leaving behind only two narrow slits. Indrajit didn't know this race of man, and had no idea how to read the facial expression. Grit Wopal, the head of the Lord Chamberlain's Ears, and sometimes Indrajit's and Fix's boss, would have known what the shipowner was thinking. He would have *seen* it, with the third eye set into his forehead.

But Indrajit and Fix were working for their own account today, and Grit Wopal was nowhere in sight.

"Yes, Oritria." Indrajit cleared his throat. "I said 'Melitzanda' because I was thinking of an important incident in the Blaatshi Epic, involving a kidnapped princess named Melitzanda. Who is also a great poet. Naturally, the similarities to your daughter's situation brought that episode to mind."

"My daughter is not a princess," the shipowner said. "I am not a king. I sail in the Serpent Sea trade."

"But princess-*like*." Indrajit smiled.

"In what respect?" The tentacles quivered.

"In deserving to be rescued," Indrajit suggested.

"I don't want you to *rescue* her," the shipowner said. "The little vixen ran away with her filthy Yeziot lover, and as far as I'm concerned, he can have her. But she took important documents with her, and I want you to get them back."

"I don't know the Yeziot." Fix's coppery-brown face brightened, his eyebrows lifting high enough almost to touch the straight hair spilling over his forehead. Fix loved nothing more than learning, unless possibly it was learning from a *book*, the pervert. "Tell me about them."

"They're ravenous maneaters," the green man said. "They're really excellent sailors, practically a one-man crew, with a huge capacity for work, and they never get tired, but you have to keep feeding them man-flesh or they go berserk."

Indrajit now worried he'd forgotten the man's name, and he checked his memory palace. There, standing on a tussock of grass beneath the steep gray cliff from which Indrajit had dived as a boy, were four frogs. Four frogs.

"Forfa," he said, "we'll get your daughter back."

"I'm vexed." Forfa's voice continued to be flat. The tentacles were curling more tightly, so apparently the curl reflected negative emotion. Or tension. "You don't appear to be listening to me."

"You don't want your daughter back," Fix said. "You want the documents."

"Yes," Indrajit agreed. "I meant we'd bring her back, with the documents. What *are* the documents, by the way?" He hoped they contained merely pictures, with no words. Fix got entirely too much approbation for his literacy as it was.

"First, demand the return of the documents," Forfa said. "Wopal said you'd be the right jobbers for the task. He said you work complex and sensitive jobs in the Paper Sook. Jobs involving contracts and so on."

Indrajit harrumphed.

"I presume she took them because they have value." Fix's voice was melodic, high-pitched, almost feminine in tone, though it emerged from the barrel chest of a muscle-bound jobber.

"Of course."

"So we'll demand them back," Fix said. "And what if she offers to sell them to us, instead?"

"I'll reimburse you," the shipowner said. "Up to 50 Imperials."

"Which happens to be our fee, conveniently," Fix said. "If you pay us in advance, we'll have the cash to negotiate."

A sound like wordless mumbling bubbled from behind the tentacles, but Forfa retrieved a brass-bound casket from a shelf behind him, unlocked it, and counted out 50 gold coins.

"What kind of poetry?" Indrajit asked.

"Eh?" The merchant grunted.

"What kind of poetry does your daughter compose?" Indrajit clarified. "Or write?" He hoped she didn't write it, but that was probably a vain wish.

"The foolish stuff," Forfa grumbled. "You know, swords and heroes and love."

"That's the *best* stuff," Indrajit said.

Forfa glared at him.

"We'll demand the documents back," Fix said, "then offer to pay for them if she says no, then steal them if we have to."

Forfa nodded curtly. "As a last resort, bring back the girl."

"That seems clear enough," Fix said.

"You have to tell us what the documents are," Indrajit reminded their client, "so we can identify them."

"They're not documents such as you would recognize," Forfa droned. "They aren't written on parchment or carved into clay."

"Good." Indrajit smiled.

Fix frowned.

"They're four long strips of leather as wide as your thumb. Each is punched with a series of holes and has knots tied along its length."

"So...not documents at all," Fix said.

"If you prefer." Forfa's face-worms bounced.

"How long are they?" Indrajit asked.

"Each is about as long as a man is tall." Forfa looked from Indrajit to Fix and back. "About as tall as you, with the long face-bone. Not your short friend."

"Short is a matter of context." Fix frowned.

"I usually call it my 'nose,'" Indrajit said, "rather than my 'face-bone.'"

Forfa shrugged. "You'll admit that it's long and prominent, and goes rather farther up your face than most noses do. Also, your eyes are rather far apart."

"And you have a plate of noodles glued to your cheeks," Indrajit said.

"Noodles?"

Fix stepped forward, putting himself physically between the other two men. "What can you tell us about where your daughter might have gone?"

"I'll have you know," Forfa said, "that my grandmother chose my grandfather from the Mating Run precisely *because* of his thick, luxurious beard."

"A beard is made of hair," Indrajit said.

"Not all beards!"

"Your daughter," Fix said. "Oritria. And the secret messages. How do we find them?"

"I never said the strip-writing contained secret messages." Forfa snorted.

"Fine." Fix nodded amiably. "The cryptic dots and knots embedded in four leather strips the length of an itinerant Blaatshi bard."

"I'm not itinerant." Indrajit sniffed. "You'll be calling me 'shiftless' next."

"The nature of the documents should not concern you," Forfa said.

"Fix is just jealous of any book he can't actually read," Indrajit said.

"I'm not concerned with the nature of the documents," Fix replied mildly, "or their contents. My question was, how do we find them? How do we find your daughter and the Yeziot?"

"You don't have to *find* them." Forfa shook his head as if he were sluicing away water. "They're hiding aboard a ship called the *Duke's Mistress*." He stepped to the door, opened it, and pointed at a two-masted, lateen-rigged ship within bowshot. "The brazen thieves. Oritria and the monster she's making off with. They sail tomorrow with the morning tide."

"Why not go take your documents back?" Indrajit asked. "You have sailors."

"I can't lose any of my sailors," Forfa said. "And my sailors might not be as cautious as I'd like around the documents. And worse, if the harbormaster were to hear I had started a fight in port, it would get back to the Lord Chamberlain—"

"I'm pretty sure the Lord Stargazer has the contract for the ports," Fix said.

"Fine, the Lord Stargazer." Forfa nodded. "But whichever of the great families is administering the port these days, if I get banned from docking here, the trade is useless to me."

"Not useless, surely," Indrajit objected. "The Serpent Sea trade has four legs, doesn't it? You could still trade in the other three. Pelth, Boné, and Xiba'alb." He grinned at Fix.

"Except," Fix said immediately, "the spices you buy in Xiba'alb you sell in Kish, to be resold to buyers from Ukel, Karth, and Ildarion. Ildarion won't buy directly from Xiba'alb because of the political tensions, and the others are too far."

"And the Pelthites don't care about spice!" Forfa sputtered. "Have you ever tasted Pelthite food? They make it savory by letting it rot!"

Indrajit nodded. "Of course. So if you can't sell here, you'd have to sail farther, or lose the entire trade."

"Farther, and across rougher seas!" Forfa snapped. "My costs would go up for the time alone, and then there's the cost of selling the risk!"

At the mention of risk-merchantry, Indrajit closed his eyes and willed the conversation to go elsewhere.

"Grit Wopal said you were discreet." The shipowner's eyes sagged with fatigue.

"How do we recognize the Yeziot?" Indrajit asked.

"He'll be the biggest man on the ship." Forfa grunted. "You won't be able to miss him."

"What's the name of the monster?" Fix asked. "And what do we do if he tries to stop us?"

"Squite." Forfa nodded, his tentacles wiggling excitedly. "Feel free to kill him. Indeed, I *want* him dead. Bring back his head, and I'll pay you an additional ten Imperials."

\* \* \*

"Do you feel like we never get quite *all* the information we'd like to have up front?" Indrajit asked.

The two men pushed their way along the busy boardwalk. Indrajit gnawed at the fried leg of a Kishi fowl gripped in his left hand

and kept his right hand near the hilt of his legendary sword, Vacho. Trying to appear nonchalant, he scanned the wharf where the *Duke's Mistress* was moored. Sailors loaded merchandise, and a large, four-armed, scaly-looking man directed their movements.

Fix sauntered, his thumbs hooked into his wide leather belt, keeping his hands near his falchion and his ax. For real fighting jobs, he'd bring a spear, but if you carried a spear around in your hand, you announced you were ready for combat, and you attracted attention. Even in Kish.

"We'll be able to identify the documents on sight," Fix said, "and Oritria must look at least *something* like her father."

"Not sure about that. Grokonk males and females look radically different, for instance."

"Like tadpoles and frogs." Fix nodded. "But most likely, we'll spot Oritria easily."

"She should at least be green."

"So the thing we don't really know is what a Yeziot is."

"The thing *you* don't really know." Indrajit cast the bone, gnawed clean of flesh, into the water. A lavender-skinned Zalapting who had narrowly missed being struck glared at him. "Mmm, I would really like some fried tamarind right now. Maybe on a bed of kelp."

"The Yeziot appear in the Blaatshi Epic?"

"How many times must I tell you," Indrajit asked, "that the Epic contains all the best knowledge of the Blaatshi? *Everything* worth knowing is in the Epic. This is why knowledge of the Epic not only enlightens the mind, it necessarily edifies the soul. One becomes a better person merely by listening."

"The Epic doesn't tell you how to find a successor Recital Thane. Or you'd have done it by now."

"Touché. This is also why, naturally, I'm interested in talking with Oritria, who is *not* a princess, but who *is* a poet. I wish to see what…edification…may be had from *her* poems."

"What do you know about the Yeziot, then?"

"Shall I declaim?" Indrajit wiped grease from his mouth with the back of his forearm. He wore a sleeveless, baggy tunic and a kilt; Fix wore a kilt only. Both men had sandals on their feet. Even in winter, Kish would experience cold rain, but would not freeze.

"Just say the line."

"Yes, I will declaim." Indrajit looked around for a platform and saw a chunk of stone carved roughly with the features of a horned skull, lying beside a brick wall at the corner of an alley. Not roughly, he realized; the sculpture had once been very fine, its cuts deep and its lines subtly curved, but it had crumbled under the teeth of wind, rain, and time into its present state. He stepped up onto the skull and turned to face Fix and the street. "Auspicious that I should have for a stage the image of our patron." The heraldic symbol of Orem Fish, the Lord Chamberlain, was a horned skull.

"Or his great-great-great grandfather."

Indrajit raised his arms and struck the third combat pose; that was the one in which his left arm imitated a stabbing spear and his right pantomimed the motions it would make if bearing a shield. "Yeziot the growler, eater of the flesh of men," he chanted, "swords in his mouth and spearheads for fingers."

A passing sailor with rope sandals and canvas trousers threw a rock and hit Indrajit in the shoulder.

Fix stroked his beardless chin. "Those are picturesque details."

"Picturesque? Perhaps you missed the part about 'swords in his mouth.'"

"Yes, yes, and spearheads for fingers. But Forfa had already told us that the Yeziot were eaters of men, so you'd expect that sort of thing. And 'growler' tells us something, I suppose. But a man may growl, and so may a dog, but have little else in common. Is there another epithet for them, or anything else that would give us more...*specific* information? Such as, I don't know, their color?"

Indrajit switched to the seventh combat pose, a crouch with an imaginary spear braced to receive an attack. "Long-limbed Yeziot, drinking blood in darkness."

A waddling merchant with a green turban wrapped around her head hissed. "Shut up and go away!"

"You see the burden of poetry lies heavy upon me," Indrajit said.

"Long-limbed," Fix said. "That's a little vague. I suppose it means tall."

"Prominent limbs," Indrajit said.

"Hmm."

"If I were Squite and Oritria, I'd hide belowdecks," Indrajit said. "At least until the ship left port."

"We could pretend we want to buy passage. Bluff our way aboard."

"Or pretend we want to ship cargo."

"Or that we're inspectors on behalf of the Lord Stargazer."

"That one would come back and bite us," Indrajit said. "We could tell the captain who we are and say we're investigating for the Lord Chamberlain. Make out that some kind of Paper Sook misbehavior has taken place. Fraud or off-book risk-merchantry or trade indoors."

"You mean insider trading. But we have no uniforms, and there are only the two of us, so the captain could easily tell us to go away."

"Right. Or we could disguise ourselves as sailors. Or leave our weapons and swim."

"I don't think leaving our weapons is a good idea. The Yeziot have prominent limbs, after all. Maybe the Epic's epithets call attention to their limbs because they're unusually strong."

"Forfa said it's like having a one-man crew, so the Yeziot are likely strong and very fast. I say we just walk on board," Indrajit said. "And if anyone stops us, we tell them we're looking for Melitzanda. Or Oritria, rather."

"What, to collect a debt?"

Indrajit stepped down off the weathered skull. "No. We'll say we want to hear her poetry. Which happens to be true."

Fix nodded, and they turned their steps toward the *Duke's Mistress*.

The ship was moored at the far end of a long, sagging wharf. Sailors with undyed cloth wrapped around their legs to form something resembling baggy trousers marched along it with baskets and large clay jars on their shoulders to trudge up a splintered gang plank and deposit their burdens in various corners of the ship, mostly belowdecks. A big man, covered with a patchwork of scales and fur, directed their motion with movements of a long, coiled whip. Indrajit and Fix walked purposefully alongside the line of sailors and then, when a gap presented itself, slipped up the gangplank.

At the top, a cracking whip stopped them.

The big man loomed over them. His scales were red, orange, and yellow, in a repeating diamond-shaped pattern. His fur, which sprouted in irregular patches, was black and oily. His legs curved back and forward again, like an exaggerated caricature of the hind legs of a dog. Or like a frog's legs, much more dramatic even than the legs of the Grokonk Indrajit had seen. He wore a harness of broad, thick leather straps. Of the man's four arms, one held a long whip and the other a falchion, a curving, one-edged sword like Fix's, only twice the size.

"Businessss?" the big scaly man asked.

"Pleasure," Indrajit said. "We have come seeking a poet."

"A poet?" The scaly man's eyes narrowed and the nostrils at the end of his long snout flared. "Thiss is a merchant ship."

"I'm Indrajit Twang," Indrajit said. "I'm the four hundred twenty-seventh Recital Thane of the Blaatshi people, and keeper of their sacred epic. You may not have heard of me, but, as a man of culture, you've no doubt heard of the poem."

"Anaxssimander Sskink mentioned you." The big red man chuckled. "You were trying to pay your tab at the Blind Ssurgeon with poetry."

"Yes." Was this big fellow a Yeziot? Indrajit didn't dare ask, nor did he dare meet the gaze of Fix, who must surely be asking himself the same question. The man's nails were long and sharp, as were his teeth. He was large and strong; was he large and strong enough to crew a ship entirely by himself? Or had that been mere hyperbole? "I'm all paid up now, though. In fact, I have cash, and look, I'll pay you. I'll give you a shiny gold Imperial if you let us go belowdecks to talk to Oritria."

The scaly man's eyes narrowed further. "You take me for a ssilly child."

"We take you for a big man with a sword and a whip," Fix said. "What race of man did you say you are?"

The scaly man growled.

Fix hesitated, then nodded. "Five Imperials. This is easy money. We'll be gone before you know it, and we won't cause trouble."

The big man held out one of his hands. Fix, who always handled the money because he didn't trust Indrajit to do so, dropped five yellow coins into the scaly red palm, and then the brute with the whip stepped aside.

Indrajit followed Fix toward an open hatch in the deck, near the front of the ship. He saw two more hatches farther back. "That could be Squite."

"He'll watch us go belowdecks, in any case, so don't look back at him."

Indrajit forced himself to keep his eyes on the plank ladder at his feet as he climbed down into the hold. "I don't want to fight that guy. I'd rather jump into the water and swim, if it comes to it."

"Fortunately, we're looking for documents that aren't water soluble."

"Documents, I feel obligated to point out, that might be hidden under the leather straps wrapped around that fellow's large, long-limbed body."

Fix nodded. "Let's find the girl before we tackle the monster."

"I wish he'd told you his name."

Light filtered down through a grate overhead, revealing a broad central open space, piled high with stacks of loose rope of a greenish fiber. The sailors carrying casks and jars descended to a second level below this one, from which arose an unpleasant odor reminiscent of a latrine. Fore, hammocks hung close together lined the walls, and left and right— port and starboard, Indrajit reminded himself—were rows of doors, close together so as to imply tiny cabins. Aft, two doors farther apart might belong to the captain or his principal officers. Indrajit's people were fishermen, but they rode the waves in small boats, and the details of a ship this large were a little beyond him.

"I guess we knock," Indrajit said.

They started at one end and rapped on the door. When it didn't open, Indrajit cracked the door and took a look inside, finding no one. Then the second door, and then the third.

"This reminds me a little bit of my youth in the ashrama," Fix said. "We'd go door to door sometimes."

"Salish-Bozar the White has a proselytizing operation?" Indrajit shook his head. "That surprises me. What did you say to people, 'come join us for the glory of memorizing useless nonsense?'"

"Basically."

"I'm shocked Salish-Bozar hasn't converted everyone."

Two irascible Zalaptings waved them away from one narrow cabin, and a sleepy Luzzazza grunted from his cot in another. A third cabin held something that looked like a sloth, gripping a beam overhead and staring with eyes like bone-white saucers. Otherwise, the starboard cabins were empty.

"Passengers haven't boarded yet," Fix suggested.

"Or they won't fill these cabins with passengers, and will stack cargo in them eventually," Indrajit countered. "Or maybe the ship's officers have cabins. Did something just move in the pile of ropes?"

"Most likely a rat," Fix said. "Ships have rats."

They crossed the central space, pausing to let sailors emerging from the hold below pass them.

"The ropes are pretty disordered, aren't they?" Indrajit asked. "Isn't that a point of pride for sailors, to always make sure your ropes are tightly coiled and neatly stowed?"

"Did you learn that from the Epic?" Fix asked.

Indrajit nodded. "It's an epithet of ships. 'All ropes tightly coiled, all sails furled tight.'"

"Maybe this captain is just less epic than the Blaatshi captains were."

They knocked at the first port cabin door, and there was no answer. Fix pushed the door open—

A woman sat on the cot inside, staring at them with golden eyes. She had green skin, and strands like tentacles hung off the front of her face. She was wrapped in a toga, and she held a wax writing tablet on her lap.

"Oritria," Indrajit said. "You have a—" He caught himself. He had almost said 'beard,' but he didn't feel comfortable finishing the sentence that way. "Tablet. Writing tablet. You write your poems down, of course you do."

He felt a little disappointed.

The green-skinned woman blinked. "Are you sailors?"

"Your father sent us." Fix kept his hands away from his weapons, but both ax and falchion were clearly visible. "We've come for the documents you took."

"What documents?" She held up her writing tablet. "This is for writing poems."

Fix sighed.

"Maybe keep an eye out for Squite, coming down the ladder and surprising us," Indrajit suggested. "Let me talk to Melitzanda, poet to poet."

Fix stepped back into the larger chamber and turned to watch the stairs.

"Melitzanda is a princess of Blaatshi legend," Oritria said. "My name is Oritria."

Indrajit leaned against the wall. He felt light-headed. "What do you know about Blaatshi legend?"

"I've read summaries of stories. The Epic itself isn't written down, of course, but in Zilander's *Ninety-Nine Riddles*, he retells a dozen or so of the tales. Including the one about Melitzanda and the harp that knew how to tell time."

"Wait, wait…what is ninety-nine riddles?"

"It's a book." The green woman's brow furrowed. "Are you Blaatshi?"

A wave of nausea hit Indrajit. "The Epic is *written down*?"

"Only some stories," Oritria said. "And in Kishi, not in the original Blaatshi. And of course, the real experience of the Epic is engaging with a Recital Thane who performs it, composing it as he goes from his stock of epic epithets. So the true Blaatshi Epic is never exactly the same twice, as no two men live exactly the same life."

"I…I'm sorry, may I sit down?"

Oritria scrambled to her feet and Indrajit fell heavily on her cot.

"Indrajit?" Fix called.

"I'm fine," Indrajit said. "Just. Is the scaly red guy coming?"

"Not yet."

Indrajit took deep breaths. "Okay, sorry, I'm a little overwhelmed. It's just…I've been here…months, I'm not sure how many, I've lost track of the time, and no one has ever heard of my people, or wants to hear the Epic, or understand what it's about, and here you are…practically *teaching* me!"

"I *am* a poet."

"Yeah." Indrajit exhaled slowly, trying to stop his head from spinning. "Listen, we're here to get the documents you took from your father."

"I didn't take any documents."

"They looked like four leather strips, with knots tied into them and holes punched through."

"I've seen those." Oritria nodded. "I didn't take them. I'm just leaving Kish, and I have to sneak out so my father doesn't stop me. He thinks the world is dangerous."

"He's right."

"Yes, but I'll never write my own epic if I don't try to live an epic life first."

Indrajit clapped his hands to his forehead. Thoughts raced through his mind faster than he could catch them. Had he finally stumbled, in the hold of this ship and trying to escape Kish, upon an appropriate apprentice to become his successor as Recital Thane? She wasn't Blaatshi. On the other hand, her greenish skin and the generally…oceanic…appearance of his features suggested she might be some sort of distant cousin. Fix teased Indrajit that he looked like a fish; Oritria looked like an octopus. A little.

But she wanted to leave. Indrajit could leave with her, of course, and they could travel the world together as he passed on the Epic and its many arts. On the other hand, where would that leave Fix? But was that any of Indrajit's concern? Fix would be fine, he would be no worse off than he had been before he and Indrajit had met and become partners. If Fix could reunite with his lost lady love by leaving Kish, wouldn't he do so in a heartbeat?

But they were here for something else. What had they come for?

"Indrajit!" Fix snapped.

Indrajit took a deep breath and stood. "We need those two documents. Four documents. The leather strips. We don't have any instruction to bring you back, so I guess your father thinks it's okay for you to travel the world."

"He does?" Oritria blinked.

Indrajit shrugged. "Anyway, listen, let us buy the documents from you. Fifty Imperials."

Fix groaned and stepped in close to the door. "At least *try* to bargain."

"It's just money," Indrajit said.

"*Everything* is just money!"

"Fifty Imperials," Indrajit repeated. "You could use the cash if you're really going to travel. And listen, maybe I could come with you."

"That's too much." Oritria took a step backward, pressing herself against the wall. "Why would you want to come with me?"

He had come on too strong. "To be poets together, on the road. You could hear the Epic, maybe even learn Blaatshi." Her eyes looked more skeptical by the second. "Also, I'm armed, so I could protect you against dangers on the road."

"I have protection," she said. "This is why I am traveling with Squite."

Indrajit sighed. He wanted to run away with this girl and explore poetry. Instead, he was going to do his job. "My instructions are to ask for the documents, then offer to buy them, then take them from you."

"I don't have them," she said again.

"Keep watching," Indrajit reminded Fix. He searched the little cabin. It took all of a minute, and he found no leather straps. Standing, he faced Oritria again and put his hand on the hilt of Vacho to look menacing. "Take off your toga." He hated himself, but it was what the job required.

"You can't torture any information out of me because I don't have the documents."

"I'm not going to torture you. I have to make sure you're not hiding them under your clothes."

She stripped, and Indrajit checked her toga. She didn't have the documents.

"You can get dressed again." He stepped back, standing in the doorway.

She left the toga on the floor where it lay.

"The captain could have them locked away," Fix said.

"Or Squite has them." Indrajit sighed. "I guess we have to go talk to the big guy."

"Let's search his room first," Fix said. "Where is Squite sleeping?"

"Right where you first saw him," she said. "It takes a lot of effort to move, and he can operate the ship from where he is right now, so he just plans to stay there until it's time to disembark."

Indrajit stared at Oritria and blinked. Something wasn't adding up.

"What does Squite look like?" Fix asked.

Then greenish cords wrapped around Fix and whipped him sideways, out of Indrajit's sight.

The thing in the center of the deck, the thing that Indrajit had taken for a pile of disordered ropes, now shuddered. It contracted, and a forest of eyestalks sprouted in its center. Indrajit drew his sword. He heard a crash and Fix cursing somewhere off to his left and out of sight. Sailors dropped their crates and scampered back up the ladder.

Then a mass of the green ropes sprang toward Indrajit like darts fired from crossbows.

He slammed the door shut. A hail of simultaneous thudding sounds erupted from the door as most of the ropes—they were really tentacles—struck the wood. Two of the tentacles slipped in through the door before it shut, and now squirmed, pinned between wood and wood.

The tips of the tentacles bore curved talons. Where they scratched the wood, they cut deep furrows, slicing easily through the planks.

Indrajit took a step deeper into the room to give himself space and sliced the tips off the two tentacles. Thick green ichor sprayed in wedge-shaped spatters across the wall.

Outside, he heard a noise that was ear-piercing shriek and deafening bellow at the same time. Then a thud. Then he heard Fix shouting, "The Protagonists!" That was a battle cry of sorts, as it was the name of the jobber company of which Indrajit and Fix were both the owners and the sole employees.

Indrajit stepped forward to open the door and join the fray, and something seized him by the throat.

It felt like a single finger, and the sudden backward tug caused him to lose his grip on Vacho. The sword clattered to the floor, and his flow of air disappeared. Indrajit staggered backward, slapping at the choking strand around his neck.

It was tightly-twisted cloth.

A toga.

Of course it was. Was Oritria innocent? Or at least relatively innocent, a woman trying to escape her father and now trying to defend her friend?

Squite the Yeziot, who looked like a tangled pile of green ropes.

Was it possible she had some darker part in this affair? She was, after all, choking him.

But she was a *poet*.

He struggled, but couldn't bring himself to smash the woman in the face with his elbow. His vision spun and was beginning to turn black, then he heard words in his ear.

Blaatshi words.

"Soft-headed Indrajit, eyes and heart blinded, he'll die and let his friend die, before he will see clearly."

The Blaatshi was grammatically perfect, perfectly intoned and accented. The lines rhymed and scanned and had impressive internal rhyme.

Indrajit swung his head back. With a crack, the back of his skull connected with something hard and heavy, and then he was lurching forward, sucking in the humid, close air of the *Duke's Mistress*'s lower decks.

He heard a heavy thud outside the little chamber and spun around to face Oritria. She stood, wrapping the fabric of the toga around her left arm; in her right hand, she held a long, thin dagger.

"Who taught you that line?" Indrajit demanded. The room swung left and right beneath his feet, as if the ship were cresting an enormous wave.

"I *wrote* it!" Oritria stabbed with the knife.

Indrajit's senses returned to crisp clarity at the last possible moment. He slapped the blade aside and swooped forward, slamming Oritria in the face with his forehead. With his long face bone, in fact.

Blood spurted from her nose and poured into her tentacles. Perversely, disgustingly, the bright red blood over the waving face-appendages reminded Indrajit of a bowl of spicy noodles.

"Liar!" he shouted.

"Blind fool Recital Thane, death now comes calling!" she howled, again in Blaatshi.

She couldn't have memorized lines, could she? Her accent was too perfect.

But what was the alternative? That a previous Recital Thane, someone of whom Indrajit was unaware, had come to Kish and taken an apprentice? And now the apprentice was attacking Indrajit?

Or could she have encountered a Blaatshi poet somewhere else, sailing with her father? Was there a Blaatshi village in Pelth, or in Xiba'alb?

But then why was she trying to kill him?

"Who taught you this?" he demanded.

She stabbed him in the side.

He pushed, knocking her to the floor. "Stop doing that!"

"Indrajit!" Fix yelled outside the door.

Indrajit scooped up his sword and rushed out into the larger space belowdecks. Tentacles whipped and flailed in all directions. Some whipped themselves through portholes or around railings, bracing the Yeziot, while others snatched up weapons—a boathook, a metal rod, an ax—and fell in a mass toward Fix, crouched in a corner with his falchion in one hand and his ax in the other.

Indrajit rushed in, sword first. Oritria was right—he would only one day be worthy of his epic poetry if he had lived an epic life in the meantime. Vacho sliced through one tentacle and then another, dropping a cudgel to the floorboards, then a huge chunk of pumice, and then an iron pot.

Pain lanced through his back.

He turned, his motion ripping the dagger from his flesh and sending it spinning along the floor. Oritria crouched like a wrestler, naked, face-tentacles writhing. "I'll let you live, Blaatshi!" she shrieked. "But you will be mine!"

Only moments earlier she had seemed coy, retiring, put off by Indrajit's forwardness. Had that all been an act?

Clearly, she wasn't made of the right stuff to be an apprentice Recital Thane.

"The documents!" he bellowed, waving his sword.

"Squite!" she yelled.

The tentacles that rushed Indrajit didn't seize him so much as *push* him, faster than a running pace, lifting him off his feet and hurling him against the wall. He managed to raise his arms at the last possible moment to protect his face and he bounced off the wood, falling to the floor.

Indrajit heard a thick growl that elevated instantly into a roar, and then he felt the heat of flame on his cheek. He raised his head, saw that a fire burned in the midst of all the rope-like tentacles and eyestalks, and then Oritria kicked him in the face.

He rolled over onto his back, groaning.

"Squite!" Oritria shrieked. "Kill the other one!"

"I'm trying!" Squite's voice sounded like the thick buzz of a saw cutting through hardwood, accented with a barrelful of rattling stones. Tentacles ripped open the doors of the ship's small cabins and dragged blankets out, trying to dampen the flames.

Oritria was looking at the fire, and Indrajit took the opportunity to grab both her ankles. He rolled toward the flames, pulling her to the ground and sending her bouncing away across the wood. He managed to find Vacho and gripped it in his hand as he stood.

"Fire!" The alarm was bellowed by the large red scaly man—who was not, after all, Squite—who now stood at the bottom of the ladder, long, curved scimitar naked in his hand.

Squite launched four tentacles at the scaled man. They wrapped around his legs, one tentacle on each, and two further tentacles whipped themselves around his sword arm. How many tentacles did Squite have, anyway?

And how many did he have *left*?

Indrajit left Oritria on the floor. One thing he was fairly certain of was that she did not possess the documents he and Fix were looking for. As four more tentacles lashed at Fix, ripping the ax from his hand and dragging him to the floor, Indrajit took two long steps and leaped forward, diving into the center of the Yeziot's body.

He felt the tentacles bunched up beneath him like corded rope. As he landed, the tentacles tensed, and stalk-mounted eyes swiveled to look Indrajit in the face.

"Drop my friend!" Indrajit howled, raising his blade.

Tentacles seized him from behind—

He swung the sword, chopping through the eyestalks entirely.

Squite squealed. A thin, soupy, warm liquid that smelled of minerals and brine sprayed from the severed stalks and washed Indrajit's face. The tentacles wrapped around him dragged him away, but they lacked coordination, and as one pulled in one direction and one pulled in another, Indrajit swung again. Like a farmer who hadn't cut the grain close enough to the ground, like a woodsman who had left too tall a stump, he mowed through the stalks a second time, cutting right above the massed central bunch of tentacles.

Squite howled and threw him against the wall again.

"You!" The scaly red-skinned man stomped across the deck and stooped to grip Indrajit by his sword belt. He raised Indrajit into the air with one arm and shook him. "Causing trouble!"

"Me!" Indrajit's vision swam in circles. He realized that he'd lost his sword, but he wasn't exactly sure where. "I'm not here for trouble, I came for..." he said, feeling faint, "the poet. And the rope-beast."

"Attacking passengers?" The four-armed man punched Indrajit in the face simultaneously with two enormous fists. His head rocked back so hard he felt his neck nearly snap, and for a moment he lost consciousness.

"Don't kill the Blaatshi!" he heard Oritria yelling, and her words woke him. "I need him!"

*Need me? For what?*

Indrajit heard thumping behind him. Fix, fighting the enormous bundle of tentacles that was the Yeziot?

They were losing. They might be defeated already. Indrajit needed a way to take some of his enemies out of the fight, immediately.

"*Need* him?" the scaly man snarled, echoing Indrajit's own thoughts. "For what?"

"That's my affair, Chark!" Oritria snapped.

Chark. Was that the scaly man's name? Or his race?

Indrajit kicked the scaly man. It wasn't much of a kick, because Indrajit's lungs were deflated and his limbs heavy, but he put all the force he could into the blow and struck Chark in the knee.

Chark hurled Indrajit to the floor and roared.

"Squite!" Oritria screamed.

Indrajit heard a louder thud, then tentacles surged over him. Oritria was screaming, and Chark ripped tentacles apart with his bare hands and slashed with his huge saber. Indrajit dragged himself out of the middle of the storm of noise and movement. He patted the floor, looking for Vacho—

And found a knotted leather strip instead.

And then another.

He gathered them together and squinted. Fire had engulfed one wall of the chamber, and it gave more than enough light for him to see that, as described, he held two lengths of leather, about his own height, holed and knotted irregularly.

And there were two more on the floor.

He was on his knees in the center of the space where Squite had...lain? Been heaped up?

The Yeziot had been lying on the documents.

Indrajit gathered up the strips and looked behind him; Squite was massive and strong, but he fought blind, and his tentacles crashed aimlessly against the ladder and wall behind Chark. Or *the* chark. Oritria was focused on the fight, screaming directions at Squite, and Chark waded into the sea of tentacles, slashing and cutting.

Indrajit spotted Vacho at the base of a wall and scooped it up with his free hand. Then he went looking for Fix in the shadowy depths of the room and found him, crumpled in a heap and bleeding from his nose. Indrajit prodded his friend.

"Can you hear me?"

"Mmmm...urggg..."

"One of the more miraculous properties of the Epic is its restorative virtue," Indrajit said. "The Recital Thane is obligated to sing over the sick and wounded to accelerate their recovery."

"By all your ugly gods, no." Fix grunted and dragged himself onto all fours. "I'm fine. No singing." Fix gathered up his ax and falchion from where they lay on the deck.

"You see, even the *mention* of the Epic has healing properties," Indrajit said.

"It's not the Epic, it's the fire. I don't want to burn to death on a ship in port."

"You started the fire. What did you do, hit Squite with a torch?"

"I threw an oil lamp." Fix shrugged. "It seemed like a good idea at the time."

Indrajit raised his friend with an arm under Fix's shoulder, and they limped toward the back of the ship, where he was reasonably confident they'd find another ladder and hatch. "Still, since I'm the one who will be composing the account of today's events...it will be the Epic that caused you to revive."

Fix growled.

"Be careful," Indrajit said. "You are growling, and you have noteworthy limbs. I may mistake you for a Yeziot."

"We didn't find the documents," Fix grunted.

"I have them," Indrajit said. "Squite was sitting on them. But after I blinded him, he moved off them to try to kill Chark."

"Who's Chark?" Fix mumbled.

"Well," Indrajit said, as he climbed the ladder toward a square of daylight, "I think it's the name of the big four-armed fellow with red scales. Or possibly he is *a* chark."

"I didn't imagine today would be so educational."

"So much to work into the Epic." Indrajit nodded. They emerged onto the deck past sailors with leather buckets full of sand and water, rushing below. "Too bad for you the knowledge is all strictly useful and professional information. You'll never qualify to be one of the Pointless by learning the names of monsters."

They turned toward the gangplank and the wharf, moving slowly but steadily.

"Selfless," Fix murmured. "The priests of Salish-Bozar are called the Selfless. And I gave that up long ago."

*****

## D.J. Butler Biography

D.J. (Dave) Butler has been a lawyer, a consultant, an editor, a corporate trainer, and a registered investment banking representative. His novels published by Baen Books include the Witchy War series: *Witchy Eye, Witchy Winter, Witchy Kingdom*, and *Serpent Daughter*, and *In the Palace of Shadow and Joy*, as well as *The Cunning Man* and *The Jupiter Knife*, co-written with Aaron Michael Ritchey. He also writes for children: the steampunk fantasy adventure tales *The Kidnap Plot, the Giant's Seat*, and *The Library Machine* are published by Knopf. Other novels include *City of the Saints* from WordFire Press and *The Wilding Probate* from Immortal Works.

Dave also organizes writing retreats and anarcho-libertarian writers' events, and travels the country to sell books. He tells many stories as a gamemaster with a gaming group some of whom he's been playing with since sixth grade. He plays guitar and banjo whenever he can, and likes to hang out in Utah with his wife, their children, and the family dog.

\* \* \* \* \*

# About the Editors

### Rob Howell

Rob Howell is the publisher of New Mythology Press, including his work as editor of the *Libri Valoris* anthologies of heroic fantasy. He's the creator of the Firehall Sagas and an author in the Four Horsemen Universe. He writes epic fantasy, space opera, military science fiction, alternate history, and whatever else seems fun.

He's a reformed medieval academic, a former IT professional, and a retired soda jerk.

His parents discovered quickly books were the only way to keep Rob quiet. He latched onto the Hardy Boys series first and then anything he could reach. Without books, it's unlikely all three would have survived.

You can find him online here:
- Website: robhowell.org
- His Blog: robhowell.org/blog.
- Firehall Sagas: firehallsagas.com
- Amazon: amazon.com/-/e/B00X95LBB0

Twitter: @Rhodri2112

\* \* \* \* \*

## Chris Kennedy

A Webster Award winner and three-time Dragon Award finalist, Chris Kennedy is a Science Fiction/Fantasy author, speaker, and small-press publisher who has written over 30 books and published more than 200 others. Get his free book, "Shattered Crucible," at his website, https://chriskennedypublishing.com.

Called "fantastic" and "a great speaker," he has coached hundreds of beginning authors and budding novelists on how to self-publish their stories at a variety of conferences, conventions, and writing guild presentations. He is the author of the award-winning #1 bestseller, "Self-Publishing for Profit: How to Get Your Book Out of Your Head and Into the Stores."

Chris lives in Coinjock, North Carolina, with his wife, and is the holder of a doctorate in educational leadership and master's degrees in both business and public administration. Follow Chris on Facebook at https://www.facebook.com/ckpublishing/.

\* \* \* \* \*

# Excerpt from
# *A Reluctant Druid*

Book One of The Milesian Accords

———————

**Jon R. Osborne**

Now Available from New Mythology Press

eBook, Hardcover, Paperback, and Audio

## Excerpt from *A Reluctant Druid*:

"Don't crank on it; you'll strip it."

Liam paused from trying to loosen the stubborn bolt holding the oil filter housing on his Yamaha motorcycle, looking for the source of the unsolicited advice. The voice was gruff, with an accent and cadence that made Liam think of the Swedish Chef from the Muppets. The garage door was open for air circulation, and two figures were standing in the driveway, illuminated by the setting sun. As they approached and stepped into the shadows of the house, Liam could see they were Pixel and a short, stout man with a graying beard that would do ZZ Top proud. The breeze blowing into the garage carried a hint of flowers.

Liam experienced a moment of double vision as he looked at the pair. Pixel's eyes took on the violet glow he thought he'd seen before, while her companion lost six inches in height, until he was only as tall as Pixel. What the short man lacked in height, he made up for in physique; he was built like a fireplug. He was packed into blue jeans and a biker's leather jacket, and goggles were perched over the bandana covering his salt and pepper hair. Leather biker boots crunched the gravel as he walked toward the garage. Pixel followed him, having traded her workout clothes for black jeans and a pink t-shirt that left her midriff exposed. A pair of sunglasses dangled from the neckline of her t-shirt.

"He's seeing through the glamour," the short, bearded man grumbled to Pixel, his bushy eyebrows furrowing.

"Well duh. We're on his home turf, and this is his place of power" Pixel replied nonchalantly. "He was pushing back against my glamour yesterday, and I'm not adding two hands to my height."

Liam set down the socket wrench and ran through the mental inventory of items in the garage that were weapons or could be used as them. The back half of the garage was a workshop, which included the results of his dabbling with blacksmithing and sword-crafting, so the list was considerable. But the most suitable were also the farthest away.

"Can I help you?" Liam stood and brushed off his jeans; a crowbar was three steps away. Where had they come from? Liam hadn't heard a car or motorcycle outside, and the house was a mile and a half outside of town.

"Ja, you can." The stout man stopped at the threshold of the garage. His steel-gray eyes flicked from Liam to the workbench and back. He held his hands out, palms down. The hands were larger than his and weren't strangers to hard work and possibly violence. "And there's no need to be unhospitable; we come as friends. My name is Einar, and you've already met Pixel."

"Hi, Liam." Pixel was as bubbly as yesterday. While she didn't seem to be making the same connection as Einar regarding the workbench, her eyes darted about the cluttered garage and the dim workshop behind it. "Wow, you have a lot of junk."

"What's this about?" Liam sidled a half step toward the workbench, regretting he hadn't kept up on his martial arts. He had three brown belts, a year of kendo, and some miscellaneous weapons training scattered over two decades but not much experience in the way of real fighting. He could probably hold his own in a brawl as long as his opponent didn't have serious skills. He suspected Einar was more than a Friday night brawler in the local watering hole. "Is she your daughter?"

Einar turned to the purple-haired girl, his caterpillar-like eyebrows gathering. "What did you do?"

"What? I only asked him a few questions and checked him out," Pixel protested, her hands going to her hips as she squared off with Einar. "It's not as if I tried to jump his bones right there in the store or something."

"Look mister, if you think something untoward happened between me and your daughter –" Liam began.

"She's not my pocking daughter, and I don't give a troll's ass if you diddled her," Einar interrupted, his accent thickening with his agitation. He took a deep breath, his barrel chest heaving. "Now, will you hear me out without you trying to brain me with that tire iron you've been eyeing?"

"You said diddle." Pixel giggled.

"Can you be serious for five minutes, you pocking faerie?" Einar glowered, his leather jacket creaking as he crossed his arms.

"Remember 'dwarf,' you're here as an 'advisor.'" Pixel included air quotes with the last word, her eyes turning magenta. "The Nine Realms are only involved out of politeness."

"Politeness! If you pocking Tuatha and Tylwyth Teg hadn't folded up when the Milesians came at you, maybe we wouldn't be here to begin with!" Spittle accompanied Einar's protest. "Tylwyth? More like Toothless!"

"Like your jarls didn't roll over and show their bellies when the Avramites showed up with their One God and their gold!" Pixel rose up on her toes. "Your people took their god and took their gold and then attacked our ancestral lands!"

"Guys!" Liam had stepped over to the workbench but hadn't picked up the crowbar. "Are you playing one of those live-action role playing games or something? Because if you are, I'm calling my garage out of bounds. Take your LARP somewhere else."

"We've come a long way to speak to you," Einar replied, looking away from Pixel. "I'm from Asgard."

"Asgard? You mean like Thor and Odin? What kind of game are you playing?" Liam hadn't moved from the workbench, but he'd mapped in his mind the steps he'd need to take to reach a stout pole which would serve as a staff while he back-pedaled to his workshop, where a half-dozen half-finished sword prototypes rested. From where he stood, though, he didn't feel as threatened. He knew a bit about gamers because there were a fair number of them among the pagan community, and he'd absorbed bits and pieces of it. Maybe someone had pointed Liam out to Pixel as research about druids for one of these games—an over-enthusiastic player who wanted to more convincingly roleplay one.

"Gods I hate those pocking things," Einar grumbled, rubbing his forehead while Pixel stifled another giggle. "Look, can we sit down and talk to you? This is much more serious than some pocking games you folk play with your costumes and your toy weapons."

"This isn't a game, and we aren't hippies with New Age books and a need for self-validation." Pixel added. Her eyes had faded to a lavender color. "Liam, we need your help."

* * *

Get "*A Reluctant Druid*" at:
amazon.com/dp/B07716V2RN

Find out more about Jon R. Osborne and *A Reluctant Druid* at:
chriskennedypublishing.com/imprints-authors/jon-r-osborne/

* * * * *

# Excerpt from *Responsibility of the Crown*

Book One of The Endless Ocean

---

### G. Scott Huggins

Available Now from New Mythology Press

eBook and Paperback

# Excerpt from *Responsibility of the Crown*

The sky was so big.

She had never been so high up on her own. Thousands of feet, it must have been. She felt as if she could fall forever in the endless blue that was the ocean below and the sky above. Already, she had to strain to pick out the bronze and violet specks that were Elazar and Merav.

Senaatha aimed for the fighters, and they bored in, lines of death shooting from their wings. Suddenly, she seemed to stutter in the air, beating her wings irregularly. She dropped, climbed, and dropped again.

*She's throwing off their aim,* Azriyqam realized. Consortium planes were fast, but they moved in long curves. They had no wings to beat—*how do they turn?* she wondered—and so they weren't capable of the fast changes in direction a dragon could manage.

Or a half-dragon. The planes sliced through the air on either side of Senaatha, and she whipped her neck around, flaming, but her fiery breath fell short of her targets.

*They must be going a hundred miles an hour,* thought Azriyqam.

Her heart sank. It was obvious, even to her, that the weapons on the aircraft reached much farther than Senaatha's flame could, and they could use them while going at full speed. Senaatha didn't dare— she'd fly right into her own breath. Even worse, the planes would not get tired. Already, they were looping around for another pass. Senaatha labored for altitude, but the aircraft climbed higher still, nearly to her own height.

*Height.* She strained against the thin air, found a weak thermal, and rode it upward. The planes settled in for their attack run. Again, the deadly lines of gunfire lashed out.

Two tiny figures dove into them. Elazar slashed downward, Merav flying practically at his wingtip. They twisted between the lines of light and danced in front of the oncoming plane. It veered in the air, yawing and rolling to avoid a collision. Slowing.

Senaatha breathed flame as it passed by her at a distance of 50 feet. The airplane emerged from the stream of flame spinning wildly, a comet of fire trailing black smoke, every surface ablaze.

Then the second plane's guns punched heavy bullets through Senaatha's right wing.

Blood flew like mist from the wounds. The dragon screamed. Engine roaring, the plane broke off in a tight turn. Its pilot had seen what had happened to his companion, and he didn't want to chance closing with the dragon, wounded or not.

He would come back to finish the job from farther away. Senaatha was in a flat glide. The bullets hadn't cracked her wing spars or she'd be falling out of the sky, but there were ragged holes in the membranes of her wing. If she strained it too hard, she'd rip it apart by the sheer force of her passage through the air.

The plane turned. Merav and Elazar beat for altitude, but she could see they were on the wrong side. They couldn't get between her and the plane, let alone be ready to dive. Then the pilot would unleash his deadly guns into Senaatha's helpless body, sending her and her human passengers into the Endless Ocean below.

It was up to her.

Already, the plane was lining up.

Azriyqam winged over and dove.

\*\*\*

Get *Responsibility of the Crown* now at: amazon.com/dp/B095CLDVMD/

Find out more about G. Scott Huggins and *Responsibility of the Crown* at: https://chriskennedypublishing.com/

\*\*\*\*\*

Made in the USA
Columbia, SC
09 November 2024